THE
RIGHT
WAY

A NOVEL

THE
RIGHT
WAY

A NOVEL

SKYLER ANDERSON

AUTHOR'S NOTE

This novel, while inspired by the author's work as a practicing immigration attorney, does not have any character based on any specific client, attorney, officer or judge. The story and characters are fictitious. Any institutions, agencies, and locations referenced in this novel are used in a way that is purely fictional. However, the U.S. immigration laws addressed herein are not fictional, and are accurately described to the best of the author's ability to do so for the time this fictional account is said to have occurred, between March 1 and July 1, 2018.

I have to start by thanking my wife and eternal partner in crime, Kim. From reading early drafts to giving me advice on the cover to embracing single parenthood while I edited, re-edited, and re-re-edited; she was as important to finishing this book as I was. I love yer stinkin' guts.

I would also like to thank my dad, Bruce, for his encouragement, insights, and suggestions, and my mom, Gloria, for her unconditional love and support.

Also, a special thanks to Jana Miller for her considerable contributions in editing and story development, and to Gary Huntsman for his insights on the early drafts.

Finally, I have to thank my fellow immigration attorneys who have helped and inspired me in the trenches, and my former, current, and future clients and their families to whom I dedicate this book.

TABLE OF CONTENTS

PART 1

CHAPTER 1

DAY 1

Thursday, March 1, 2018

IT'S ALMOST MIDNIGHT. A Hispanic man in his early forties sits alone on a barstool, staring blankly at an open but untouched bottle of beer in a small town in northern Utah. The beads of condensation once peppering the outside of the bottle evaporated long ago as the beer slowly rose to room temperature over the past three hours. The man is clean shaven and neatly dressed in a light-blue dress shirt tucked into his khaki pants. He feels his cell phone vibrating in his pants pocket but does not respond. Without looking he knows it's his wife calling. Again. The extended vibration at the end lets him know she has left voicemail. Again. He doesn't move. The redness of his eyes and the occasional welling up of tears are the only signs of life.

The bar would be completely silent if not for a large flat-screen television suspended from the far wall, which carries the undivided attention of the bartender, the only other person still in the bar. He too appears to be in his early forties but is a white man with a patchy beard and greasy, unkempt brown hair just starting to grow over his ears. A wet terry-cloth rag is draped over his shoulder, dampening the black polo shirt bearing his name, Stan. After numerous failed attempts at conversation with his only remaining customer, Stan stands alone, leaning against the other side of the bar, watching the repeat of the evening news. It will soon be time to close for the night and clean up. He turns at the sound of a small bell announcing the entrance of another customer.

"Roger!" he says enthusiastically as he recognizes one of his regulars. "Good to see you. How ya been, man?"

"Can't be that good if I'm here on a weeknight," Roger says, laughing. "Double shot of tequila, please, Stan."

"You got it," Stan says, reaching for the bottle. "You know we're closin' up soon, right?"

"Yeah, I know, I know. I'll be quick."

Roger sits two seats down from the Hispanic man and turns to him as Stan gets his drinks.

"Howdy, friend," he says, extending his arm towards the man to offer a friendly handshake. "Roger's the name. And you?"

The man says nothing.

"No hablas English, amigo?" Roger asks, smiling, his hand slowly retreating.

Still nothing.

"Don't bother, Rodge," Stan says, walking over with a shot glass of tequila in each hand. "He seems to be the introverted type. Not much for conversation, I've found. But he don't bother nobody else, so he don't bother me."

Roger turns his attention back to Stan and they begin discussing tonight's college basketball games, proffering their conflicting but equally confident opinions on the likely winner of the upcoming national tournament. To their surprise, the still-silent man at the end of the bar stands up quite suddenly, jerking his arm across the bar and knocking over his bottle of beer, which spills down his shirt and pants. He shakes them off, bends down to pick up his now-empty bottle, and stumbles awkwardly towards the exit.

"You okay, buddy?" Roger asks, rising from his seat.

The man says nothing and leaves the bar. As the door closes, Roger walks quickly over and peers through the small diamond-shaped window on the door. He sees the man open the driver's side door of an old white Pontiac, throw his empty bottle onto the passenger-side floor, climb into the car, and turn the ignition.

"You're not gonna let this guy drive outta here like this, are you, Stan?!" Roger asks in concern, turning back to the bartender.

"He's fine."

"Are you crazy, man?" Roger furrows his eyebrows in disbelief. "Did you see him? He could kill somebody out there! Plus, you could get fined if this guy gets busted."

"I'm telling you," Stan says with a tone of calm assurance. "He's fine. He's been here all night and never even touched that one beer I sold him. At least not 'til he spilled it all over himself."

"Sounds like a real whack job," Roger says, raising his eyebrows and smiling.

"Yeah," Stan says with a laugh. "But there's no shortage of those around here—present company *in*cluded."

Roger laughs, returns to his seat, and continues talking to Stan.

Outside of the bar, the Hispanic man begins to drive slowly down a dark, lonely street, staring blankly into the night. His lack of attention is apparent as he periodically weaves just slightly in and out of his lane and reacts either too soon or too late to the changing of the stop lights on every other block. He doesn't get far before he sees the reflection of red-and-blue lights in his rearview mirror. Still emotionless, he slowly pulls to the side of the road and puts his car into park. He's still looking forward moments later when a police officer taps on his window with a large, metal flashlight. He rolls down the window and looks up at the officer, who has the light pointed directly into his face. The man instinctively turns away.

"License and registration, please," the officer says coldly.

"Yes, sir," the man answers, his voice cracking through his dry throat after uttering his first words in hours.

He opens his glove box, releasing a large stack of poorly organized documents that spill onto the passenger-side floor. Sensing the officer's growing impatience, he quickly picks up and sorts through the documents until he finds his registration. The officer's flashlight steadily follows every movement of the man's hands, even as he hands him the document.

"And your license, please?" the officer asks after quickly scanning the registration.

The officer leans closer as the man reaches into his back pocket and pulls out a bulging brown leather wallet, cluttered with a combination of money, receipts, and credit cards. He pulls out his identification and hands it to the officer. The officer squints suspiciously, pointing his flashlight from the card to the man's face and back again, comparing the two.

"Wil—Wil-*fred*-o—Wilfredo Gonzalez?" asks the officer with a strong gringo accent to which the man long ago became accustomed. "What, is that like Mexican for Wilfred or somethin'? Did I say that right?"

"Close enough," the man says quietly. "My friends call me Fredy."

"Okay, Wilfredo. Got it."

The officer reviews the identification carefully, shaking his head with a half-smile as he reads to himself the bold print across the top of the card:

DRIVING PRIVILEGE
NOT VALID IDENTIFICATION

"So, you got one of them driving privilege cards, eh?" the officer asks, turning over the card to inspect the reverse side as if questioning its validity.

Fredy smiles nervously and looks down without responding.

They both understand the significance. In 2005, the State of Utah began issuing temporary driving privilege cards instead of driver licenses to Utah residents who could not provide a valid social security number. Fredy is an "illegal immigrant," an "illegal" for short, or, as defined by Congress, an "alien." Those words alone do not necessarily carry any sting—at least not for Fredy. Although he understands those who find the terms offensive, it's always the intent of the speaker that matters more to him. He's never embraced the notion that well-meaning people defending an "alien" or "illegal immigrant" should have to apologize for their word choice. He's observed that those who demand as much often hurt the cause they purport to help, creating conflict where they might otherwise create compromise: an endless war of words serving as little more than a distraction from the more significant legal issues ignored for decades.

In any case, Fredy *feels* like an alien. He felt like an alien when he was the only Spanish-speaking kid in his middle school struggling with a new language. He felt like an alien when, after mastering the new language and excelling in high school, he had to cut short and limit his further education and employment while his peers moved forward. He feels like an alien now, as a police officer smirks upon reading the bold notice of his alienage on his driving privilege card. It makes little sense, then, to patronize him now by calling him a "non-citizen," a "non-traditional immigrant," or even a "human being." Under the law he is an *alien*. Referring to him any other way would only appease the sensitivity of well-intentioned white people.

But none of this is new to Fredy, and it occupies no more than a passing thought in his mind as he anxiously waits for the officer's next move. Before the officer can say anything else, he turns to his right in response to flashing lights in his peripheral view from another police car pulling up close behind his own. This second officer steps out of the car, carrying his own flashlight, and walks towards Fredy's car. The first officer points his flashlight back inside Fredy's car as he peers inside for a closer look. His light reflects off the glass of the empty beer bottle on the passenger-side floor. The officer turns the flashlight directly to Fredy's eyes, causing him to squint and turn away.

"All right, how much you had to drink tonight, Wilfredo?" he asks.

"Excuse me, sir?" Fredy says.

"To drink!" the officer says sternly. "Cerveza. How much, amigo?"

"Nothing," Fredy says.

"Don't jerk me around, buddy," the officer says angrily, having lost all patience.

By this point the second officer is standing next to the first with a scowl on his face nearly mirroring that of his peer.

"I can smell the beer," the first officer continues. "You got bloodshot eyes, and I can see an empty bottle right next to you. So I'm gonna ask you again, how much have you had to drink tonight?"

"I know, but I didn't drink anything."

"All right, I guess we're gonna have to do things the hard way. Please step out of the vehicle. It's one thing when you people sneak into my country illegally and at least respect the rest of our laws, but I'm not gonna let you put innocent U.S. citizens' lives in danger by drinking and driving. You're only making things worse on yourself by not cooperating."

"Maybe a quick call to our friends at immigration will help straighten things out for us," the second officer suggests. "You want me to see if ICE wants him while you start the field test?"

"Sure, why not?" the first officer says with a sly smile. "Couldn't hurt."

ICE is the commonly used acronym for the U.S. Immigration and Customs Enforcement, which is essentially the immigration police. Also known as ERO, formerly known as INS, and not to be confused with CBP and TSA. It falls under DHS and is represented in court by OCC or OIL. Given ICE's limited resources, the federal government has a long history of prioritizing its enforcement by focusing on serious criminals. Even with this prioritized enforcement, the understaffed immigration courts have worked for several years with a backlog of hundreds of thousands of cases. These priorities regularly shift and evolve (or devolve, depending on one's perspective) from administration to administration at the whim of the current president. People with actual *convictions* for driving under the influence have long been considered priorities for removal. Under the current Trump administration, however, priorities have been expanded to include anyone ICE deems to pose a risk to public safety. This has been interpreted broadly by those actually implementing the priorities to essentially include everyone living illegally in the United States.

With the blessing of the first officer, the second officer walks back to his car and makes a call to a contact number he has with local ICE operating in Salt Lake County. He watches the first officer instructing Fredy to blow into a breathalyzer while he waits on hold for the next several minutes. By the time he has spoken to an ICE officer about the suspected DUI, Fredy has finished all of the field sobriety tests and is leaning against his car and, to the surprise of the second officer, is not wearing handcuffs.

"What'd he blow?" the second officer asks as he returns, pointing to the breathalyzer still in the first officer's hand.

"I couldn't get a good read on it."

"Did he pass the field test?"

"Yeah, good enough. I don't think we got enough to arrest him. It's obvious he's been drinking, but not enough for a DUI as best as I can tell. I thought about citing him for an open container at least, but the bottle was empty. What'd ICE say? Did you actually get a hold of anyone?"

"Yeah, I did. They asked us to hold on to him and they'll send someone over."

"Really?" the first officer says, raising his eyebrows in surprise. "That's a first for me. Good to know. All right, we can hold him a little longer. Did I ever tell you that one of my cousins had a daughter killed in a DUI accident by one of these illegals?"

"Are you serious?" the second officer asks with a mixed tone of empathy and anger as he glares at Fredy in disgust, shaking his head.

Fredy can feel the animosity of the officers towards him grow as they begin to discuss the details of the tragic death, as if he himself were the culprit. It reaches a level of discomfort for him where he almost feels the need to accept some level of responsibility and apologize. This obligatory feeling of guilt by association—despite the absence of any true association—is a familiar one for him. He's accepted the fact that, for many, his own life decisions will never define him as much as those of the most violent legal or illegal immigrants living in the United States at any given time. He's a scofflaw, a job stealer, a tax evader, and a terrorist wrapped into a single person. A living representation of a poorly defined and poorly understood problem.

But this does not feel like the best time for Fredy to object to the unfairness of opinions based more on stereotype than fact. Instead, Fredy stares blankly at the road in silence as his thoughts immediately turn to his family still waiting for him at home.

CHAPTER 2

DAY 3

Saturday, March 3, 2018

A SMALL GROUP OF PARENTS SITS IN A VARIETY OF FOLD-OUT LAWN CHAIRS ON A LARGE, OTHERWISE EMPTY FIELD OF GRASS IN FRONT OF AN ELEMENTARY SCHOOL. Immediately behind them stand half a dozen mature pine trees with long-reaching branches shading the southwest corner of the field. To the parents' left, set back safely from the residential road leading to the school, is a large playground. The base of the playground is partly covered with faded brown wood chips, with sporadic patches of hard dirt ground. Several children, at least half of whom are wearing matching blue soccer jerseys, are running back and forth between a large swing set, a cold metal slide, and a freestanding, web-shaped jungle gym.

"Such a beautiful day, isn't it, Lori?" says one of the women sitting in a fold-out chair on the field.

"Oh, I know, I love it," Lori says with a smile, taking in a deep breath and looking up at the clear blue sky. "I thought this winter would never end. But you know as well as I do we'll get at least one more snowstorm before winter's really gone."

"Stop it, Lori, you'll jinx us!" the other woman says, playfully slapping her arm.

Lori, like most of those sitting near her, is a middle-aged white woman. She is wearing a white, fitted T-shirt, light-tan capri pants, and brown leather sandals. Her medium-sized silver hoop earrings sway back and forth with her every movement. In contrast to the brown or varying shades of blonde hair of her peers, she appears to have embraced the early signs of old age with her striking, solid-grey hair, cut just shy of her shoulder. A pair of hot-pink sunglasses with dark lenses rests on top of her head and holds her hair back behind her ears. Taking advantage of the pause in conversation, she looks down at her watch. Again.

"It's almost eleven thirty already," she says. "It's not like Coach to be this late. At least not without sending a text or something."

"Or sending his poor wife to cover for him," the other woman says, laughing. "Were you here last fall when he had a work emergency or something, and so he sent Sarah to try to run the practice? I've never seen so much chaos on a soccer field—and that's saying a lot for this group."

"In all fairness," Lori says, with a playful tone, "she was about twenty months pregnant at the time."

"Oh, that's right. I can still picture her hobbling across the field trying to keep the kids focused. *Children!*" she says in dramatized, loud but sweet voice. *"Stay together! Please, stay together!"*

They both laugh.

"Sarah's the best," Lori says, smiling sincerely. "I tried texting her a while ago, but I still haven't heard back."

"I hope they're okay."

"They live just down the street from my house," Lori says. "I'll stop by on my way home to check in if they don't show up soon."

"Maybe the kids are just sick or something. Oscar's seemed to be doing great since he got out of the hospital."

"I know, he's such a little fighter. And a real inspiration to my boy. Ethan's got so much more confidence now. I just love to see that. Between you and me, he used to be a bit of a wuss. Crying and whining over nothing. I mean, I love him to death, but sometimes I just wanted to shake him and tell him to man up a little bit."

"You're terrible, Lori," the other woman says with a laugh.

"I'm serious though. But playing with Oscar and working with Coach has really toughened him up. It's just so—"

Lori stops short at the familiar sound of her son yelling in the distance. Instinctively she stands and turns to the playground, scanning it until she sees him in the middle of an angry game of tug-of-war with another child over the only unused swing.

"You've gotta be kidding me," Lori says slowly and quietly to herself, shaking her head with an increasingly stern expression as she bends to pick up her purse. "I guess that's my cue," she says to the other women with a forced smile as she begins a fast-paced walk towards the playground.

"Ethan Reed!" she shouts as she continues walking.

Ethan abruptly lets go of the swing and looks towards his mother. He instinctively starts running in the opposite direction but quickly thinks better of it, realizing it would only be worse for him once she inevitably catches him. Accepting defeat, he turns around and slowly walks towards his mother, who is now just about twenty feet away.

"All right," she says sternly. "Get your stuff together; we're going home."

"But I came back!" he says in his defense. "I'm sorry, mom! I didn't even get to play soccer yet."

"Well, Coach isn't here anyways, and you've already made me get up. So you blew your chance at another twenty minutes of playing. Come on, let's just go."

Realizing there's no chance of changing her mind, Ethan starts crying through unintelligible complaints, which his mother doesn't care enough to even attempt to decipher. She's now walking back towards the other parents, her right arm lagging behind as she drags her unwilling son by the hand. The majority of the other parents are folding up their chairs and calling after their own kids as Lori walks by with her son, who is still crying.

"I guess we'll need a little more work with Coach on that *manning up* business," Lori says, forcing an awkward smile as she stops briefly to fold up her chair before continuing to walk with her son.

They stop at a white Toyota Camry parked in the street at the edge of the field. Lori opens the back door, prompting her son to begrudgingly climb into his seat. She closes the door behind him, and by the time she has opened her own door, her son is silent and perfectly content. She turns back to him in surprise and sees that he has found some old sucker wedged in his seat, which he is now unwrapping and getting ready to put in his mouth.

"Why, thank you, son," Lori says, reaching back to take it and putting it in her own mouth.

Ethan scrunches his face into a grimace but says nothing more. Lori turns back to the front and begins fishing through her purse. Having found her keys, she inserts them and turns the ignition, leans back abruptly on her seat, and releases a heavy sigh. She sits quietly for a moment, debating on which of her various weekend errands to take on first. Ultimately, she decides to stop by Sarah's house before anything else to make sure everything is okay and, if so, to casually remind Coach that he missed practice.

It's an older neighborhood surrounding the elementary school, with all of the homes having been built in the 1950s. No two homes are exactly the same, inside or out, but most are made of varying colors of brick. The residents are generally either very old and the original owners, or a revolving door of young married couples renting from the heirs of the original owners. Lori and Sarah are two of the few exceptions in the neighborhood, married couples in their forties with children. That was the most obvious reason they inevitably became friends, but certainly not the only one. Both women have what some insecure men have described as "strong personalities." They seem to look for opportunities to share their unsolicited, sole dissenting opinion on any given topic just for the fun of it. Somehow this common trait has strengthened their friendship, even as they have often found themselves passionately disagreeing on trivial topics. They both respect their shared ability to firmly challenge the other, and then to be firmly challenged, without taking offense. Lori smiles as she reflects upon their last such debate as she continues to drive towards Sarah's home. Something about whether it ever made sense for someone to say they "could care less" instead of "couldn't care less," neither willing to back down after taking their initial position. Lori can't recall what side she took at the time, but she knows she may well take the opposite one in a future debate.

A few minutes after leaving the elementary school, Lori is within sight of Sarah's home, which is wedged in the corner of an L-shaped street. She pulls into the driveway and puts her car into park but leaves it running.

"I'll be right back, Ethan," she says, turning back to her son before opening the door. "Control yourself and maybe we'll go out for lunch when I'm done with my errands."

"Okay, Mom," Ethan says with a hopeful smile at the thought of possible redemption.

Lori steps out of her car and begins walking to the front door of the home. The paved pathway leading to the steps of the front porch is cracked and missing sizeable pieces of cement on the corners and edges, as are the steps to the porch itself. The brightly painted yellow door contrasts the dark-grey bricks. Lori stops short of knocking as she hears yelling coming from inside. She turns her ear to the door and moves closer, straining to make out the words piercing through the sound of crying children.

"I can't do this by myself! This house is disgusting!"

Lori can only assume the voice is Sarah's, though if she weren't standing outside Sarah's house, she would've never guessed it.

I thought I *was the mean mom,* Lori thinks to herself. *This isn't normal.*

She starts to turn to walk away from the house but stops.

Maybe there's something I can do to help. But it's really none of my business. No, of course it's my business; she's my friend.

Ultimately, Lori decides to ring the doorbell, hoping it might help defuse things. She hears a moan of frustration in response, followed by an order for the children to go to their rooms. A long minute later, the door opens halfway. A white woman with light brown hair pulled back in a messy bun peeks through the open door. She is wearing a baggy red shirt with a large wet spot in the front, light-grey sweatpants, and mismatched socks but no shoes. She forces a half-hearted smile and mumbles a barely audible "Hi" beneath her breath.

"Sarah," Lori says with an uncharacteristically enthusiastic tone. "How are you?"

"Fine," Sarah says shortly, unable or unwilling to feign interest in conversation. "Just really busy right now, as you can probably tell."

"Oh, that's good," Lori says, fumbling through her words. "No, I don't mean that's *good*. It's just—we all were—I mean I, *I* was just wanting to make sure everything was okay since we didn't see Fredy and Oscar at practice today. So that's good that you're just busy. How's Fredy?"

Such an uncomfortable conversation is unusual between these two friends, leaving Lori unsure of what to do or say next. Sarah stands silently for an extended moment, only adding to Lori's increasing feelings of awkwardness. Just as Lori begins to open her mouth to break the silence, Sarah drops her head into her hands, sobbing.

"Oh no! What is it, Sarah?" Lori says, instinctively stepping inside the home and hugging her.

They continue to stand without saying anything for what feels to them like several minutes but is closer to only one. Sarah is now crying into Lori's shoulder as Lori gently rubs her back in support.

"They took him!" Sarah finally says, still sobbing, partially muffled by Lori's shoulder where Sarah continues to rest her head. "They took Fredy! They're taking him away!"

"Who took him?" Lori asks frantically. "Who?"

"Immigration!" Sarah says forcefully into Lori's shoulder.

Lori pulls back in shock, her hands still holding Sarah's arms tightly.

"Immigration?" Lori says in a tone conveying her disbelief. "Why would immigration have anything to do with *Fredy*?"

Sarah looks back over her shoulder to the empty room behind her, gently pulls Lori with her to the porch, and closes the front door behind her.

"They're going to deport him," she says, her voice cracking.

Lori is baffled by the statement, replacing her expression of shock with one of skepticism. This can't be right. Sarah must be mistaken. No doubt it's a simple misunderstanding that they can quickly resolve without all this fuss.

"They can't deport him, Sarah," Lori insists assuredly, placing her hands on Sarah's cheeks as a gesture of comfort. "I know there's been a lot of things in the news right now and everyone seems to be deportation crazy all of a sudden, but Fredy has the same rights as every other U.S. citizen, no matter where his family's from. Someone has obviously made a mistake. But don't worry, we'll get it all figured out."

"You don't understand," Sarah says, pushing Lori's hands down and still crying. "He's *not* a U.S. citizen. His parents brought him here when he was a kid. They didn't qualify to come here legally, but they couldn't provide for their kids anymore in Mexico, so they just came here illegally."

Lori's face changes abruptly from one of confidence to shock.

"I never would've thought," she says, trying to maintain a calm and comforting tone. "But I'm sure we can get this all figured out. Even if he's not a citizen, *you* are. And all of your kids too. I'm sure there's just some paperwork or something you need to fill out to get his citizenship."

"We already tried all that," Sarah says, still crying. "Years ago. Something was wrong with the paperwork or something, I don't know. I don't know what to do; I don't know what I'm even saying! I still haven't even told the kids yet. They think he's helping my brother with some project out in California."

Lori hugs Sarah again, still trying in vain to comfort and assure her friend.

"Sarah, you and Fredy are family to us; you know that. Why didn't you tell us sooner? Maybe we could've helped."

Sarah doesn't respond, instead gently crying on her shoulder. Lori hugs her tighter.

"Well, we'll help you figure this out," she insists. "Greg is still out of town, but I'll talk to him as soon as he gets home on Monday, and if we have to get a lawyer or whatever, we'll do it. Maybe we can sponsor him ourselves or file a petition or something, but we'll figure this out, I promise."

Sarah is still crying. Lori, though not normally an emotional person, soon finds herself crying too. She feels overcome by sadness and empathy for her friend, who for some reason doesn't share her assurance that everything will be fine. These feelings are soon competing with increasing anger at whoever or whatever did this to her friend. She wants answers and an apology, and she wants them now. But she says nothing. They will find a solution soon enough. For now, the two friends will stand in silence, holding each other for the next several minutes on the porch outside of Sarah's home.

CHAPTER 3

DAY 4

Sunday, March 4, 2018

FREDY IS LYING ON TOP OF THE COVERS OF A THIN MATTRESS ON A METAL BUNK BED IN AN EIGHT-BY-EIGHT-FOOT CELL AT THE CACHE COUNTY JAIL IN LOGAN, UTAH. He's wearing a navy-blue prison jumpsuit and white socks. A pair of jail-issued neon-orange sandals is sitting at the end of his bed. To his immediate left is a cold cinder-block wall that has been painted white. To his right and below him is a small, silver aluminum sink attached to a wall. A single matching toilet sits next to it with a four-inch-wide rim at the top of the bowl for sitting, but no lid. The back of the toilet has a carved-out circular slot where half a roll of toilet paper sits. In front of him is a wall, at the far-right corner of which is a grey metal door.

He's reading a tattered old copy of The Book of Mormon that was left in the cell by the prior occupant of the top bunk. For the past several minutes, his attention has been devoted to a single passage that he has read again and again.

"... he denieth none that come unto him,
black and white,
bond and free,
male and female ...
all are alike unto God ..."

A Hispanic man lying on the bunk below Fredy turns his legs over the side of his bed onto the cold concrete floor to which he has become accustomed, pushes himself up to his feet, and stretches his arms as he lets out a large, exaggerated yawn. He puts his hands on the metal support of the top bunk, trying to make eye contact with Fredy, who is still reading. Fredy keeps reading, prompting the man to forcefully shake the top bunk to get his attention.

"Hi, Julio," Fredy says quietly without turning from his book.

Julio laughs.

"So, I take it you're going to church with the Mormons today, amigo?" Julio asks with a smile, looking at Fredy's book.

Julio, like Fredy, is fluent in English but, unlike Fredy, has a strong Mexican accent. Fredy assumes Julio must be in his mid- to late-thirties but hasn't bothered to ask. During the past few days, Fredy has gotten to know enough about his cellmate to see they have very little in common. He sees no point in investing too much of his time talking with Julio, especially since he expects to be home soon. But Julio's reference to church has caught Fredy off guard, prompting him to turn to look directly at him and abruptly sit up.

"They let us go to church here?" Fredy asks, surprised.

"Yeah, of course, man. They can't take *God* away from us. But I bet they would if they could, you know? I never been to so much church in my life until I got here, man. I go with the Mormons, and the Catholics, and any other cult that will take me. I even used to go to their twelve-step AA classes, even though I never drink and I don't believe in God!"

Julio belts out a raspy, deep chuckle, seeming well pleased with his joke.

"It beats hanging around here all day like some *pendejo*. But they ain't gonna let you go today, man, if you don't got your written request approved by ICE yet."

Fredy is surprised and disappointed.

"I didn't know I had to do that," he says. "Or that they even had church."

"Yeah," Julio says. "It took ICE like three months to approve my request to go to the church meetings."

"Three months?!" Fredy says with a mixed tone of shock and disappointment. "Why didn't anyone tell me I had to make that request?"

"They don't tell you nothing that actually helps," Julio explains. "The guards will just say, *'You guys is different,'* and *'You guys ain't entitled to nothing because you're illegals.'* But I told them, we ain't all illegals here, man; I *got* my green card. I could've been a U.S. citizen already too, like my parents are now, I just never got around to all the paperwork. But nobody here cares about any of that. And they don't know nothing about immigration cases anyway. They've only had ICE bringing people here for just over a year now. At first they had me in Utah County, and then they moved me to Alabama, and then they brought me here."

"Does ICE ever come by?" Fredy asks.

"Yeah," Julio says. "They stop by the dayroom every Tuesday to lie to everyone for fifteen to twenty minutes."

"What do you mean?" Fredy asks.

"They come to supposedly answer your questions, but they mostly just like to scare the new people into signing their deportations," Julio says. "They'll tell everyone that they've already been ordered deported, or that there's nothing they can do so they shouldn't waste their time and money getting a lawyer. Or they'll act like they care about you and say, *'I can help you get outta here real fast, just sign these papers and we can get you back to Mexico right away.'* They like to mess with people. They think it's funny. Hey, I laugh at it sometimes myself, you know, to tell the truth. But they don't try that with me no more, because they know that I already know they're all a bunch of liars."

Fredy feels discouraged by Julio's response but is unsure of how much to trust him.

"But you said they had AA classes too, right?" Fredy asks in an attempt to change the course of their conversation.

"Nah, man," Julio says. "Not here. They got them, but not for us, they say. Because we're *different*, remember? But they had them back in the Utah County Jail. All kinds of stuff. Anger management and domestic violence classes. You could even get jobs in the kitchen. It helped to pass the time. But not here, man. Not here."

"That's too bad," Fredy says. "Those classes might've been helpful. Between you and me, I've had some problems with alcohol in the past."

Julio seems surprised, both by the admission and by the first sign of an open and honest conversation with his new cellmate.

"A good little Mormon boy like you drinking the devil's potion?" Julio asks, laughing. "*¡Qué barbaridad!*"

"I wasn't always a member," Fredy explains. "I got baptized about a year and a half ago is all. I haven't drank for almost two years now, but for a while it was pretty bad. I never drank much until my sister was killed in Mexico. That messed me up pretty bad. I was pretty much an alcoholic by the time the missionaries knocked on my door."

"*¡Ay caray!*" Julio says in surprise. "*They killed your sister, man?* What happened?"

"Sorry, I don't talk about that," Fredy says, immediately regretting his implicit invitation for such an obvious follow-up question.

"No, that's cool, man, that's cool," Julio says, not pressing the issue further. "You said you came from Guerrero, Mexico, right?"

"Yeah," Fredy says.

"I heard some crazy stuff about Guerrero," Julio says. "That place is *loco* right now, man. But pretty much everywhere is these days. Even where I grew up in Mexico didn't used to be so bad, but now it's a mess too. And they just keep sending more and more of the crazy ones back there, so it's not safe for good people like you and me, you know? It's just getting worse and worse, man. I probably would've started drinking too if that happened to my sister."

"Well, that's kinda how I ended up here," Fredy admits with some reservation and embarrassment.

"What, the Mormon boy started drinking again and got himself into some trouble?" Julio asks, laughing.

"Almost," Fredy says. "It was the anniversary of my sister's death last Thursday. That's always a hard day for me, but it was just a bad time. My son Oscar had to be hospitalized a few months ago, right at the end of last year and into the beginning of this year, and we had just gotten the bills to pay two full years' worth of deductibles at once, which was—"

"Wait, what happened to your kid, man?" Julio interrupts.

Fredy pauses briefly, debating whether or not to share this part of his life with Julio. With some hesitation he decides to answer Julio's question.

"Well," Fredy says, "apparently my wife and I are both *carriers* of cystic fibrosis, which neither of us knew until after we had kids. Because of that, our son was born with cystic fibrosis, but our girls are just carriers like us."

"See, that's why you always gotta wear protection, man," Julio interrupts again. "You never know where these women have been before you, you know?"

Fredy glares at Julio with disdain, silently questioning whether the comment was a poorly timed attempt at humor or genuine ignorance. He's unsure which of the two possibilities would be more troubling. Ultimately, he responds.

"It's a genetic disease that causes infections in the lungs, if that was your way of asking," Fredy explains. "It's *not* an STD."

"Hey, man, I don't judge," Julio says, unsuccessfully holding back a smile. "This is a safe place for all your darkest secrets."

"Just forget it."

Fredy lies back down on his bed and picks up his book while Julio laughs.

"Okay, okay, I'm sorry, man, I'm sorry," Julio says. "Go on, go on. You had a lot of medical bills to pay, right? Then what else happened?"

Fredy pauses for a moment, contemplating whether or not it would be more productive to continue talking or just cut off the conversation completely. Reluctantly he sits back up and finishes his story.

"Yeah, so we'd just got all of the medical bills," Fredy continues. "Business was slow. And it was starting to create some tension at home with my wife. And to be honest, I was just feeling angry at life. Angry that I was stuck in this immigration limbo, where I've pretty much already hit the ceiling of what I can achieve here. I wanted to be an architect or an engineer, but without legal status I couldn't get past the application process for scholarships or schools, so eventually I just started up my own landscaping business.

"It wasn't even my idea to come here in the first place," Fredy continues. "My parents brought me here when I was a kid. I mean, don't get me wrong, I'm glad they did, but I feel like I've been punished my whole life for a decision I didn't have any part of. And now my own family is being punished too. All the while my kids keep getting older, and taking care of them is getting more and more expensive. And I know this is nothing new. It's the story of my life. But everything just seemed to be falling apart in that moment, so it was hitting me harder than usual. And then I noticed the date on my phone was the anniversary of my sister's death, and that was it for me. I was done. I went to the first bar I saw on my way home from work, and I just sat there and sat there for who knows how long."

"What stopped you from drinking?" Julio asks.

Fredy pauses briefly to consider the question before responding.

"My family," he says, confident with his conclusion. "I just kept thinking about what it would do to them if I started drinking again. They were the reason I stopped in the first place. I was always so close with my boy, Oscar, but our daughter Katie was born just after my sister was killed. She was almost three before I stopped drinking, and I really just hadn't been there for her like I had been for my son. I felt like she didn't even know me—which was completely my fault, of course. And I could see my son drifting away from me too. So I knew I had to stop, but I felt like I was in so deep at that point. I don't think I ever could've done it without God walking me through it all."

Fredy looks down pensively for a moment. He briefly reflects on these moments in his life but then wonders if he has made Julio uncomfortable by bringing God into the conversation. His intent is certainly not to preach, much less convert. But he feels compelled to acknowledge the fact that he did not do this alone. Having reached this conclusion, Fredy continues.

"I mean, it's not like God walked through my front door and just took away all my problems," he says with a short smile that quickly fades back into a more serious expression. "But He helped me find a way to deal with them and overcome them. He gave me a second chance. And so did my family. And last year we had another daughter, Veronica—we named her after my sister. She's never had to see me like I was back when I was drinking, and I promised God and my wife that she never would. And I just kept thinking about all of this as I'm sitting there staring at this bottle of beer—for hours, it seems like. I knew that if I took just one drink that I'd be throwing everything away. So I left."

"Good job, amigo," Julio says, seeming uncharacteristically sincere. "How'd you end up in here then?"

Fredy shakes his head as he reflects on the night of his arrest. "It was late, so I was pretty tired, and still kind of a mess," Fredy says. "I got pulled over because some officer thought I must've been drinking. It didn't help that I spilled the beer all over myself as I was leaving, and then decided to bring the bottle with me."

"Why'd you bring that?" Julio asks, scrunching his face in confusion.

"I don't know," Fredy says, shrugging. "It sounds stupid now, but in the moment I thought it would be a good reminder in the future to not let myself get back to this place. Some kind of souvenir or something to help keep me motivated."

"Yeah, you're right, that *was* stupid," Julio says, laughing. "So what'd they charge you with?"

"Nothing. They called ICE after they saw my driving privilege card."

"Are you *kidding* me, man? Everybody's got one of those. I've never heard of the police calling up ICE for that. Things is getting crazy out there now, man, *con ese payaso* Trump."

Fredy, not wanting to dwell much longer on issues beyond his control, changes the subject to a more comforting one.

"What time did you say church started?" he asks.

"Both the Mormons and the Catholics are at eight o'clock for one hour," Julio says. "It was better when they had me at the Utah County Jail, because they had them at different times, so I could kill two hours instead of just one."

"Perfect. It's gotta be close to eight now. Hopefully they'll let me go with you today, since I'll be outta here way before three months have passed to get approval."

"Yeah, if by 'outta here' you mean back in Mexico," Julio says, laughing. "They can take care of that real fast for you, man. But if you want to fight your case, you'll be here a lot longer than three months, unless you can get a bond. I been with ICE for almost two *years* now, man."

Fredy doesn't even attempt to hide his immediate feelings of shock and defeat. Julio laughs.

"I'm just messing with you, man," he says. "But that's the kinda stuff you'll hear on Tuesday when ICE comes to lie to us for fifteen to twenty minutes."

"So how long have you really been here?" Fredy asks.

"Oh, I *have* been here for two years already, but it's because the judge wouldn't give me a bond. He wouldn't even give me a bond *hearing*, man. But you got family here, right? U.S. citizen kids? U.S. citizen wife? Right?"

"Yeah, that's right," Fredy says confidently. "And I've paid all of my taxes and never got in any real trouble before this."

"Then you should be fine, man. I seen drunk drivers and wife beaters and all kindsa people get outta here with a bond. You don't got nothing to worry about."

"But *you're* still here. Even though you got a green card, right?"

"Yeah, yeah I got my green card. But they won't let me out because they say I supposedly raped some girl."

Fredy feels a sense of shock and disgust roll down through his body. He hadn't dared ask Julio previously about how he ended up here, despite his legal immigration status. Fredy does his best to hold back any visible reaction but says nothing.

"It's all just a big lie though," Julio continues. "I know she wanted it. She just changed her mind later, or during, or whatever, I dunno, man. But you can't be changing your mind in the middle of it like that! That's not right! What was I supposed to do? *¡Soy un hombre!* But my lawyer said that it don't matter that she was fine with it at first, because she was only fifteen. So I guess she can't consent or whatever. *I didn't even know she was fifteen!* I mean, obviously I knew she wasn't *eighteen*, but it's not like I'm gonna card her or something, man."

Julio laughs, and Fredy forces a barely perceptible half-smirk without responding.

"So I just had this public defender, you know?" Julio continues. "And they don't care about helping you actually fight a case. They're all the same. *Plead guilty, plead guilty*, they say. *It's better for you, it's better for you.* So I did, man, you know, I did, and now here I am. I didn't do no extra time for the conviction, though. Full credit for time served—that's the only good thing my lawyer did—but I been locked up for almost *two years* with immigration now. Can you believe that? Way longer than for my actual conviction that put me here in the first place. The immigration judge says my felony is *aggravated* supposedly, so they want to take my residency away and won't give me a bond. But I'm gonna fight them on this one, man. I'm not gonna just lay down plead guilty like last time. I already filed my appeal, so now I'm just waiting. If I lose I'll file another one, but I ain't going back to Mexico, I'll tell you that much. Even if they kick me out, I'm just gonna come right back, you know?"

To Fredy's surprise and relief, their conversation is cut short by an interruption from one of the guards passing by.

"The church meetings are starting in five minutes," says the guard, stopping and turning towards Julio and Fredy's cell. "You goin' today, Julio?"

"Of course," says Julio with a tone even more sarcastic than his norm. "Now that I have found my sweet Jesus, I don't want to ever lose him again."

"Could I please go too, sir?" Fredy asks.

The guard looks down at his list and pauses, debating in his mind how to use this small measure of power afforded him.

"All right," he says, looking up, seemingly pleased with himself for his benevolent act of mercy. "You can go today. But you gotta get in your written request right away, *got it?*"

"Yes, sir!" says Fredy, jumping down from his bed. "Thank you, thank you."

. . .

A group of about fifteen men are sitting in a medium-sized room at the Cache County Jail designated for religious services, behavior courses, and other miscellaneous meetings. Some are convicts and some are aliens. Some are white, some are black, and some are brown. Some are sincere believers, some are curious, and some have ulterior motives. But all are sinners, all are equals, and all are welcome.

A white man dressed in a suit and tie is seated at the front of the room, facing the others, who are all dressed in matching navy-blue jumpsuits, spread out between four short rows of metal fold-out chairs. Fredy takes a seat in the front row after seeing Julio sit in the back row. Next to the white man in front is a small table with a portable CD player and a dark green hymn book matching those beneath each of the chairs in the small congregation. He looks down at his watch. It's now 8:03 am. He stands to welcome this week's participants. His appearance suggests he is in his mid to late fifties. His white dress shirt is tucked tightly into his light tan pants with his large, firm stomach hanging over his waistband, partially concealing his silver belt buckle. He is wearing wide wire-framed glasses, and his dark brown hair is combed over a poorly hidden bald spot, pressed firmly against his scalp with a large amount of hair product. What stands out more than anything, to Fredy, is his large, glowing smile, too infectious to be fake.

"Welcome, brothers," he says with a jovial tone that complements his smile. "I'm thrilled to see such a large group here today. For those of you who don't know me, which is almost all of you I think, my name is Brother Robert Moore, and I'll be conducting this morning's meeting. First, we'll sing hymn number twenty-nine, 'A Poor Wayfaring Man of Grief.' You'll find a hymn book under your chairs. Brother Neo Adebayo has offered to be our music leader today, so we'll invite him to come forward. After the opening hymn, Brother Octavio Gomez will give us our opening prayer."

Neo, an African alien sitting in the front row, stands on cue and walks to the front of the room holding a hymn book. He looks to the left, where Brother Moore is preparing to press *play* on his portable CD player. Neo begins to wave his free hand once the music begins, leading the congregation in 4/4 time, the only musical time signature he knows. This particular song is actually written in 6/8 time, but since no one in the congregation knows how to follow a conductor, it makes no difference. Those in the congregation who actually participate sing poorly but sincerely after the music begins. Most of the voices, however, are buried under Brother Moore's overly confident, echoing vibrato.

At the close of the song, a Hispanic alien, Octavio, stands up in the front without a reminder to offer the prayer. He folds his arms and looks to the crowd, waiting for them to follow his lead before bowing his head and closing his eyes.

"Dear Lord, *Señor bendito*," he says. "We thank you this day for your unconditional love for us, your children. We know we have all done wrong in your eyes, Señor. Some more than others, of course. Bless us, sweet Lord, with your grace and forgiveness. Help us to make things right. In Jesus' name, amen."

"Amen," the congregation says in a broken unison.

Brother Moore stands and walks back to the front center of the room, his smile as forceful as ever.

"Thank you, Brother Adebayo and Brother Gomez," he says, looking directly at the men who are now seated again, before turning his attention back to the full congregation. "I see some new faces today, which is great. By a show of hands, for how many of you is this your first time in a Mormon meeting?"

Three men raise their hands.

"Great," Brother Moore says. "I always like to know that from the outset so I can make sure to try to speak in a way that is understandable to anyone not familiar with our church. The first thing you should know is that it's not actually called the Mormon Church; it's the Church of Jesus Christ of Latter-day Saints. People have always called us *Mormons* because of our belief in scriptures called The Book of Mormon. It's kinda like calling Malcolm X a *Koran* instead of a Muslim."

Brother Moore laughs softly, clearly pleased with what he believes to be a clever observation. Those few regular attendees know this particular line to be one of his favorite attempts at humor, despite the absence of even an encouraging courtesy laugh.

"You may have noticed that I introduced myself as *Brother* Moore," he continues, "and that I referred to some of the others in our group as the same. That's because we believe that we are *all* brothers and sisters, as children of the same heavenly parents. It doesn't matter what we look like, where we come from, or what we've done. We are all family, and we are all equal in God's eyes."

"Tell that to ICE," Julio says to the man seated next to him in the back of the room, prompting them both to laugh quietly.

Brother Moore continues undeterred.

"We believe that God wants us to be happy," he says, "We believe that Jesus Christ showed us the path to that happiness, and also provided a way back to our Heavenly Father. We believe that Christ suffered the pains of *all* mankind, and that He knows how to comfort each of you, even when no one else can.

"We believe that God can guide and speak to us as individuals, but also to His prophets, who guide His church. Through ancient prophets in Jerusalem and that part of the world, we have His words in the Holy Bible. Through ancient prophets in the Americas, we have The Book of Mormon. We believe that God has continued to speak to prophets to guide His church in our day. Through modern prophets we have learned many important truths, like our belief that families can be sealed together for eternity in sacred temples, so that we remain a family unit after this life. Marriage does not have to be until *death* do you part.

"Does anyone have any questions or comments before I continue?"

The congregation sits in silence for an extended moment. Some are looking around the room as if waiting for someone to take the lead. Brother Moore's introduction reminds Fredy of his first several meetings with the missionaries in his home. It was Sarah's idea to invite them in after they had knocked on their door one Saturday morning about two years ago. Despite being raised Catholic and passively believing in God, Fredy had never considered himself very religious. But as of late, Fredy had found himself communicating quite regularly with his creator. Not in praise or devotion, but in anger, cursing Him almost daily as the heartless, soulless being who sat idly by while his sister suffered and died alone in Mexico. Fredy had been willing to look past prior unanswered prayers, but this was his breaking point.

Although initially annoyed by his wife's invitation to the missionaries to come into their home, Fredy soon saw this as a fortunate opportunity to take his religious grievances to someone he could actually see. If God was bold enough to send His messengers to Fredy's front door, Fredy would be happy to at least be able to shoot the messengers. And so he did, as the two inexperienced and painfully naive young men quietly and patiently listened to Fredy's hostile mockery of everything they held sacred. Fredy found the short visit to be strangely therapeutic and, somewhat facetiously, invited them to come back anytime—an invitation they happily accepted, facetious or not.

The next few weekly meetings were much like the first, but Fredy slowly began to replace his comments and complaints with questions. While their answers were often far from satisfactory, they prompted him to start to look at things in a new way. He had never talked to anyone, not even his wife, about the specific details of his sister's death, other than to say that she had been murdered and no one would likely ever be arrested or charged in Mexico. He felt it was his cross to bear alone, and in so doing he had, in fact, felt terribly alone off and on for the prior three years. Even as Fredy continued to keep those details to himself, for the first time since his sister's death, he didn't feel completely alone in his sadness. He began to feel that something greater than himself was suffering alongside him and could comfort him. That comfort grew with the missionaries' teachings about eternal families and the promise that he would be with his sister again, and that his own small family would not end at death. Fredy is reminded of these initial feelings of comfort that ultimately led him to baptism six months later, as he now sits in a small room with a dozen other men listening to Brother Moore's references to Christ's love and eternal families.

Fredy raises his hand, accepting Brother Moore's open invitation to share his own thoughts. After receiving Brother Moore's blessing to speak, Fredy stands and turns to the others.

"I wanted to just say a few things," Fredy says. "The Lord has brought me through some hard times in my life."

Fredy pauses for an extended period of time, fighting unsuccessfully to hold back his tears.

"Looks like your roommate needs some extra love from you, amigo," says an inmate seated next to Julio, laughing quietly. "Maybe you can hold him extra close tonight."

"Don't be jealous now," Julio responds, laughing as well.

Brother Moore looks sternly at the two, raising his index finger to his mouth as a silent instruction for them to be quiet, in stark contrast to his generally happy demeanor. They smile in response but, not wanting to be forced to return to their cells, follow his order.

"I don't care that I'm in here," Fredy continues. "Well, I *do*, obviously, but that's on me. I probably should've done things different, I guess. But what's killing me is that it's hurting my family more than anything. I can't help thinking it would've been better if I never got married or never had kids, so they wouldn't have to suffer too. I feel like Abraham when he finally got his son, but then he was commanded to sacrifice him. I feel like God must have felt when Jesus was praying to him on the cross, saying, '*Why have ye forsaken me?*' I keep waiting for some angel to walk into my cell and tell me that my trial has passed and my family will be saved. And I haven't even been here for a full week yet!"

Fredy laughs softly and wipes the tears from his eyes. Others in the congregation laugh softly and shortly in response.

"But I just want to say," Fredy continues, "that I know that God loves me. I know that Jesus felt the pain that I feel now. The pain that my family feels now. But like Brother Moore was saying about temples, my family has been sealed together *forever*. God made me that promise. So I know that I will be back with them soon. And in the meantime, I know that He can comfort me and take care of my family. And I know He can do the same for all of you too. He hasn't forgotten us, so we can't forget Him. And I know that in the end He will save me from deportation and I will be back home with my family. I guess that's all I want to say, in Jesus' name, Amen."

"Amen," the congregation says, again in a broken unison.

CHAPTER 4

DAY 5

Monday, March 5, 2018

"You're kidding me," Greg Reed says to his wife in disbelief. "Fredy's an illegal?"

Greg is a tall, thin white man in his early forties. His short, straight, mostly brown hair is graying, more so on the sides than anywhere else, with a hairline that has been slowly retreating over the past several years. He works in sales and got back into town from a weekend business trip earlier today, but Lori waited until Ethan was in bed before telling him about Fredy.

"Don't call him *an illegal*!" Lori shoots back at her husband, who's sitting next to her on the couch in their small living room. "What's wrong with you?" Lori lightly slaps her husband's shoulder in disbelief.

"Well, what I am supposed to call them then?" Greg says, sounding genuinely surprised by the chastisement.

"*Fredy*, Greg," Lori says. "You can call him *Fredy*, just like you always have before. He's still *Fredy*. Are you serious?"

"All right, you're not being fair, Lori. Of course he's still Fredy. It's not like I was going to start calling him *the illegal* or something. This is just something I didn't know about him before. I knew he was a landscaper, a soccer coach, a Mormon, and a nice guy. I just didn't know that he was also an illegal, okay? It caught me off guard, I guess."

"Well, they don't like being called illegals, Greg. It's an offensive term."

"I'm sorry if I can't keep up with all the politically correct words of the day. And how do you know what *they* don't like to be called anyways? That sounds a bit presumptuous of you to try to speak for an entire subgroup of people. I never knew you were so racist." Greg smiles with his sarcasm.

"Oh, shut up, Greg! Race has nothing to do with this. I'm sure we have some white Canadians here illegally too. Not all illegals are Mexican."

"Not all *what*? Not all *illegals*, you say? Now you've done it, Lori. You've gone and offended me."

"That's your fault! You put that word in my head."

Greg laughs.

"It's not funny, Greg. We need to do something."

"Okay, okay, just calm down. I'm sure it's just a matter of filling out some paperwork or something. I mean, his wife's a citizen. His kids are all citizens. He should've just taken care of all of this a long time ago the right way instead of waiting until it all caught up to him like this."

"Well apparently, it's not as simple as all that. Sarah said they tried to get his citizenship years ago but that it was denied for some reason. I don't know the details, but she's pretty worried about it all. She's only been able to talk to him once since the immigration police took him last week. They won't give her any more information, or even take a message for her or anything."

"Wait, what?" Greg says, surprised. "He's in *jail*? He's got a wife and kids. It's not like he's out there raping and killing people like some of these other illeg—I mean some of these other *people from other countries*. Somehow all of those ones seem to be able to get out of jail with no problem to commit more crimes. Why are we wasting tax money locking up people like *Fredy*?"

"I don't know," Lori says, shaking her head. "It doesn't make any sense. Sarah said he's been here since he was a kid, so it's not like it was his fault his parents brought him here. It's probably *your* fault for voting for that Trump."

"Oh, come on, Lori, are you serious? He was better than the alternative."

"I'm not so sure."

"Well, you didn't even vote at all, so I don't think you can chime in now. Anyways, it's not like Donald Trump is down at some Utah jail holding the door shut on Fredy. He's not the *king* of America, like Obama thought *he* was. There's gotta be more to this. Can't they just pay a bail or something?"

"I don't know. Sarah hasn't been able to get any more information yet, and he's already been in jail for four days now. It doesn't sound like they have much money to spare though, especially after Oscar was hospitalized just a few months ago. And now with Fredy not working—Sarah just doesn't know what to do."

"Well, why doesn't their church step in and foot the bill here? I'm sure they've been paying all kinds of tithing to help build all those fancy temples. Why can't Mormons step up and actually help some of their own?"

"She's not asking us for any money, Greg. But let's be clear—if she did, you know I'd give it to her without a second thought. The problem is nobody knows what the problem is, so Sarah doesn't know how to even start to solve it. Meanwhile she's turned into a single mother overnight, the kids don't know what's going on, it's all just such a mess."

"That's terrible," Greg says, shaking his head. "Well, why don't you tell me what our plan is? I'm sure you have something in mind."

Lori smiles.

"Well first, I just need you to come home early on Wednesday this week so I can help Sarah take the kids up to the jail in Logan to go see him."

"*Logan?* Why is he all the way out in Logan? That's like two hours away from here. Or is that Trump's fault somehow too?"

"Probably," Lori says, only somewhat sarcastically, before continuing. "All I know is he's in Logan and Sarah has to make the appointment twenty-four hours in advance to take the kids out to go see him, and she can't do that alone, so I need you to be at home with Ethan on Wednesday."

"Okay, okay, what else? I'm sure you've got more up your sleeve than that."

"Of course I do," Lori says emphatically. "For whatever reason, Fredy couldn't get his citizenship through his wife, so *we're* going to be sponsoring him."

"And *there* it is," Greg says, laughing.

"Is that a problem for you?! Who was the one who taught *your* son to play soccer? Who helped *your* son to get some actual confidence and learn to work with a team while you were out on the road? You know for a *fact* that Fredy would do whatever he could to help you if things were reversed, so don't start acting like this is—"

"I know, I know, I know," Greg interrupts, raising both hands in a sign of surrender and defeat. "Take it easy. I'm just giving you a hard time. This whole thing is just so stupid. They got the wrong guy, it's as simple as that. This can't be what our immigration laws are supposed to do. Just figure out what we have to do and where I have to sign my life away and let's get this done. I'll do whatever we have to do."

"You better," Lori says with a soft smile. "And I don't want any more of this back talk from you."

Greg laughs.

"I missed you too, my love," he says.

"All right, I'm gonna call Sarah," Lori says, already walking towards the hallway leading to their bedroom to get her phone.

Greg sits down on the couch, and before more than a minute

passes, he takes his phone from his pocket and begins aimlessly browsing through random local and national news stories. It's more of a reflex than an actual interest in any specific current event or topic, and one that regularly occupies more of his time than he would prefer. He quickly finds himself surprised by a number of immigration-related stories. Not surprised by the intensity of the debate, which by now is the norm, but surprised by how Fredy's face has forced its way into these debates in a very uncomfortable way.

Greg recalls the rage he felt when former President Barack Obama issued an executive order protecting from deportation hundreds of thousands of immigrants brought to the United States illegally as children. The order, called Deferred Action for Childhood Arrivals, or DACA, remained highly controversial through the years that followed, particularly during the 2016 presidential campaigns. Although DACA only granted temporary work authorization and relief from deportation, Greg and other critics viewed it as nothing short of complete amnesty. That, Greg argued, was something only Congress could do. Not that he wanted Congress to do as much, but that was beside the point. Greg had strongly opposed the idea that anyone should receive any kind of immigration benefit, much less citizenship, after having broken the law. He was equally opposed to making an exception for the children they brought with them. If they're still children, he argued, they need to just leave with their parents. But if they're adults now they can no longer blame their parents, and should do the right thing and leave on their own.

Greg was disappointed when current President Trump did not revoke Obama's executive order on day one of his presidency like he had promised. But Trump redeemed himself in Greg's eyes last September when Attorney General Jeff Sessions announced the better-late-than-never end to DACA. Greg reluctantly accepted the six-month window provided to current DACA holders to file one last renewal to phase out the program. While both Trump and Sessions presented this window as an opportunity for Congress to act and provide a permanent replacement of DACA, Greg was certain Congress would never actually do anything. He was right. Now, six months later, Congress had yet to even vote on one of the many proposed DACA replacement bills. Although a federal district court judge from California preserved DACA beyond the six-month expiration date, Greg was also convinced the Supreme Court would ultimately overrule this miscarriage of justice by some liberal, Trump-hating anarchist posing as a judge.

Now, reading a story of demonstrators marching in support of DACA, Greg feels conflicted on the issue for the first time. It has never occurred to him that one of these people could be someone he knew, or worse yet, someone he actually liked. The shock of it all is just now registering with Greg. He feels ashamed for his initial reaction of casual sarcasm when his wife told him about Fredy. Somehow, what for years had been a black-and-white argument of principle is now smeared with varying shades of ugly, ambiguous grey. It's always been easy for Greg to dismiss hypocritical, bleeding-heart liberals pleading on behalf of millions of nameless, faceless aliens invading his country. But this is no longer just another political debate. This is a friend. A good friend. A good man.

Greg feels sick as his mind begins replaying dozens of moments with Fredy, now with a knowledge of his life-long secret. He feels tormented by memories of all the political conversations he's initiated with Fredy at neighborhood barbecues, family parties, and even after their sons' soccer games. Particularly those throughout the presidential primary elections in 2016 and during the first year of Trump's presidency. Fredy is the polar opposite of the stereotypical caricature Greg always envisioned during those discussions on immigration. Fredy is a hard worker, an entrepreneur, and a family man. A *real* American. Not one of those job-stealing freeloaders invading, exploiting and destroying the greatest nation on earth. Greg can now almost see the pain that must have been behind Fredy's eyes as he politely smiled and nodded in response to these and other statements.

The passing question of why Fredy never told Greg about this part of his life is quickly replaced by the more convincing question of why *would he* ever have told him. *I was a bad friend,* Greg thinks. But Fredy had to have known Greg never meant *him*, even if he had known the truth about Fredy. It wasn't *him*; it was *them*. Or was it? Greg has never carved out any exception in his mind for the *good* illegal immigrants in the past, nor did he accept the fact that such a thing existed. How good could they be if they broke the law? He certainly never thought of the families of those people or how the deportation of a single person could have such a negative impact on his community.

What would happen to Sarah if Fredy were deported? What about those amazing kids of theirs? And how would this impact Greg's own family, he wonders. His son would be devastated to no longer be a part of the soccer team that Fredy both created and coached. He thinks about all that confidence his son has gained, particularly after Fredy made him the "team captain," a title based more on friendship than merit. But that would just be the start. Greg knows that without Fredy's income, Sarah would never be able to afford to stay in their home. Would that be the end of their family friendship? Due to the dynamic of the neighborhood, with mostly very old and very young couples, there is not another kid his son's age in the whole neighborhood. Nor is there another couple Greg and Lori have cared to get to know beyond superficial pleasantries.

The discomfort of Greg's new feelings of doubt and guilt soon makes room for feelings of anger. But anger at whom or what, he's not quite sure. He doesn't blame Fredy for staying in the United States, even after becoming an adult. Although he argued for as much in the past, these arguments are unconvincing to him now when applied to Fredy. Greg is also not prepared to direct his anger at the law or the lawmakers that created what he still believes to be necessary limitations on immigration. Ultimately, Fredy's parents become the easiest target. If *they* had never brought him here in the first place, none of this would have ever happened. Why didn't they just do it the right way? Maybe Fredy still could have eventually ended up in their neighborhood, even if it took him a little longer to get into the United States.

Still convinced that the just laws of his country would ultimately protect people like Fredy and his family, Greg resolves to help find that solution to the problem created by Fredy's parents. He drops his phone on the couch, stands up, and walks down the hall to his bedroom. Lori has just finished her call to Sarah and looks up as Greg walks in.

"All right," he says. "Did you get it all figured out? Where do I sign? Let's get this done."

Lori smiles.

CHAPTER 5

DAY 7

Wednesday, March 7, 2018

FREDY IS NOW ACCUSTOMED TO THE DAILY ROUTINE OF LIFE IN THE CACHE COUNTY JAIL. *Accustomed* may be a poor choice of words, but he at least knows what to expect. Lights on for the morning headcount at 6:00 am, and lights out after the evening headcount at 10:30 pm. Ten to fifteen minutes for breakfast at 6:30 am, lunch at 11:30 am, and dinner at 5:30 pm. Never anything very good to eat, to no one's surprise, but they get milk with breakfast and at least some kind of minced meat with dinner. Sometimes they even get some low-quality cookies.

Everyone roams freely in the day room, where they also eat their meals, from 8:00 am to noon, and then again from 5:00 pm to 9:00 pm. The day room has tables and chairs for sitting, although usually not enough, and a thirty-inch television suspended from the wall. Some sit and talk. Some walk around or do push-ups or sit-ups. Others watch the television. Every Sunday, religious leaders come to teach for an hour, and every Tuesday ICE comes to, according to Julio, "lie to everyone and scare the new people for fifteen to twenty minutes."

Cell time is the hardest time of the day, from 6:00 am to 8:00 am, noon to 5:00 pm, and then finally from 9:00 pm until morning.

Some read, some try to sleep, and some cry. It's the lack of distraction that proves to be the most difficult, especially for those like Fredy who have little in common with or struggle to be around their cellmates. They are left largely to thoughts of what they stand to lose and the uncertainty of what's to come.

As Fredy goes through the motions of his new routine, his mind is constantly focused on what he would be doing at any given moment if he were back with his family. He is surprised by many of the daily annoyances of life that he misses so much now that they're gone. He misses his wife pulling his blanket off of him in the middle of the night and the wheezing sound she makes breathing through her nose all night. He misses the sound of his kids fighting over the remote control or their spot on the couch. He misses changing his baby daughter's diapers at the end of a long day of work when he is ready to collapse but it's "his turn." He feels this short time away from his family has been a sort of blessing, as it has left him recommitted to better prioritize his time once he's back home.

When he's not deep in thought during his cell time, Fredy passes the vast majority of this time reading—avoiding, when possible, conversation with Julio, whose mere presence has caused him discomfort ever since he told him about his criminal history. Fredy is lying on his bed reading a paperback copy of *Uncle Tom's Cabin* he checked out of the jail library when he is disrupted by one of the guards.

"We got visitors," he says loudly outside of Fredy's cell.

Fredy sits up abruptly at attention but relaxes and slowly lies back down as Julio stands up and begins walking towards the guard. "It's about time they showed up," Julio says. "I only got like two bucks left on my account."

"It's not your parents, Julio," the guard says, raising his hand motioning for him to stop. "I'm sure they'll be back here soon enough, but not today. I don't know how that sweet old mother of yours puts up with you anyway."

"Are you kidding me, man?" Julio says with a poorly restrained smirk. "I'm her pride and joy. So who is it then?"

"Someone for Mr. Wilfredo Gonzalez," the guard says.

"That's me!" Fredy says with excitement, tossing aside his book and jumping down from his bed. "Is it Sarah?"

"No idea," the guard says. "You comin'?"

The guard extends his left arm, directing Fredy to walk out of his cell, which he eagerly does. Fredy walks anxiously down the halls of the jail, occasionally turning back to the guard behind him for additional guidance or instructions but receiving none. He stops at a locked door.

"Please move five steps to your left and put your hands on the wall," the guard says.

Fredy obeys the orders without question. The guard watches Fredy cautiously as he pulls out a key ring attached with a zip string to his belt. The guard looks down at the key ring, quickly rotating through them until he finds the right one. Fredy's excitement is readily visible as he imagines his wife and kids waiting for him on the other side of the door. The guard unlocks and holds open the door, motioning for Fredy to enter an unlit room.

Even before the guard turns on the light, Fredy sees a single round metal seat, centered on a metal cylinder fastened to the floor in a room less than half the size of his cell. The guard turns on the light. Instead of a person, Fredy sees a thirteen-inch television with a built-in camera immediately above the screen and a corded telephone attached to the left side. It is bolted on top of a steel counter spanning the back of the room. Whatever disappointment he initially feels from the impersonality of the visiting arrangements vanishes at the sight of his wife and the older two of his three kids on the black-and-white television screen.

"Sarah!" Fredy shouts. "Sarah, I'm so glad you finally came."

"You gotta talk into the phone, sir," the guard interrupts in a slightly harsh tone softened by a smile. "I'll be back in twenty minutes. Just ring the buzzer by the door if you wanna come out sooner."

The guard closes the door, leaving it locked as Fredy grabs the phone before sitting down in front of the television screen.

"Sarah!" Fredy shouts into the phone. "Can you hear me? Can you hear me okay?"

Fredy sees Sarah look directly into the camera and quickly cover her mouth, appearing to conceal her emotions in front of the kids. After a brief pause, she responds.

"Yes, I hear you, Fredy!" she says. Her voice echoes through the phone, breaking through mild static. "Why haven't you called me again?" she asks. "It's almost been a whole week and I have no idea what's going on."

"I know. I'm sorry," Fredy says. "They only let me make that one call to you that first night. I asked about making other calls, but they said that someone needed to put money on my account. I wrote you a letter to see if you could put some money on my account, but I didn't have money on my account to pay for a stamp," Fredy says, instinctively laughing after describing his predicament for the first time out loud.

"Where's Veronica?" Fredy asks upon noticing their baby doesn't appear to be in the room.

"She's out in the lobby with Lori," Sarah says abruptly. "I can only do so much on my own."

"I know," Fredy says. "I'm sorry, I didn't mean for—"

"Just wait a second, Oscar," Sarah says, turning away from the camera to her son, Oscar, who is standing to her left, impatiently tugging at the metal cord on the phone while their four-year-old daughter, Katie, restlessly sits on her lap. "Mommy's still talk—I said no, Oscar! Just wait!"

"Well, why can't we go see him, mom?" Oscar asks angrily. "You said we could see him!"

"We do see him, Oscar," Sarah says, pointing to the television screen on her end. "Look, there's your daddy right there."

"No. You said we could *see* him," Oscar says. "I want to see him.

I want to hug him."

"Here," Sarah says, handing the phone to Oscar. "Just talk to your dad for a second."

Sarah stands up and puts Katie down on the floor, leaving an empty chair for Oscar to use as he talks to his father.

"Hi, Dad," Oscar says. "Is that really you on the TV?"

Fredy smiles warmly at the sound of his son's voice.

"Yes, that's me, buddy," he says, waving to the camera. "I see you too. You look so big. Have you been working out? Your muscles have definitely grown in this past week."

"Your voice sounds weird, Dad."

"Yeah, I know. It's like when we play with your Batman walkie talkies, right? Kinda cool, huh?"

"No," Oscar says, shaking his head with a frown. "I don't like it. When are you coming home?"

The question stings Fredy, prompting him to pause briefly before responding.

"I don't know, buddy," Fredy says. "I hope really soon. How's school going?" he asks, hoping to change the subject.

"Why are you even here?" Oscar asks, unwilling to follow his father's lead to more trivial topics. "What did you do wrong?"

"We're trying to figure that out really soon, okay?" Fredy answers. "Tell me about school."

Oscar sits quietly for a moment, his face slowly turning more upset. "I hate those stupid police," he says. "I hate them!"

"It's not their fault," Fredy says with a frown. "They're just doing their job. They're not bad people. It's nobody's fault."

"How can it be their job to steal my dad?" Oscar asks through a burst of tears. "That's not a job! I hate, hate, hate them. I hate them!"

Oscar drops the phone as his crying brings on a fit of heavy coughing and wheezing, which Fredy can hear through the receiver of the phone even as it continues to sway back and forth by the cord. Fredy instinctively reaches towards the screen to help, only to be immediately reminded of his current uselessness. He stands up and starts to shout instructions to his wife on how to help Oscar. Although Sarah cannot hear Fredy, she's essentially following his orders. Sarah pulls Oscar's right side close to her front and puts her left arm around his back. She cups her right hand and starts clapping against Oscar's chest, using an airway-clearance technique Oscar's respiratory therapist taught them as a way of dislodging the mucus buildup typical of cystic fibrosis. After what feels to Fredy like several minutes, Sarah is able to help Oscar calm down and begin to breathe normally. Fredy sees his wife hug their son for a moment, and he can see that they're talking to each other briefly before Sarah picks up the phone and hands it back to Oscar.

"Are you okay, buddy?" Fredy says anxiously.

"Yeah," Oscar says, still sniffling but no longer crying.

"Did Mom bring the portable nebulizer?"

"I said I'm fine, Dad!" Oscar says curtly, making it clear that his anger at the situation has not passed.

Fredy sits silently, unsure of how to respond for a moment.

"This world has enough anger and hate, Oscar," Fredy finally says. "You have to choose if you want to make this world better or worse. Hate never made anything better. Hate's not gonna help you be Mom's big helper and take care of your little sisters. I need your love to be stronger, buddy. Your love for me, and for Mommy, and for your little sisters. Can you do that for me?"

Oscar pauses before responding, slowly regaining his composure.

"I don't know," he finally says, looking down at his feet. "I don't know if I can do that."

"Well, *I* know," Fredy says. "You're the strongest kid I've ever met, Oscar. Look at you. You got out of the hospital just a couple of months ago, and you already look stronger than me. And look how fast you shook off that coughing, like it was nothing. You're getting stronger and stronger every day. So can you try for me, buddy?"

"I guess so," Oscar says with a half-smile. "I can try."

"Good boy," Fredy says. "Mom needs you to be strong now, okay?"

"Okay," Oscar says. "But when will you come home?"

"I don't know yet."

"Will you *ever* come home?"

"Of course, buddy, of course. I'm saying my prayers every day, and I know God will bring me back home soon. And I know you're saying your prayers too. Do you remember when we all went to the temple together last year? What did we do?"

Oscar smiles and waits a moment before responding.

"Got sealed together," he says softly.

"For how long was it?" Fredy asks. "I can't seem to remember. Was it just for—a couple of *weeks*?"

"No," Oscar says.

"Nine *months*?" Fredy asks.

"*Forever*," Oscar says, smiling now more than ever.

"That's right, buddy. God made a promise to us that we will be together forever. And He'll keep that promise. And I promise you that I'll be home soon, okay?"

"Okay."

"All right, Oscar," Sarah says. "Why don't you say bye to your dad and take Katie out to Lori for a minute so Mom and Dad can talk?"

"Bye, Dad," Oscar says.

"Bye, buddy," Fredy says. "I love you to the moon and back."

"I love *you* to the moon and back," Oscar says, leaning towards the small screen and kissing the black-and-white image of his father and then laughing at the gesture.

Oscar hands the phone to his mother as he stands up from his chair and takes his younger sister by the hand as they walk towards the door. Sarah opens the door and motions for Lori to come. After closing the door, she picks up the phone, sits down, and begins talking to her husband.

"I don't think you should be making promises like that, Fredy," she says.

"Like what?" Fredy says in genuine confusion.

"That everything's gonna be fine, and that you'll be out soon. We don't have any idea what's gonna happen."

"Of course we do," Fredy says reassuringly. "We know how all this ends, Sarah. We made a promise to God and He made a promise to us. He will keep us together forever; we just gotta stay faithful."

"Yeah, I want to believe that too, Fredy; you know I do. But even if that's how it all *ends* once we're all dead and gone, we got a lot of life left. You can't make promises to our kids like that, Fredy. *I'm* the one that has to be there at home when they're crying at night for you. *I'm* the one that's gonna have to answer every night why you're still not back like you promised. And worse yet, like you said *God* promised. God did *not* make that promise to you, and you know it."

"But I have faith, baby. God already got me through harder times than this, and He'll get us through this too."

"That's fine, Fredy. I'm trying to have faith too. But faith without works is dead, right? So we gotta figure out what we're gonna do before just throwing our hands up and letting God do it all for us. So what are we supposed to do?"

"Okay, you're right, you're right. I'm sure this has been harder on you than anyone. But I'm doing everything I can to figure this all out. Hold on a sec."

Fredy leans his head to his left, holding the phone against his shoulder, freeing both hands to pull out some folded-up paperwork from the pocket of his navy-blue jumpsuit. He unfolds and irons them out with his hand on the table in front of him and begins looking through the documents.

"Okay," he says, "they gave me a bunch of documents on Saturday, mostly just generic forms. But I just found out yesterday that my hearing has been scheduled for March 14th at 8:00 am."

"What?!" Sarah says in shock. "Not for whole other week?! How can they keep you there for so long without a bond hearing?"

"I don't know, baby, that's just what they told me. I got the notice right here."

Fredy lifts up the notice and holds it up near the camera as if Sarah would somehow be able to make out the contents on the small screen in front of her. Sarah looks away.

"I'm not sure we can make it another week, Fredy," she says desperately.

"Of course you can, Sarah. I was in Mexico for like four months after my sister died. It was hard, I know, but you made it work."

"Yeah, but my brother was still single and living with us at the time helping out, and I was still working back then. What about all your clients? How are we supposed to keep your business going? We only have your income now."

"Did the jail release my cell phone to you?" Fredy asks. "I filled out all the paperwork for that."

"Yeah, I got it in here," Sarah says, lifting up her purse. "But how's that supposed to help me?"

"Just call Trevor. He knows the schedule and all my clients and can take care of everything until I get out. You won't have to worry about a thing. Everything will be fine."

"Well, what about—it doesn't matter, I'll figure it out. Do you got the address for the court?" Sarah asks as she begins fishing through her purse for a pen.

"Yeah. Tell me when you're ready."

Sarah eventually finds a pen but no paper, so she holds it over the palm of her left hand ready to write, the phone held to her ear with her shoulder. She writes and confirms the address Fredy gives her, and the time. She raises her eyebrows and sighs in frustration when Fredy asks her to also write down the three phone numbers of attorneys on a list of free legal service providers he has in his documents. By the time she's done, the better part of her left forearm is tattooed with critical legal information.

"I already told the immigration officers that I want a bond hearing," Fredy says. "So just see if one of those attorneys can help me with that next week. Shouldn't be too complicated, but they told me it would probably take a day to update the system once the judge gives me a bond. But you can pay the bond the day after my hearing they said, so I should be home by the end of next week. Just one more week, baby. We can do it."

"Well, how much will we have to pay for the bond?" Sarah asks. "With Oscar's medical bills coming all of a sudden, we were already late on our rent when you were arrested. The church will be able to help with the rent, but this all happened right at the beginning of the month, just as all the bills were coming in. I don't think we're gonna have much left to pay your bond. I still can't believe we even have to pay one."

"I'm sure it won't be too much compared to others," Fredy says. "I don't have a criminal history like a lot of the people in here, so it might just be a couple of thousand bucks, but it could be closer to five thousand or so."

"Five *thousand?*" Sarah asks in shock. "Or maybe even more?! We can't afford that right now, Fredy, you know that!"

"Well, I'm sure we can figure something out," Fredy says. "Maybe we'll have to sell my car or something just for now, but if I have to get a second job to get caught up, then I'll do it. Everything will be fine."

Sarah remains seated in silence, her emotional steam slowly—almost imperceptibly—building until she explodes.

"Stop saying that!" she shouts. "Everything's *not* fine, Fredy, and you can*not* keep telling me that it's all just gonna work out! You don't know that. Nobody does. You're in jail, Fredy! Look at you!"

Sarah pauses, covering her mouth with her hand and looking down.

"You look like some kinda *murderer* or something in that jumpsuit," she says, her voice now deepened and slowed by her crying.

"Like, like just some *criminal*. That's how they see you, Fredy, and that's how they're gonna treat you. You've seen the news just like everyone else. You know what everyone in the country thinks about people like you. Stop pretending you don't know how serious this all is!"

Sarah stops talking, her increasing sobs having overpowered her speech. Fredy sits quietly for a moment, looking helplessly at the image of his wife. The growing burden of having brought these hardships upon those he loves most weighs heavily on his optimism, threatening to crush it.

"I'm sorry, Sarah," he finally says. "I'm so sorry. I never meant for this to happen to you. I should've done things differently, I know."

"*What?*!" Sarah says, frustration and anger replacing her sadness. "What should you have done different? Should you have never met me? Never loved me? Never married me? We *tried* to do things right. We tried to fix things, to pay their fees and go to their interviews and all of that. But that wasn't good enough for them. I just can't understand how this can really be happening to us. That this could happen to anyone. I don't understand. I'll never understand."

"I'm sorry," Fredy says again.

"Stop apologizing!" Sarah shouts. "Why are you *sorry?*!"

Fredy waits before responding, unsure himself of the answer. As often as he has found himself trembling at the thought of the hardships his family is enduring in his absence, it would be a lie to say that he regrets any decision that led to the formation of his beautiful, perfect little family. Everything good in him he attributes to them. He likes to believe as well that they are at least somewhat better off because of him. Still, he feels sorry. But why?

"I'm sorry you're hurting," he finally says.

Sarah looks back up at the television screen. She reaches forward to touch it, gently rubbing the small black-and-white image of her husband.

"Me too," she says with a sad smile.

They sit in silence for a moment just looking at each other. Ultimately, Fredy breaks the silence.

"I love you," he says.

"I love you more," Sarah says with a slightly less sad smile.

CHAPTER 6

DAY 9

Friday, March 9, 2018

"ALL RIGHT, LET'S GO, LET'S GO, LET'S GO!" shouts an unseen man from somewhere outside of Fredy's cell, startling him awake. "Everybody move!"

It's still very dark in his cell, but quite loud with a lot of movement and talking in both English and Spanish. Fredy opens his eyes and sees a light outside of his cell and several men loudly marching past his door. Fredy rubs his eyes and sits up.

"What's going on?" he asks, hoping Julio is awake too and will hear him over the noise outside their cell.

"It's Friday," Julio says. "That's what's going on. Deportation and transfer day."

"Why so many?" Fredy asks. "Are they really deporting that many people today? Some just barely got here."

"A lot of them, yeah," Julio says. "Some don't got the stomach for the fight in jail, so they just give up. Or maybe they believed ICE's lies on Tuesday. But some are probably being transferred to Vegas or Colorado. That's where they send a lot of them ever since ICE lost their contract with the Utah County Jail. Most don't stay here long. *You* could be next," he adds, laughing. "You got your luggage packed up? Or should I call the butler to gather your belongings?"

"Whatever," Fredy says, at this point not believing most of what Julio tells him. "I talked to ICE on Tuesday, and they didn't say anything about transferring me."

Julio laughs as heartily as one possibly can after having been woken up at four in the morning.

"When do you think they told me I was going from Utah County to Tucson, genius?" Julio says. "And then two days later to Alabama for ten months? And then all of a sudden here? They told me at four in the morning, ten minutes before I left, like the rest of these fools. That's why it's so loud. They're mad. Real mad. Some of them just found out they're going."

"So you're telling me that nobody knew they were leaving today?" Fredy asks incredulously.

"No," Julio says. "Some of them probably knew, but they're as loud as the rest of them because they just don't care about nothing, you know? They got nothing to lose now. They don't care that some of us gotta stay here and try to sleep while we can. Mostly the Hondurans—they're the worst. They're just dirty people who don't care about nobody else, you know? Even worse than the Guatemalans."

"That's not true," Fredy says, sitting up before leaning over his bed to look directly at his cellmate below. "I've got good friends from Honduras and Guatemala. What's wrong with you?"

"Whatever you say, man," Julio says, laughing. "I keep asking them to let me room with a respectable Mexican, but somehow that's never happened yet after more than two years now."

"You do know that *I'm* Mexican, right?" Fredy asks.

"Oh yeah," Julio says, laughing. "I forgot. But you're not a *real* Mexican, so it don't matter. You're more gringo than Latino."

"Well, according to the gringos, we're all Mexicans," Fredy says. "As long as we've all got brown skin and look like we habla Spanish."

"True," Julio says. "But the gringos is a special breed of stupid."

"Even the brown gringos like me?" Fredy asks, shaking his head and then rolling back over on to his pillow.

"*Especially* the brown gringos like you," Julio says, laughing more than ever.

If Fredy cared at all about what Julio thought about him, he might have continued to challenge his blanket statements. But he doesn't. And this is nothing new to Fredy, having lived most of his life marginalized between two worlds. He's too gringo to be Mexican and too Mexican to be gringo. He's not a real Latino, and not a real American. As an "alien," he's arguably not even a real person. But, again, this is nothing new to Fredy, and it doesn't occupy his thoughts as he is more interested in sleep than deep inner reflection at the moment. He rolls over in his bed to face the wall and attempts to cover his ears with his pillow as the group of aliens continues to walk past noisily. Some seem to intentionally talk louder as they pass any unlit cells.

Having given up on the possibility of sleep, and having no interest in talking more to Julio, Fredy is left now to his thoughts. He knows that each voice he hears walk past his door belongs to a living, breathing human being. A father, a son, a brother, a husband, a neighbor, and a friend. Some have been in the United States for only a short time. Others have been here as long as Fredy or even longer. Some have serious criminal histories, some have recent minor offenses, and some have completely clean records. Some sat next to Fredy in his small church meeting less than a week ago as they all faithfully prayed for divine intervention from the same God. But they're all going—in a best-case scenario, to a holding facility in Nevada or Colorado, a six- to eight-hour drive away from their family and, if they have one, their attorney. But others are taking a much longer and perhaps permanent trip to a distant country now more foreign than native. Fredy spends the next two hours lying quietly on his bed, thinking of and praying for them, ultimately being interrupted by the 6:00 am headcount for the remaining few men. Their now-empty beds will be filled by the end of the day.

. . .

"Law office. How can I help you?" answers a woman after Sarah waits through three rings on her cell phone.

Just moments ago, Sarah managed to get both her four-year-old, Katie, and her baby, Veronica, to sleep, and only about fifteen minutes past her daily goal of 2:00 pm. It was no small feat coordinating their two competing nap schedules, but one that has blessed her with a window of almost of a full hour a day to attempt to accomplish something before Lori brings Oscar home from school. Sometimes she gives in to the temptation to join them in their nap. But today she is continuing her efforts to find an attorney for Fredy's bond hearing.

"Hi, can I talk to the attorney, please?" Sarah says to the woman.

"Which one, ma'am?" the woman asks. "We have a few that share the office space here."

Sarah frowns as she looks at the last of the three names of free attorneys she wrote on her arm during her visit with Fredy. By the time she was able to transcribe them over to actual paper later that night, she was left with a lot of guesswork.

"Uh," she says, making no effort to conceal her uncertainty, "Jasmine—*Barista?*"

The woman laughs. "You mean Jasmine *Bautista?*" she asks.

"Yeah, sorry," Sarah says. "I must've written it down wrong."

"Are you a current client of Ms. Bautista?" she asks.

"No, I got her name from my husband," Sarah says. "She was on some list of free attorneys."

"Oh, really?" she says. "Can you please hold for a minute?"

Before Sarah can answer, the line is taken over with smooth jazz music, indicating she has already been placed on hold. Sarah looks down at her watch to check the time, confirming she still has plenty of time before Oscar will be home. She already spoke with the other two attorneys on Fredy's list yesterday. The first one told her she was short-staffed and no longer able to take on any new cases. The second told her he was no longer interested in practicing immigration law at all. Sarah left a message with Jasmine Bautista—or Jasmine *Barista*—yesterday but had not heard back, prompting her to try again today. After about two minutes on hold, the woman returns to the call.

"Ms. Bautista can speak to you now," she says. "Please hold and I will transfer you."

Sarah hears two rings before the phone is picked up.

"Hello, this is Jasmine."

Sarah pauses for a moment, unsure if the attorney is going to say anything else or if she should speak first. The prolonged silence confirms the latter.

"Hi," Sarah ultimately says. "Are you an immigration lawyer?"

"Yes, I am."

"Okay, but are you still taking new cases?" Sarah asks hopefully.

"Yes, I am."

"Oh, great," Sarah says enthusiastically. "My husband has a hearing in the immigration court on the fourteenth and we wanted to get a lawyer to help him."

"The fourteenth of *this* month? So next week? That's not giving me much time to work with. Is there any reason you're just now looking for a lawyer?"

"Well, I've been calling people for a couple days now, and I left a message with your office yesterday too. My husband got your name off some list of free attorneys."

"Oh, really?" Ms. Bautista asks with a tone of obvious surprise. "That must be an old list that he got somehow. I was dropped from that list last year."

Her response makes Sarah nervous. How good of an attorney could you be if you got kicked off of a program for providing *free* legal assistance?

"What do you mean *dropped*?" Sarah asks in hopes of a reasonable explanation.

"Nothing to worry about," Ms. Bautista says, seeming to sense Sarah's reservations. "The branch of the Department of Justice that determines who can and cannot be on the list of free legal service providers has just added a bunch of extra hoops we have to jump through before being included on the list they hand out to everybody. I thought I did everything they asked for, but then I saw I had been dropped from the list. Last I heard there wasn't anyone left on the list for the Utah court, which is probably why your husband got an old list instead of the current empty one."

Sarah sighs heavily. "All right," she says. "Well, we'll just have to try to figure something else out, I guess."

"No, no, not necessarily," Ms. Bautista says. "I still represent people for free or discounted prices when I can, depending on the type of case. I'm just not on the official list anymore, that's all."

"Oh, okay, great," Sarah says with a tone of restored hope. "We're not looking for any handouts or anything—we can figure out how to pay you once my husband is out of jail—we just don't know how much his bond is going to be until after his hearing next week. He was saying it could be *thousands* of dollars. So obviously we want to make sure we can get enough money together for that first."

"Oh, he's detained?" Ms. Bautista asks.

"Yes," Sarah says nervously. "Is that a problem?"

Ms. Bautista pauses for an uncomfortable amount of time for Sarah before responding.

"I'm sorry," she says. "I don't do detained cases anymore. It's just too fast-paced for me and my little office here. We never seem to have enough time with the deadlines and everything to do the kind of quality work I demand from myself."

"*Fast*-paced?" Sarah asks in confusion. "But my husband was arrested on March 1st and they're just barely giving him a bond hearing on the 14th."

"Oh, I understand how slow it feels to the family, and obviously the people actually detained. But for the amount of work required and the complexities of immigration law, I just always felt like I was doing my clients a disservice with rushed work back when I still did detained cases."

Sarah doesn't respond, pressuring Ms. Bautista to continue.

"I'm sorry," she says. "Even on the old free legal services list, it should've specified that I wasn't doing detained cases. But are you sure he has a hearing scheduled in *Utah*? He's still in Utah?"

Sarah pauses, confused and somewhat nervous by the tone of the question.

"Yes," Sarah says slowly. "I'm sure. He gave me the court address in West Valley. Is that a problem?

"No. It's not a problem. I heard they occasionally still do detained hearings here in Utah, but ICE has been transferring most of the detainees out of state for a while now. Which is a huge headache to communicate with the client, and coordinate with the court, and decide if you're better off with an attorney in the same state as the family and the evidence or the client and the court. Which is another reason I stopped doing detained cases. So, no, it's definitely not a problem; it's a good thing actually. Well, depending on the judge, I guess. Sometimes we have better luck with the judges in other states, but sometimes they're worse. It's a crapshoot really, but—sorry, none of this is relevant to your husband's case."

"Okay, but do you know of any other lawyer that might be able to help us just with this bond hearing?"

"Unfortunately, no. I understand the predicament you're in, working with limited funds that you'll want to save to pay the actual bond before spending that all on an attorney. But I don't know of anyone else taking on free detained cases or allowing payment *after* the bond hearing. They're all going to want that money up front. But if your husband is able to get released, I would certainly be willing to take a closer look at his case to see what I can do to help."

She pauses, appearing to be expecting a response from Sarah but receiving none. Sarah has no words. She feels discouraged, though not completely surprised, that none of the advertised free legal service providers will be able or willing to actually provide any free legal services. Life experience has helped her develop a healthy skepticism, which is generally balanced out by Fredy's relentless optimism. But now she is starting to feel skeptical of Fredy's optimism. Ms. Bautista continues.

"Do you have any other questions I can help you with?" she asks.

"No," Sarah says. "I don't think so. Thanks anyway."

Sarah ends the call and sighs. She was cautiously hoping to have better news for Fredy when he calls tonight. Now that she has been able to add money to his account for phone calls, they agreed that it didn't make much sense for her to drive eighty miles just to see each other on a small screen. Especially after they learned that Sarah could do the same for thirty minutes a day from home on their laptop computer. But until the Cache County Jail approves Sarah's online application to do so, Fredy is calling once a day at 8:00 pm.

She thinks back on Fredy's reassurances that his case is far less complicated than most of the people he has met so far. She knows that once Fredy gets out of jail, they will be able to figure out the rest. They just need him home. Worried that this new piece of bad news may discourage her husband, she resolves to prepare herself to sound as optimistic as possible when Fredy calls. Off and on throughout the rest of the afternoon, she will rehearse different versions of the conversation in her mind until she is comfortable with her script.

CHAPTER 7

DAY 14

Wednesday, March 14, 2018

THIRTY-THREE ALIENS DRESSED IN NAVY-BLUE JUMPSUITS ARE SITTING CLOSE TOGETHER ON THREE ROWS OF WOODEN BENCHES INSIDE A SMALL COURTROOM. All of them have handcuffs around their ankles and wrists, which are fastened to a chain around their waists. Some are talking quietly to each other, but Fredy is sitting anxiously in silence in the front row. A dark wooden fence-like barricade stands directly in front of him, stretching across the room, at the end of which is a wooden swinging gate leading to the open area of the courtroom. Upon entering, one finds two large desks, both accompanied by two leather chairs with wooden armrests. Behind the desk to the left sits a government attorney, logging on to a black laptop as he skims through a large bin full of files on the floor to his left. The desk to the right is empty.

In front of the desks reserved for attorneys, raised above the rest of room by a single step, sits a large judge's bench, with smaller desks on either side reserved for the court interpreter and court clerk, both of whom are seated and quietly waiting. Behind the judge's bench is an empty red leather chair, directly behind which is a large gold circle displaying the seal of the Executive Office for Immigration Review next to a standing pole holding an American flag. The quiet conversations filling the room come to an abrupt halt as a man in a black robe opens the door in the back right corner of the room behind the clerk's desk, prompting the clerk in front of him to immediately stand.

"All rise!" she says, cuing everyone in the courtroom to follow her lead.

After standing with the rest, Fredy turns around, bobbing his head from side to side in an attempt to see between the people behind him in search of his wife. She's not there. Fredy turns back to the front of the courtroom to check the time on the large circular clock hanging on the wall to his left. It's 8:04 am.

She's late, Fredy thinks. *I told her to come early.*

After nearly two weeks away from his family, he's anxious to actually touch his wife again.

She'll be here soon, Fredy reassures himself.

During their last phone conversation, she told him that she had not been able to get any of the attorneys from the free legal services list to help. But Fredy feels certain, despite Julio's negative description of public defenders, that whatever attorney the judge appoints to him should be able to manage a case as simple as his.

"Thank you. You may all be seated," the judge says after taking his own seat.

He's a heavy-set white man with squinted brown eyes, a long, pointed nose, and a wide, clean-shaven jaw. The front and top of his head are completely bald, with short-trimmed dark brown hair circling the lower half of his head. The loose skin of his neck drapes down from the bottom of his chin to the white collar of the dress shirt under his black robe. The judge turns to the government attorney assigned for the master calendar hearings for the day.

"Good morning, Mr. Richter," he says in his low, raspy voice. "How are you?"

"I'm doing well, Judge," Mr. Richter says. "Yourself?"

"Just another day in paradise," the judge says.

Mr. Richter smiles politely and musters out a half-hearted courtesy laugh. The desk immediately to the right of the government attorney, reserved for the aliens and their counsel, is still empty. The judge turns his attention to the gallery beyond the parties' desks, quickly scanning by all the new faces before stopping at a familiar one.

"Mr. Radley," he says to a tall white man in a suit and tie just walking in, "you appear to be the only attorney here so far. Is your client ready to proceed?"

"Yes, Your Honor," he says. "Can the court please call the case of Mr. Luis Garza? The last three digits of his alien number are 407."

Mr. Radley motions for a man seated in the row in behind Fredy, who stands and slowly walks sideways through the small space between the other seated men and the wooden bench in front of him. An ICE officer stands ready to meet him once he reaches the end of his row. The officer unlocks the handcuff to one of the alien's hands, leaving the other secured to the chain around his waist. The handcuffs around his ankles remain attached, easily doubling the number of steps he would otherwise require in making his way to the seat next to his attorney.

The judge turns to his immediate left where his clerk, a Hispanic woman in a black pantsuit, sits in front of a computer monitor and a stack of blue folders. Familiar with the routine, she requires no further instruction and begins fishing through the stack of folders in search of the alien's file. She stops at what is by far the largest of the files, and the only one requiring the added support of a large rubber band wrapped around it. She picks up the file with both hands and passes it to the judge, who is smiling and shaking his head.

"I could've told you that one was Mr. Radley's case without even opening it," the judge says facetiously, in reference to the size of the file.

Mr. Radley laughs. "I'm just doing my part to make sure you have no shortage of reading material before your hearings, Your

Honor," he says. "I feel a moral responsibility to see to it that you're never bored."

"Your arguments are generally very *creative*, if not entertaining, Mr. Radley, but certainly never boring."

"I will take that as a compliment, Your Honor."

"As well you should. Give me just a moment to get the recording going," the judge says as he turns to his own computer monitor, fidgeting with the equipment until the recording starts.

"We are back on the record," the judge begins, a more robotic and serious tone replacing his natural one. "It is March 14, 2018. This is Immigration Judge Samuel O. Lanzotti conducting removal proceedings in the matter of Mr. Luis Garza. All parties are present. On behalf of the respondent is—"

"Shane Radley," Mr. Radley says, instinctively following the cue of the judge's pause.

"And," the judge continues, "on behalf of the Department of Homeland Security is—"

"Jonathan Richter," Mr. Richter says.

"Today we are scheduled both for bond and removal proceedings," the judge says. "At our last hearing, the respondent, through counsel, denied all of the allegations and charges contained in the Notice to Appear. Specifically, the respondent denies that he was convicted of possession with intent to distribute cocaine and that his conviction is an aggravated felony. Mr. Radley, how would you like to proceed?"

The judge's reference to a "Notice to Appear" jumps out at Fredy. It's the first thing that has any semblance of meaning to him, as he recalls reading the same on one of the many documents one of the ICE officers gave him at the jail after his arrest. This passing feeling of understanding reminds him of his early efforts at learning English in middle school, straining to understand his gringo peers with only a few sporadic words in his limited vocabulary—like *hello* or *happy* or *friend*—standing out in the onslaught of gibberish. Now, like then, it is not enough to help him understand the actual context, but it still gives him a sense of hope of understanding, even if it is a false hope.

Legalese is a foreign language even for most native English speakers. Immigration law legalese is a dialect understood by even fewer. For aliens, the immigration court is a foreign country within a foreign country. With his hands still cuffed and linked to the chain around his waist, Fredy struggles to sort through his paperwork until he finds the one titled *Notice to Appear*. He begins to read to himself his charges again. After reading and re-reading the document in its entirety, he is still not sure of its true significance. He turns his attention back to the ongoing hearing.

"Your Honor," Mr. Radley continues, "no one is disputing the fact that Mr. Garza sold drugs—"

"*¿Qué pasa, Shane?*" his client whispers in panic to Mr. Radley. "*I told you, it wasn't mine. I'm innocent.*"

"Quiet," Mr. Radley shoots back quietly but forcefully, cupping his hand over the portable microphone on the desk in front of him. "Nobody's gonna believe that; just let me do the talking."

"Is everything all right, Mr. Radley?" the judge asks, scrunching his face in confusion and concern.

"Yes, Your Honor," Mr. Radley continues. "Everything is perfect. As I was saying, no one is disputing that Mr. Garza sold drugs in a drug-free zone. Specifically, that he sold cocaine to a minor within one hundred yards of a high school."

"It sounds like Mr. Garza's counsel has made the government's closing arguments for us," interrupts Mr. Richter, seeming to hold back a laugh. "I guess with that we'll rest our case."

"You've been resting your whole professional career, Richter," Mr. Radley says, turning to his adversary with a smile. "Why stop now?"

"All right, that's enough," the judge says. "Can we wrap this up? It seems that we're in agreement that Mr. Garza has a conviction for selling cocaine, which is clearly an aggravated felony under the Act. I fail to see how he can possibly qualify for a bond, much less any relief from removal."

"Respectfully, Your Honor, no, we are not in agreement," Mr. Radley says. "Mr. Garza's conviction for selling cocaine is not a *conviction* for selling cocaine, and thus not an aggravated felony."

"Good grief," Mr. Richter says, sighing. "Here we go."

"Enlighten me, Mr. Radley," the judge says. "But make it fast, as you can see I have a full calendar today."

"Certainly. I'd like to direct the court's attention to Mr. Garza's submission of evidence marked as Exhibit 3. Pages thirty-five through thirty-seven show that Mr. Garza was initially charged with a first-degree felony for possession with intent to deliver a controlled substance in a drug-free zone. The amended charging document at pages forty-one through forty-three shows that this charge was amended to a third-degree felony, dropping the reference to a drug-free zone. Mr. Garza pled guilty to this amended charge."

"Exactly, Your Honor," says Mr. Richter. "We're all on the same page here. Mr. Garza was convicted of selling cocaine, a federally prohibited controlled substance, even with the dropped reference to a drug-free zone. That's clearly an aggravated felony."

"Not so fast," says Mr. Radley. "He was only charged with distributing a *controlled substance*, not cocaine. And Mr. Garza's written statement in support of the guilty plea similarly only references an unspecified *controlled substance*. As Mr. Richter knows, *or should know*, Utah law defines controlled substances more broadly than federal law. So Mr. Garza's offense could have simply involved benzylfentanyl instead of cocaine, which is a controlled substance under our state law but not federal law."

"Benza—what, Mr. Radley?" the judge asks, furrowing his eyebrows and grimacing in disbelief.

"Benzylfentanyl, Your Honor," Mr. Radley says. "Which the Board of Immigration Appeals recognized in a published decision is a substance that would not trigger removability. As you can see on page seventy-one of Exhibit 5, our state schedules include benzylfentanyl as a controlled substance. Furthermore, I've submitted several examples of cases prosecuting possession of that substance, thus showing a realistic probability that—"

"This is ridiculous, Your Honor," interrupts Mr. Richter. "We all know it was cocaine. The police report makes that clear, and Mr. Garza admitted as much through counsel just two minutes ago. His conviction obviously didn't involve benzyl-whatchamacallit. It was *cocaine*! Plain and simple."

"All right then," says Judge Lanzotti, turning back to Mr. Radley. "Are you suggesting that I am to *ignore* the undisputed facts in this case?"

"Yes, I am," Mr. Radley says confidently. "The facts are irrelevant. As I'm sure this court is aware, U.S. Supreme Court case law makes clear that a conviction is defined as the minimum conduct necessary to satisfy the elements of the offense. While Mr. Garza may have actually sold cocaine, his conviction was for selling an unspecified controlled substance, which under state law could have been benzylfentanyl, rather than cocaine. While he may have *committed* an aggravated felony, he was not *convicted* of an aggravated felony for immigration purposes."

Judge Lanzotti sits pensively. He turns back to review the documents in Mr. Garza's very large file. Mr. Radley sits quietly with a barely perceptible smirk. Finally, the judge turns back to the government attorney.

"Mr. Richter," he says. "Do you have a response?"

"Your Honor, this is—this is ridiculous," Mr. Richter says. "We all know what happened here—"

"But does that matter for this issue of law?" the judge interrupts.

"Yes, Your Honor. We rest on our prior arguments."

"What arguments?"

"We—we rest, Your Honor. It's an aggravated felony; he was

convicted for selling a federally controlled substance, whether the charging document specifically says so or not."

"All right," the judge says. "I am granting bond in the amount of $15,000. Is there anything el—"

"Actually, Your Honor," Mr. Radley interrupts.

"Let's not push your luck, Mr. Radley," the judge says, raising his eyebrows. "That is a very reasonable bond given these circumstances."

"To be sure, Your Honor, no question," Mr. Radley says. "And as you know, we submitted a substantial amount of evidence for the bond hearing to show that Mr. Garza is neither a danger to the community nor a flight risk. But I don't believe we even need to get to a bond hearing today. My arguments this morning are specifically in support of my written motion to terminate proceedings, marked as Exhibit 4. Given Mr. Garza's lawful permanent resident status, and the government's inability to prove removability, I ask that this court terminate these proceedings and order that my client be released immediately."

The judge sits quietly for a moment before turning to the government attorney.

"Mr. Richter," he says. "What's the government's position on the respondent's motion?"

"Again, Your Honor," Mr. Richter says. "We believe this is an aggravated felony conviction."

"Very well," the judge says. "I am granting the respondent's motion to terminate proceedings. Does the government wish to reserve appeal?"

"Yes, Judge," Mr. Richter says.

"Mr. Radley?" the judge asks, turning back to the alien's attorney.

"No, Your Honor, we will waive appeal this time," Mr. Radley says with a confident smile bordering on arrogance.

"Okay, thank you to both of the parties," the judge says. "I have a full calendar today, so I will draft a written decision in this case by then end of the week. Anything else from either party before I close the record?"

"No, Your Honor," both attorneys say in unison.

"This hearing is closed."

The judge turns to his right to turn off the recording equipment and then turns back to the attorneys.

"And that's my only case today, Your Honor," Mr. Radley says as he picks up his large file and begins to stand. "May I be excused?"

"Certainly. Good day, Mr. Radley," the judge says.

"Same to you," Mr. Radley says.

Shane Radley walks out of the courtroom, leaving a room full of aliens with a renewed sense of hope. Fredy is smiling for the first time since he entered the courtroom. While he never wavered in his faith that God would ultimately deliver him, he feels a new excitement at the thought that it may be much sooner than he had expected. He's thinking very little about just how much he didn't understand of the preceding case, focusing instead on what he does understand. The *alien* won! David slew Goliath. Sure, he did so with the help of an attorney who came to court prepared for the fight, but that was in the case of a convicted drug dealer. A felon. A living representation of the immigrant stereotype prompting so many U.S. citizens to passionately advocate for increased deportations and an impenetrable wall on the southern border. And *he* won. Not just a bond, but his entire case. Even if Fredy can't do any better than to get a public defender unfamiliar with his case, he feels more assured than ever that he will be home soon, and maybe even today.

CHAPTER 8

DAY 14

(continued)
Wednesday, March 14, 2018

ATTORNEY SHANE RADLEY WALKS DOWN THE HALL OUTSIDE OF THE COURTROOM STILL BEAMING WITH PRIDE FROM HIS VICTORY. As no other private attorney has arrived, Judge Lanzotti turns back to the gallery of aliens.

"It doesn't appear that anyone else is represented today," he says before turning to his right to the court interpreter. "I'm going to begin with the group advisals. Ms. Orozco, can you please interpret?"

"Yes, Your Honor," she says.

The judge turns to his audio equipment to start the recording and then turns back to the portable microphone in front of him.

"This is Immigration Judge Samuel O. Lanzotti," he says. "Conducting removal proceedings at the Salt Lake Immigration Court, March 14, 2018, in the matter of the following respondents…"

The judge pauses after reading four to five names and alien numbers in order to allow the Spanish interpreter to translate. After getting through the thirty-two remaining aliens, the judge begins reciting his memorized template of legal advisals, pausing periodically to allow time for translation.

"In these hearings you have rights," the judge says. "First, you have a right to be represented by counsel at no expense to the government, or to represent yourselves. You have the right to present evidence and to testify on your own behalf. You have the right to present witnesses, and to question any witnesses called by the attorneys for the Department of Homeland Security. If you do not agree with my final decision in your case, you may file an appeal to the Board of Immigration Appeals within thirty days. If any of you do not understand these rights, please raise your hand."

The judge pauses briefly, scanning the room for raised hands. Of course, all of the hands remain handcuffed to the chains around the aliens' waists, limiting the ability to actually raise them any more than a few inches above their laps, but as far as Fredy can tell, no one appears to attempt to do so.

"Let the record reflect that no one rose their hand and everyone understood the group advisals," the judge says.

With the formality of explaining the legal rights of more than thirty unrepresented aliens taken care of—all in one shot, no less—the immigration judge is ready to proceed with the individual cases. Fredy is surprised to hear his name called first. He looks to the back of the room. Sarah's still not there. He stands up quickly, causing his paperwork to fall to the ground. He kneels down quickly to retrieve it but finds himself boxed in by the wooden barricade in front of him, the bench behind him, and the legs of the men seated on either side of him. The men, seated tightly on the bench already, move over as best they can to give him room. One of them slides some of Fredy's documents close to him with his foot. Fredy feels a similar sense of impatience from the authority figures around him as he did when his belongings spilled out of his glove box on the night of his arrest.

Having retrieved his documents, Fredy leans back and upward, straining to rise to his feet without the aid of his hands. Now standing, he turns and walks sideways between the wooden barricade and the others seated in his row until he reaches the ICE officer waiting for him with the keys. While the officer begins to unlock one of his handcuffs, Fredy looks to the back of the courtroom, looking again for Sarah. She's still not there, triggering a half-frown on Fredy's face that he quickly resolves to bury under a forced smile.

I can do this, he thinks. *I'll be fine, and I'll be home soon.*

He turns to the front of the courtroom just as the court clerk is handing the judge a thin blue file. Fredy is struck by just how small his file is compared to the prior case. He thinks initially about the absence of any exhibits or motions or arguments on his behalf by an experienced attorney. But he doesn't dwell on this thought long, recalling that the prior alien's case file was no doubt filled largely with criminal records. Fredy's small file is a *good* thing, he thinks.

"Good morning, Mr. Gonzalez," the judge says after Fredy has taken his seat behind the empty desk. "What is your best language?"

"English, sir. My Spanish is a little rusty," Fredy says, smiling at the judge.

"Please raise your right hand to take an oath," the judge says after raising his own right hand.

Fredy follows his lead.

"Do you solemnly swear or affirm that you will tell the truth, the whole truth, and nothing but the truth throughout these proceedings?"

Fredy feels a sense of the solemnity of the oath he is about to take. To him it is more than just a promise to tell the truth to some judge. He feels as if he's simultaneously recommitting himself to his family, as their sworn protector and provider. It is for them he is fighting. It is for them he will prevail. He pushes back his shoulders confidently and looks deep into the judge's eyes.

"Yes, sir," Fredy says. "I swear it. I swear it."

"Thank you," the judge says. "Do you want to proceed today without an attorney?"

"Thank you, sir. My family can't afford to pay for a lawyer while I'm in jail, so I'd like to just have a public defender for today, please."

"I'm afraid not. As I informed you in the group advisals just moments ago, you have a right to be represented *at no expense to the government.* That means you can hire an attorney, or you can contact one of those attorneys on the pro bono list provided to you."

Fredy is surprised and shaken by the response.

"So I can't have a lawyer?" he asks.

"I didn't say that, Mr. Gonzalez," says the judge with a tone of increased annoyance. "You may *pay* for an attorney *yourself,* or you may see if someone on that list in front of you is willing to take your case for free."

Fredy looks down at the list of three attorneys. He frowns, recalling his last phone call with his wife when she told him that none of them were able to take on his case. He explains this to the judge, who offers the most sympathy he can manage to fake.

"I'm sorry to hear that," the judge says. "Would you like to proceed today without an attorney, or would you like me to give you a couple of weeks to try to find an attorney?"

Fredy sits pensively for a moment before responding. He's sure he could figure out a way to get an attorney if he could just get out of jail.

"Could I have a bond, sir?" he asks.

"I haven't gotten to that yet, Mr. Gonzalez," the judge says. "First, I need you to tell me if you would like to proceed without an attorney today. If so, we can talk about a bond. If not, you will have to come back in two weeks with an attorney."

Two *weeks?* Fredy thinks. He recalls his video visit with his wife last week and knows she couldn't possibly handle another two weeks of this. Fredy is not so sure he could either. And it's not like he has a terribly complicated case like the last one, or even like his cellmate, Julio.

"I would like my bond today," Fredy says. "I don't need an attorney."

"All right," the judge says. "But we haven't gotten that far yet, Mr. Gonzalez. First, we must address your charges in these proceedings. I have a document in front of me titled a Notice to Appear. According to the second page, purporting to bear your signature, you received a copy of this document, is that correct?"

"Yes, sir, I remember that," Fredy says, recalling having just reviewed it during the prior hearing.

"I will be marking the Notice to Appear as Exhibit 1," the judge says. "I now will ask you to respond to the charges. First, the Department of Homeland Security alleges that you are not a citizen of the United States. Is that correct?"

"No, sir."

"So you *are* a U.S. citizen?"

"No," Fredy says, stirred by the question. "I mean, no, I am *not* a U.S. citizen."

"So the allegation that you are *not* a U.S. citizen is true?"

"Yes, sir. It's true. I'm *not* a U.S. citizen."

"Next, they allege that you are a native and citizen of Mexico. Is that correct?"

"Yes, sir. I was born there, but I've lived here since I was twelve."

"Okay, so you admit that charge as well," the judge says, making an apparent checkmark on the document in front of him. "Very good. They also allege that you arrived in the United States at or near an unknown place, on or about an unknown date. Is that correct?"

"No, sir," Fredy says defiantly, attempting to restore his confidence. "The date is not unknown. My parents brought me here in 1989. I only went back to Mexico once for four months after my sister was killed in 2013, but other than that I have been here pretty much my whole life. I graduated from high school in—"

"I understand, Mr. Gonzalez," the judge interrupts. "That's not relevant right now. I don't need your life story; I just need you to respond to the charges. Homeland Security is simply alleging that at some point, at a place, and on a date unknown *to them*, you arrived to the United States. Is that correct?"

"No, sir, they know when I came. I already told them everyth—"

"Okay, that's fine," the judge interrupts again, his tone increasing in volume corresponding with an increase in Fredy's anxiety. "But the government wasn't there with you at the border when you entered, were they?"

"No, sir."

"So they don't know for sure, do they?"

"No, sir."

"So is it correct that the date and place is unknown to them, or do you want to deny that allegation?"

"It's okay, sir."

"That's not responsive to my question, Mr. Gonzalez. Do you admit the allegation or not? A responsive reply would be yes or no. 'It's okay' leaves ambiguity on the record about your pleadings. So I will repeat the question. Do you admit or deny that you arrived in the United States at or near a place unknown *to the government* on a date unknown *to the government*?"

"I'm sorry, sir, I didn't mean—"

"I'm not asking for an apology, Mr. Gonzalez; I am asking for your pleadings. I have more than thirty other cases this morning that I need to get through in addition to yours. If you're not ready to plead to the charges I would be happy to set the matter out for an additional two weeks for you to review the Notice to Appear."

"No, sir, I admit it," Fredy says in panic at the thought of two more weeks in jail. "It's true, it's true."

"Very well. Allegation number four is that you were not admitted or paroled after inspection by an immigration officer. You have indicated that you, in fact, entered the United States on two occasions, is that right?

"Yes, sir."

"And were you inspected and admitted or paroled by an immigration officer on either of those occasions?"

"No, sir."

"So do you admit the charge?"

"Yes, sir."

"The Department of Homeland Security charges that you are inadmissible under section 212(a)(6)(A)(i) of the Immigration and Nationality Act, as amended, in that you are an alien present in the United States without being admitted or paroled, or who arrived in the United States at any time or place other than as designated by the Attorney General. Do you understand this charge?"

At this point Fredy only understands that somehow his case is not going well, and his questions don't seem to be helping.

"Yes, sir," he lies. "I understand."

"Do you admit or deny the charge?"

"I admit it, sir."

"Okay, then I am sustaining the charge of inadmissibility. What country does the government wish to designate in the event of removal?" the judge asks, turning to the government attorney.

"Mexico, Your Honor," says Mr. Richter.

"So designated," the judge says. "Mr. Gonzalez," he continues, turning back to Fredy, "are you afraid that you would be harmed, persecuted, and/or tortured in Mexico on account of your race, religion, nationality, political opinion, and/or membership in a particular social group at the hands of a government official, or a person or group of people that the government is unable or unwilling to control?"

Fredy stares blankly at the judge, his mind fishing through the wordiest, most incoherent question he recalls ever being asked. In essence, Fredy ultimately concludes, he is being asked if he is afraid of returning to Mexico. *Of course I am*, Fredy thinks to himself, *after what happened to Veronica there*. But at this point, he doesn't dare provide anything more than a one-word response to the judge.

"Yes," he says.

The judge turns from Fredy back to the government attorney.

"It sounds like asylum or withholding of removal may be the only forms of relief from removal for the respondent; do you agree, Mr. Richter?" he says.

"Well, not even asylum, most likely, due to the one-year issue, so probably just withholding or CAT. But we would not oppose a voluntary departure if the respondent wants to accept that today."

"You may be right about asylum. But let's not get ahead of ourselves with talk about voluntary departure just yet. We're still scheduled for a bond hearing today as well."

This turn in the conversation between the judge and the government attorney both startles and worries Fredy. *Is the judge actually asking the guy trying to deport me if there's anything I can do to stop him?* Fredy wonders in disbelief. *This is worse than having no lawyer at all.* He feels as if the judge has appointed his enemy to represent him. Could anyone honestly expect an adversary to develop any kind of viable strategy for his own defeat?

"Mr. Gonzalez," the judges says, turning back to Fredy, "in that black tray in front of you is an application for asylum, withholding of removal, and/or protection under the Convention Against Torture. Please take one of those, complete it, and bring two copies to your next hearing, which will be on—"The judge turns to his left, waiting for his clerk to tell him his next available date.

"The 22nd," the clerk says.

"On March 22, 2018 at 8:00 am, Mr. Gonzalez," the judge says. "If you do not complete any applications for relief, they may be deemed abandoned. Now, Mr. Gonzalez, we are also scheduled for a bond hearing today. Would you still like me to consider your bond motion without an attorney present?"

"Yes, please, sir."

"Very well. You have the burden, Mr. Gonzalez, of showing you have no criminal conviction requiring mandatory detention, and then that you would not be a danger to the community or a flight risk if released on bond. Do you understand?"

Fredy's prior confidence is replaced by panic and fear. He struggles to focus and does not understand.

"Yes, sir, I understand," he says.

"Very well. Do you have any evidence that you would like me to consider in meeting your burden of proof?"

"Evidence, sir?"

"Yes, evidence. Anything to show me that you qualify for and should be granted a bond?"

"No, sir, I don't have anything with me here today, but—"

"Mr. Richter," the judge says, turning back to the government attorney. "Anything from the government?"

"Yes, Your Honor," Mr. Richter says. "May I approach?"

"Certainly."

Mr. Richter picks up two small stacks of paper, pushes his chair back, and stands up. He walks between the two desks towards the judge, dropping one of the stacks on Fredy's desk and then handing the other to the judge. Fredy slides the papers over in front of him. His attention is initially drawn to a black-and-white copy of a picture of his face and a copy of two of his fingerprints on the lower half of the first page. After realizing the upper half of the first page is limited to his basic biographical information, he turns to the second page with his left hand, his right hand still cuffed to the chain around his waist. On the second page he finds typed notes in small print under larger headings, including, "Entry Data," "Immigration History," and "Criminal History." Before he has had a chance to even skim through the information, the immigration judge calls his name.

"Mr. Gonzalez," the judge says, "I have just received a five-page document from the government. The first document is a Form I-213 prepared by the Department of Homeland Security. The Form I-213 alleges that you were detained by ICE during an investigation for driving under the influence of alcohol. Is that correct, Mr. Gonzalez?"

Fredy is startled by the question but responds quickly.

"Yes, sir," he says. "But I didn't drink anything. I had only—"

"So," the judge interrupts, "you're telling me that both the police and the ICE officers are liars, Mr. Gonzalez? That you have been falsely charged?"

"No, that's not it, sir."

"On that night of—" the judge pauses, glancing quickly at the Form I-213 for the specific date of incident. Being quite familiar with the form, which is submitted in most immigration cases, the judge is able to find the sought information almost immediately. "Here we are," the judge continues. "On the night of March 1, 2018, were you or were you not driving prior to your detention, Mr. Gonzalez?"

"Yes, sir," Fredy says, "but I—"

"Prior to driving, Mr. Gonzalez," the judge interrupts, "did you drink any alcohol?"

"No, sir," Fredy says with conviction. "None at all."

"Mr. Richter," the judge says, turning to the government attorney, "are there any pending DUI charges for Mr. Gonzalez?"

Mr. Richter turns to his file, quickly flipping through the pages before responding.

"I don't have anything here, Judge. However, my notes reflect that the officer found Mr. Gonzalez *had* been drinking, and that there was an empty beer bottle in his car."

"Is this true, Mr. Gonzalez?" the judge asks.

"It's true that there was an empty bottle in my car," Fredy admits, "but I wasn't drinking."

"Whose bottle was it, Mr. Gonzalez?"

Fredy pauses and sighs in frustration before responding.

"It was mine," he admits. "I know that I shouldn't have done it, but I—"

"Now it sounds like you're acknowledging that you did, in fact, violate the laws of the United States, above and beyond our federal immigration laws. Just moments ago, I was led to believe you may have been the victim of some elaborate conspiracy between the local police and ICE. So I'm glad we got that cleared up. Mr. Richter, do you have anything else on this?"

"Nothing on the DUI, judge."

"It was *not* a DUI, sir," Fredy says forcefully.

"I understand, Mr. Gonzalez," the judge says. "However, *you* have the burden of proof. Can you prove that you have not been charged with a DUI as you assert, or that you had *not* been drinking and driving on the night of March 1, 2018?"

"How am I supposed to prove that, sir?" Fredy asks.

"I would be happy to consider any and all forms of evidence that you may have," the judge says. "Do you have anything other than your own testimony?"

"No, sir, I don't have any evidence," he says. "But I can promise you that I don't have any charges, and that I wasn't drinking that night. I haven't drank a drop of alcohol for almost three years now, and I—"

"Okay, Mr. Gonzalez, I have heard and considered your testimony, in addition to the contradicting information from U.S. Department of Homeland Security and a local police officer," the judge says. "Let's just table all that for a moment. Before we go any further, is there any *other* criminal history I should be aware of? And let me be *very* clear. Have you *ever* been cited or arrested or charged for *any* criminal offense?"

Fredy frowns at the judge's emphasis on the word *ever*. After a brief pause, he responds.

"Just once, sir," Fredy says. "It was more than twenty years ago. I got cited for shoplifting. It was really stupid. I'm embarrassed to even talk about it, but it was so long ago, sir."

"And how old were you at the time, Mr. Gonzalez?" the judge asks.

"Eighteen, sir," Fredy says, still frowning.

The judge looks back down at the documents submitted by the government attorney in search of Fredy's date of birth. After finding it, he instinctively looks up and to his left, as if in search of an answer to an unvocalized question.

"So that would have been in about 1995," the judge says after calculating the math in his mind. "Did you serve any time for this?"

"No, sir," Fredy says emphatically, followed by an abrupt change in his demeanor. "Well, not exactly," he continues sheepishly. "What I mean to say is that I wasn't sentenced to go to jail, but I ended up getting a warrant on this case after the fact."

Judge Lanzotti smiles and shakes his head, seeming to convey without words his conclusion that Fredy is just another liar in the hot seat trying to talk his way out of a difficult situation.

"Is that right, Mr. Gonzalez?" he asks sarcastically. "I'm sure that was just another misunderstanding and that it somehow wasn't your fault."

Fredy sighs heavily in exasperation.

"No, Your Honor," he says. "I mean, there *was* a misunderstanding, but it was my fault. The judge said I had to pay a fine, but then I got a notice in the mail from the store to pay something directly to them. I assumed that was the same thing, so once I paid that I thought I was done. But I should've checked with the court, so that was my fault. Then I graduated from high school and moved without giving the court my new address, so I didn't get the notice they sent me to return to court for the fine, and I got a warrant. I didn't even know about it until a few years later, when I got stopped for speeding and I got arrested because of the warrant."

A look of surprise on the judge's face suggests that somewhere in the middle of Fredy's explanation he found something he actually deemed relevant.

"So you were arrested a few *years* after the theft?" he asks Fredy. "Do you recall approximately when that arrest was?"

"Yes, sir," Fredy says. "I know exactly when it was, because it was on New Year's Eve at the end of 1999 and I was driving home with my wife late that night. But I hadn't been drinking, sir. My wife bailed me out that next morning. I explained the misunderstanding to the judge and he just let me pay the fine but extended my probation for another year. But I was able to get that terminated early, after about six months, so by June or July of 2000."

"It sounds like this would have been after the expiration of the Transition Period Custody Rules for mandatory detention, Mr. Richter," the judge says, turning to the government attorney. "Does the government have anything on this theft?"

Mr. Richter flips through his file in search of confirmation, then turns back to the judge.

"No, sir," he says.

"Do *you* have any documentation on that offense, Mr. Gonzalez?" the judge asks, turning back to Fredy.

"No, sir," Fredy says in surprise. "Like I said, it was more than twenty years ago. I was only eighteen when it happened, but I was able to get it all dismissed later. I mean, I might have something at home in my files or something, but I don't have anything here."

"Okay, Mr. Gonzalez," the judge says. "I'm denying your request for bond."

Fredy is dumbstruck as the judge continues.

"You carry the burden of proof, Mr. Gonzalez," the judge says. "I am finding that you have *not* established that you are not subject to mandatory detention based on your theft conviction. I might also note that there is evidence you may be a danger to the community based on a possible DUI, but it appears that charges still may not have been filed. In any case, you have not convinced me that you would not pose a danger to the community if you were released."

Fredy's confusion is surpassed only by his increasing anger. Before he is even given an opportunity to make his case, to talk about his family and his work and his twenty-nine years of life in the United States, the hearing comes to an abrupt halt with no bond at all. And this immediately after the prior alien was released despite a far more recent conviction for selling drugs.

"Mr. Gonzalez, would you like to waive or reserve appeal?" the judge asks.

Fredy doesn't respond.

"Mr. Gonzalez, would you like to waive or reserve appeal?" the judge asks again.

"What?" Fredy asks curtly.

"Again, as I already explained during the group advisals," the judge says, slowly and condescendingly, no longer even attempting to veil his complete loss of all patience with a single *pro se* case taking up this much of his time. "If you think my decision is wrong, you can file an appeal to the Board of Immigration Appeals to try to convince them that *I* am wrong and *you* are right. If you want to do that, you must, as I stated before—*reserve appeal*. You then must file a written notice of appeal within thirty days. You must serve a copy of the same on the Department of Homeland Security. If you are able to convince the Board of Immigration Appeals that I am wrong, then they may send your case back to me to consider a bond amount. However, an appeal of my bond decision will not stay your removal proceedings. I will continue to hear your case and determine whether you qualify for any form of relief from removal. Do you understand these rights *now*, Mr. Gonzalez, after I've explained them to you for the *second* time today?"

Fredy stares angrily at the judge, furrowing his eyebrows and clenching his teeth. His eyes instinctively look downward towards the judge's bench and will not return to the judge for the rest of the hearing, even as they continue to communicate.

"Yes, I understand, *sir*," Fredy says.

"Would you like to appeal my decision today?" the judge asks.

Fredy doesn't respond, still staring blankly below the judge. He begins thinking about his cellmate, Julio, and his nearly two-year-long appeal, and wonders, *What's the point?*

"Mr. Gonzalez," the judge says. "As you can see, I have a lot of cases today. Would you like to appeal my decision or not?"

"No!" Fredy says abruptly.

"Very well," says the judge. "Mr. Richter, does the government waive or reserve appeal?"

"We waive."

"Okay, that will be all for today," the judge says. "Mr. Gonzalez, we'll see you next time. Please come prepared to file any and all forms of relief at your next hearing in two weeks."

Fredy turns his head to look back to the gallery. Sarah's not there.

CHAPTER 9

DAY 15

Thursday, March 15, 2018

"OSCAR!" SARAH YELLS DOWN THE STAIRWAY LEADING TO THE BASEMENT IN HER HOME. "Are you ready? Lori will be here in two minutes to take you to school! Let's go!"

She's holding her baby, Veronica, who she's feeding a bottle of formula. With her left hand holding Veronica and her right hand pulling a clean shirt over her squirming four-year-old Katie's head, Sarah holds the bottle pressed between her chin and chest.

"Hurry, hurry, Katie," she says, nudging her daughter to put her arms through her shirt on her own. "We're running late—*again*. But I guess that's the new normal around here."

Sarah feels her cell phone vibrating in her front left jeans pocket just before it starts playing the ringtone she chose randomly two years earlier, *Everybody Dance Now* by C+C Music Factory—a poor choice in retrospect.

"Of course," Sarah says, sighing in frustration and rolling her eyes.

She puts Veronica on the floor, who immediately starts to cry as the bottle leaves her mouth. She pulls the phone out of her pocket and smiles largely as she recognizes the phone number from the Cache County Jail.

"It's Daddy!" she says excitedly to Veronica and Katie.

She answers the phone and hears the familiar pre-recorded introduction asking her to authorize and accept the call from the jail.

"You are receiving a call from an inmate at—"

Sarah takes the phone away from her ear, already familiar with the process, and presses 1.

"Fredy?" she says before she hears him. "Can you hear me? Did you get the bond?"

"Where were you yesterday?" Fredy asks abruptly without saying hello.

"During the hearing, you mean?" Sarah asks. "I was there the whole time."

"No, you weren't," Fredy shoots back. "Don't you think I checked? I had *no one* with me yesterday. No attorney, no family, *nothing*. It was a disaster!"

Sarah is both startled and concerned by Fredy's tone, but also upset by his criticism directed at her. After a brief pause she responds.

"I'm not *lying*, Fredy," she says. "I had to call around for days to get rides and babysitters for all of *our* kids so I could make sure I could be there. It's been *just a little* hectic the past couple of weeks."

"So, what then, it was too hard so you just gave up?" Fredy says bitterly. "It's only been a couple of weeks and everybody's already given up on me and moved on?"

"You're not listening, Fredy. *I was there!*" Sarah says forcefully. "I got there an hour early. Some lady at the front desk said she'd tell me when you were up and that I had to wait in the lobby, so I did—for *three hours*, Fredy. Watching other family members come and go the whole time. So I finally go ask how much longer it'd be, and she says *'Oh, uh, sorry, hahaha, it looks like he's already done.'* She didn't even care, and it was *her* fault! Then she said you were down in holding, and that I'd have to go to the jail if I wanted to see you."

Fredy does not immediately respond. The pause in conversation gives Sarah time to replace her initial feelings of resentment of his accusations with growing anxiety.

"This is—this is just unbelievable," Fredy says, with a tone only moderately less hostile. "I feel like the whole world is conspiring against me, Sarah. Like it's personal with me."

"So what happened yesterday? Why didn't you call me last night?"

"What happened is this judge they got me is out of his mind. Right before I went up he lets some drug dealer—*a felon!*—out without thinking twice, and then he says *I* can't have a bond because of that stupid shoplifting thing more than twenty years ago."

Sarah drops to her knees in defeat.

"You didn't get the bond?!" she says desperately.

"No!" Fredy shouts. "That's what I'm telling you."

"But—but why? I—I—I don't understand."

"I don't either, Sarah. They got me locked up with some child rapist, and as far as this judge is concerned, we're the same. He didn't even let me talk about anything important. Not you, the kids, nothing! I told him I've been here since I was a kid, and it wasn't my decision to come here, but he said that's irrelevant. *Irrelevant?!* All that's relevant is I tried to be *cool* in high school with my idiot friends and stole some stupid discman, and then a couple of weeks ago I *almost* drank before driving because, for some strange reason, I sometimes feel a little depressed when I'm reminded of my sister's *murder* in the country they wanna send me to now."

"So he didn't give you any bond at all?"

"No! That's what I keep telling you. It was like he didn't even consider it. Like he had already made up his mind."

"So what happens now?"

"What happens now is this psychopath is gonna deport me! I can't go back to Mexico, Sarah. I can't. There's nothing there for me but death. No family, no home, no help. Nothing. I'm scared, baby. I've never been so scared in my life. I never thought they could really do this to me. But they're gonna do it. They really are. This judge will do it. He doesn't care. Please help me, baby, please."

"You have thirty seconds remaining on this call," a recorded voice interrupts. The emotionlessness of this almost inhuman messenger feels intentionally cruel.

Veronica is now screaming, Katie is tugging at Sarah's shirt, and she can hear Lori's short double honk from her car letting her know she's waiting outside for Oscar. Sarah feels as if her heart has stopped, and she can't breathe as she starts crying. Just moments ago, she felt as if she would barely make it through another morning without Fredy. Now, images of a life's worth of unnecessary heartache and struggles consume her mind, preventing her from knowing how to respond.

"I don't know what to do," Sarah says, still crying. "What can I do?! What can I do?!"

"I *have* to get a lawyer, Sarah. That's my only hope. This judge doesn't believe anything I say; I need a white guy in a suit to say it for me. I need someone who can understand all this stuff and say the right words. Shane Radley. I need you to find Shane Radley. He's an immigration lawyer. I don't have his number, but you gotta find it. Please. I know he can help me. Please, baby, please."

"I'm trying, Fredy, I am. But you know we don't have any savings. The church had to pay our rent for us this month, and I've been borrowing money from Lori to pay Oscar's medical bills that were already past due when you got arrested. I don't know how we can do it."

"Just please find a way, baby. Remember, Shane Radley. I can't do—"

"Goodbye," interrupts a recorded message again, ending the call.

"Fredy?" Sarah says into her phone to silence. "Fredy!"

...

Inside the reception area of a two-story office space sits a young Hispanic woman in her early twenties behind an L-shaped receptionist desk. Her straight black hair is neatly pulled back in a ponytail, and she's wearing a white, form-fitting dress shirt and black slacks. She's drafting a billing statement on the computer in front of her when the phone rings, to which she immediately turns her attention. She answers, instinctively looking to her left at a sheet of paper hanging from the wall, titled *Mandatory Script*, which she has already memorized but continues to read out of habit.

"Thank you for calling Radley & Associates, buenos días, my name is Luciana, how can I help you today?"

The inclusion of "buenos días"—or "buenas tardes" between noon and closing—was calculated by Mr. Radley as a way of quickly conveying to the caller that the receptionist is bilingual, thus saving her at least three seconds on each phone call having to answer if she "*habla*-ed *español*." However, the one or two seconds spent saying "buenos días/tardes" is wasted anytime an English speaker calls, and at least half the time, Spanish speakers still ask for confirmation of bilinguality. Careful calculation of the time spent on the amended bilingual script would show it as a net loss of billable hours. But Mr. Radley feels better under the false assumption of added efficiency. This particular call is from an English speaker, so another "buenos días" has been wasted. At least, Luciana believes it's an English speaker. It's initially hard for her to discern, as the woman's voice coming through is buried under heavy breathing and uncontrollable sobbing.

"I'm sorry, ma'am, can you repeat that? I'm having trouble understanding you. Something about your husband?"

Luciana scrunches her eyebrows, almost squinting, as she strains to make out the caller's request.

"Okay, so you would like an appointment with Mr. Shane Radley, is that right?"

Luciana raises her eyebrow with sincere empathy as the caller continues.

"Oh my. That's awful. I understand. So do you—"

She stops short, interrupted by the caller, which continues for the duration of the call.

"Um, yes," Luciana continues. "Mr. Radley charges $250 for an initial consultation. However, if you retain him for your case, he will credit that payment towards the total cost of your case— ... Oh, okay, yes, to your *husband's* case then... I know this must be so difficult for you; I'm so— ... Oh, yes, I assure you, Mr. Radley is an excellent attorney, and he will give you an honest assessment of your husband's case. If anyone can help him, he can— ... No, I'm so sorry, but Mr. Radley is booked for the rest of the week, I'm afraid. But he could meet with you on Monday morning at 11:30. Will that work for you? ... I really wish I could, but that's the soonest we can possibly get you in. Mr. Radley is very— ... Oh, okay, then, yes, great, we will see you then."

Luciana gets the information she needs to finish adding the appointment to Mr. Radley's calendar, and then she hangs up the phone, slouching forward as if she has just been handed a bag of bricks. She puts her hands over her face and sighs.

"Paula!" she whines in desperation.

Paula is working in an office down the hall from the reception area when she hears Luciana. Had this been the first such cry, Paula may have been concerned and come quickly. But this has become a common occurrence in Mr. Radley's office since he hired Luciana two months earlier.

"What is it this time, hija?" Paula says through a nearly audible smile as she stands up from her desk and walks slowly to the reception area, more out of obligation than genuine concern.

"We had another bad one," Luciana replies. "She was a real mess. I feel so bad for her. This is *terrible*, Paula! How have you done this for so long?"

Paula smiles, amused by her coworker's sensitivity.

"You just can't think about it, hija," Paula says. "You'll go crazy in this job if you do. We do what we can and we help a lot of people, but it's an uphill battle for most of our clients, and a lot of them are going to lose in the end. We can't control that. Some of our clients have done some stupid stuff and made things harder for themselves, but Shane has still been able to help a lot of them. I told you he won that case for Luis yesterday, didn't I?"

"The drug dealer?" Luciana says, genuinely surprised by the news. "No! Are you serious? I didn't think that guy had a chance."

"Yeah," says Paula, snickering. "Can you believe that? You were at lunch when Shane got back yesterday. You shoulda seen that white fool parading around here, so pleased with himself. You'll never see such a giddy gringo as Shane after he wins a case."

"So maybe he can help this lady's husband too. Oh Paula, I hope so. She started talking about all their kids. And one has some medical problem, some breathing problem or something, I dunno. But it sounds so awful."

"Well, if anyone can help him, Shane can."

"Yeah, *if she can afford him.*"

Paula laughs. "Yeah, that's true," she says. "Shane mostly takes the less sympathetic and harder cases with the serious criminal histories. It probably makes it easier to charge a lot of money and not feel bad about it."

"And to not feel as bad when he loses, I'm sure too, since some of these guys actually deserve to be deported."

"No, he *hates* losing," Paula says emphatically. "He doesn't care what his clients have done."

"But some of them have done horrible things. Don't *you* ever feel bad helping them stay here?"

"I used to at first," Paula admits. "I've talked to Shane about it a few times. He made some pretty good points. By the time clients come to us, they've already served a full sentence for whatever crime they committed. Plus, their sentence ends up getting extended most of the time whenever they're detained during their immigration case, so they get punished *more* than U.S. citizens for the same crime, even if they got green cards."

"Yeah, but some of these people give the rest of us Latinos a bad reputation. They assume we're all criminals."

"They're gonna do that anyways, hija, you know that. At least we get to stick it to the man every once in a while. It's like, fine, you think we're *all* criminals, huh? Then, here, you can keep some of the worst of us," Paula says with a laugh.

"But think about some of the people his clients have hurt here," Luciana says. "What about their families? Some of his clients never had a right to be here in the first place. If they had never broke the law in the first place to come here, those people they ended up hurting would've been safe."

"Shane says that's just an argument politicians use to push their agendas."

Luciana squints her eyes in confusion. "But it's true, isn't it? Like that girl in New York or New Jersey or New *somethin'*, I can't remember where it was. But you know, that girl in the news who got shot by some immigrant who had already been deported before. If he wasn't here, she'd still be alive. How can Shane deny that?"

"So, yeah, she'd probably still be alive if stronger immigration laws had kept him out of the country," Paula says, almost appearing to concede the point. "But she'd also still be alive if stronger gun laws had kept him from getting a gun in the first place. Both sides have already made up their mind on who or what to blame before the crime even happened. Either guns are to blame or immigrants are to blame. But they all at least seem to agree that we can't just blame the guy that actually did it because that wouldn't help their agenda. That's why most of the time, the proposed solution is some new immigration or gun law that wouldn't've even prevented the crime they're using as a justification. It's just politics, hija."

Luciana sits thoughtfully in silence for a moment, not quite convinced but initially unsure of how to respond. "Okay, fine," she finally says. "But seriously though, don't you think that some people have done such horrible things that they should just be deported?"

"Ask Shane. He'll tell you that deporting someone won't magically rehabilitate them. If they're going to continue to commit crimes even after their sentence, deporting them won't change that. If anything, they'll just commit even *more* crimes and hurt *more* people in another country. The police in Mexico don't do anything. Honduras, El Salvador, Guatemala. It's a joke down there. They're all run by *los pandilleros y los carteles*. No one even calls the police 'cuz they assume they're all bought off, and truth be told, a lot of them are. So deporting these people is just saying we don't care who they hurt as long as they're not Americans. Just look at that El Chapo guy. How many times has that *pendejo* escaped from *top security* prisons south of the border? Even with all the problems we got with the police here, I'll take them over *la policía mexicana* any day!"

"No wonder Shane's a lawyer," Luciana says. "He's got an answer for everything."

"I know, right?" says Paula, nodding with a wide smile.

CHAPTER 10

DAY 18

Sunday, March 18, 2018

APPROXIMATELY TWENTY MEN BETWEEN THE AGES OF TWENTY-TWO AND FORTY-FIVE ARE SEATED ON GREY, METAL FOLD-OUT CHAIRS IN A LONG RECTANGULAR ROOM IN THE SOUTHWEST CORNER OF A MEETINGHOUSE OF THE CHURCH OF JESUS CHRIST OF LATTER-DAY SAINTS. Most are wearing different styles and colors of long-sleeved dress shirts and ties. Some are wearing dark brown, black, or blue suits. An apparent black sheep of the flock is wearing an untucked dark-green polo shirt with khaki pants and tennis shoes. Half of those seated in the back row have their chairs leaned back on the rear two legs against the wall. Most are talking quietly to the men next to them, while a few sit quietly, patiently waiting or looking down at their cell phones. Some phones are opened to digital copies of holy scripture, while others are opened to video games. At the front of the room, facing the group, sit three men all dressed in suits. One of them stands and walks to the center of the room, placing a book on a small table in front of a white board stocked with dry erase markers.

"Welcome to elders quorum, brethren," he says. "How is everyone today?"

The elders quorum of the Church of Jesus Christ consists of a group of men, generally not very "elderly" but as young as eighteen years old, who have been ordained to what they call the Melchizedek Priesthood. They do not work full time in the Church and are not paid for their services in their individual callings. In holding this priesthood, members believe they are authorized to do certain works in the name of Jesus Christ, such as blessing the sick and presiding in leadership positions in the church, as President Samuel Taylor, who just began the meeting, is currently serving as the elders quorum president. His first and second counselors, Brother Walsh and Brother McLeod, remain seated behind him facing the rest of the elders.

"Before we turn the time over to Brother Halpert for our lesson," President Taylor continues, "I just wanted to invite everyone to fast and pray on behalf of Brother Fredy Gonzalez. He and his wife and kids got baptized about a year and a half ago, as many of you know, but he's been teaching the kids in primary for a while now so he hasn't been to many elders quorum meetings with us. But I've seen him at almost all of our service activities, so some of you might know him better from there. Anyways, they're going through some challenges right now. My neighbor Greg and his wife, Lori, are very close with the Gonzalezes and have been helping the family. I understand that he's in immigration custody now, trying to figure out his status or something—I'm not sure exactly what—but I just wanted to invite us all to—"

"Well, why was—sorry for interrupting," says one of the other elders in the room. "But why was he arrested by immigration? Is he here illegally? I don't know if it's appropriate for you to ask us to be fasting and praying for someone if they're facing punishment for a crime. How could he even get baptized if he's breaking the law literally every day?"

President Taylor pauses after an unsuccessful attempt to conceal the surprise in his face to the question and then calmly responds.

"I don't have all the details, Brother Warner," he ultimately responds. "But I know that Sister Gonzalez and her kids are having a very difficult time right now. And I know that Brother Gonzalez is a good man and would be the first to help any of us if the tables were turned. So I just—"

"Are you kidding me, Warner?" says another elder, Brother Turner, who is sitting in the back of the room, bringing his previously reclined chair forward onto all fours. "There's absolutely nothing wrong with what our elders quorum president just asked us to do. Jesus taught us to love our neighbor as ourselves, and to help the sick and the afflicted and *the imprisoned*. And that what we've done to the least of us, we've done to *Him*."

"Sure, Jesus taught us to love one another," Brother Warner says, turning back to Brother Turner. "But we've also been taught to honor and obey the law, and that our choices have consequences. The Lord cannot look upon sin with the least degree of allowance."

"But that's not your place to judge," Brother Turner says back quickly with an increasingly animated tone. "You don't know the facts any more than any of the rest of us. Fortunately for you, nobody's gonna deport you for *your* sins."

President Taylor stands quietly, his eyebrows raised, no longer even attempting to conceal his surprise by this unexpected debate. This is not his first exposure to a heated debate mixing politics and religion, but it's certainly the first he's observed in the middle of a church meeting—and one he's responsible for running, no less. Unsure of how exactly to intervene, his silence allows the debate to continue as a third elder offers his opinion.

"I think that maybe Brother Warner was just meaning we shouldn't pray that people will escape the inevitable consequences of their sins," says another elder, attempting unsuccessfully to find a peaceful middle ground. "But maybe instead pray that they will repent and find peace through Christ, even if the temporal consequences cannot be avoided."

Brother Turner shakes his head in disbelief as he continues. "Did you ever think that maybe it's not *their* sins but *our* sins and the sins of this nation that are bringing about this so-called invasion from the southern border?" he asks. "That the white Gentiles have had their time on top, refused to repent, and now the Lord himself is bringing these descendants of the House of Israel as the rightful heirs of this land? That the first shall be last, and the last shall be first? Their land became ours, and now our land becomes theirs. Do you really want to be praying against *God's* will?"

"All right, all right," says Brother McLeod, the second counselor of the presidency, who is now standing next to President Taylor. "We're getting into some deep doctrine and interesting theories here, but all President Taylor asked us to do is *pray* for Fredy and his family. Let's not lose sight of that. I'm not sure how this turned into something controversial. Frankly, I expect that we'll come together to do a lot more than just pray for the Gonzalez family, or any family in need of any kind, for any reason. The question we should be asking is what *more* can we do, *in addition to* praying? President Taylor, is there more we can do right now?"

"Thank you, Brother McLeod," says President Taylor, grateful for his counselor's intervention. "My wife will be reaching out to Sister Gonzalez to see if we can help with a couple of meals or something, so we'll keep everyone posted on how we can help once I have more information. But this is not some requirement to pray for them. No one will be monitoring your personal prayers. We're not going to kick you out of the quorum if you don't pray for them—"

"Aw man, I thought I'd found my way out," says the black sheep, triggering some laughter that cuts through the tension in the room.

"I'm happy to direct you to the exit if you'd like to leave," says President Taylor with a playful smile. "I'm kidding, of course. Anyway, I wasn't intending on taking up this much time, but as an elders quorum presidency we felt that it was appropriate to *invite* everyone to fast or pray for Fredy and his family and support them any way that you can. Whether or not you accept that invitation is, of course, up to you."

President Taylor sits down after turning the time over to Brother Halpert for the lesson. The lesson is on faith but quickly evolves into a discussion on service and charity, driven largely by the mention of the Gonzalez family at the beginning of the meeting. Despite the initial tensions in the group, the discussion becomes one of the more meaningful and memorable ones this particular group has had. Four minutes before the end of the hour, Brother Halpert ends the lesson and asks for a volunteer to say the closing prayer, after which they all leave, except for President Taylor and his two counselors, who are still sitting.

"Well, looks like we dodged a bullet today, didn't we?" President Taylor says to his counselors after the other elders have left.

"What, that little debate about praying for Fredy at the beginning?" says Brother McLeod. "Yeah, that was really weird. Brother Halpert did a great job of defusing all that with his lesson though. It turned into one of our better meetings, I think."

"Yeah," says Brother Walsh. "But it's a good reminder about why you gotta just keep politics out of church as much as possible."

"But there was nothing political about what I said, was there?" President Taylor asks.

"Well, as soon as you said Fredy was in *immigration* custody, it became political for some people," Brother Walsh says. "I don't know what it is about immigration that gets people so riled up. It's like we weren't even talking about Fredy anymore, or almost as if we never were. You might as well have endorsed nationwide amnesty from the pulpit as far as some of them were concerned."

"But not Brother Turner," President Taylor says.

"No," Brother McLeod says, laughing. "Definitely not Turner. I knew he was going to have something to say about the subject. You could just see the fire building up in his eyes while Warner started going off on his tangent about not praying for Fredy."

"Between you and me, I'm on the same page with Brother Turner on this one," President Taylor says. "At least his underlying point, though he could use a little more tact and a little less fire."

"Oh, I agree," Brother McLeod says. "I can't believe anyone could honestly feel scripturally justified in not *praying* for someone, or *serving* them, no matter how they ended up where they are."

"I just don't like the idea of using the scriptures to fight with people on either side of any argument, including my side," President Taylor says. "That's not the point, ya know? They're supposed to inspire us to build up other people with our actions, not cut other people down with our words. Even if someone *is* wrong, the scriptures weren't meant for beating the truth into someone. They're meant for *inviting* others to come unto Christ and the happiness that comes with that. We should be loving and serving them whether they accept that invitation or not."

"I agree," Brother Walsh says. "The funny thing about Brother Turner though is he's probably the *last* person in the quorum who would actually step up and *do* something to help the Gonzalez family when it comes down to it. Unless it were marching in some highly publicized protest. He's always got a lot to say, but with all the opportunities we give these guys for actual service, I've yet to see Turner show up and—"

"All right, all right," President Taylor says, interrupting. "I know I'm the one who brought this all up again, so I'm sorry, but it's just starting to feel like a bit of a gossip session now. But I don't think we should stop trying to find ways to help the Gonzalez family. Any thoughts on how to follow up in the next week or two with the quorum without a repeat of today?"

"Frankly, I'm still surprised that this even happened today," Brother McLeod says. "For some people it's hard to tell where their religious beliefs end and their political opinions begin. It's easy enough to cherry pick scriptures to support both sides of most issues. It's almost like some people start building their faith on their polit-ical party rather than on Christ. I bet some members would rather die as a martyr for the Church than change their political position on taxes or immigration—and I mean both sides of the issues." Brother McLeod pauses thoughtfully for a moment and shrugs before continuing. "I don't know if anyone has the *right* answer on those issues. But it's strange how deeply that stuff can get mixed up in the gospel."

"Yeah, I think you're right," President Taylor says. "Well, let's go ahead and start our presidency meeting. My wife's gonna kill me if I leave her alone with the kids for too long. Brother McLeod, can you give us the opening prayer?"

"Sure," Brother McLeod says.

"And just to be clear before you start," President Taylor adds. "Praying for Fredy *is* mandatory for *you*."

"Understood," Brother McLeod says with a smile.

...

Fredy is lying on his bed in his cell, staring blankly at the ceiling, neither reading nor speaking, both of which he has done very little since his hearing four days ago. Julio is lying on his own bed, quietly singing some Spanish song Fredy has never heard before. After finishing, he pulls his knees into his chest, points his feet upward, and forcefully kicks the underside of the top bunk. Fredy doesn't respond.

"Yo, Fredy!" Julio says. "You ready to worship the Lord with me on this glorious day of the Sabbath? It's almost time to go, man."

"I'll pass."

Julio laughs. "Is that really all it took to lose the faith, amigo?" he asks. "It don't sound like you were ever really a believer. But that's cool, man, that's cool. I ain't either, but at least I ain't a hypocrite about it. God knows where I stand, and I still stand there. But you? You had such bee-uuu-tee-ful thoughts to share with us all just last week. You even forced up some tears there, man. How'd you do it? Did you take some acting classes or something?"

"Just shut up, Julio."

"Whoa," Julio says, laughing heartily. "Looks like I hit a nerve. The truth hurts, man. At least that's what they tell me, but what do I know?"

"Nothing. That's what you know. Nothing. You know nothing about me, so just shut up!"

Julio gets out of his bed, stands and leans his left hand on the metal support of Fredy's bed, forcefully pointing his right index finger at Fredy as he responds. "I know enough to know you were singing praises for your sweet Jesus last week when you still thought things were going to be easy for you. When you thought your God would save you. That you were special or something. But you ain't the only fool in here that believes all those lies. And plenty got it worse than you. But you had no problem loving your God during *their* hard times. Because *your* God lives and dies based on how *your* life is going, don't he?"

Julio pauses as if expecting an answer to his question. Once it is clear he will receive none, he continues.

"Yeah," he says. "Who cares if God lets the rest of the world rot and die, right? He'll at least get your love as long as you're doing okay."

Julio laughs and steps back away from the beds.

"But, hey," he says. "What do I know? I'm just a humble sinner."

A guard knocks on the door.

"You guys going to one of the churches today?" he asks.

"Just me today," Julio says, smiling as he glares back at Fredy. "My brother here is having a little faith crisis, you could say. But I am still true to *my* Lord."

Julio walks out of the cell, leaving behind Fredy, who is still staring motionless at the ceiling of his cell.

CHAPTER 11

DAY 19

Monday, March 19, 2018

LORI IS SITTING NEXT TO SARAH IN THE RECEPTION AREA OF RADLEY
& ASSOCIATES, ATTORNEYS AT LAW. They arrived fifteen minutes
before Sarah's 11:30 am appointment, and it is now more than twenty
minutes past. Lori has given up on attempting small talk with Sarah,
who has said very little since she picked her up this morning. They
both look up when they see a man in a suit walk down the hall into
the reception area.

"Wilfredo?" he says.

"That's us," Lori says, sitting upright abruptly, and pointing
towards Sarah. "This is his wife."

"I'm Shane Radley," he says. "Is English okay? If not, I can have
Paula come and translate for us, because I don't *habla* so good."

"We're American," Lori says.

"Okay, that's fine, I'm not gonna ask you to show me your papers or anything," Shane says. "I just need to know if you both *habla*
English?"

"Yes," Sarah says, confused.

"Okay, great," Shane says. "Come on back."

They follow Mr. Radley from the reception area down a short
hallway. He opens the door and waits for them to walk in before

following them into a large office. They smell the artificial air fresh-
ener plugged into a socket behind Shane's large desk, outside of their
view. There are two large leather chairs with padded armrests in front
of the desk, behind which Shane sits in a larger, rotating leather chair.
Lori and Sarah follow his lead and sit down. Their eyes are naturally
drawn to the various diplomas, degrees, and certificates hung on the
wall to their right in expensive-looking solid wood frames. Shane
quickly brings their attention back to the purpose of their visit.

"So, tell me about this Wilfredo guy," he says.

Lori looks to Sarah to respond. She sits there quietly for a moment, grimaces, and starts to silently cry, appearing unable to answer
for the time.

"Sorry, Mr. Radley," Lori says. "She's having a very hard time
as I'm sure you can imagine. They have three kids at home. They're
all U.S. citizens. Sarah too. She was born in California, so I just
can't figure out what the problem is and why Fredy can't just get his
citizenship. They're such great people, I don't understand what—"

"Well, let's try to figure that out," Shane interrupts. "I'm guessing Wilfredo—or Fredy? You call him Fredy?"

"Yes," Sarah says.

"Okay, so I'm assuming that Fredy is in ICE custody right now
and that's why he's not here with us today, is that right?"

The complete absence of emotion in the question, coupled with
Sarah's overabundance of emotion, causes her to burst into tears
again.

"Is she gonna be okay?" Shane asks, turning to Lori. "Maybe
she'd be more comfortable waiting in the reception area with Luci
while you and I talk. You seem to have a handle of the basic facts
here, and Luci's great with these kinda emotional problems."

"No, she's fine," Lori says forcefully. "And she needs to be here.
But yes, Fredy is with immigration, or with—*ICE*, did you say?

"Yeah, ICE. U.S. Immigration Customs and Enforcement,"
Shane says, quickly moving on. "Okay, got it. And how did Fredy

come into contact with ICE? Does he have any criminal history in the United States?"

"Oh, heavens, no," Lori says. "Well—not really. Just a misunderstanding, I think. It's so silly. He was just a kid at the time, wasn't he Sarah?"

"Well," Sarah says, having regained her composure, "he had just turned eighteen, so—"

"Okay," Shane says. "So he'd be charged as an adult then. What was the charge?"

"It was just a stupid thing," Sarah says. "And there hasn't been anything else ever since. This was way back in like—"

"Right," Shane says, clearly trying to move the conversation along, "but what was he convicted of?"

"Shoplifting."

"Got it," Shane says, turning to his monitor and quietly reading aloud his notes as he types them. "Theft conviction, possible CIMT, possible agg fel."

Sarah and Lori look to each other in confusion without saying anything. Shane turns his revolving chair to his left to a landline phone and pushes the speaker button.

"Yeah," says a woman's voice coming through the speakers of the phone a moment later.

"*Hola*, Paula, *mi amor*," Shane says. "See if you can dig up any court dockets for a theft conviction for a Mr.—"

Shane pauses, apparently having forgotten the name of his potential new client, and turns to his notes for confirmation before continuing.

"Yeah, for a Mr. Wilfredo Gonzalez," he continues. "He's my 11:30 appointment; you should have the DOB or anything else you need in the client intake."

"You got it," Paula says before hanging up.

"So while we're waiting on that," Shane says, turning back to Sarah and Lori, "why don't you tell me a little more about Fredy. He's got a USC spouse and three USC kids, but what—"

"USC?" asks Sarah.

"Sorry," Shane says. "U.S. citizen. A U.S. citizen wife, and some U.S. citizen kids, right?"

"Yes," Sarah says. "We have three kids."

"And how long has Fredy been in the U.S.?"

Sarah pauses before answering, unsure of the exact date. "Since he was about twelve, I think," she finally says.

"Okay, so what year was he born?" Shane asks.

"1977," she says.

"Okay." Shane turns back to his monitor, still whispering his notes and making additional comments to himself as he types them. "Born in '77, so he never qualified for DACA, but sounds like a possible 42B."

Shane continues to look at his monitor, no longer turning back to the women as he speaks to them.

"How did Fredy enter the U.S.?" he asks. "Papers? No papers?"

"Well, his parents brought him here illegally when he was a kid, so it wasn't his choice or anything. But he—"

"Got it," Shane says, still typing. "No papers—EWI when about twelve, okay."

The majority of the rest of the conversation leaves Sarah feeling like a human checklist, as she has given up on providing anything more than one-word answers.

"Entry through the desert or a port of entry?"

"Desert."

"Were they detained at the border?"

"No."

"Was Fredy ever deported?"

"No."

"Was Fredy ever a victim of a crime in the U.S.?"

"No."

"Was he or any close friend and/or family member ever

threatened or harmed in any way in Mexico?"

"Actually, yes," Sarah says. "His sister, Veronica, was murdered in Mexico in 2013. That's why Fredy was—"

"Murdered?!" Shane says enthusiastically, actually turning back to look at Sarah briefly before looking back at his monitor again. "*Nice.* That could be helpful if worse comes to worse.

"So," he continues, more thinking aloud than talking to anyone, "we got at least four USC qualifying relatives, ten-plus years of U.S. presence, and sister killed in Mexico. That gives a possible 42B option, but we'd have to look into the hardship issues for that and the shoplifting conviction. If not that, maybe asylum, but we'd have the one-year filing deadline issue, so maybe just withholding or CAT. Better option would be to bond him out, admin close for a provisional waiver, then take a VD. OCC isn't stipulating too much these days, so it'd probably be an opposed motion to admin close. But now that Sessions has referred the admin closure issue to himself, it's only a matter of time—"

"Excuse me," Lori says, interrupting Shane's conversation with himself. "Can you maybe dumb that down a little bit for us over here? I think I speak for the both of us when I say that we have no idea what you've been saying since we got here."

"Oh, don't worry about it," Shane says. "I'm just running through a few things in my mind here. *I* understand it, and, in the end, that's what matters most, right? Here's the bottom line—"

Shane is interrupted by the sound of an incoming interoffice call. He turns back to his phone and pushes the speaker button again.

"What do you got for me, Paula?" he asks.

"Nada," she says.

"That's Mexican for nothing, right?" Shane asks with a smile, knowing that calling the language Mexican instead of Spanish always gets an easy rise from his lead paralegal, whose family is from Venezuela.

Paula doesn't respond.

"Love ya, Paula," Shane says, still smiling, before hanging up. Shane turns back to Lori and Sarah.

"All right," he says. "Paula couldn't find anything on the theft for some reason, but we can look into that more later if we have to. But as I was saying, the bottom line is that this is an open-ended kinda case. A lot of question marks still, but with what you've told me so far, and with the different options it looks like he has or may have, I would need a $7,500 retainer up front for this case. We'll probably run through that pretty quick with this being a detained case on the IJ's priority calendar, so I would expect you would have to replenish that retainer by the end of the month. We accept cash or credit cards, or a combination of the two. No checks."

"Wow," Sarah says, raising her eyebrows in shock. "I didn't think it would be so expensive. But you can get him his citizenship?"

"That's a *long* way down the road still," Shane says. "Right now, the priority is stopping his deportation. *If* we can do that, then maybe three to five years later we can get him his citizenship."

"Wait," Sarah says. "So there's no guarantee that you can even stop his deportation? What are we paying for then?"

"No, there's no *guarantee*, per se, that I can stop his deportation," Shane says. "Nobody can guarantee *that*. But I *can* guarantee that if anybody in this state—or even in this country—can do it, *it's me*. You're paying for *me*, not a guarantee on the outcome. I'm not some contractor you pay to build a house or something. *I'm* the product, and frankly the best you'll find out there. There's still a lot I don't even know about Wilfredy's case. It's going to take a lot of time to get a full grasp on everything, and, unfortunately, that takes more time than I am willing to give for a $250 consultation fee. Once I've really started digging into the case, then I will have a better idea on his chances."

"So we have to pay you *before* you can even give us an idea of his chances?" Sarah asks.

"Yeah. Like I said, these cases are complicated."

"Well, maybe this will change things," Lori says in a tone of forced optimism, attempting to move the conversation in a more positive direction. "My husband and I have known Fredy for years, and we were both born here. We'd both be willing to do whatever it takes to help. Can *we* sponsor him to get his citizenship?"

"No, that won't work," Mr. Radley says abruptly.

Lori raises her eyebrows, feeling disoriented by his unexpected response without explanation.

"Why not?" she asks.

"It just doesn't work that way."

"Okay, well, do you have a payment plan or something?"

"Lori!" Sarah whispers forcefully. "We can't afford that!"

"No," Shane says. "I don't deal with payments. If things go south and Wilfred's back in Mexico, you know as well as I do that those payments aren't gonna keep coming in."

"Well, would you consider a discount in this case?" Lori asks. "Fredy is just such a wonderful guy, and I'm sure—"

"No," Shane says with a tone of cold indifference.

"All right," Lori says. "Well, maybe we can just—"

"Look," Shane says, standing up and walking towards the door of his office. "It sounds like you just can't afford my services. I wish I could take every case for free; I really do. I'm in this for the people. I love the Mexican people. And we all know they put our food to shame. But I have a business to run, employees to pay, etcetera, etcetera, yada, yada, yada, you know how it goes. But you can always go see if the church or law school clinics can help you out, if you at least want *some* kind of representation. Better than going solo at least—*maybe.*"

"What do you mean?" Sarah asks, starting to stand in response to Shane's less-than-subtle invitation for them to leave.

"There are some free immigration clinics you can check out," Shane says. "They might be able to help you out for free or a discounted rate. But sometimes you get what you pay for, so buyer beware."

Shane leans out the open door of his office, his left hand rested against the door frame and the right holding fast to the door knob.

"Paula!" he shouts down the hallway.

"Yeah?!" Paula shouts back.

"Get these ladies some of those pamphlets for the pro-bono clinics on their way out, por favor!"

"You got it!"

With that taken care of, Shane extends his hand directing Sarah and Lori to leave his office and then closes the door behind them.

...

Lori and Sarah are sitting across from each other in a small booth at their favorite soup-and-sandwich restaurant near their home. Lori suggested they take advantage of Greg's offer to babysit for what they both anticipated would be a much longer and productive consultation with the attorney. The restaurant is considerably less busy than what they've come to expect on their semi-regular Saturday girls' night out. The relative silence of the restaurant seems to amplify the silence between these old friends. Neither seems to know what to say.

Despite her best efforts, Lori can't come up with a positive spin on their meeting with Mr. Radley. Particularly after learning, without explanation, that she and Greg will not be able to petition for Fredy to get citizenship like they had hoped. She can't begin to imagine how Sarah must be feeling right now, and she feels frustrated by her own inability to provide any meaningful comfort. It's no surprise to Lori that her friend has not been her typical talkative and happy self during the past few weeks. But she *was* surprised to see Sarah order the crab salad avocado melt rather than her usual chicken pesto sandwich. *A strange choice of her*, Lori thinks. While Sarah remains silent, her face after the first couple of bites attests that she is already regretting her purchase. This seems to Lori to be a safe topic of conversation.

"I knew you shouldn't have gotten that crab salad mess," Lori says.

"What?" Sarah says, feigning confusion. "I didn't say anything."

"Your face says it all," Lori says.

They both laugh.

"Seriously, though," Lori continues. "You can't expect to get any kind of quality crab in Utah."

"I don't even think it's real crab, so what's the difference where it comes from?"

"Well, I'm sure there's some combination of aquatic life mangled up in there that had to be transported in some dirty, musty old semi-truck out here to Utah. Imitation crab salad is like the hotdog of the sea. Nobody knows what's really in it."

They laugh again. Sarah looks down at her sandwich and smiles, and then looks back at Lori. For the moment she seems relaxed. Almost happy even. For the next several minutes they talk about the most trivial, random topics they can think of, just like they used to before Fredy's arrest. It seems to Lori that her friend is back, no doubt temporarily, but even that's progress she's happy to embrace.

"I can't tell you how much I needed this," Sarah says.

"I still think you should've stuck with the chicken pesto," Lori says.

Sarah laughs harder than the joke warranted, but clearly with sincerity.

"No, I mean *this*," Sarah says, extending her arms and scanning the restaurant. "Just to get out and not think about anything that matters. Just feeling normal for an hour, ya know? I can't even begin to put into words how completely overwhelmed and lost I've been for the past few weeks without Fredy."

Lori says nothing. She's been making a conscious effort not to bring up anything to do with Fredy or the kids or their discouraging consultation with Shane Radley for more money than Sarah had to spare. Now that Sarah has brought Fredy up herself, Lori's still not quite sure how to respond. Sarah continues.

"It's like I had no idea how much he was doing every day for our family until it all became *my* responsibility alone overnight."

"Well, you know we'll always be here for you, Sarah," Lori says reassuringly.

"Of course I know that. But so much of this is beyond what I could ever ask of anyone other than Fredy. I can't call you in the middle of the night and tell you it's *your* turn to feed Veronica. Or ask you to temporarily take over Fredy's business so I can still be there to help with the kids' homework, get them to their practices and lessons, and actually be a regular presence in their lives. Or to lay opposite me on the couch and rub my feet every night while I unload all of the daily stresses of my life on you.

"As chaotic as our lives seemed three weeks ago, I never realized what an amazing team Fredy and I were. We had a sort of unspoken syncness—if that's even a word—I don't know how to put it exactly. We both had *our* responsibilities, ya know, just the normal life stuff that we divided between ourselves through the years. But we would always know when the load was getting to be too much for one of us, and the other would immediately adjust, I guess, to keep a balance that I didn't really recognize or appreciate until it was gone.

"But now I feel like I've been so consumed with the thoughts and pressures of everything I have to do that used to be *Fredy's job*, on top of all of my normal responsibilities, that I end up accomplishing nothing but somehow keeping my kids and myself at least *physically* alive at the end of the day. And my best friend and biggest supporter is gone," Sarah says softly, her voice slightly cracking. She looks past Lori, appearing to space out, and then looks down at the table and continues. "Even if he were doing absolutely nothing to help me right now besides standing beside me or holding me at the end of the day, that alone would be such an amazing support for me right now. But I can't even touch him. And I think the worst part is I have no idea how long it's going to be like this. So I can't even tell myself that it's just another week, or two weeks, or two months, or whatever it is. I have no idea. I have no control. And so I do nothing. Day after day after day, I accomplish nothing, because I can't even begin to think of where to start."

Lori doesn't respond, instead showing her support with a silent facial expression of genuine sympathy. To her surprise, Sarah smiles.

"But right now," Sarah says, returning to a more cheerful tone, "in this exact moment, the only problem I have is finding a way to force down this awful sandwich, and I'm loving every second of it. Thank you for bringing me here, Lori. And please thank Greg again for watching the kids."

Lori reaches over to Sarah's hand across the table and smiles.

"Anytime, Sarah," she says. "I mean that. *Any*time."

They sit in silence for a moment, continuing their meal. Sarah stands up with her empty paper cup and walks to the middle of the restaurant to fill up her soda. She returns to the table with a calm smile.

"Ya know, he's not without his fair share of shortcomings," she says.

"Who?" Lori asks.

"Fredy," Sarah says. "He's gotta be the most stubborn man I've ever met," she says, smiling, looking past Lori, as if recalling dozens of past experiences supporting her claim. "Once he gets something in his head, there's no getting it out. And don't even try to tell him he's wrong."

"Sounds like someone I know," Lori says. "And by someone I *know*, I mean someone I *married*."

They both laugh.

"And our little Oscar is just a spittin' image of him," Sarah says, shaking her head, appearing to picture him in her mind. "For better or worse. He's only ten years old and he thinks he's invincible. He's refused to let his cystic fibrosis slow him down at all. I mean, you've seen him out there on the soccer field. He can be coughing and wheezing, but he won't stop running after that ball. He doesn't have the patience half the time to sit down and catch his breath. There's something in that Gonzalez blood, I guess. They just think they can do it all without any help from anyone."

Lori smiles sweetly without responding, and Sarah takes another drink of her soda. A moment later she continues. "I'm sure that's been the hardest part of all of this for Fredy," Sarah says.

"What's that?" Lori asks.

"Having to rely on so many people right now," Sarah says. "I told him on the phone the other day that I was thinking about looking into getting signed up for food stamps and some other government assistance, just until we can get things figured out, and I could tell it was making him sick inside. I probably just shouldn't have even told him about it. I know it makes him feel like less of a man somehow, knowing he can't take care of his family without any help from anyone."

"Well that's stupid, Sarah," Lori says, finally engaging the serious topic she's been avoiding. "Fredy's done more than his fair share of helping other people, and so have you. So if the Gonzalez family needs to call in some favors and ask for a little help, then Fredy needs to man up, swallow his pride, and accept the help."

"I know," Sarah says. "And it's not like we have much of another choice. But Fredy could use some convincing still. Maybe this whole thing is just God's way of forcing him to learn some humility, which I would welcome." She smiles.

"Well, you know I'm not big on religion," Lori says. "But I'd be the first to recognize divine intervention if the male ego mystically disappeared."

They both laugh and then sit in silence for an extended moment. Sarah takes the last bite of her sandwich then wipes her mouth with the same crumpled napkin she's been using throughout their meal.

"It really isn't all that bad," Sarah says.

"What?" asks Lori. "This whole situation?"

"No," Sarah says. "The sandwich."

Lori smiles and shakes her head, happily accepting the implicit invitation to return their conversation to more trivial matters for the next forty-five minutes.

CHAPTER 12

DAY 22

Thursday, March 22, 2018

"GOOD MORNING, EVERYONE. We're back on the record," Judge Lanzotti says into his portable microphone, having already started the recording for his first master calendar hearing for the morning.

Fredy is sitting at the desk reserved for aliens and their attorneys, again without an attorney. He feels sick.

"This is Immigration Judge Samuel O. Lanzotti," the judge continues. "Conducting continued removal proceedings in the matter of Mr. Wilfredo Gonzalez. The respondent is again present."

Fredy turns around to the gallery of aliens. Only a small portion of those present at his last hearing are still there, many having been ordered removed already. But it's not *their* faces Fredy's looking for. Sarah's not there. He feels alone. The judge continues without pause.

"The Department of Homeland Security is represented by Assistant Chief Counsel Jonathan Richter," he says. "The Spanish interpreter, Claudia Sarmiento, is on standby."

Fredy turns around again. Still no one. He feels defeated. Before he turns back to face the judge, he is startled to hear the judge call his name.

"Mr. Gonzalez," the judge says. "At the last hearing, you indicated that you did not require use of the Spanish interpreter. Do you still feel English is your best language?"

"Yes, sir," Fredy says.

"Also at the last hearing, I provided you—"

"Excuse me, sir," Fredy interrupts timidly. "I'm sorry. But I think my wife might be here. She said she would come."

The judge pauses briefly before turning the clerk to his left.

"Do you have anything on that?" he asks the clerk.

The clerk flips through his stapled print-out of today's cases, confirming with his handwritten notes that a family member did, in fact, check in. He apologizes to the judge for the oversight and offers to go himself to the lobby to find Fredy's wife. The mere thought that Fredy will soon see his wife replaces all of his fear with a level of joy he does not recall ever feeling before. Not just her voice or a blurry black-and-white image of her on the other side of two sets of glass. *Her*. Having already seen the ICE officer deny the request of a prior alien's child to hug his father, Fredy knows he won't be able to touch her or even talk to her. But that doesn't diminish the happiness he feels in this moment, which nearly overpowers him as he sees her walk into the courtroom.

They don't dare attempt to speak or even wave to each other as Sarah is guided by the ICE officer to take a seat in the empty back row. Instead, they just stare at each other for an extended moment, both fighting the impulse to even blink. Fredy feels as though God Himself is manifesting His incomparable love for him through her, His most pure and beautiful child, mercifully crafted and preserved for this precise moment. It doesn't matter what happens to Fredy next. If he were to be ordered deported or even executed. Nothing else matters in this moment.

"As I was saying, Mr. Gonzalez," the judge continues. "At the last hearing, I provided— "

The judge pauses upon seeing that Fredy still hasn't turned back to face him since his wife walked into the room.

"Mr. Gonzalez," he says, attempting to regain his attention.

Fredy doesn't move.

"Mr. Gonzalez!" the judge says again, raising his voice.

Fredy turns around slowly and smiles at the judge, who has now lost all power over him.

"Mr. Gonzalez," the judge says. "At the last hearing, I gave you instructions to come prepared with any applications of relief you intended to file. The court provided you with an asylum application. Are you prepared to file anything today?"

"No, sir," Fredy says, no longer smiling but still not intimidated.

"Why not?"

"My wife has been trying to get me an attorney. She is going to go to a free clinic she was told about, but they only do it on the first Tuesday of every month, so she hasn't been able to go yet."

The judge turns to his left, where a three-month paper calendar hangs on the wall.

"That wouldn't be for almost another two weeks. On April 3, 2018. Are you asking for a continuance until after that date, Mr. Gonzalez?"

"Yes."

The judge sits quietly, considering the request, then turns to the government attorney.

"Mr. Richter," he says. "What is the Department's position on the request for a continuance?"

"No objection, Judge."

"All right, Mr. Gonzalez," the judge says, turning back to Fredy. "I'm granting your request for a continuance. In light of your ongoing detention at the cost of the government, I'm scheduling your next hearing for the next available date after the clinic your wife intends to attend, which will be—" the judge pauses as he turns through his hearing calendar on his desk. "Thursday, April 5, 2018 at 8:00 am."

"That's fine," Fredy says.

"Now, Mr. Gonzalez," the judge says with the tone of a father rebuking his child with a final warning. "I want to be perfectly clear that I expect you to come prepared to file any applications for relief at your next hearing—with or without an attorney—or I will have no choice but to move forward on your case, potentially issuing an order of removal. Is that understood?"

"Yep," Fredy says, smiling defiantly.

"All right, then, this hearing is closed."

...

Approximately forty-five aliens are in the day room at the Cache County Jail in Logan, Utah. It is almost 9:00 pm, which means it will be time for the nightly headcount and then back to their cells for the night. Julio has been walking slowly around the walls of the room for the past twenty minutes, part of his nightly light-exercise routine. Fredy, who just got off the phone with his family, walks over to join him for his last couple of laps around the room.

"Hey, Julio," Fredy says. "I've been wanting to talk to you about something for a while."

"Yeah, I had a feeling you did. But I'm sorry, man, I don't like you like that, you know?"

"What?" Fredy says, surprised.

"How can I put this?" Julio says, briefly pausing before continuing. "I love you, man, but I'm not *in love* with you. You're not the first guy whose heart I had to break in here."

"Shut up," Fredy says, with a short snicker.

Julio laughs, and Fredy can't help but laugh with him. He's started feeling an unexpected kinship with Julio. On the outside, there's no question they would never be friends. But here, with limited options and their shared circumstances, Julio's the closest thing he has to a friend.

"Seriously though," Fredy says. "I wanted to thank you."

"*Thank me?*" Julio asks in surprise. "For what?"

"For what you said to me on Sunday. It may not have been your intention, but you really gave me a lot to think about. You were right. You were absolutely right. It was easier for me to have faith when I thought everything was gonna work out quick and easy for me. And you're right, my faith never wavered when I saw other people around me with their own hardships. They have their families too, and some of them have lived in the U.S. even longer than the both of us. I was being a hypocrite, and you helped me see that."

"Well, that's nothing new for you believers, man, so don't feel too bad," Julio says, his grin widening. "Hypocrisy is like the one thing that unites all the different churches, you know?"

"Yeah," Fredy says. "Maybe. I guess anyone who believes in something bigger than himself sooner or later will fall short of those beliefs. And it's easier to just try to justify it somehow instead of actually changing. But I don't wanna be like that. God walked with me through the hardest time of my life after my sister was killed, and I walked away from Him pretty quick after times got hard again. But all week I've been praying for some kind of sign that God was still there, that He hadn't forgotten about me. And He answered my prayers today. My wife was at my hearing this morning, and as soon as I saw her I could feel, through her, that He was still with me. Nothing good happened at the hearing really. I mean, everything the judge said just felt like a stay of execution really. I can't say that I know what will happen, but I know that God will be with me, even if I get deported and lose everything God has given me. And I don't think I would've had that experience if it weren't for you, so I—"

"Okay, okay, man," Julio interrupts. "I got it, I got it. But you're using up all your best material. You're not gonna have anything left for Sunday, you know? So save some of that for Brother Moore, okay?"

Fredy smiles, accepting Julio's response as the closest thing he will ever get to "you're welcome." Fredy looks over at the large, circular wall clock across the room to his left as he continues to walk around the room with Julio. It's now 8:55 pm.

"Hey, Julio," Fredy says, familiar by now with Julio's nightly routine. "It's almost nine o'clock. You better hurry if you still want to make your call."

"Oh yeah," Julio says, looking behind him towards the only available phone in the day room.

No one is there, which is typical at this time of day. By 8:30 pm all of the other aliens have already made whatever phone calls they had to make that day. Julio walks slowly towards the phone without thinking much about it. The process has become almost unconscious at this point. He picks up the phone and enters first his account number to access the money on his books, and then the 1-800 number for the Executive Office for Immigration Review case information hotline, both of which he memorized long ago. In fact, by this point, he could recite the entire recorded hotline by heart. Approximately three seconds after entering the phone number, without even waiting for a single ring, a prerecorded voice begins speaking.

"Welcome to the automated case information—"

Julio presses 1 to continue in English. Every other night, he presses 2 to continue in Spanish, for the sake of variety.

"The alien registration number, also known—"

Julio enters his nine-digit alien number without waiting for further instruction.

"You entered—"

Julio presses 1 to confirm he entered the correct number.

"The system shows your name is—"

Julio presses 1 to confirm his name.

"For your next—"

Julio presses 4 for decision information.

"Your appeal was dismissed on Thursday, March 22, 2018."

This is new. For more than eighteen months now, Julio has heard the exact same recording every single night, telling him that his appeal was received on October 14, 2016 and that it is currently pending. He is startled by this unexpected change in his routine. There is no further explanation provided, and no actual person to talk to. Why was it dismissed? What does that mean? Julio frowns briefly and then shrugs it off, feigning indifference, and hangs up the phone. *I guess I gotta start on my next appeal then*, Julio thinks calmly to himself before returning to his walk around the room for the next two minutes before the nightly headcount. At least that will be something new to do.

...

DAY 23

Friday, March 23, 2018

"All right, let's go, let's go, let's go!" shouts an unseen man somewhere outside of Fredy's cell, startling him awake. "Everybody move!"

Fredy opens his eyes and grumbles in annoyance. Somehow, the weekly 4:00 am transfers and deportations always seem to catch him by surprise. Sometimes when he's sleeping, he will have passing moments of believing he's at home next to his wife. Of all the inevitable reminders of reality, the early-morning transfers and deportations are by far the harshest of them all. As usual, there is a lot of loud talking in both English and Spanish, peppered with occasional yelling from a distance. But this time, it's just outside Fredy's cell.

"Yo, Julio!" someone shouts.

Fredy recognizes the voice as ICE Officer McAllister.

"I got a present for you, amigo," Officer McAllister says. "We got your decision yesterday, so I thought I'd get you somethin' real nice. A one-way ticket to beautiful *Mexico*, compliments of Uncle Sam. Let's go! Ándale, ándale, amigo! Arriba, arriba!"

"You can keep walking, *pendejo*," Julio says, rolling over. "I ain't going nowhere. I'm filing another appeal."

"You can file whatever you want from Mexico," Officer McAllister says sternly. "Now get up!"

"Save your routine for the newbies, McAllister," Julio says. "I know my rights, so you can't scare me with your lies. I got thirty days to file an appeal to the Tenth Circuit, and that's what I'm going to do. So just keep on walking, man. Your services are no longer needed here."

Officer McAllister looks out the door to his left and shouts, "Hey Johnson, we got a tough guy over here! I may need a hand."

Fredy is now sitting up nervously, while Julio continues to lie down calmly until Officer McAllister and Officer Johnson walk into his cell and begin to pull him out of his bed.

"*Oye!*" Julio shouts. "I told you I ain't going nowhere, man! I'm filing an appeal, so—hey, get your hands off me. I got rights, man! I'm a lawful resident! I had my green card for eleven years!"

"Not anymore you don't," Officer McAllister says, pulling Julio by one arm while the other officer pulls him by the other. "We got a decision from the Board of Immigration Appeals, so you got a final removal order. We don't have to wait for any more bogus appeals you wanna file."

"You guys are gonna lose your jobs for this one, man," Julio says. "I'm gonna sue you all!"

The officers laugh. Julio is standing now with an officer on either side of him holding his arms as they slowly walk towards the door of the cell. They firmly tighten their grip in response to Julio's futile efforts to pull himself free.

"Go for it," Officer McAllister says with a tone of cold sarcasm. "Next time I'm on vacation in Cancun, you can stop by and serve me the papers in person. Maybe I'll even buy one of your tamales for a couple of pesos."

"I'll serve you a lot more than papers if I ever catch you in

Mexico, ¿*me entiendes?*" Julio says, no longer struggling.

Officer McAllister stops abruptly and turns to face Julio. "You threatening me?" he says. He slowly moves his angry face closer to Julio as if daring him to say another word. Julio stands in silence without looking away.

"That's what I thought," Officer McAllister says, nodding his head slowly. "That's what I thought."

The officers continue to hold Julio by both arms, even though he's no longer resisting, as they walk out together in silence. Fredy is left alone in his cell for the first time since his arrest. The sight of his only "friend" finally being deported fills Fredy with an almost overpowering feeling of the reality of the danger he too faces. *What will become of Julio?* Fredy wonders. *Will he really try to come back? Will he really be prosecuted, sentenced to imprisonment, and deported again if he does?* Fredy begins to wonder about Julio's family in the United States. His elderly U.S. citizen parents who faithfully visited and added money to his account every month for the past couple of years. He imagines the countless other innocent victims impacted by the permanent loss of a family member or friend through all the deportations he's seen in just three weeks.

Inevitably, Fredy's thoughts turn to his own family. Julio's now-empty bed makes him think of his empty half of the bed in his own home. Julio's cell bed will be filled with a new alien by the end of day; but who or what will fill the now-empty space in Julio's family? Who or what will fill the empty space in Fredy's family? Is this really in the country's best interest, as so many people argue? Fredy recognizes that this is surely not an easy question to answer. He understands there are legitimate concerns about the safety of the United States, and everyone has an interest in seeing the law obeyed. But he has been detained long enough to see a significant number of people contributing more good than bad in this country, whose deportations no doubt caused more harm than benefit. He's not sure exactly where Julio would fall on that sliding scale, in light of his criminal history and apparent lack of any real remorse. But still, he feels sad. Sad for Julio's family. Sad for the permanency of Julio's punishment. Sad for the dozens of others accompanying him on the same flight to the same fate. Fredy prays silently in his cell for the remaining few aliens until the 6:00 am headcount.

PART 2

CHAPTER 13

DAY 34

Tuesday, April 3, 2018

AN OLD SILVER HONDA CIVIC PULLS INTO A NEARLY FULL PARKING LOT IN FRONT OF A LARGE BUILDING IDENTIFIED ON A SIGN OVER THE FRONT DOORS AS THE SALT LAKE YOUTH & ADULT LEARNING CENTER. It is 4:55 pm. After parking in the closest spot to the entrance he can find, a white man in his late twenties exits the car holding a large book in one hand and a tattered, black cloth laptop bag in the other. He's dressed neatly in a navy-blue suit with a light-blue tie. His dark-blond hair is parted to the right, only slightly modernized from when his mother used to comb it for him as a child. He walks past a large plastic folding A-frame sign at the end of the parking lot near the edge of the sidewalk advertising a FREE LEGAL CLINIC TONIGHT, with a Spanish translation immediately below. He pulls open a heavy blue door into the building and walks into a large lobby with glossy white tile reflecting the light of the sun coming in through the large windows.

"Hola, Ernesto," he says after seeing a bald, middle-aged Hispanic man with a mustache mopping the lobby floor. "How are you?"

"*Oh, estoy super bien, Señor* Todd," Ernesto answers. "They'll be happy to see you here tonight, amigo. It looks like they already have a big crowd of people, and it's not even five o'clock yet."

"Yeah, I heard there have been a lot of calls lately," Todd says. "I just hope I can help out some. Some of these cases are a little too complicated for me."

"But you're the lawyer, man," Ernesto says, laughing. "If it's too complicated for *you*, what are these poor fools coming to you for advice supposed to do?"

"Well, in my defense, I've only been practicing law for a couple of years. I've talked to some immigration lawyers who've been doing this for more than twenty years, and they still say they're left scratching their heads with some of these legal issues."

"*Híjole!*" Ernesto says dramatically, his word of choice for expressing any level of surprise. "Twenty *years*?! And they still don't got this figured out? Are you kidding me, man?"

"I know, it's crazy. On the one hand, it makes me feel better when I don't always know the answer. But on the other hand, it doesn't give me much hope for my future if they still don't have it all figured out after so much time."

"Well, what's a smart white boy like you doing in immigration law anyways? Why don't you do that big corporate law stuff and make some real money for yourself? You didn't think this one through too well, did you?"

"What, you want me to sell out? And miss out on your good company every month?" Todd says with a smile. "I wouldn't think of it."

"You're crazy, man," Ernesto says, laughing. "But seriously, Todd. It means a lot to these people what you're doing here. God bless you, boy. And God bless your family."

"Thanks, Ernesto."

"How's your little one doing?"

"Nora's doing great," Todd says, smiling. "Thanks for asking. Here, let me show you a new picture I took of her the other day."

Todd puts down his laptop bag, reaches into his pocket, and pulls out and opens an old cellular flip phone, one of the few still in existence in 2018, then shows him a picture of a nine-month-old baby girl. Her thin, short blonde hair is pulled into a short ponytail on the top of her head, held in place with a thin pink rubber band. Her mouth is wide open with toothless smile.

"*Hijole!*" Ernesto says. "Will you look at that little beauty? You must have a very pretty wife to make a cute little baby like that, because that sure ain't her daddy's looks."

"You can say that again," Todd agrees with a grin.

"Oh, I'm just messin' with you. You're very pretty too."

"I bet you say that to all the lawyers," Todd says, raising his eyebrows and smiling as he picks up his laptop bag and slowly starts to walk away.

"Yeah, but I only mean it with you, Señor Todd."

"I knew we had something special," Todd says, looking back to Ernesto while still slowly walking away. "See ya later."

"Yes, you will. I don't got nowhere else to go." Ernesto laughs and goes back to mopping.

Todd walks past the lobby and turns to his right down a hallway. Between the echoing sounds of his dress shoes walking across the tiled floor, he hears muffled conversations increasing in volume as he nears the end of the hallway. He turns into a large room that is normally used as a children's library but is currently full of adults seated and spread out over a dozen long rectangular desks. Some have kids with them, who, taking advantage of the location, are skimming through a pile of children's books. A couple other children are not as easily entertained and can be seen running through the aisles of books, hiding from and chasing one another without a hint of parental intervention.

"Oh great, Todd, you made it," says a black woman wearing a dark-purple pantsuit. "Thanks for coming again this month. We've got a full house tonight."

"Yeah," Todd says. "It sure looks like it, Tina. Any other attorneys here yet?"

"We got a few," Tina says. "But so far you're the only immigration attorney, and we mostly have people with immigration questions tonight. So we'll probably have you just sit back at the attorney table as much as possible and work through the volunteer law students instead of individually with each person."

"No problem. Whatever you need."

Todd walks over to the attorneys' tables and takes his seat at the one labeled "IMMIGRATION LAW." Before it's even five o'clock, when the clinic is scheduled to begin, a female law student walks up to Todd, her arms bent upward with a notepad and pen held tightly in her hands above her chest. Her face is beaming with excitement and energy.

"All right, Todd," she says enthusiastically. "I think I have an easy one for you to start with tonight."

"Not likely, Emma," Todd says, smiling. "But I love your confidence. What do ya got?"

"So," Emma says, "this guy and his wife came to the United States in about 1998. *No* criminal history, has his *own* business so no false documents for working, and they have *four* U.S. citizen kids. So they just want to see if their kids can petition for them. I assumed yes, since they're all U.S. citizens and he has a clean record and everything else looks good, but I thought I'd check with you to be sure."

"Well, that all depends," Todd says. "Which you'll find is the same answer to every immigration question. How old are the kids?"

Emma looks down at her notes, frowning.

"I'm not sure," she says, appearing embarrassed that she didn't think to ask. "I'll be right back."

She picks up her notepad and walks quickly to the back of the room, where a Hispanic couple is sitting close together. Todd can't hear them over the chatter throughout the room, but he sees Emma writing notes as the couple speaks to her, after which she abruptly returns to his table.

"Okay," she says as she sits in a chair across from Todd, partially out of breath. "The kids are fifteen, eleven, nine, and six."

"Okay, but are they boys or girls or a combination of the two?" Todd asks.

Emma's shoulders drop and she lets out a large sigh as she admits she didn't think to ask, and begins to stand to go back to ask them.

"No, no," Todd says, reaching out to stop her as he laughs. "I'm kidding, I'm kidding. That one doesn't matter. Sorry, I couldn't resist."

Emma sits back down but does not laugh or even smile.

"Okay, so the current answer is *no*, they can't petition for their parents," Todd explains. "At least not yet. U.S. citizen children can't petition for their parents until they're at least twenty-one years old. But even after the kids are twenty-one and petition for their parents, that doesn't necessarily mean their parents will qualify for legal status if they've been in the country illegally. So sometimes getting an approved petition doesn't even matter."

"Then what's the point?" Emma asks.

"For the government to get filing fees, I guess," Todd says with a smile. "Not really. Well, at least *I hope* not really. There are just multiple applications that have to be filed to get legal residency, and it's possible to qualify for some of the steps but not all of them. Do you know if they entered the U.S. legally?"

Emma stares blankly for a moment.

"I don't think so," she says, looking down at her notes for confirmation. "But I know I asked that one, just give me a sec." She turns back to her first page of notes and smiles, apparently relieved that she asked the question.

"Okay, nope, they didn't enter legally," she says. "Does that make a big difference, even though they have U.S. citizen kids and they've been here for so long? I know last month you told me that there was no problem for a guy to get residency from his U.S. citizen wife even though he had been in the U.S. for like fifteen years after his visa expired."

"That's true, but it was the original legal entry that made the difference in that case, even though he overstayed for many years afterwards."

"So is there anything this guy can do six years from now once his oldest kid is twenty-one?"

"It depends," Todd holding back a smile.

"Of course it does," Emma says with a sigh. "Because this guy said that his cousin also entered the U.S. *illegally*, at the same time as him and his wife, and he was able to get his green card even though he has like, three DUIs. But these two here tonight don't have any criminal history at all, so they assumed it would be even easier for them."

"Well, if this guy's cousin really entered illegally and was still able to get residency, he probably qualified under 245(i)."

"What's that?"

"It's a law that allows people who had an immigrant visa petition filed for them on or before April 30, 2001 to apply for residency without leaving the United States, even though they entered illegally. But only if they were illegally present in the United States on December 21, 2000, unless, of course, the petition was filed on or before January 14, 1998, in which case they could've come illegally after December 21, 2000. But that goes without saying."

"What?!" Emma says with a tone of exasperation, prompting Todd to laugh shortly. "How are you supposed to keep track of this stuff? Why do all these different dates make a difference?"

"Because immigration law is done by patchwork," Todd says. "Congress just keeps adding small pieces of reform on top of a giant pile of incoherence. It's like a history lesson every time I look at a new case. So anyway, my guess is that this guy's cousin probably has a U.S. citizen brother or someone who filed a petition before the cutoff date in 2001. Then, after he married a U.S. citizen, he was able to pay a fine and apply for residency here instead of having to leave."

"Okay," says Emma slowly, carefully deciding which of the

dozen questions she now has is the most pressing. "But they both entered *illegally* and they've both been here the same amount of time. The only difference is this guy's cousin might have a U.S. citizen brother, but these two here have no criminal history. I would think that no criminal history would be more important than having a U.S. citizen brother."

"That's because you're thinking logically. That won't help you much in understanding immigration law."

"But what about their kids? I hate to use the term, but aren't they supposed to be *anchor babies*? Doesn't sound like much of an anchor."

"Usually not. If they are *anchors*, they have a very, very, very long chain—a minimum of twenty-one years long. But in most cases, even after that, if the parents entered illegally, they will have to leave the United States for an immigrant visa interview. And once they leave the United States, they trigger a ten-year bar and only qualify for a waiver if they have a U.S. citizen or lawful resident *spouse* or *parent*. So if all they've got are the kids, that's another ten years on top of the twenty-one years, and it's ten years they have to spend *outside* of the United States, so it doesn't exactly anchor them to the U.S. in most cases."

"Wait, wait, wait," Emma says, squinting her eyes in confusion. "Why do they get a ten-year bar when they *leave* the U.S. for an immigration interview? Isn't that what everyone *wants* them to do? To go back home and do it the right way?"

"Again with the logic," Todd says, still smiling. "It's frustrating, I know. And sad, really, because it affects real people's lives. But the law says that if you've been in the U.S. for more than one year illegally, you trigger the ten-year bar once you *leave* the U.S., even if the reason you are leaving is to visit family, attend a funeral, or even go to an immigrant visa interview. So for most people, it creates an incentive to just stay here unless they qualify for a waiver of the ten-year bar, which in this case it sounds like they don't, right? The only family they have here legally is the kids?"

Emma is fairly sure that is correct but reviews her notes anyway in hopes of finding that she missed something. She didn't.

"Yeah, that's right," she says.

"Okay," Todd says. "Unfortunately, they're looking at a minimum of sixteen years, assuming they leave the U.S. to wait out the ten years once they get an approved petition. But who knows what the law will look like at that point. Hopefully better."

Emma sits quietly, frowning.

"So this is just another case of waiting and hoping in vain for the laws to change?" she asks.

"'Fraid so," Todd says.

Emma stands up without saying more, drops her hands to the sides, her notepad in one and her pen in the other, and walks back to give them the bad news. Todd feels the vibration of his cell phone in his front left pocket. He takes out his phone and finds a text from his wife, Julie.

> Guess who just took three steps? :)

Todd smiles and responds:

> At 9 months old? That's gotta be some kinda world record. She must have her father's advanced intellect. At this rate she'll be talking by the time I get home.

Todd sits waiting and smiling in anticipation of a response, which he receives less than a minute later.

> By the time you get home? Oh... do you still live here? Nora and I haven't seen you for a while, so we assumed you found a new family.

Todd laughs quietly and responds:

> No. No new family yet. It's not for lack of trying though. It's a tough market right now for new families, so it's not the best time for me to upgrade just yet. I'll keep you posted though. Let me—

"Okay, Todd," Emma says, interrupting and startling Todd, who is still texting his wife. "Oh, sorry, I can come back later if you're busy."

"No, you're fine," Todd says, putting down his phone. "What do you got for me?"

"Well, actually I think you might need to talk directly with this one. This lady's husband has been in jail with ICE for like a month already and she said they're gonna deport him this week maybe. Is that something we can even help with? I've never come across this at the clinic before."

"That makes two of us. Most of my work is family-based immigration, naturalization, and stuff like that. I've never actually represented anyone in immigration court. I know some of the basics, I guess, but I'm not sure how much help I can be if they're gonna deport him this week. What'd you find out?"

"To tell you the truth," Emma admits sheepishly, "once she said her husband was already in jail and about to be deported, I didn't even know what to ask. I felt so horrible I didn't even *want* to ask her anything. I'm sorry. She has a big folder of documents though."

"That's okay, Emma. We can only do so much with this little clinic here, but I can at least go back and talk to her." Todd pushes back his chair and walks around the table to Emma. "Why don't you sit in on this one with me?"

"Ok!" Emma says excitedly. "That'd be great!"

Emma leads the way to one of the long tables in the back of the room where Sarah is sitting alone with a large folder of documents in front of her. She's staring blankly with a melancholy gaze at the back of the heads of the two people seated at the table in front of her. She turns her head and looks up as she hears Emma walking back to her table. Sarah is visibly surprised and pleased to see with her a man whose shirt and tie lead her to assume he's one of the attorneys. Emma had explained to her that the clinic does not have a large enough volunteer staff for the attorneys to be able to personally talk with all of the clients, so she wasn't expecting to be able to do so. Sarah instinctively stands up to greet them, smiling.

"Oh, thank you, sir," she says, looking at Todd. "Thank you so much."

"Don't thank me yet, I haven't done anything. I'm Todd Becker," he says, extending his hand to Sarah, who graciously accepts it.

"I'm Sarah, Sarah Gonzalez."

Todd and Emma pull out chairs on the opposite side of Sarah and sit down. Sarah follows their lead and sits back down.

"So, I understand that your husband is detained right now," Todd says. "And that immigration may be deporting him this week? Is that right?"

"Yes, sir," Sarah says, causing Todd a fleeting feeling of discomfort being referred to as "sir" from a woman he assumes is easily ten years older than him. "His name's Fredy," she continues. "He's been in jail for more than a month now and he has his last court this Thursday. The judge said he has to file his asylum application or be deported."

"Why was he arrested?" Todd asks.

Sarah recounts the details of Fredy's arrest as she understands them. Sensing Todd's skepticism that Fredy had not actually been drinking the night of his arrest, Sarah begins describing Fredy's history of alcohol abuse following the death of his sister, Veronica, and their subsequent conversion to the Church of Jesus Christ of Latter-day Saints. She talks about Todd's service in the community, the free community soccer team he formed, and other examples of help he has given to people in his church and his neighborhood. Todd knows that most of this will not ultimately be relevant. Even if Fredy had actually been charged and convicted for a DUI, that would not prevent him from qualifying for relief from removal if he were otherwise eligible. And even if Fredy is as great of a person as Sarah claims, that will not necessarily prevent the judge from deporting him. Relevant or not, Todd listens.

"Fredy sounds like a great guy," Todd says, taking advantage of a pause in Sarah's prolonged answer. "I'm sorry this is happening to your family. But I'm gonna need a little more information to know if there's anything he can do to stop his removal."

During the next fifteen minutes, Todd gets a fuller understanding of the facts of Fredy's case. He learns that Fredy's parents brought him to the United States from Mexico in the summer of 1989, when he was twelve years old. His parents enrolled him in school, where he learned English, ultimately graduating from high school with honors in 1995. Sarah shows Todd a copy of Fredy's diploma and explains that they began dating while they were both still in high school. Fredy first started working in 1993 when he was sixteen years old and has worked continuously ever since, until ICE arrested him last month. Sarah shows Todd a large folder with Fredy's taxes dating from 1993 to 2016 and explains that they have not had a chance to file his taxes for 2017 yet, but that she hopes to soon. Todd learns that Fredy was cited for shoplifting in 1995 when he and a couple of his friends attempted to steal a discman from an electronics store, the name of which Sarah can't remember. Because Fredy had just turned eighteen earlier that year, he was charged as an adult, even though he was still in high school at the time. Although Sarah admits she wasn't there, she insists Fredy was very apologetic about the whole thing before the judge, admitted his guilt, and paid the required fine. Years later, after she married Fredy, they were easily able to get the conviction erased from his record through an expungement since he had no other criminal history. Sarah shows Todd the petition for expungement, the corresponding order, and all of the other old court documents they saved.

Sarah and Fredy continued dating after high school, ultimately getting married in 1998. They have since had three children: Oscar, Katie, and Veronica, born in 2007, 2013, and 2017 respectively. Oscar was born with cystic fibrosis, for which he was hospitalized as recently as a few months ago. Veronica, the baby of the family, was named after Fredy's sister who was murdered in Mexico. Todd now has enough information to begin to identify the different options Fredy might have. Several come to mind. Because Fredy married a U.S. citizen in 1998, she could have petitioned for him at any point before April 30, 2001 and he could have been given a waiver for his (or rather, his parents') unlawful entry into the United States. However, Sarah says that they didn't think to worry about Fredy's status until several years later, after their son was born.

"So that means they can't get residency in the U.S., right?" Emma says with a smile, excited to have spotted the issue, but feeling bad immediately after, realizing the negative implications for the human being seated in front of her. "Sorry," she says, looking down with embarrassment.

Sarah continues to explain that in 2008, they hired a notary to file Fredy's immigration papers because they couldn't afford an attorney, but it was denied the following year. Sarah pulls out a document titled DECISION from the U.S. Citizenship and Immigration Services.

"Why did you file an application for residency?" Todd asks Sarah after reading the first half of the first paragraph. "Without a legal entry or a pre-2001 petition, he didn't even qualify to attempt to file this."

"So I was right?" Emma says. "I *knew* it!"

"Are you kidding me?!" Sarah asks. "We never completely understood why the application was denied. I thought it was because he had worked in the U.S. illegally or something, but we paid like two grand to that guy who did our paperwork."

"Plus filing fees, I'm sure," Todd says.

"Yeah!" Sarah says. "That was like another fifteen hundred."

Todd shakes his head. This is far from the first time he has seen non-attorneys, and even some actual attorneys, charge thousands of dollars to file some immigration application that has no hope of possibly being approved. He continues reading the decision.

"Okay," Todd says in confusion, still looking down at the document. "It says he supposedly made a false claim to U.S. citizenship? Do you know what that is about?"

"Yeah," Sarah says. "That's what I was talking about. We went to our interview and there was this real nasty woman. It was like she already decided we were liars from the very beginning, that our marriage was fake or something. Even though by this point we had been married for ten years and had a kid together. Then she started asking us how he had been working in the United States, and he told her that his mom got him a social security number when he first got here and that he had used that. So she said that she couldn't approve it until she'd seen some forms from all his past jobs—I can't remember what it was called—"

"An I-9?" Todd asks.

"Yeah, that's it," Sarah says, nodding her head. "So we went around for like five weeks trying to dig up all of his I-9 forms, and then after we sent them in, they denied it anyways."

"I'm assuming at least one of those forms had a check on the U.S. citizen box," Todd says.

"Maybe. I don't remember," Sarah says. "But Fredy didn't fill out those forms. All of his bosses knew he was here illegally, but he had a social security number his mom got him, so that's all they cared about."

"Did he sign any forms when he started his new jobs?" Todd asks.

"Yeah," Sarah says. "He signed those forms, but he didn't fill them out. I don't think he even read them. They just said they needed him to sign some forms before he started."

Todd continues reading the decision but then stops abruptly.

"Wait," he says, looking up at Sarah. "Did they make him sign an affidavit at the interview with immigration?"

"I remember that he signed something there. The officer wrote it all, but I can't remember exactly what it said."

"Well, according to this decision, it says he admitted that he made a false claim to U.S. citizenship to get his job. Is that true? Did he sign that?"

"I don't know. Maybe. The interview wasn't going very well at this point, and she said she needed a statement or something from Fredy before they could make a decision. I think we thought it would help to just admit that he was working illegally, even though he was paying all his taxes and stuff."

This is not good, Todd thinks to himself, frowning. Fredy shouldn't have even filed that application in the first place. He is puzzled why immigration would even have an interview and ask for additional evidence once it was clear he didn't qualify. An obvious fishing expedition by an overzealous immigration officer, exploiting the fact that Fredy didn't have an attorney present. Todd runs through the multiple missteps in his mind. What Fredy *should have* done after missing the 2001 filing deadline was apply for an immigrant visa and waiver from Mexico. He could have been back in the United States after just a few months or so, with lawful permanent residency, and by now even U.S. citizenship. Today he may have been able to do the same, without even leaving the United States until the waiver was approved, only requiring a week or so of separation from his family. But now Fredy can't do any of that. There is no possible waiver for making a false claim to U.S. citizenship. It would have been better had Fredy instead committed an act of domestic violence against his wife, which *would*, in contrast, allow for a waiver. But this supposed false claim to U.S. citizenship has drastically limited Fredy's options moving forward. Todd is angered that some incompetent or dishonest "notary" not only stole their money, but also stole their alternative, viable option. Stole their future.

"Well," says Todd, still frowning, after an extended period of silence. "It looks like he would've qualified for DACA at least."

"What's DACA?" Emma asks.

"Deferred Action for Childhood Arrivals," Todd explains. "It's for people brought here by their parents when they were kids. It was one of President Obama's executive orders. President Trump revoked it last year, but a couple of federal court judges have preserved it for now, at least for renewals. So if Fredy ever applied for it in the past, he could always try to renew it."

"Is that the same as the DREAM Act?" Emma asks.

"It was based on the proposed DREAM Act that never got through Congress," Todd says. "DACA's really just a Band-Aid on a broken leg, no permanent solution, but it's been a great temporary benefit for a lot of people. I've done a ton of these cases. Unfortunately, we can't do any new applications for people who never had DACA."

"Actually," Sarah says, interrupting the lesson. "We already tried that one too a few years ago, but it was denied."

"Why?" Todd asks. "Do you have the decision with you? Tell me you didn't go back to that notary, did you?"

"No, no," Sarah says, shaking her head. "We just did it on our own this time. I don't have the decision with me here, sorry, but I'm sure it's at home."

"Okay," Todd says. "Well you said he's been here since he was twelve, and that he graduated high school. When was he born?"

"January 9, 1977," Sarah says.

Todd pauses for a moment, thinking to himself before responding.

"Ah, that's why," he says, having finished his silent calculation. "He's too old. He had to have been younger than thirty-one when

President Obama signed the executive order in 2012. I always thought that was the dumbest of all the requirements. He's essentially being punished for being *more* tied to the United States than everyone who actually qualifies for DACA. That's too bad. Unfortunately, that was just more lost filing fees for something he didn't qualify for."

Todd sits silently, thinking.

"Well," he says. "It sounds like his best option now would be to apply for cancellation of removal before the immigration judge."

"The judge said he had to apply for asylum," Sarah says.

"Asylum would be a distant 'Plan Z' in my opinion," Todd says. "I hear the immigration judges here deny the vast majority of those cases. Truth be told, I hear they deny most of the applications for cancellation of removal. You used to just have to show *extreme* hardship to your U.S. citizen family to get it approved, but Congress decided it was okay with causing extreme hardship to our citizens, and so they raised the standard to *exceptional and extremely unusual* hardship. But with your son's medical history, I think he actually has quite a strong case. He just needs to also show that he's been in the U.S. for at least ten years, which we can easily show with all of these tax records. And that old shoplifting conviction would just be a petty offense since he doesn't have anything else. If he can get cancellation of removal, then he could get his residency and eventually his U.S. citizenship, even with the problems with the other applications you filed."

"That's great!" Sarah says. "So you can help us?!"

Todd is startled by the question.

"Well," Todd says, slowly, "I've never actually represented anyone in court. It would take a lot of work to get up to speed, and I'm just working on my own. I don't even have a receptionist."

"I could help!" Emma says excitedly.

Todd looks at Emma but doesn't respond. Sensing Todd's reservations, Sarah intervenes.

"It's all right," Sarah says as she begins to put the documents back inside her large folder. "You've already helped us more than anyone since this whole mess started. Thank you so much. At least now we know that maybe he can try to cancel his deportation."

Todd sits quietly thinking to himself, knowing full well how far in over their heads Fredy and Sarah are.

"Removal," Todd final says.

"What?" Sarah asks.

"Cancellation of *removal*," Todd says. "They don't call it deportation anymore. It's *removal* now."

A trivial distinction, to be sure, and one that Todd hasn't bothered correcting dozens of times in the past. Half the time Todd says deportation rather than removal himself for convenience. But if Sarah and Fredy don't even know the correct word for what it is they're fighting against, how can they possibly be expected to prevail? He knows that Fredy doesn't stand a chance with his wife effectively acting as his legal advisor. But he also knows that he would fare much better with an attorney with actual experience in removal proceedings. Whether it's the blind leading the blind, or the nearsighted leading the blind, chances are they'll all end up at the bottom of a ditch.

Todd thinks of his own family. His wife, Julie, and their nine-month old daughter, Nora. He thinks of the emotional, financial, and psychological hardship it would be for them if he were suddenly gone forever. He recognizes that Sarah's family would suffer even more than his own, with her significantly longer marriage, two more kids, and one with serious medical problems. Todd also knows that there is no second chance for Fredy. If he cannot stop his removal, there's no coming back. Ever. The senselessness of this clear outcome triggers mixed feelings of frustration, sadness, and anger. Motivated in varying degrees by a combination of these emotions, Todd takes a bold and defiant stand.

"I guess I'll see what I can do," he says.

CHAPTER 14

DAY 35

Wednesday, April 4, 2018

TODD IS SLEEPING—POORLY—IN A BED IN A SMALL, DARK BEDROOM AT JUST PAST THREE IN THE MORNING. He is moving and rolling around even more than his wife could attest to being the norm. He feels a cold spot on Julie's side of the bed and pushes himself up in panic. Half awake, and less than half conscious, he stumbles out into his daughter's room immediately opposite his own. He turns on the light to an unoccupied room.

"Julie!" he shouts. "Nora!"

They're gone! His family is gone! He feels overwhelmed by increasing panic and fear. Still not completely aware of what's happening, Todd stumbles into the hallway wall, making his way towards the dark living room of their apartment. Before he can say anything else, he comes to an abrupt halt at the sound of a forceful whisper.

"Be quiet! What are you doing?"

Todd squints through the darkness at the shadow of his wife sitting in a rocking chair in the corner of the room, nursing Nora. By this point, Nora is generally sleeping through the night, but she will still occasionally get thrown off her normal feeding schedule and demand a late-night snack.

"What? What are you doing out here?" Todd says, struggling to understand what's going on, having still not completely woken up.

"What does it look like I'm doing, crazy?" Julie says, looking down at her nursing baby.

Still somewhat emotional from the temporary scare of finding his family gone, and torn between a dazed desire to hold his child and nature's demand that he go back to sleep, Todd offers to help.

"Well, that depends," Julie says. "Have those lactating pills I've been giving you started to work?"

"What?" Todd says, unable to comprehend.

"Do you have any boobs?" Julie says more forcefully.

"What?" Todd says, still confused. "What?"

"Just go back to sleep," Julie says, laughing. "You're no use to me now."

Todd, with reluctance that quickly turns to gratitude, follows his wife's instructions to go back to bed.

...

Todd is dressed in the same navy-blue suit he wore the day before, the only one he has, but a different tie. Red today. A strong choice, he thinks. He stands up from the kitchen table as he drinks the remaining milk in his bowl of cereal. After putting the bowl in the sink, he bends down to kiss Julie, and then Nora, who she is holding while still seated at the table. They say their goodbyes and love yous as Todd opens the sliding glass door at the back of their kitchen, leading to the concrete stairway down to the parking lot in the back of their small apartment complex.

"Thanks again for your help last night, babe," Julie teases, clenching her lips tightly in an apparent effort to hold back a smile.

"What?" Todd says, confused.

"You don't remember, do you?" she asks, now laughing. "You never do."

"Remember what?"

"I'll tell you later. Just go, you're gonna be late."

Todd follows her command and walks down the stairs with his black laptop bag. Sitting inside his old Civic, he stares forward without moving, his hands resting on the steering wheel. After an extended hesitation, Todd reluctantly decides to take the hour-and-a-half drive north to the Cache County Jail to meet Fredy. It's early still, so after reaching the I-15 North freeway entrance, Todd finds less traffic than he's used to. The wide, overcast skyline is covered with different shades of blue, purple, and pink, pushed through the clouds by the rising sun. To his right are large mountains, still partially covered by the winter's snow. The beauty of it all feels like home to Todd and is a stark contrast to Tucson, Arizona, where he grew up. Tucson will always be an important part of Todd, where he still has family ties and fond memories, but Utah has become his *home*. Given the purpose of this long, quiet drive, Todd's thoughts quite naturally turn to Fredy, a man he has never met. He suspects Fredy largely feels the same about his own Utah home, even as his childhood in Mexico will always be a part of him. But certainly not a part of him that could ever, at this point, feel like *home* again. Utah is his home, which just happens to be in the United States of America. By all accounts, it's a home that Fredy has done more than his share to care for. But that somehow is irrelevant now.

As Todd continues his long drive, he perceives his surroundings the way he imagines Fredy would. Every other town he passes seems to have a large American flag hung and waving high along the side of the freeway, both before and after passing Exit 331 for the Hill Air Force Base. What mixed feelings Fredy must feel when seeing the same, Todd thinks. Symbols of the country he loves, a country not quite ready to love him back.

As Todd passes a police car inconspicuously parked under an

overpass, he nervously checks his speed, feeling the natural sensations of fear that an authority figure may have caught him in the wrong. The feelings quickly pass upon confirming through his rearview mirror that no lights are flashing and the police car remains parked. But he suspects these are feelings that have not so quickly passed, and have come much more frequently, during Fredy's nearly three decades in the United States. Todd personally knows of victims of crimes too afraid to report those crimes to the police because of their immigration status. How sad is it, Todd thinks, that those who are meant to protect our society—and in fact consistently do so day after day—could elicit so much fear and suspicion, rather than trust and respect.

By the time Todd reaches the I-15 exit to U.S. Route 91, the sky has darkened significantly from the expanding rain clouds, and it has started to lightly rain. Now, driving past the small town of Brigham City, Todd reflects upon Brigham Young, the city's name-sake. Brigham was the second prophet of the Church of Jesus Christ of Latter-day Saints, of which Todd is also a member. Brigham, like Fredy, had a challenging journey to Utah before finding his own home. Brigham's route into Utah, ironically enough, is now called Emigration Canyon. Fortunately for Brigham, Todd thinks to him-self, Emigration Canyon was not blocked by a wall or any Customs and Border Protection officers. Simpler times, Todd supposes. At least in some respects. Todd passes a number of bright-yellow deer migration signs, urging drivers to proceed with caution for their presumably legal migration.

Todd's engine begins revving as he climbs the hills weaving through the canyon, fast approaching the city of Logan. He passes a number of farms on either side of the highway as he gets closer, snow-capped mountains still encircling him. He sees in large black lettering LOGAN next to smaller lettering EST. 1866, on top of a multi-colored brick wall, welcoming him to the city and prompting him to confirm the address of the Cache County Jail he has written on a sticky note and put on his dashboard. After making his way through the south side of the city, passing a number of fast food restaurants, businesses, a Catholic cathedral, and the historic Logan Tabernacle, Todd comes to a stop at 200 North Street. To his right he can see one of his church's temples, where families come together with the promise of being sealed together for all of time and eternity. To his left, in the distance is the Cache County Jail, serving as temporary housing prior to the ultimate tearing apart of dozens of families every week, sealed or not. Todd wishes he were turning right but frowns and reluctantly turns left.

After driving a couple of miles down the road, Todd sees a large, wide brick building to his right and turns into the parking lot, passing a large green-and-white sign reading "Cache County Sheriff's Complex," a large yellow sheriff's badge serving as a backdrop. After parking, Todd gets out of his car with his laptop bag and walks towards the building, following the signs pointing towards the jail in the far southeast corner of the building. He pulls open a heavy white metal door with a large, double-reinforced glass window. To his left is the only person he can see, a woman seated on the other side of a glass window with a wooden counter along the wall to Todd's left. Todd begins to take out his wallet as he approaches her window.

"Hi, I'm an attorney," he says, showing his Utah State Bar card in case she doubts his word. "I'm here to meet with a client of mine."

"Please sign in," the woman says without turning away from her computer monitor, pointing to a clipboard on the counter on Todd's side of the window to his right.

Todd picks up a pencil tied with a thin string to a clipboard with a sign-in sheet. He searches the room for a wall clock, ultimately finding one on the wall behind him, and writes his name, the time, and the type of visit.

"Name?" she says after hearing Todd put down the pencil, still without turning from her screen.

"My name?"

"The inmate's name, sir."

"Oh, of course. Wilfredo. Wilfredo Gonzalez."

The woman begins typing on her keyboard in search of the name.

"Looks like he's here with ICE. Is that correct, sir?"

"Yes, ma'am. I'm his immigration attorney, or at least I'm—"

"Do you have a signed G-28, sir?" the woman interrupts.

A G-28 is a form specifically designated for attorneys to attest that they are representing aliens before USCIS, ICE, OCC, or CBP. Not to be confused with an EOIR-28 for attorneys representing aliens before an IJ, or an EOIR-27 for attorneys representing aliens before the BIA.

"I have a G-28," Todd says, opening his laptop bag and flipping through his documents until he finds it. "But it's not signed yet."

"I can't let you see him until you have a signed G-28," she says. "Sorry, that's ICE's policy."

"But I can't have a signed G-28 until I see him."

"That may well be, but rules are rules," she says, pointing to a bright-yellow piece of paper taped to the counter on Todd's side of the window to his left.

Todd begins reading in disbelief the instructions for attorney visits with detained aliens.

"How can I ever get him to sign a G-28 if I can't see him until I get it signed? Is this a joke?" asks Todd, frustrated at the thought that he may be turned away after a two-hour drive.

"No, sir. This is very serious. It's for the protection of the detainees."

"Fine," he says, putting down his laptop bag and then taking a pen out of the inner breast pocket of his suit. "Give me a second."

Todd signs next to Wilfredo's name on the G-28 and then holds it up against the window for the woman to see.

"I am authorized by my client to sign on his behalf," Todd says. "Here is your signed G-28. May I please see my client now?"

The woman looks over the form, reviewing Todd's signature

next to a handwritten "OBO Wilfredo Gonzalez." Todd doubts the legitimacy of this unauthorized signature only slightly less than the legitimacy of the jail's G-28 policy. But he does his best to feign confidence as the woman squints suspiciously at the form.

"All right," she ultimately says. "Everything appears to be in order. I'll tell the guards to bring your client to attorney room number 2."

"Thank you," says Todd in disbelief.

He starts to laugh quietly but stops short upon catching a stern look from the woman. Todd walks across the lobby to the opposite wall and attempts to open a beige metal door with the number 2 stenciled in white paint. It's locked. He tries again, then looks back to the woman at the front desk but hears the door unlock before he has a chance to speak. He opens the door and finds two plastic chairs pushed in under a steel counter in front of two large, double-reinforced windows separated by a metal frame. No one is on the other side yet. Todd expected to find a telephone to speak to Fredy on, but instead he observes several rows of small holes running up either side of the metal frame dividing the two large windows, through which he hears the echoing of voices and footsteps. After no more than a few minutes, Todd is startled to see the door open.

Fredy walks into the small room on the other side of the glass. He seems both confused and disappointed to see a white stranger in a suit looking at him. Knowing that tomorrow may well be his final hearing, he had probably hoped to see his family while he still can.

"Hello?" Fredy says after sitting down.

"Hi, Wilfredo?" Todd says.

"Fredy. Who are you?" Fredy asks suspiciously.

"Sorry, my name is Todd Becker. I'm an immigration attorney. I spoke with your wife yester—"

"You're here to help me?!" Fredy interrupts with excitement. "Oh, thank you, sir, thank you. I've been praying every day for someone to help me somehow. God bless you, sir. God bless you."

"Well hold on, hold on," Todd says, feeling the need to

immediately manage Fredy's expectations. "I don't know if I *can* help you. But I promised your wife that I would at least try to talk to you about your case."

"Oh, that's fine, thank you, sir, thank you."

"Before I do anything, I need you to understand that I don't have any experience in immigration court. I am an immigration lawyer, but I focus on family petitions and naturalization. This would be a first for me."

"You're white and you got a suit and tie," Fredy says. "Between you and me, that's what seems to matter most with this judge I got."

"Why do you say that?" Todd asks, laughing.

"With all due respect, this guy's an obvious racist," Fredy says. "He gives me no bond and no hope right after he gives some white attorney everything he asks for for his client. His client had a *felony* drug conviction, and this guy Radley got him off scot-free."

"*Shane* Radley?" Todd asks.

"Yeah, that's him," Fredy says.

"The problem is not that the judge is racist," Todd says. "It's that the law is stupid. The judge is sworn to honor, interpret and uphold *stupidity* in many cases. Shane is great at navigating through the stupidity. I'm still working on it. I still haven't quite been able to abandon my impulse to find common sense and consistency in the law, which, frankly, has made it harder for me to understand and remember it sometimes. It's also why I've avoided the immigration court so far, where things can get really messy. And I don't have any staff to help me—well, other than Emma, a volunteer law student."

"I'm not worried, Mr. Becker," Fredy says. "God has sent you to me. He is greater than all. I know He will deliver me. I know it."

Todd sits quietly for a moment, suddenly overwhelmed with the burden of the sum total of a man's hope for his family and his future. He realizes that there is nothing he can say to take that hope away, and he doesn't really want to anyway. Maybe God *did* lead him to Fredy, Todd thinks. He can't think of a clearer example of divine intervention than a successful outcome with a case left in his inexperienced and incapable hands. If God chose a poor carpenter to raise His Only Begotten Son, and an uneducated farm boy to restore His church in 1830, as Todd believes, then maybe this isn't as impossible as Todd originally thought. It certainly seems to be God's MO to do His work through the underdogs.

"Well, before I can know if I can help you," Todd says, "I need to know some more about you."

"Of course, of course. Ask me anything, Mr. Becker."

"Well, the first thing I'll ask is that you call me Todd," Todd says with a grin.

"You got it, Todd," Fredy says, smiling back.

CHAPTER 15

DAY 36

Thursday, April 5, 2018

TODD IS STANDING AT THE END OF A LINE OF PEOPLE, MOSTLY HIS-
PANIC, IN A SMALL LOBBY WAITING TO PASS THROUGH A METAL DE-
TECTOR AT THE MAIN LEVEL OF THE IMMIGRATION COURT IN WEST
VALLEY CITY, UTAH. A short, heavy Hispanic woman is removing
a number of gold bracelets and large earrings and placing them in a
rectangular plastic bin at the end of an x-ray conveyor belt. Past this
first round of security, a guard is waving a metal detector wand up
and down the inner and outer legs of a tall man leaning forward with
his hands against the wall. A second security guard is sitting on a
chair on the left side of the conveyor belt, watching a screen revealing
the contents of the items passing through. A third security guard
is managing the line of people, ensuring that they remove all metal
items before passing through.

This is worse than the airport, Todd thinks to himself. He looks
down at his watch. It is 7:58 am. He sees that he has received another
text message from Emma, who wisely arrived at the court thirty
minutes early to observe Fredy's hearing at 8:00 am. Todd opens the
text and reads it.

> Judge not here yet... but Fredy is the only one here today so
> he'll be up as soon as Judge comes out!!!

Todd is now at the front of the line, shuffling his belt, watch, wallet, and phone into a small bowl and placing his laptop bag in a larger bin. It's now 8:02 am.

"You're going to have to remove your computer from the bag, sir," a guard says to Todd, pointing to his laptop bag.

"Of course I am," Todd says, quickly pulling it out and putting it back into the bin before starting towards the walk-through metal detector.

"Hold on, sir," the guard says. "You need to wait until your belongings have gone through."

Todd reaches into his pocket for his phone to check the time again, only to recall that it is going through the x-ray conveyor belt. He scans the room anxiously until he finds a circular wall clock. It's now 8:04 am.

"Okay, sir," a guard on the other side of the walk-through detector says. "Come on through."

Todd walks through slowly with his arms close to his sides, being sure not to touch the inner sides of the detector. To his relief, the detector does not alarm. He quickly pushes all of his belongings into his laptop bag, not bothering to even put on his belt, and quickly walks towards the elevator, asking the occupants in English and then Spanish to please hold the door. They do so. It's now 8:06 am. After a painfully long minute they reach the second floor with the immigration court. Todd walks as quickly as he can without running out of the elevator and into a lobby. He sees and follows a sheet of copy paper taped to the wall to his left saying IMMIGRATION COURT with an arrow pointing to a doorway which opens into a seating area in front of a clerk's window. Down a hallway to his left, past a row of unoccupied chairs, Todd hears a deep voice addressing Mr. Wilfredo Gonzalez. Todd follows the sound of the voice down the hall and into a courtroom where Fredy is sitting alone at a desk in front of the judge.

"Your Honor," Todd says interrupting the judge, almost out of breath. "I apologize. I was just retained to represent Mr. Gonzalez if I may."

The judge sits silently with a scowl on his face, clearly not pleased with the disruption. He looks down to his file, flipping through the first few pages before looking back up towards Todd.

"Have you submitted your notice of appearance, young man?" the judge asks him. "I don't see anything in the file here."

"I have not, Your Honor," Todd says, sighing as he recalls his run-in with the jail clerk over his signed G-28 just yesterday. "Is that something I can file with the court later today maybe?"

"Well, that's not typically how we do things here, Mr.—?"

"Becker, Your Honor. Todd Becker."

"Okay, Mr. Becker. You've kinda put the cart before the horse here, so to speak. There's an order to these things. I'll allow you to appear on Mr. Gonzalez's behalf today—assuming of course that's what Mr. Gonzalez wants. Mr. Gonzalez," the judge asks, turning to Fredy, "would you like Mr. Becker to represent you in your removal proceedings today?"

"Oh yes, sir, yes, please."

"Very well. I will allow you to do so, Mr. Becker. But please file your written appearance with the court clerk before you leave and be sure to serve a copy on the government."

"Certainly. Thank you, Your Honor, and again, I apologize for not having that already."

Todd sits down next to Fredy, still catching his breath. He is visibly flustered.

"You came!" Fredy whispers excitedly, leaning over to Todd. "Oh, thank you, sir, thank you."

"Don't thank me just yet," Todd says nervously, pulling a file out with copies of some of the documents Sarah gave him.

Fredy turns to look to the back of the courtroom, prompting Todd to do the same. Emma is sitting next to Sarah, who has a smile so big it appears it may burst at any moment. She waves to Fredy, who responds with a thumbs-up with his one free hand. She makes eye contact with Todd, tilts her head to the side, raises her eyebrows and mouths a sweet "thank you" to him with a face of true sincerity and gratitude. Todd can feel almost a physical presence of restored hope radiating from Fredy and Sarah, which only serves to convince him further of his own inadequacies. The judge has turned on the recording and starts speaking to the parties.

"It is April 5, 2018," he says, beginning his robotic, memorized introduction. "This is Immigration Judge Samuel O. Lanzotti conducting removal proceedings in the matter of Mr. Wilfredo Gonzalez. All parties are present. On behalf of the respondent is—"

The judge pauses, looking towards Todd, who is nervously reviewing his notes from his meeting with Fredy at the jail. After an uncomfortable silence, Todd looks up to the judge. Todd's lost eyes seem to silently plead for merciful guidance from the judge.

"You need to state your appearance for the record, Mr. Becker."

"My appearance, Your Honor?" Todd asks, less sure of himself now than before the judge attempted to nudge him in the right direction.

"Just state your name, son. Appearing on behalf of the respondent *is*—"

"Oh, yes, sorry, Your Honor. Todd. Todd Becker, sir."

"On behalf of the Department of Homeland Security is—"

"Debra Kaiser," says the woman representing the government today.

"At the first hearing," the judge continues, "the respondent appeared *pro se* and entered pleadings to the Notice to Appear, admitting the four factual allegations and conceding the corresponding charge of inadmissibility. The Court designated Mexico as the country of removal in the event that removal should become necessary. At the next hearing, the Court granted the respondent's request for a continuance in order to obtain legal counsel. The respondent was told to come today prepared to file any and all applications for relief from removal. Mr. Becker," the judge continues, turning now directly to Todd. "Does your client have any applications that he would like to file with the court today?"

"I do not actually, Your Honor," Todd says. "Not yet anyway, but I wanted to see if we could first talk about a bond hearing for my client."

"No, we cannot, Mr. Becker," says the judge. "Mr. Gonzalez previously made a request for bond, which request was denied. He waived appeal. We are scheduled for removal proceedings today. I have already taken pleadings. Your client was instructed to come prepared with any and all applications for relief that he intends to file. This court is troubled to learn that these clear instructions were not followed."

"Yes, Your Honor," says Todd. "I understand. But I think there may have been a misunderstanding at the last bond hearing about Mr. Gonzalez's arrest. It's my understanding that he actually *passed* the field sobriety tests, and that he has never even been charged with any DUI, so—"

"Mr. Becker," the judge interrupts, making no effort to conceal his annoyance. "You are welcome to file a *written* motion for a bond hearing. While the regulations permit an oral motion for an *initial* bond hearing, you must file a *written* motion for any subsequent request. Assuming, of course, you can demonstrate that there have been changed circumstances since Mr. Gonzalez's last bond hearing, I would be happy to grant your motion. However, we are not sched-uled for a bond hearing today."

"I understand, Your Honor," Todd says nervously, his already limited confidence now all but destroyed.

"Are you at least prepared to tell me what, if any, forms of relief Mr. Gonzalez *intends* to apply for, if not today, Mr. Becker?" the judge asks.

"Oh yes, Your Honor, yes I am!" Todd replies, excited to get a question for which he believes he has an intelligent answer. "I'm sorry, I've just started working on this case; let me just check my notes here."

Todd looks back through his notes, attempting to reorient himself. Feeling almost a burning sensation from the judge's piercing and impatient eyes, Todd begins fumbling through his response before he feels completely ready to do so.

"Yeah, okay," he says. "I—I think he would qualify for cancellation of removal, sir. He has been in the United States since about 1989, and he has three U.S. citizen children and a U.S. citizen wife too, so—oh, and one of his kids actually has some medical problems, Your Honor, cystic fibrosis, so I think he has a pretty good case for cancellation of removal, actually. I mean, I know it's a high standard, but I think he's—"

"That's fine, Mr. Becker," the judge interrupts, "I don't need a full summary of your case right now. Would you like me to set the matter over for filing of an application for cancellation of removal?"

"Yes, please, Your Honor," Todd says.

"Any objection from the Department, Ms. Kaiser?" the judge asks, turning to the government attorney.

"No objection to a continuance for attorney preparation," Ms. Kaiser says. "But I do think there may be some issues on eligibility for cancellation of removal. Our initial screening of Mr. Gonzalez's criminal history came back negative, aside from the DUI investigation. But after Mr. Gonzalez mentioned a shoplifting conviction, we dug a little deeper. The FBI rap sheet just came back showing an apparent theft conviction from 1995 in Utah. I don't have any information on a sentence—I'm assuming this was expunged, which is why we couldn't find it before—but it says it was a class A misdemeanor, and so potentially an aggravated felony. May I approach, Your Honor?"

"Yes," the judge says.

Ms. Kaiser stands up and drops a stapled, two-hole punched stack of documents on the desk next to Todd as she walks up towards the judge, handing him a copy of the same.

"I was already aware of this, Your Honor," Todd says, skimming quickly through the pages. "My understanding is it was for shoplifting a discman back when Mr. Gonzalez was in high school. It was just a misdemeanor though, so it couldn't be an aggravated felony, Your Honor. It's just a petty offense, so he should be fine."

"Well, counselor," the judge says, "That's not necessarily true. Several misdemeanors fall within the definition of an aggravated felony under the Act, including some misdemeanor theft convictions. Mr. Gonzalez carries the burden of proof, which may be challenging if he did, in fact, have his record expunged. You will need to provide the court with evidence that this conviction is not an aggravated felony, or, for that matter, a crime involving moral turpitude, unless it meets the petty offense exception."

"Yes, Your Honor," Todd says.

"How much time would you like to prepare, Mr. Becker?"

"If I could have at least a couple of weeks, Your Honor."

"Let me check my calendar," says the judge, turning the page of a folder placed immediately in front of him. "It appears that I am now booked out for the next three weeks, actually. It seems Homeland Security been busy filling up my calendar with new respondents. Are you available April 26, 2018? That is my next available date."

"Yes, Your Honor," Todd says without bothering to check his calendar. "I will make that work."

"Okay, then, Mr. Becker," the judge says. "To be very clear, I expect you to come prepared to file any and *every* application for relief from removal that your client has, or may have, any interest in pursuing. I do not intend to grant any more continuances in this matter. Understood?"

"Yes, Your Honor," Todd says.

"Anything else from the parties before I close the record?" the judge asks.

"Nothing from the Department," Mr. Kaiser says.

"No, Your Honor, not for the respondent either," Todd says.

"This hearing is closed," the judge says, before turning off the recording. "And we're off the record."

The judge stands without saying more, prompting the others in the courtroom to do the same until he has left through the door in the back of the room.

"That was a disaster," Todd mumbles under his breath.

"What?" Fredy asks.

"Oh, nothing, nothing," Todd says. "I'll be in touch soon."

Fredy smiles as the ICE officer instructs him to stand and walk over to him so he can cuff his free hand. He turns to Sarah and quickly tells her he loves her and that everything is going to be fine before he is led by the ICE officer down to holding until he can be transported back to the Cache County Jail.

...

It's now 11:41 pm. Todd is sitting in front of a small fold-out square table, staring into the glowing light of his laptop computer in an otherwise dark room. To his right is a large immigration book, now peppered with sticky notes and dog-eared pages from his research during the past several hours. To his left is a still-untouched plate of spaghetti that has cooled again after having already been reheated once by Julie. She has since decided not to bother again. Behind him in a small crib, Nora is swaddled and has been sleeping for about four hours now. She stirs suddenly and starts to cry at an unexpected disruption.

"Are you kidding me?!" Todd yells, slamming his hand down on his desk, having temporarily forgotten both the late hour and the fact that his home office is doubling as a nursery.

Todd is standing next to Nora's crib, putting her pacifier in her mouth when Julie opens the door abruptly.

"What happened?" she asks nervously.

Todd turns to Julie with a guilty face, mouthing a *sorry*. He's able to comfort Nora quickly, and within a minute or two she's asleep again. Julie is still standing outside the door as Todd quietly walks out to meet her. Her expression of concern is replaced with one of confusion and mild annoyance.

"All right, lawyer man," she says. "I think it's time you call it a night. You have officially lost your mind."

"I know I have," Todd says as he softly closes the door behind him, prompting them to walk towards their bedroom. "But it's the government's fault."

"Isn't it always?" Julie asks as she sits on her side of the bed, leaning up against the headboard. "What has Uncle Sam done to you this time?"

Todd sighs heavily and pauses, unsure of where to begin. He sits on their bed across from Julie with his legs crossed. A moment later he has settled on a starting point.

"So basically, ninety percent of the ridiculous immigration laws I'm always ranting and raving about," he begins, "and a bunch more I've just discovered tonight, all stem back to the same genesis of stupidity."

"What's that?"

"IIRIRA," Todd says.

"Ira who?"

Todd laughs.

"*Ira-Ira* is how it's pronounced, apparently," Todd says. "I-I-R-I-R-A. It stands for the Illegal Immigration Reform and Immigrant Responsibility Act."

"That's a mouthful," Julie says.

"I know," Todd says. "That's just another example of how little thought was put into the stupid thing. The least they could do is come up with a catchy acronym, like the *DREAM* Act, for the Development, Relief, and Education for Alien Minors. Even

Trump came up with *VOICE* for his Victims of Immigration Crime whatever it was—"

"Okay, okay," Julie interrupts. "You're losin' me here. Focus, Todd, focus. What's the problem with this Ira guy?"

Todd laughs softly at this characterization.

"If you're gonna humanize this law, why do you gotta assume it's a guy?" Todd asks. "Maybe it's short for Irene?"

"I can already tell he's far too stupid to be a woman," Julie says.

"Touché," Todd says, smiling. "Okay, so back to this Ira *guy*. Ira shows up in 1996, an election year of course, and decides to show everybody just how angry and stupid someone can be under the right circumstances."

"Okay," Julie says. "What'd he do?"

"Well, first he decides that the best way to pass common sense immigration reform is to remove all of that overrated common sense. He starts by redefining basic English. A *conviction* no longer has to actually be a *conviction*. A *term of imprisonment* is redefined so that it doesn't require any actual *imprisonment*. And an *aggravated felony* doesn't have to be *aggravated* or even a *felony*. But only when dealing with noncitizens, of course."

"Of course," Julie says, nodding her head facetiously.

"So, say you've got some 'real' American," Todd continues, "and he gets charged with a class A misdemeanor shoplifting offense that's dismissed after paying fines and complying with his probation, and his whole sentence is suspended so he doesn't spend even a single day in jail. If a noncitizen did the exact same thing, Ira would say this guy has a *conviction* for an *aggravated felony* with a *term of imprisonment* of 365 days. He would group this guy together with actual aggravated felons like murderers and rapists, treating them all exactly the same."

"That's stupid," Julie says. "Why'd he do that?"

"I don't know," Todd says, shaking his head briefly and then suddenly smiling. "But I have a theory."

"I'm sure you do," Julie says, laughing softly. "Do tell. I'm on the edge of my seat here."

"So am I!" Todd says, playing along with Julie's sarcasm. "And I already know what I'm going to say, but it's *that* interesting!"

"Carry on, counselor."

"Thank you, I will. So my theory is that Ira is trying to scare white people."

Julie rolls her eyes and shakes her head, unsure of how to initially respond.

"Is this really what you've been working on all night?" she ultimately asks, thinking back on the plate of cold spaghetti still sitting on Todd's desk.

"No, of course not," Todd says, smiling. "I've been studying what the law actually says. I'm just making this part up as I go along. But it sounds as good as any other reason I can think of at the moment. Maybe Ira thought he could make white people scared of all those evil *aliens* by describing even rehabilitated petty offenders as *convicts* and *aggravated felons*. He takes all these scary words with commonly understood meanings, but then he applies them equally to everything from murder to shoplifting."

"You should try that out at your next hearing," Julie says, rolling her eyes. "Your Honor," she says, in the low, confused voice she always uses when pretending to speak for Todd. "I object, uh, clearly this is uh, uh, just another attempt to scare the white man."

"Maybe I will," Todd says emphatically, feigning offense.

Julie laughs.

"All right, fine, maybe it's not to scare white people," Todd says. "But Ira was definitely trying to justify what he did next."

"Oh, wait, there's more?" Julie says sarcastically. "Do tell."

Todd continues undeterred.

"So next, Ira goes and takes his scary, redefined words and tells the mindless masses that we just can't stand for having all of these *convicts* and *aggravated felons* in *our* country. Why, that just sounds downright sinful—because Ira is a devoutly religious man, you know."

"It sounds like it," Julie says.

"Oh yeah," Todd says. "And not just a twice-a-year, Easter Sunday, Christmas mass kinda religion. This guy kneels before the feet of his sweet Beelzebub on a *daily* basis."

"Please continue, Mr. Becker," Julie says in an effort to keep her husband focused.

"All right, all right," Todd continues. "So you've got these words like *conviction* and *aggravated felony*—don't even get me started on *crimes involving moral turpitude*—that all *sounds* so terrible that Ira can pretty much do whatever he wants without having to actually analyze an individual case. He doesn't care if you're an illegal immigrant who just got here, or a lawful permanent resident of twenty years with a dozen U.S. citizen kids. He doesn't care if you committed the crime yesterday or decades ago. Because an aggravated felony just *sounds* like it must be a horrible crime, so we shouldn't have to worry about the details, and just lock 'em all up with *mandatory* detention. *No bonds for anyone!* he says. Even if they can prove they're not a danger to the community or a flight risk, and even if their cases go on for months or even years. Ira doesn't care how much it costs either. He just puts it all on his daddy's credit card, which his daddy has no intention of paying off anyway."

"Naturally," Julie says.

"And once you've been branded as a so-called aggravated felon, there's no saving you from Ira. There's almost *no* way to stop your deportation or for you to *ever* come back. And Ira doesn't care if that ends up hurting the country he claims to love. He'll gladly banish the sole provider of a family and then just whip out his daddy's credit card again to pick up the tab for the government aid for thousands of now fatherless families."

"That's terrible," Julie says, replacing her playful sarcasm with sincerity.

Todd stares pensively past his wife for a moment before continuing.

"But somehow, everybody just loved this Ira guy when he showed up," Todd says. "The Republican-run Congress, the Democratic President Clinton, and all the shortsighted, fear-driven voters—they all wanted to be best friends with Ira. It didn't matter how quick to anger and slow to forgive he was. He got the mobs so riled up about the actual serious criminal immigrants that we all willingly looked the other way while he banished thousands of people who provided more good than bad to our country."

"This Ira guy sounds like a real douche," Julie says.

Todd laughs.

"Now *that* sounds like an argument I can actually use in court," he says. "Much better than that scaring-white-people theory.

"Your Honor, may it please the court," Todd says in an exaggerated, pretentious voice. "It is indeed true that the law *is* the law, but that Ira guy is a real douche."

"I like it," Julie says, laughing.

"Maybe you should be the lawyer," Todd says.

"No, I have too much self-respect for that," Julie says with a smile as she grabs and pulls over the blanket on Todd's side of the bed, exposing the mattress and motioning with her head for him to lie down beside her.

Todd smiles. He recognizes that his mind is long past the point of functioning clearly, and, somewhat reluctantly, accepts his wife's implicit invitation to go to bed.

CHAPTER 16

DAY 41

Tuesday, April 10, 2018

"Thanks again for letting me work with you on this case, Todd," Emma says.

"Of course," Todd says. "This is the kind of stuff that will teach you how to actually be a lawyer, far more than any of your law school classes."

Todd and Emma are sitting at a booth in a fast food restaurant a few blocks from Todd's home. Emma has her laptop in front of her and a few remnants of their lunch on a plastic tray pressed against a wooden barrier at the far end of their table. The generally muffled squeals and screams of a dozen children periodically echo through the restaurant every time someone opens the glass door to enter or exit the play area directly behind their booth.

"Sorry we had to meet here," Todd says, reaching for the last of his fries. "I'm looking into getting one of those virtual offices, but for now I'm still working from home most of the time, so this has become my go-to spot for lunch meetings with clients. It's not the most professional environment, but you can't beat the free Wi-Fi."

"No, it's fine," Emma says, smiling. "Don't worry about it."

"So, I got your email with your research," Todd says. "Why don't you give me an overview of what you understand to be the issues and we'll work through them together?"

"Perfect," Emma says enthusiastically. "Well, actually, I wanted to ask you something first. I was reading a story over the weekend about some new *zero-tolerance* policy that the attorney general announced. Something about prosecuting everyone who enters illegally. Is this something else we need to be worried about for Fredy?"

"Yeah, I saw that too. I haven't had a chance to read up on that much, but my understanding is that it will just apply to people stopped at the border."

"So what's gonna happen to them?" Emma asks.

"Well, usually people caught at the border just get sent back with a voluntary return or an expedited removal order, unless they're requesting asylum. They could technically charge all of them for a misdemeanor offense of illegal entry, but that hasn't happened in the past because there's not enough resources and they're lower-priority offenses."

"What do you mean?" Emma asks.

"It's like with people speeding," Todd says. "Under the law, an officer could technically pull over and ticket every single person who drives even a single mile over the speed limit, but that's never gonna happen because that would be a terrible use of limited resources. So this will be interesting. AG Sessions is mad that Congress hasn't given more resources for border protection and a wall, so he's gonna try to somehow prosecute *everyone* stopped at the border, even without the additional resources he'd need to actually do it."

Emma sits quietly, thinking of the possible implications.

"Anyway," Todd says. "Let's get back to Fredy."

"Right," Emma says, shifting her focus back to the purpose of their lunch meeting and looking down at her notes. "Okay, so the government attorney and the judge said Fredy's shoplifting charge could be an aggravated felony even though it was a misdemeanor. So I started my research there and found a case stating that the term 'aggravated felony' is 'a term of art' and 'does not mandate that the crimes *actually be felonies when the literal language of a particular subparagraph includes offenses that are misdemeanors.'"*

"Term of art, eh?" Todd says sarcastically, thinking back on his conversation with his wife last night. "That's one way to describe it. Abstract art, I guess."

"I know," Emma says. "I couldn't believe it. But according to the law, a shoplifting offense like Fredy's can be a so-called aggravated felony if it has a sentence of at least one year. I had to read that one twice because it's written weird in the law. Hold on, let me find it."

Emma scans through her notes until she finds the quote she's looking for.

"Here it is," she says. "It says an aggravated felony under section 101(a)(43)(G) is *'a theft offense (including receipt of stolen property) or burglary offense for which the term of imprisonment at [sic] least 1 year.'* That *sic* part threw me off. I'm embarrassed to admit I had to look up what it means. I guess it's not actually a part of the statute. It was added by the editor of the book to show that the grammatical error is a direct quote of the statute, and not a typo in the book. Apparently, in 1996 this statute was amended and they took out the word 'is' by mistake, so it now says in the actual statute an 'offense for which the term of imprisonment at least 1 year,' instead of '*is* at least 1 year.'"

"Yeah," Todd says. "Ira's an idiot."

"Who's Ira?" Emma asks.

"He's that 1996 law that's responsible for most of the things I've been teaching you at the clinics that don't make sense."

"Well, it definitely seems like it was rushed. That's a pretty obvious grammatical error. It makes it seem like there wasn't that much thought or review put into this thing. I mean, how do you forget such an obvious word like *is*?"

"Well, this was back during Clinton's presidency," Todd says. "Remember how he said he didn't understand the meaning of the word '*is*' during the Monica Lewinsky hearings? Maybe the Republican Congress also struggled with the word and intentionally left it out."

Emma sits quietly in confusion.

"Sorry," Todd says. "Lame joke. Go on."

"Okay," Emma says. "So, the documents we got from Fredy's wife for his shoplifting citation don't say anything about a sentence, but I figured there's no way it could've been for a year to be an aggravated felony. All it says is that it was a class A misdemeanor. So I looked up Utah law and found that you can actually be sentenced up to 365 days for a class A misdemeanor. I was shocked. I have a cousin whose ex-husband was convicted for domestic violence, and he didn't spend a single day in jail, so how could shoplifting get you a year in jail?"

"It won't," Todd says, shaking his head. "You'll never see anyone spend anywhere close to a year in jail for shoplifting, probably not even a single day. What usually happens with a class A misdemeanor in Utah is the judge will give a sentence of 365 days, but then immediately suspend the entire sentence. So in the end there's no time in jail, but Ira treats it like the shoplifter was sentenced to a full year."

"That's so stupid," Emma says. "This is a *state* offense. Doesn't it matter that the *state* says there is no imprisonment?"

"Not at all," Todd says. "Even though a lot of people think the local police should help enforce federal immigration laws, federal immigration law completely ignores what state law says about state offenses. So if you've ever been caught speeding, which is a class C misdemeanor in Utah, then according to Ira, you may have a 90-day term of imprisonment on your record because that's the maximum possible sentence."

Emma shakes her head in disbelief. "Okay," she says. "But I started looking at the actual state statute he was convicted under, Utah Code section 76-6-412, and it says that in order to be a class A misdemeanor, the value of the property stolen must be between $500 and $1,500."

Todd sits back, startled, this being the first thing Emma has told him that he hadn't already figured out for himself. Emma continues, confirming Todd's suspicions.

"So I went back and looked at his citation," she says. "And it says that the discman he tried to steal was valued at only $115."

Todd smiles widely, feeling a sense of hope for the first time since he reluctantly agreed to take on Fredy's case.

"Does that mean—"

"He got an illegal sentence!" Todd interrupts with excitement. "That's great! Well, it's not *great*, it's horrible, actually. I mean, this guy just can't catch a break. But that's great news for us. So what does the law say about trying to steal property valued at only $115?"

"Hold on, let me check," Emma says as she begins turning through her notes.

"Here it is," she says. "It says if the value of the property stolen is less than $500 then it is a class B misdemeanor, which has a maximum sentence of—"

"Six months!" Todd interrupts. "So no aggravated felony! Even if they try to say it's a crime involving moral turpitude, it would be a petty offense. Awesome work, Emma!"

Emma smiles with excitement at the thought that she may have just made the breakthrough they needed to save Fredy and his family, or to at least give them a chance. Her research on the immigration consequences of aggravated felonies has previously left her with little hope that Fredy would be able to stop his deportation or ever come back to the United States. She read about lawful permanent residents of several years, with strong family ties in the United States, having their applications for citizenship denied and being deported for life, based on old convictions classified as aggravated felonies. She read about immigrants with strong asylum claims, victims of horrific violence in their native countries, being denied the opportunity to even apply for asylum based on the same. Even with her still-limited exposure to immigration law, she knows enough to know that if they cannot conclusively show that Fredy's conviction is not an aggravated felony, there is likely not much more they can do. The overwhelming feelings of joy in potentially playing a small role in helping Fredy seem to solidify her previously uncertain decision on whether to pursue immigration law as her career path.

"The only problem," Todd continues, "is that the immigration judge won't care that the sentence was illegal. He has to take it at face value, so we'd have to get it fixed in the criminal court, which would be another first for me. But we might not have to worry about that. I have another theory I was going to tell you about."

Emma sits upright, anxious and almost excited to hear what Todd has to say.

"Fredy's conviction was back in 1995, before Ira came around in 1996," Todd begins. "Back then, a theft offense had to actually be a felony to be considered an aggravated felony. So he would've had to have had a sentence of at least five years for it to have been an aggravated felony back in '95, which he clearly did not."

"So there's no way this could've been an aggravated felony," Emma says. "So we can get him a bond, right? And get him cancellation of removal? And he can stay here, right?!"

"Maybe," Todd says with a tone of cautious optimism. "But let's slow down a minute. I wanna check with some other local immigration lawyers to make sure we're not missing anything else."

Todd reaches down to his bag and pulls out his laptop. He begins addressing an email to a local chapter of immigration lawyers that he is a member of while Emma sits quietly, smiling.

Hello all,

Another quick question from the rookie to make sure I'm on the right track here. Client pled guilty to a class A theft back in February of 1995 and presumably got a suspended 365-day sentence. He got it expunged several years ago. DHS says it may be an aggravated felony. I know the expungement doesn't help him, but I think he may have actually had an illegal conviction. Under Utah Code 76-6-412, a class A misdemeanor has to involve property worth more than $500. But my client's theft was only for property valued at $115. It's actually on his citation! So he should've been charged as a class B misdemeanor, which wouldn't be an aggravated felony, and it would be a petty offense. Right? Also, I did some research on 1995 immigration law and found that before IIRIRA became law in 1996, a theft conviction had to have a sentence of 5 yrs instead of 1. So at the time of his conviction it clearly would not have been an aggravated felony, right? Let me know if I'm missing anything. Thanks in advance.

--

Todd Becker

Becker Law, LLC

"Come on," Todd says, closing his laptop and putting it back in his bag. "Let's call it a day. Great work, Emma. Dessert's on me. You like shakes? I'm super-sizin' today, so you don't wanna pass this up."

"I'm okay," Emma says with a grin.

...

"Is it gonna be another late night?" Julie quietly asks Todd, who is sitting in front of his laptop in his office/nursery.

It's 9:30 pm, and Nora has been sleeping in her crib behind him for almost two hours now.

"No," Todd says. "I just finished an application for a new client that has to go out tomorrow. I'll be done in a minute."

"Okay," Julie says as she quietly closes the door and walks into their bedroom.

Before closing his laptop for the night, Todd decides to check his email. He sees a few responses to his immigration question for Fredy's case from earlier that day. The first is from Caitlynn Preston, an attorney he respects very much and who he has called upon numerous times for assistance with his more complicated applications for residency or citizenship.

> I avoid the immigration court like the plague, so I'm not the best person to ask, but it sounds like your on the right track. Good work. You're client's lucky to have you.
>
> Cheers!
> Caitlynn
>
> ***Sent from my iPhone. Please excuse any typos***

Todd smiles with more assurance and opens the next email from an attorney whose name he doesn't recognize.

> I can't believe our government is wasting our limited resources on cases like this. My kid's doing some bake sale so her class can buy books, but our government has plenty of money to lock up and detain non-violent immigrants and send our troops half way across the world to die for nothing!?! Sorry, you caught me in one of my moods.
>
> End of rant.
>
> -Saul

Not exactly responsive to Todd's question, but he appreciates the enthusiasm. Before Todd has a chance to close his laptop, he sees another response come in. This one is from Shane Radley. If anyone knows the answer, Shane does, Todd thinks as he opens the email response.

Sorry, rookie, a swing and a miss! But I gotta say, I love that you're swinging at least. Welcome to the blood bath.

You're right that the *current* version of the Utah statute requires property valued at $500 or more, but you always, always, always have to check the version that existed at the time of the offense. I've attached a pdf of the 1995 amendments of the Utah statute for your reference. See that up until March 20, 1995 you could get a class A misdemeanor w a 365-day sentence for stealing property worth as little as $100. It wasn't until 2010 that it went up to the current $500 amount. So no illegal conviction (at least not on that ground - keep swinging though, you might hit something else). The most ridiculous part of all is that your guy—or girl... *because ladies steal too, ya buncha misogynists* :) —but I digress... the most ridiculous part of all is that your guy/girl would've been a thousand times better off under immigration law had s/he committed this exact same offense *yesterday* instead of more than two decades ago, because then it would have just been a class B misdemeanor and not a supposed aggravated felony.

As far as your "Plan B" goes, unfortunately the 1996 amendment to the definition of an aggravated felony applies retroactively. *See, e.g.,* IIRIRA § 321(b), 8 U.S.C. § 1101(a)(43) ("... the term [aggravated felony] applies regardless of whether the conviction was entered before, on, or after the date of enactment of this paragraph."). So, in other words, it doesn't matter if the conviction wasn't an aggravated felony at the time he pled guilty, because on an otherwise beautiful fall afternoon on September 30, 1996, Billy C. and the Republican thugs in Congress flexed their stupidity, waved their magic wand of tyranny, and POOF! thousands of minor offenses instantly changed from petty offenses to aggravated felonies overnight. In short, your client can't benefit from the good changes in state law after the conviction, but at the same time is stuck with the bad changes in immigration law after the conviction.

And these are just a few of the reasons why Caitlynn (and other attorneys on this listserv) "avoid the immigration court like the plague…"

You might look into 212(c) options, if he qualifies for that. But IIRIRA will definitely apply. Sorry…

Shane M. Radley, Esq.
RADLEY & ASSOCIATES, LLC
Email: Shane@RadleyLaw.com

CONFIDENTIALITY NOTICE: This message is confidential and may be privileged. Unauthorized use or distribution is prohibited and may be unlawful.

Having finished reading the email, Todd stares blankly past his laptop at the wall behind his desk. He feels hopeless and defeated. It seems Ira has thought of everything. It's as if he has anticipated every possible scenario or loophole that could somehow allow even a little common sense or compassion to squeeze its way through. Todd resents the fact that first Judge Lanzotti, and now Shane Radley, have left *him* feeling stupid for still not quite comprehending the stupidity of the law. He's reminded of his first several months during his proselytizing mission in Argentina for his church, struggling to muster out the simplest of thoughts in a language still quite foreign to him. He recalls some well-intentioned listeners politely nodding during his message, offering unintentionally condescending words of encouragement, like "Yeah, you got that word right," "Close enough," or "I *think* I understand you." He felt like they were just humoring him when his intent was to teach them, rather than the other way around. A humbling experience to be sure. Others were less kind, belittling even his best efforts. The most frustrating part of all was that he had learned enough to understand what they were mocking him for, but not enough to defend himself. Not a day would go by without some random person passing him in the street shouting, "Hello! Hello!" or "One, too, tree, forrr, fibe!" Most days he didn't mind. Sometimes he laughed with them. But then there were days like today, when he was working so hard, believing he had made real progress, only to be kicked back down.

The further Todd travels through the labyrinth of immigration law, the more certain he becomes that no rational mind could have possibly played a role in its creation. The more he learns, the less he understands. The more he understands, the less he wants to understand. Echoing through his mind is one of the most common battle cries in this deeply divided political issue: "The law is the law." But is it? Is some man-made, *malum prohibitum*, civil immigration offense really an unwavering standard for morality? Obviously not, Todd thinks, if Fredy's single youthful indiscretion can be viewed as a relatively minor offense on the day it is committed, only to be redefined after the fact as equivalent to murder, rape, and sexual abuse of a minor. Ironically, this federal redefining of the law happened even as the very community in which Fredy's offense was actually committed came to view it as *less* egregious, not more. Why, then, such hostile opposition to the mere thought of amending the law *again*, to provide a reasonable path to legalization, at the very least for people like Fredy who are so obviously a benefit to this country?

Todd thinks of the political pundits demanding five-year mandatory minimum sentences for so-called aggravated felons who reenter the United States. He thinks of the millions of Americans who would support such a new law as "common sense," based on the false assumption that Congress similarly used such "common sense" when defining seemingly simple terms like *aggravated felony* or *conviction* or *term of imprisonment*. Do any of these people know that an aggravated felony need neither be aggravated nor a felony? Or that a conviction does not have to be a conviction? Or that a term of imprisonment requires no term of imprisonment? Does anyone actually believe that first-degree, premeditated murder and Fredy's shoplifting offense should carry the same permanent immigration consequences? Todd's growing animosity towards the law in general begins to almost overshadow his sincere concern for Fredy as an individual.

Pushing aside his instinct to give up, Todd leans back in his chair, takes in a deep, slow breath, and resolves to start from scratch. Working under the light of his computer screen, he opens his immigration law book back to the page tabbed as "Aggravated Felonies" and begins re-reading the section he now knows he still does not understand. From there he goes to an exceptionally dry section of the book dedicated to the legislative history of IIRIRA. Just as he feels he's starting to make some progress, he is startled back into reality by the creaking sound from the opening of his office door and the intruding light from the hallway.

"So much for two minutes," Julie says in a tone that is equally sarcastic and unsurprised, conveying a message of *I told you so* without needing to say the actual words.

Todd looks at the time in the upper right corner of his laptop. It's now 10:17 pm.

"Sorry," Todd says, looking back to his wife as he closes his laptop for the night. "I guess I lost track of the time. Again."

He forcefully closes and rubs his eyes, strained from the abuse of his unrelenting focus on the small rectangular glow of his computer screen in an otherwise pitch-black room. There must be *something* he can do, he thinks as he quietly walks out of the room. He just hasn't figured it out yet. But he will. Of this much he feels certain.

But not tonight. Ira wins tonight.

CHAPTER 17

DAY 46

Sunday, April 15, 2018

TODD IS SITTING IN THE LIVING ROOM OF HIS APARTMENT, SUNK IN THE HOLE OF "HIS SPOT" OF A WELL-USED BROWN COUCH THAT HAS MOLDED ALMOST PERFECTLY TO HIS BODY SHAPE. He still looks for opportunities to tell guests he got it for less than a hundred bucks at his favorite second-hand store after he and Julie got married three years ago. Todd was in his last year of law school at the time, and with the birth of their daughter less than two years later, Todd is still winning the argument that it's too soon for an upgrade. He hears Julie down the hallway in the bathroom, fishing through the small plastic bin used to carry makeup and other womanly things whose purposes Todd has neither identified nor cared enough to ask about. Nora starts whimpering, but not yet crying, from her crib in the office/nursery directly across from the bathroom that Julie is now leaving.

"Are we going to your family's house for dinner tonight?" Todd asks in a voice loud enough to be heard down the hall, already knowing the answer.

"We do every Sunday," Julie answers as she opens the door to the office/nursery to pick up Nora, who is now past the point of calmly whining for attention.

"Will John Jacob Jingleheimer Schmidt be there?" Todd asks,

still sitting on the couch, not offering to help even as they are minutes away from leaving.

"He always is," Julie answers.

She's now in the living room, carrying Nora with one hand, as she uses the other to pick up a portable car seat by the front door and place it in the center of the room. She kneels down and begins to buckle in her daughter.

"But you know how Nora feels about him," Todd says, still not moving. "Don't you care about her feelings?"

"She'll survive," Julie says, smiling at her daughter, who squirms in her car seat as Julie forces her arms through the straps and buckles her in.

Todd and Julie have some variation of this exact conversation almost every week. Nora's birth nine months ago allowed Todd to add her to the routine conversation as an attempted scapegoat. Julie is the only daughter of seven children and the second born in her family. Her parents, Randy and Rose, named their first son Jesse, after Julie's maternal great-grandfather. After noticing the coincidental use of the letter R for both of their first names and the letter J for both of their two children, Julie's parents—or rather, Julie's *mother*—decided it would be "fun" to continue the trend with the rest of their children. Randy was ultimately able to convince Rose not to limit themselves further to J names that also had exactly five letters, like Jesse and Julie, but compromised with her request that they take their names from the holy scriptures. As the number of children increased, so increased the uniqueness of their names. Next came John, then Jacob, then Jeremiah, then Jude, and finally little Jedidiah. Todd has always clashed with Julie's older brother, Jesse, who is just a couple of years older than Todd but infinitely wiser by his own estimation. The others he has generally found to be tolerable individually, but they can't help but follow Jesse's lead when they are all together, effectively morphing into an extension of their older brother. Todd refers to them collectively as "John Jacob Jingleheimer

Schmidt." He says it's easier. Julie has suggested it might actually be easier to call them "her brothers," but Todd insists somehow it would not.

Todd and Julie strategically found an apartment just over forty-five minutes away from Julie's parents' home. Close enough for regular visits and occasional free babysitting, but far enough to discourage daily unannounced visits from Julie's mother. Approximately forty-seven minutes after leaving their apartment, Todd parks on the street in front of his in-laws' home as, per usual, John Jacob Jingleheimer Schmidt has taken up all of the remaining free space in the large driveway wrapping around the far left side of the house.

Todd opens the door to his car, steps out, and pulls the lever on the side of his seat to fold it forward so he can get his daughter out of his two-door car—a weekly unwelcome reminder that it will soon be time to upgrade his vehicle. He walks around the back of his car with Nora and meets up with Julie at the end of the long sidewalk path leading to their front door. It is a large, two-story brick home, inside of which Todd and Julie's apartment could fit comfortably half a dozen times. Todd sees Rose through one of the wide windows between neatly trimmed bushes running along the front of the house. She opens the front door with a big smile on her face, extends her arms, and takes a series of short, quick steps out the front door to meet them. After hugging and welcoming her daughter, she bends down to kiss and baby-talk to Nora in the car seat that Todd has now rested on the sidewalk path just short of the porch.

"Come in, come in," Rose says, now walking up the steps to her porch. "You're just in time. Dinner will be ready in about fifteen minutes."

After walking into the home, standing in the large entryway, Todd sees to his right that a normally empty decorative wood table is overflowing with reds, whites, and blues. Visible through a large plastic bag are no fewer than fifty small American flags attached to short wood sticks. Next to that is a stack of pleated cloth fans, fully opened into half circles. A large wreath of false red, white, and blue roses is partially covered by similarly decorated garland, and streamers.

"Your house is looking very patriotic, Rose," Todd says to his mother-in-law.

He has tried in the past a time or two to call her *Mom*, but it seemed to just make them both uncomfortable. John Jacob Jingleheimer Schmidt didn't seem to approve either.

"Oh, yeah," Rose says, smiling enthusiastically. "I volunteered to help with the Pioneer Day parade for the city this year. It's still a few months away, so I've just been picking up little things here and there that I think will look nice on our float."

Todd smiles at the thought of the upcoming parade.

"I always think it's kinda funny to see all these American flags out here every year for Pioneer Day," he says as Julie's older brother, Jesse, walks past them into the kitchen to Todd's right.

Jesse stops abruptly and turns back.

"Why would you say something *stupid* like that?" Jesse asks before his mother can respond.

"Jesse!" Rose says. "Don't be rude! We don't say *stupid* in this house."

"How about *estupido* then, for Todd's sake?" Jesse says, smiling and putting his arm around his mother. "You must've forgot to press 2 for español."

Rose gently pushes her son away with a forced and unconvincing face of disapproval, to which Jesse responds with only more laughter. *This has to be a new record*, Todd thinks to himself. They haven't even sat down yet and Jesse's already at it.

"I wasn't trying be unpatriotic or anything," Todd says. "I just think it's a little amusing, or ironic I guess, seeing a bunch of U.S. flags on Pioneer Day when it's basically a celebration of the pioneers' *escape* from the United States. That's all."

Todd's comment brings Jesse's amusement to an abrupt halt,

instantly transforming his smile into a scowl.

"Just because none of your clients respect the flag even after they've stolen all our jobs and benefits doesn't mean you can expect us to do the same," Jesse says. "*Our people* respect the law and this country. You and your amigos just can't seem to accept the fact that the law's the law."

Julie, sensing Todd wants to respond, gently touches his arm and intervenes.

"True, Jesse," Julie says, feigning agreement with her brother. "The law *is* the law, but I think we can all agree that that Ira guy is a real douche."

"Julie!" her mother says in horror, turning to her daughter. "Language!"

"What?" Julie says with a false tone of confusion. "It's French, mom. I'm pretty sure it means 'beautiful child of God.'"

"I don't like that, Julie," Rose says.

"Who's Ira?" Jesse asks.

Todd and Julie smile without saying more.

Todd grew up in Arizona and didn't move to Utah until after he returned to the United States following a two-year proselytizing mission for his church in Argentina. Pioneer Day, a state holiday in Utah, was something new for him. Perhaps if he had grown up celebrating the holiday, he may have just waved his American flag with everyone else without appreciating the irony. Not that Todd is opposed to waving American flags or celebrating his pioneer heritage. It's just the context that he finds amusing.

After the formation of the Church of Jesus Christ of Latter-day Saints in 1830 in New York, the early members struggled to find a safe place where they could live together in the United States. They went from Ohio to Missouri to Illinois in the span of about fifteen years. They were persecuted, driven from their homes, and even subject to a state-sanctioned extermination order. Shortly after the assassination of founding prophet Joseph Smith, the main body of the Church moved west and kept moving west. On July 24, 1847, these pioneers successfully escaped violent persecution in the United States and started their new lives in the safety and security of Mexico. It wouldn't be until the following year that this portion of Mexico would become a U.S. territory, and another fifty years before it became the State of Utah. But the very first 24th of July celebration was one of safety and freedom *from* the United States.

Through his work with Central and South American immigrants fleeing violence and poverty in their own countries, Todd has often felt his work was a way of returning the favor on behalf of his ancestors. He recognizes the obvious differences between the two migrations. There were no immigration laws to enforce or to obey in 1847 when the pioneers entered that unsettled area of Mexico. For all Todd knows, the Mexicans neither knew nor cared that anyone was there. It's not like they were moving in on the Mexicans' beautiful beach property a little further west in what would later become California. They were content instead with a barren desert with a giant, putrid, salt-ridden water hole posing as a lake. But Todd appreciates that the motives behind both migrations are certainly comparable. No one necessarily wanted to abandon their home and native country but instead acted out of necessity.

Todd recalls reading about the history of his church's Perpetual Emigration Fund, which was established two years after their arrival to the Salt Lake valley in 1847. Through the fund, converts living abroad could borrow money to pay for their travel to the United States until they were able to get established and repay the money, which would then be used to help others do the same. He also recalls reading further about the U.S. government's subsequent attempts to limit future immigration of converts to his church, ultimately passing an act that disincorporated the Perpetual Emigration Fund. He can't help but think about the many members of his faith, like Jesse, who adamantly proclaim "the law is the law" in the immigration debate today, even without having any actual understanding of what the law says. Would they have said the same about prior laws preventing members of *their* church from immigrating or voting? Or the infamous state-sanctioned extermination order? Obviously not all laws are created equal. But it seems to Todd that few are interested in debating the merit, or lack thereof, of specific immigration laws of the United States, preferring instead to make passionate, throwaway one-liners.

Todd didn't intend to start a debate at Julie's parents' house with his comment about the Pioneer Day parade—although by now he should've known better. People like Jesse have in the past, and will no doubt in the future, interpreted these kinds of observations as intended to attack their country, their religion, or both. Others take the observation as an invitation to launch into a hateful tirade on the perceived hypocrisy of organized religion in general or Todd's religion specifically. Few and far between are those Todd has found who can have such a conversation without either taking or making offense. For his part, Todd loves his country and his church, despite the complicated history between the two.

It could've been a short, simple discussion at the family dinner table. There could've been disagreement without issue. In theory there still could be. But Todd has learned his lesson—at least for tonight. He limits his conversation for the rest of the evening to the beautiful spring weather and Nora's sleeping schedule. Not exactly thought provoking, but safe enough for a Sunday family dinner.

...

Katie is sitting on Sarah's lap at their kitchen table with an excited smile, staring intently at a laptop computer screen in front of her. Veronica is sitting in her highchair to Katie's right, and Oscar is sitting in a chair to her left. An intentionally off-key and overly dramatic voice echoes through the static of the computer speakers.

"Happy birthday, dear Kaaaa-tieee! Happy biiiirth-daaaay tooooo yoouuu! Hooooo!"

Katie's smile bursts into a laugh and she begins to clap at the image of her father on their nightly video call. Sarah rotates the laptop on the table so it faces a small cake with five lit candles, and helps Katie move to the chair directly in front of it. On the wall directly behind her hangs a large poster board with colorful hand-drawn bubble letters saying "HAPPY 5TH BIRTHDAY, KATIE! WE LOVE YOU!" On the reverse side is a similar message for Oscar, which Sarah used five months ago for his birthday.

"Make a wish, baby girl," Fredy says. "And make it a good one; you only get one a year, after all."

Katie scrunches her face thoughtfully for a moment, smiles, and then blows out four of the five candles on the first try, but gets the last one with one more quick blow.

"I wished for a flying horse!" she says excitedly.

Fredy and Sarah laugh.

"You're not supposed to tell us," Oscar says with a cold, authoritative tone. "Now your stupid wish will never come true."

"Oscar!" Sarah says. "It's her birthday; just be nice."

"What'd he say?" Fredy says, struggling to follow the conversation with Oscar out of his view.

"Nothing," Sarah says. "He's just having one of his days."

"Turn the screen so I can see him," Fredy says.

"It's fine I said," Sarah says.

"Come on, turn it, Sarah," Fredy says. "I wanna talk to my son."

Sarah reluctantly humors Fredy's futile attempt to discipline their son through a small video image projected from more than eighty miles away. While she knows it makes Fredy feel better, she also knows it has thus far proven to only fuel Oscar's defiance. Over the past several weeks, Sarah has observed a concerning change in Oscar's behavior. Where he once looked forward to the nightly video or phone calls with Fredy, he now seems disinterested, annoyed even.

His generally active and social personality has been replaced with a more reserved and introverted one. Although this did not initially surprise Sarah given the circumstances, it's only worsened in the past couple of weeks, with no sign of relenting. Sarah shakes her head and rolls her eyes at the sound of her husband's well-intentioned discussion with Oscar.

"Okay, fine," Oscar says in an annoyed tone once he seems to have heard all he deems necessary of his father's lecture. "I'm gonna go watch TV now."

Oscar stands up and begins walking away.

"Oscar, come back here!" Fredy says. "I'm not done talking to you!"

Oscar continues walking and Sarah does nothing to stop him, instead turning the screen back to her and Katie.

"Katie, why don't you go watch TV with your brother for a minute," she says, which instruction Katie quickly follows.

"What are you doing?" Fredy says in frustration. "I wasn't done talking to Oscar. And I still wanted to talk to Katie about her birthday."

Katie continues running undeterred to catch up to her brother.

"You're just gonna have to let this one go, Fredy," Sarah says.

"What are you talking about?" Fredy asks.

"There's only so much we can control right now. And even less that *you* can. We're all going through a hard time together, but it seems to have affected Oscar the most. I'm really worried about him."

"I know it's been hard for us all, Sarah. But it's all gonna be over soon. My next hearing is in less than two weeks. God has already answered our prayers and sent us a lawyer to fix everything for us. Just keep reminding Oscar that it'll all be over soon."

"I've tried talking to him, Fredy. I try all the time, but he's completely closed off to me. It's just getting worse. I really think we need him to talk to somebody. Someone to help him work through these feelings and—"

"What, like some kinda shrink?" Fredy asks with a tone that seems equally surprised and offended. "Some psychiatrist or something? What are you talking about? It's just a tough time right now; there's nothing *wrong* with him."

"There's nothing wrong with getting some help, Fredy. I'm not saying he's crazy or anything. I just think it might be good for him to have some help talking through his feelings."

"What do you think he's got parents for? What, so we're gonna start paying someone to talk to our kids for us? That's ridiculous."

Sarah sits quietly for a moment, debating how to respond. She's felt an increasing frustration with Fredy's understandable desire to continue parenting with at least his words, while leaving all of the corresponding action to her. His simple and sincere faith and hope, while welcomed and appreciated by Sarah, has proven insufficient to overcome the everyday challenges of their new life. *Has it really only been six weeks?* Sarah thinks to herself in disbelief. With no clear idea of how many more weeks may remain, Sarah resolves to reclaim some of the lost control over her life.

"I haven't decided anything yet," she says. "But I'm gonna just have to do whatever I think is best."

Fredy pulls his head back in surprise.

"That's not how a marriage works, Sarah. We're a team. We decide what to do *together*—*especially* when it comes to our kids."

"Fredy," Sarah says, pausing for a moment before continuing. "You're just gonna have to leave this one to me."

"But I—"

"*Fredy*," Sarah interrupts with a stern tone. "I need you to just trust me for now with what's best for our kids while you're away. I love you, I support you, I need you, but we're not working under normal circumstances right now. Of course I'm going to ask you for your opinion and take that into consideration, but until you're here with these kids every day again, I have to be the one making the final decisions here."

Fredy sits in silence for an extended moment. Even through her small laptop screen, Sarah can tell from his thoughtful expression that Fredy is forcing aside whatever impulse he may have to continue to argue in his defense. She knows that by her reclaiming some of the lost control over her life, she's asking Fredy to give up even more control than he's already lost. Fredy looks down and sighs before looking back into the camera at his wife.

"Okay. I'm sorry, you're right," he says. "I know it's been tough, but it'll all be over soon. I promise. Our kids are lucky to have such a tough mamma who doesn't take any crap from anybody—not even her own husband." Fredy smiles.

"*Especially* not her own husband," Sarah says, humor in her voice but without a smile. "And don't you forget it."

Fredy laughs.

"Can you at least call Katie back to open her presents before I have to end my call?" Fredy asks.

"I didn't hear a *please*," Sarah teases.

Fredy laughs again.

"Pretty please with a cherry on top," he says.

"All right," Sarah says. "That's better. I'll go get her."

"Wait," Fredy says abruptly before she is able to stand up. "Did you get it for her?"

"Did I get her what?"

"A flying horse."

Sarah laughs.

"No," she says. "This is going to be a very disappointing birthday for her."

CHAPTER 18

DAY 47

Monday, April 16, 2018

AFTER DAYS OF FRUITLESS RESEARCH, TODD RELUCTANTLY ACCEPTS THE FACT THAT THE POSITIVE FACTORS SURROUNDING FREDY'S SHOP-LIFTING CONVICTION HAVE TURNED OUT TO BE ONE OF HIS BIGGEST PROBLEMS. Because his criminal history is limited to an isolated, minor offense more than two decades ago, he easily qualified to erase it from his record through a legal expungement. But the State of Utah's reward for good behavior and rehabilitation is somehow a negative factor in his immigration case. Todd already knew that federal immigration law generally refuses the recognize the majority of state laws dismissing or expunging a state conviction. But expunging the conviction, effectively erasing it from existence, leaves Fredy without a way to readily access his record. The Department of Homeland Security need only argue his conviction *might* be an aggravated felony, unless Fredy can conclusively prove that it's not. Without his complete records, he can't prove anything. Having no experience in criminal defense in general, much less expungements, Todd feels he's gone as far as he can on his own. He calls or emails every attorney he knows in hopes of finding someone who's encountered this problem before.

"Sorry, sweetie," one says. "I don't do criminal work."

"Hmmm, that's a new one for me," another says.

"Wait a minute," yet another says. "You want to *un*-erase a conviction? Why would anyone ever want to do that? I wouldn't even know where to start."

Every person he speaks to has a different reason why they can't help, but they all have the same solution: *talk to Shane Radley*. Todd sighs in desperation at the thought. He resolves to swallow his pride and sends Shane a flattering email, asking to take him out to lunch to "pick his brain." Shane's response is only slightly less condescending than Todd anticipated:

> Happy to help, rookie. This town could use a few more attorneys who know what they're doing on cases that require actual lawyering and creativity. Let's meet at the Mexican place on Main and 4th South for lunch mañana at 1:30.
>
> Shane M. Radley, Esq.
> **RADLEY & ASSOCIATES, LLC**
> Email: Shane@RadleyLaw.com

> CONFIDENTIALITY NOTICE: This message is confidential and may be privileged. Unauthorized use or distribution is prohibited and may be unlawful.

. . .

DAY 48

Tuesday, April 17, 2018

Todd has arrived early for his meeting with Shane Radley at a Mexican restaurant with no name. He's sitting inside at one of no more than ten tables of different styles, shapes and colors. He's facing the front entrance of the restaurant, looking at a painting of a Mexican woman leaning forward and rolling tortillas with a stone rolling pin on a stone base. Her hair is not pulled back and hangs freely on either side, partially covering her face. The left sleeve of her loose, white shirt has fallen off her shoulder and hangs on the side of her arm. Todd has seen this painting before but cannot recall where.

The arguing in Spanish coming from the kitchen behind him temporarily draws Todd's attention away from the painting, and he smiles as he strains to make out the conversation. This comes to an abrupt halt when Todd hears the front door open loudly and sees Shane walk in the restaurant. He's wearing a light grey suit, pink-and-white tie, and a caramel-colored brown belt with matching shoes. He scans the room until he makes eye contact with Todd, who is now standing.

"Ted, is that you?" Shane says.

"It's Todd," Todd says, walking over to shake Shane's hand. "But yes, it's me."

"I don't remember meeting you in person before, but I figured you were a safe bet, being the only other white dude with a tie here."

Todd instinctively looks down at his tie and laughs nervously. They walk back to the table Todd has chosen and sit down.

"Actually," Todd says, "we *have* met a couple of times before at—"

Todd stops mid-sentence and turns to a heavy-set Hispanic woman who has walked over to their table. She pulls a white note pad out of the front pocket of her black apron and a pen out from the back of her hair, which is tied back in a loose bun. She turns first to Shane.

"The usual, *Señor* Radley?" she asks.

"*Sí, mamita, gracias,*" Shane says with a smile, using up almost half of his entire Spanish vocabulary in his response.

"And for you, *señor?*" she asks, turning to Todd.

"*¿Cómo está la carne asada aquí?*" Todd asks. "*¿Es muy picante?*"

"*Para mí, no, pero para los gringos yo creo que sí,*" she says with a smile.

"*Perfecto, así me gusta,*" Todd says. "*Entonces me gustaría uno de esos, y un Jarritos de piña, por favor.*"

"*Bueno,*" she says as she finishes writing the orders, and then she turns back towards the kitchen.

Anywhere else in the United States, a Hispanic waitress may have been surprised to have a gringo customer place his order in almost perfect Spanish. Shane may have been surprised as well. In Utah, however, it's far from uncommon, with the large number of people who have served religious missions in Spanish-speaking countries. Although it's a fair assumption that most white Spanish speakers in Utah are some level of members of the same faith, the fair assumptions end there. Some returned from their missions with a newfound love for foreign cultures, which continues for the rest of their lives. Some dreaded the entire experience and only went in the first place because of family or social pressure. Some continue faithfully in their church, while others attend at their convenience for special events, while others still simply haven't gotten around to formally resigning.

"You been here before, Ted?" Shane asks.

"No, I don't think so," Todd says, no longer bothering to correct Shane. "It smells good though, and I love Mexican food."

"Yeah," Shane says. "This place is a lot better than that *Cafe Rio* crap everyone's always raving about. To tell you the truth, I've never eaten there. I went in there once to see what all the fuss was about. So I'm standing there in line, right, looking at the menu, and I happen to glance over the shoulder of the cashier and see some big sign plastered on the wall saying, '*This Organization Participates in E-verify*.' Like they were proud of it or something. Are you kidding me? You can't trust some gringo or *legal* immigrant to make your tacos, man, come on! Illegals know that every burrito they roll here for whitey might be their last, so they put their heart into it, ya know? You can taste the fear in those burritos. So I just left and came back here."

Shane laughs while Todd forces an awkward smile in an attempt to hide his discomfort.

"So, tell me about this client of yours," Shane says.

Had Shane paid more attention when he met with Fredy's wife just a few weeks earlier, he may have recognized this case from Todd's detailed overview. But he did not, so he does not.

"Interesting issues," Shane says. "Could definitely be worse though. It reminds me of one of my old cases—I'm sure you've heard about it; it was a pretty big deal. So the government's trying to deport this client of mine who qualified for residency under 245(i). But he had a few convictions for domestic violence, harassment, etcetera, etcetera, blah, blah, blah. A couple of them were pretty ugly, to be honest, so I had my work cut out for me. Long story short, I win the case and I get him his residency. But then six months later the idiot goes and beats his girlfriend to *death*. The moron kills her! I told him he had to just stay away from her; I told him I was gonna charge him double next time he came knocking on my office door. But no one ever listens to me, Ted, they never listen."

Todd fails to see how Fredy's case could have possibly reminded Shane of this drastically different set of facts. He might normally just politely nod and entertain Shane's excuse to share one of his victories with a captive audience, but instead he finds himself repulsed by this casual description of the loss of a human life. Shane seems to perceive Todd's unspoken reaction, and perhaps even hoped for it, but continues without pausing.

"That one might even be too much for *me* to help him with," Shane says. "Assuming he ever gets out of jail to face an immigration judge again, which isn't likely. He's lucky he dodged the needle on that one. But people always ask me if I feel bad for helping him stay here. Or they just outright blame me for that girl's death, because if it weren't for me helping him he wouldn't have been here in the first place. But that's just a racist double standard."

Todd involuntarily squints his eyes in confusion, equally surprised and curious how racism could possibly be a factor.

"How so?" Todd asks, genuinely interested in some clarification.

"Just think about it, Ted. What if I had been the *government* attorney? And I gotta say, if I had been, there's no question this guy would've been deported the first time around. But what if he went on to get himself a new lady friend back in Honduras and killed *her* instead? Nobody would blame *me* for her death, even though arguably it would've been my fault he was there instead of here. Nobody would even care about it. And in Honduras, chances are he wouldn't even be in jail right now. Chances are he would've hurt *more* people and been able to buy off the crooked police down there. So if we're really gonna be throwing around credit and blame for what some other fool does, then maybe I should get credit for the fact that my client only killed *one* woman and will be in jail for the rest of his life, instead of probably killing half a dozen women in Honduras. But we only care about the deaths of white Americans in this country. Nobody cares about whoever dies south of Texas. That's not our problem."

Todd tries his best to follow Shane's arguments, which continued uninterrupted even after the waitress returned with their food. But before Todd can even make a comment or ask for further clarification, Shane has moved on to a new topic.

"Ya see, Ted, it's never been about solving the underlying

problems causing crime, violence, and poverty in the world," Shane says. Todd nods politely and continues to eat his carne asada, which, as warned, is a little too *picante* for his gringo tongue. "Immigration law is just a battle over where we stick the less desirables and which lives we value more. No one actually tries to rehabilitate anyone. That's too hard. It's much easier to stick 'em in a cell—or better yet, just kick 'em out of the country and have someone else deal with them. It's like that old saying, 'Give a man a fish, he eats for a day. Teach a man a fish, he eats for a lifetime.' That's what all these right-wing nut jobs say until they see how much more trouble it'd be to actually teach a man to fish, so they just throw him a fish and send him on his way to bum a fish off someone else the next day."

Todd nods his head while he continues eating his food. He has all but given up on contributing to Shane's monologue, which jumps to a new point faster than Todd can respond to the last one.

"Then you got these religious right morons. Anytime we're talking about abortion, gay rights, or teaching evolution in public schools, they start waving their Bibles, *or Books of Mormon out here in God's country*. But those good books get tossed aside when the topic turns to immigration. Turn the other cheek, lest thou wast smote by a man with no papers!" Shane says dramatically in a mocking, pious tone. "Forgive thy neighbor seven times seventy times, lest thy forgiveness was petitioned thee en español! Put not thy wife away save for fornication, and good Mormon families are eternal, lest one of thy family members be one of those dirty illegal aliens, then verily, verily, thus saith the Lord, I shalt smite thine family to smithereens! Don't get me started, Ted."

"It seems like I already have," Todd says.

"Yeah, it doesn't take much," says Shane, laughing. "But then they always insist, 'we're not splitting up families; they can *all* just go to Mexico and live happily ever after.' Basically blaming *them* for supposedly allowing their own family to be split up. But at the same time, just look at your case. You got a US citizen mom and three US citizen kids who somehow can't expect that their dad and husband should be able to legally live in *their* country, but it's somehow reasonable to expect them to be able to so easily legally immigrate to Mexico because *one* of their family members is a Mexican citizen by birth? And that's putting aside the fact that they'd never be able to provide for themselves out there, and that they'd have constant targets on their backs because of the assumption they got a ton of money comin' from the U.S. And these kids aren't even those so-called anchor babies. They weren't just born on the right side of the line; they're '*real*' Americans who passed through the sacred American vaginal canal."

For the first time since Shane started talking he pauses long enough to eat some of his food. Todd doesn't know where or how to start to respond. He's slightly annoyed by the number of stereotypes Shane has fallen back on to make his points, insulting his faith as if it were to blame for the strong opinions of some of its loudest members. Having moved from Arizona to Utah, Todd went from being a member of a minority religion to a majority one. In so doing he feels he's somehow lost the right to be able to defend his church against stereotypical criticism. The most frustrating part of the conversation is that Todd finds himself agreeing with a lot of Shane's underlying points, but he can't imagine him actually convincing any fence-sitters with these kinds of inflammatory arguments. Instead, they only provide ammunition for the other extreme, as both sides find fewer and fewer reasons to ever compromise. But Todd sees no point in highlighting these points of disagreement, particularly since he's in desperate need of Shane's help. Instead, he takes advantage of this rare pause to try to veer the conversation back on course, as Todd has almost finished his meal.

"Yeah, I see what you mean," he says in a forced agreeable tone. "You make a lot of good points. But from a practical standpoint, what do you think is the best way for me to get started in *my* case?"

"Oh, right, that expungement thing," Shane says, the inflection in his voice suggesting he'd forgotten the purpose of their lunch meeting. He finishes chewing the large bit of food he just spoke through, wipes his mouth, and takes a small drink before continuing. "Yeah, so you'll just need to file a written Motion to Unseal Expungement, Reduce Degree of Conviction *Nunc Pro Tunc*, Issue Certified Copies, and Reseal Expungement."

Todd opens his eyes wide in confusion, prompting Shane to laugh condescendingly.

"I know," Shane says. "It's a bit of a mouthful, but it should get the job done. I can email you an example. Actually—" Shane pauses and pulls out his cell phone "—I'll just text my assistant to have her send you one right now and save us both some trouble."

Todd sits quietly and patiently as Shane navigates through his phone for the next minute or so.

"All right," Shane says, putting his phone back into the inner pocket of his suit coat. "Done. You'll just have to go down and file it at the court in person, since you won't be able to pull up the case number. Just be sure to include any expungement docs your client may still have."

Todd is surprised at the seeming simplicity of the process, particularly given how long it took Shane to get around to actually explaining it.

"About how long do you think it would take to get a decision on that?" Todd asks.

"Probably a month or so," Shane says, causing Todd to cringe nervously with Fredy's next hearing just more than a week away. "It won't be at the top of anyone's list of priorities, and it will likely leave the clerks, and maybe even the judge, scratching their heads for a while. Unless you can actually get the prosecutor to stipulate, but I don't even bother with that anymore. They just always give their standard reply these days that they won't make any special deals for immigrants that they wouldn't for U.S. citizens. I'm not one for groveling at the feet of power-tripping prosecutors, so I just prefer to duke it out in court. It's funner that way anyways."

"Great," Todd says, looking at his watch and standing up. "Thank you so much, Shane. I really appreciate everything. I gotta run now, but please let me take care of lunch today." He reaches for his wallet in the back pocket of his pants.

"Don't be silly," Shane says. "Lunch is on me. I'll consider it an investment in you."

"What do you mean?" Todd asks in confusion.

"I've found that helping other attorneys just enough to get them to *try* to take on these crimmigration cases turns out to be the best referral service money can buy," Shane explains. "Most people don't even get all the way through their first of these cases before they refer it over to me to clean up their mess, and then go on to refer me for every other single one of these cases that follow. So, thank you in advance for the referrals, and I insist, Ted, lunch is on me."

...

DAY 49

Wednesday, April 18, 2018

Todd is anxiously pacing back and forth in his home office/nursery with his cell phone in his hand. His lips are moving, but only a few choice words or phrases are actually vocalized, and even then just above a whisper. He feels very much like when he was in his late teens and early twenties, building up the courage to call a girl to ask her out on a date, rehearsing and revising a mental script before finally just pressing the send button on his phone and hoping for the best. Finally, he presses send. He comes to an abrupt halt in the middle of the room and freezes as the phone rings. After a fourth ring, he is half-tempted to hang up and resolve to call back another time, but the phone is answered before he's able to act on the impulse.

"Good afternoon, district attorney's office," a woman says on the other end of the line.

"Hi!" Todd says, much louder than he intended, his voice cracking slightly, prompting him to cough to clear his throat. "Excuse me. Sorry. I'm trying—well, yeah, um, my name is Todd Becker, and I'm an attorney."

"Hello, attorney Todd Becker," the woman says softly.

Todd can tell by her tone that she's smiling on the other end, whether out of sympathy, condescension, or a combination of the two. Todd cringes and continues.

"Yeah, so I wanted to know who I would need to talk to about an old case that was prosecuted by your office."

"How old?" she asks.

"It was back in 1995," Todd says. "So pretty old." He laughs nervously.

"Let me see if we still have anything on it," she says. "Do you have a case number?"

Todd gives her the case number but explains that the case was expunged a number of years ago, so she might not be able to find anything on it. After a couple of minutes' worth of effort, she confirms that they don't have anything on it but offers to transfer him to the duty attorney, James Boren, which offer Todd enthusiastically accepts. Mr. Boren picks up his phone abruptly after a single ring following the transfer of the call.

"This is Boren," he says.

His voice is gruff yet indifferent, a stark contrast to that of the woman with whom Todd has just been speaking. Todd introduces himself and provides as sympathetic of a summary as he can of Fredy's predicament. He talks about Fredy's wife and kids, and the many years he has been in the United States. He explains that for whatever strange reason, federal immigration law doesn't recognize the expungement that Fredy got in his case. His confidence has increased significantly now as Todd has thoroughly convinced himself of the reasonableness of his request, and of the injustice of Fredy's situation.

"Eh," Mr. Boren says, interrupting Todd after a few minutes of entertaining his plea. "We can't be doing these special deals with illegal immigrants that we wouldn't make with U.S. citizens."

Todd is startled and somewhat disappointed by this response but recalls that Shane told him to expect as much. He was certainly prepared for the possibility that Fredy's case would be dismissed as just another sob story full of mildly interesting but legally irrelevant details. But not quite ready to give up, Todd continues.

"Of course," Todd says. "I wouldn't expect you to give my client some *special* deal just because he's facing immigration consequences. But is there any reason you wouldn't make this deal with a U.S. citizen?"

The pause in the conversation that follows gives Todd hope that his argument is being considered, motivating him to continue to make his case.

"*I* think," Todd continues, "it's not that you wouldn't be willing to make this deal with a U.S. citizen, it's just that a U.S. citizen wouldn't ever ask for such a deal. Why would he? For a U.S. citizen, an expungement actually does exactly what it's supposed to do—it goes away. But if it didn't for some unforeseen reason, is there any reason you wouldn't consider this same request for a U.S. citizen? Especially where this happened more than twenty years ago, and there is no other criminal history. As far as the state is concerned, the conviction doesn't even exist. There is no conviction, and I'm not asking you to change that. But the fact is that, for my client, the promise of an expungement erasing his conviction turned out to be false. I'm just asking you to sign off on something that will keep the promise of his expungement erasing his conviction."

After another pause, Mr. Boren finally responds. "Fine, I'll take a look at your draft," he says. "Just email it to me, what do I care?"

Todd is immediately overcome by happiness and hope, feelings that have become a rarity since he agreed to take Fredy's case. He senses this initial victory is prompted more by the prosecutor's desire to end the conversation and avoid having to go to court on an old case than by the persuasiveness of Todd's arguments. But in an area of law where victories are scarce, Todd graciously takes whatever he can get.

"Great!" he says enthusiastically. "Right away, I'll send it now."

Todd ends the call, drops his phone on his desk, and instinctively starts a variation of his standard "happy dance," reserved for special occasions like this. He's interrupted shortly thereafter by his wife's laughter after she opens his door.

"I haven't seen those moves for a while," she says as she walks into the room towards her husband.

"Jealous?" Todd says, still dancing, poorly, despite the interruption.

"Very," Julie says with a smile. "But not as jealous as all the other girls who couldn't find themselves a man with these sexy moves. If it weren't the middle of a work day, I might start getting some funny ideas."

"A little afternoon delight, you mean?" Todd says, dancing closer towards his wife. "I think that can be arranged."

Julie laughs.

"I'm afraid you're more than I can handle right now, Mr. Becker," she says. "Maybe later."

"Your loss," Todd says, still dancing, hoping to extend for as long as possible his feelings of happiness from another small victory.

CHAPTER 19

DAY 57

Thursday, April 26, 2018

"IT IS APRIL 26, 2018. This is Immigration Judge Samuel O. Lanzotti, conducting removal proceedings in the matter of Mr. Wilfredo Gonzalez. All parties are present. On behalf of the respondent is—"

"Todd Becker," says Todd confidently, secretly proud of himself for immediately following the judge's cue to state his appearance on the record. Another small victory.

"And," continues the judge, "on behalf of the Department of Homeland Security is—"

"Debra Kaiser," says the government attorney.

"Mr. Gonzalez," says the judge, turning to Fredy, "do you still want Mr. Becker to represent you today?"

"Yes, sir," Fredy says happily.

Fredy smiles at the sight of his once-small file on the immigration judge's desk, which is now a respectable size. Prior to the hearing, Todd met with Fredy at the jail and gave him a detailed update on his case. Even without seeing the file on the immigration judge's desk, Fredy knows what's inside. There's a motion for a new bond hearing, with evidence that Fredy's twenty-three-year-old conviction was unexpunged, reduced to a class B misdemeanor, and then re-expunged. He doesn't understand the reason this was all required, but he knows that his misdemeanor conviction will now somehow no longer be considered an aggravated felony. He knows that his chances of getting a bond are now very good, if not guaranteed. But more than that, he knows that Todd has put together a very thorough and large application with evidence to stop his deportation, all of which is sitting on the desk in front of him, ready for filing.

"Mr. Becker," the judge says, turning his attention back to Todd. "These proceedings were continued to provide you time to prepare and file any and all applications for relief on behalf of your client. Are you prepared to do so today?"

"Yes, Your Honor," Todd says, sitting upright with conviction and holding up the large packet of documents. "I have an application for cancellation of removal with supporting documents to show the required physical presence, good moral character, and that his qualifying U.S. citizen family members would suffer exceptional and extremely unusual hardship in the event of his removal. In the alternative," Todd continues, picking up a significantly smaller packet, "I have also prepared an application for asylum, withholding of removal, and relief under the Convention Against Torture. I don't anticipate that this court will need to get to that alternative application given the strength of the cancellation of removal case, but I prepared it just in case."

Todd is stunned by the contrast in how he feels in court today compared to the last hearing. He is prepared and confident. Fredy feels even more confident.

"Any objection from the government, Ms. Kaiser, if I set the matter over for a final individual hearing on all applications for relief?" the judge asks.

"No objection to the scheduling, Judge," Ms. Kaiser says. "However, I believe there remain some issues for eligibility for both asylum and cancellation of removal, even aside from the respondent's criminal history. For asylum, his application is filed well outside of the one-year filing deadline from the date of his last entry into the

United States. And for cancellation of removal, I don't believe he can show the continuous ten years of physical presence. My notes reflect that Mr. Gonzalez testified at his first hearing that he returned to Mexico to see a sister or some family in 2013."

"My sister was *murdered*," Fredy says defensively, standing up. "I went to support my family."

"Mr. Gonzalez, sit down!" the judge says sternly. "Please have your attorney speak for you unless you are testifying."

"I'm sorry, sir," Fredy says, returning to his seat. Todd leans over to him, putting his hand on his shoulder, and whispers reassurances to Fredy that he will take care of the arguments.

"Regardless of the reason," Ms. Kaiser continues, "Mr. Gonzalez testified that he left the United States for a period of four or five months within the past ten years, according to my notes. I wasn't the attorney at that hearing, but Mr. Richter is pretty meticulous with his notes, so I have no reason to doubt them."

"Yes," says the judge, "I actually made a note of the same myself. Thank you for reminding me about that. Sounds like you may have an issue establishing the ten years continuous presence, Mr. Becker."

"Well, Your Honor," Todd says, "he's been living in the United States for almost thirty years. That was just a temporary visit due to some pretty extraordinary circumstances. I think that he was certainly justified in—"

"Counselor," the judge interrupts. "I would refer you to section 240A(d)(2) of the Immigration and Nationality Act, which makes clear that a single departure for more than ninety days cuts off continuous presence, regardless of the reason. Your client testified under oath that he was gone for more than ninety days in 2013. These proceedings commenced in March of 2018, less than ten years after his return to the United States. I'm inclined to agree with the Department on this one."

"Okay," Todd says. "But he didn't even have an attorney when he made those statements, and I don't think he—"

"Now hold on, sir," the judge interrupts sternly. "Your client was clearly advised of his right to obtain counsel before moving forward with his case. He *chose* not to. Mr. Gonzalez speaks English quite fluently, and he volunteered the information to this Court, *under oath*. Now, if you're suggesting that Mr. Gonzalez's answer on a factual issue would have somehow changed after speaking to an attorney, then I think we have an issue of credibility, if not false testimony under oath. Does Mr. Gonzalez wish to recant his sworn testimony before this Court?"

Todd feels his prior assurance wavering and is unsure of how to respond.

"May I have a moment with my client?" Todd asks.

"Certainly," the judge says, reaching over to pause the recording of the hearing. "We're off the record."

Todd turns to Fredy, moves in close to him, covers the microphone with his right hand as an extra precaution, and begins whispering.

"Are you absolutely, one hundred percent sure that you were gone for more than three months?" Todd asks.

"I'm sure," Fredy says. "I know because I already had to miss the birth of my daughter Katie in April. So I promised my wife I'd figure out a way to get back in time for our anniversary on July 15th. So just over four months."

Todd sighs heavily in frustration.

"Is it *possible* that you're wrong?" Todd asks. "Is it possible that there is some documentation to show that you were really here during part of that time? Anything? Your testimony alone won't be enough if it changes now, but if there's even a possibility that there is some *proof* you were gone for less than ninety days, we can explain that you were just mistaken before, or that you were nervous or whatever."

"I'm sorry, Todd," Fredy says. "But I have no doubt in my mind that I was gone for more than ninety days. There is no way there can be any proof that I was here because I wasn't. Is it that big of a deal?"

"Well, it shouldn't be, but it is," Todd says. "It means you can't apply for cancellation of removal anymore, which was by far our best option."

"Why not?" Fredy asks.

"It's all Ira's fault, I'm sure," Todd says, assuming the 1996 law has once again come into play.

Fredy responds with a face of confusion.

"Wrath?" he asks. "Is that supposed to be symbolic or something? The wrath of society? The wrath of Trump?"

Todd is initially puzzled by the comment, but then half-smiles upon recalling that "ira" is Spanish for "wrath" or "rage" or "anger." He also recalls that when spelled with an accent mark, "irá" translates into English as "will go." The law pronounced "Ira-Ira," then, could be interpreted to mean "*The Wrath Will Go Forth.*" *That seems appropriate,* Todd thinks. Perhaps it's too cruel and stupid of a law to be humanized with the name *Ira.* Nor is it fair to those good people who may happen to share that name (apologies, Mr. Kurzban). Cruel stupidity is without question a common impulse of wrath and rage, which wrath and rage (and cruel stupidity) did, in fact, go forth upon President Clinton's signing of it into law. Maybe Congress had put some thought into its chosen acronym after all—certainly more thought than was put in the law's substance.

Rather than take another victim into the labyrinth of immigration law, Todd offers Fredy a simpler but equally true response.

"Yes," he says. "It's all wrath's fault."

Todd turns back to the judge and tells him that he's ready to proceed, prompting the judge to restart the recording and announce that they are back on the record.

"Your Honor," Todd says after the judge invites him to continue. "It appears that Mr. Gonzalez, despite living in the United States for almost *thirty* years, somehow cannot, *under the law,* prove he has lived here continuously for the past ten years."

"So I presume he will be withdrawing his application for

cancellation of removal?" the judge asks.

Todd pauses, not wanting to admit defeat on what moments ago seemed like such a strong case. Two hundred pages of evidence suddenly completely irrelevant. Reluctantly, Todd concedes. The immigration judge accepts Fredy's alternative application for asylum, withholding, and protection under the Convention Against Torture. Plan Z is now the only plan left.

"All right then," the judge says. "I can give you my next available hearing date, which is in about two months, on June 28, 2018. Now, that date is on my detained calendar, so if Mr. Gonzalez were to be issued a bond today and be released from ICE custody, then that date would change."

Sensing Fredy's panic at the prospect of another two months in jail, Todd turns to him and quietly reassures him of his certainty that he will get a bond today and may be out of jail as soon as tomorrow. Fredy smiles and nods with gratitude and then turns back to smile at his wife in hopes that his unwavering faith may prove contagious. Todd turns his attention back to the judge, confirms that he has no conflicts with that proposed date, and states that he is ready to proceed with the bond hearing. The judge nods to the clerk to his immediate left, signaling for her to enter the date in the computer and to provide a written copy of the hearing notice to both parties.

"All right," the judge says after his clerk has returned to her seat. "Now with respect to your request for a new bond hearing, Mr. Becker, I have certified copies of a motion you were somehow able to get a Utah state court judge to sign off on *un*expunging his case, reducing it to a class B misdemeanor, and then *re*-expunging the case."

"That's right your, honor," Todd says with a smile, a small level of his hope restored by the prospect of Fredy's release from custody. "So he is no longer subject to mandatory detention as an aggravated felon. Also, the motion was based on constitutional grounds under the Supreme Court's decision in *Padilla v. Kentucky*, which held that a non-citizens have a constitutional right to be advised of the immigration consequences of a plea agreement."

The judge snickers under his breath and shakes his head.

"Yes," he says. "I couldn't help but notice your reliance on the *Padilla* case, despite the fact that that decision came out more than fifteen years *after* your client's plea agreement. Which is why I'm surprised you got a judge to sign off on this when the Supreme Court has made it clear that *Padilla* does not apply to cases predating that decision."

Todd looks nervously through his file, thrown off by his oversight on what should've been such an obvious red flag. He finds his own citation to the *Padilla* case, which clearly identifies 2010 as the year of publishing. But why should that matter? He can't help but ask himself the question. If Congress can define minor theft offenses as aggravated felonies after the fact, why can't the Supreme Court require protections after the fact? Of course, Todd doesn't dare vocalize these questions, and he is frustrated with himself for not anticipating and researching this issue sooner.

Todd feels an almost overwhelming emotional weight of pressure from the perceived expectations from both the judge and his client to provide an intelligent response to the issues raised, but he has nothing. How does this keep happening? No amount of preparation and research ever seems to be enough to prepare him for the seemingly endless number of issues that arise in immigration court. Todd's feelings of guilt increase as Fredy has become a sort of legal guinea pig for him, suffering the consequences of all of his untried legal experiments, which may prove to benefit future clients far more than Fredy. In what feels like an act of mercy, the judge ultimately provides an answer to his own question.

"However," the judge says, ending the uncomfortable silence, "the case law is clear on the point that an immigration judge must give full faith and credit to a modification of a conviction when it is based on constitutional grounds."

Todd's prior feelings of panic are immediately replaced with resentment. If the case law is so clear, why the need for this commentary from the judge? It feels like the judge is just toying with Todd's obvious nervousness and inexperience for the sake of his own amusement. Pushing aside these unhelpful feelings the best he can, Todd sits upright with a renewed determination and continues.

"Yes, Your Honor," he says. "As I was saying, I believe it is clear that Mr. Gonzalez is not subject to mandatory detention, which now brings us to the issue of danger to the community and flight risk. We have submitted with our bond motion proof of payment of taxes, character statements, community service, and about fifty pages of other evidence showing his strong family and community ties and the absence of any reoffense. I believe this very clearly shows that he is neither a danger to the community nor a flight risk."

The judge nods pensively before turning to the government attorney to ask her for the government's position on the bond request.

"Your Honor, the government believes that Mr. Gonzalez is still ineligible for a bond, regardless of whether he is a danger to the community or a flight risk or not."

Todd jerks his head towards the government attorney and scowls in shock. What can she possibly be talking about? Why are they pushing so hard on a case like Fredy's? Todd's mind is racing with questions and frustration as Ms. Kaiser continues to explain her position.

"Even assuming the respondent's conviction reduction were valid for immigration purposes," she continues, "it's still an aggravated felony because of his suspended sentence of 365 days."

Todd almost laughs out loud at the argument, which he feels far more prepared to address than others raised today.

"Your Honor," he interrupts, his anger having now completely overpowered his initial amusement at the government's argument. "The law is *very* clear on this point. First of all, the government hasn't even attempted to argue that Mr. Gonzalez is a danger to the community or a flight risk, quite frankly, because that argument would be ridiculous in this case and they know it. Secondly, this Court has already found that the reduction is valid for immigration purposes. And it's been amended to a class B misdemeanor, which Ms. Kaiser knows very well carries a maximum possible sentence of six months. It is legally impossible for a conviction for a class B misdemeanor to have a sentence of 365 days. I mean, come on, Your Honor, this is crazy."

Judge Lanzotti pauses pensively, appearing, to Todd, to agree with his arguments before turning back to the government attorney and asking her to respond.

"Counsel for the respondent is mistaken," she says, glaring over at Todd and leaving him with a feeling that if it wasn't personal before, it is now. "It might also be said that it is legally impossible for the respondent to rely on a 2010 Supreme Court decision to clean up his conviction from 1995. But as Your Honor just stated, we have to accept the order from the state court as it is written. And as it is written, the *degree* of the conviction was reduced, but the actual *sentence* was not. All we have from the respondent on the actual sentence is the original judgment with a suspended sentence of 365 days. So it is the Department's position that this offense remains an aggravated felony despite counsel's creative legal work outside of these proceedings."

Todd is again left speechless, his mind tossed mercilessly through a sea of contradiction and lunacy that was somehow wrapped up with a pretty bow and presented as "the law." Before he can even begin to consider responding to the government's argument, Judge Lanzotti has fully accepted it and denied Fredy's request for a bond. Not even the audible gasps from Fredy at his side or Sarah in the gallery behind him are enough to pull Todd back into the reality of this moment. He feels numb, powerless, and defeated. Something is wrong, terribly wrong. This can't be what the law was supposed to accomplish, but if it is then it is corrupt to its core. Finally, Todd responds, after the judge asks him for the second time if he wants to reserve appeal of his decision.

"Yes," is all he can muster. Though he knows it's pointless, as the immigration judge will issue a final decision in Fredy's case, for better or worse, long before any bond appeal would ever be decided. But Todd feels that he has no other choice but to continue to play his part in a system which appears more and more to him to be nothing more than a farce. One in which the unbending letter of the law lets some serious criminals dodge harsh immigration consequences, while unleashing the full *wrath of Ira* onto obviously rehabilitated, good, productive members of society. Society loses, but the law wins. Ironically, this is the outcome that society itself seems to be advocating for, as so many of its members passionately argue against its own best interests. *This can't be what was intended*, Todd tries again and again to convince himself. *It can't be. Or is it?*

CHAPTER 20

DAY 68

Monday, May 7, 2018

"I JUST CAN'T BELIEVE IT'S ALL COME DOWN TO THIS," Lori says with frustration to Todd, pacing back and forth in a small office, having declined his invitation to sit.

Lori is the first person to meet Todd at his new virtual office in downtown Salt Lake City. It's a small, simple office space with a single desk. In the lobby is a receptionist to greet all of the incoming clients and customers and then notify the applicable business of their arrival, giving the appearance of a personal assistant. Offsite is a call center, forwarding phone calls as if they too were personal receptionists. This significant upgrade from Todd's prior office/nursery is due largely to Fredy. For the past several weeks, Fredy has been telling every new alien he meets that Todd is the best attorney out there. When Todd asked Fredy how he could possibly see him as the "best," given his inability to win a single battle in court thus far, Fredy simply stated that he listens and he cares. Rather than identify the several other attorneys who meet that same description, Todd accepted the compliment—and the referrals. He has promised Julie that he won't take on more than two big cases for free at a time, so the referrals from Fredy have significantly increased Todd's business in a short period of time. Many of Todd's new clients have already been released on bond or been granted some immigration benefits despite having more serious criminal histories than Fredy. *No rhyme or reason to the wrath of Ira*, Todd finds himself regularly thinking.

After his loss at the bond hearing, Todd spent the next several days trying to find a way to once again *un*expunge Fredy's case to reduce his suspended sentence to six months, consistent with the prior reduction to a class B misdemeanor. Despite his best efforts, Todd has been unable to persuade the prosecutor to sign off on such a motion. To Todd's surprise, the prosecutor candidly admitted that he received an angry call from a Mr. Richter with the Department of Homeland Security shortly after Fredy's last hearing, who convinced him that his cooperation with Todd was interfering with a federal immigration case. The irony, if not hypocrisy, of Mr. Richter's own interference in a *state* criminal proceeding proved insufficient to persuade the prosecutor to ignore the outside pressure.

Todd can't help but think back on Shane's thank you for the future referrals for cases that he knew Todd would inevitably screw up. He wonders if by leaving out the actual sentence reduction in the sample motion he gave Todd that Shane set him up for failure. But he doesn't dwell on these thoughts for too long, and ultimately, he gives Shane the benefit of the doubt. He accepts the fact that he alone is responsible for this case and any mistakes along the way.

Ultimately, Todd concluded that the only way he can correct this particular mistake is to have another attorney file a new motion with the state court arguing that Todd provided ineffective assistance of counsel by failing to include in his motion a sentence reduction. Despite his initial fear of what that might mean to his career if he had a run-in with the Utah State Bar, Todd advised Fredy to consider that option and even gave him the phone numbers of a few attorneys he had come to know and trust through his expanded practice in removal proceedings. Fredy and Sarah refused. Todd is the first person with any knowledge of immigration law, even if an imperfect knowledge, who they have trusted and felt actually cared. Todd was unable to convince them otherwise, even with his assurances that he would be fine and that he would still help them with the immigration case. This expression of gratitude and loyalty from Fredy and Sarah increases his dedication and motivation to find some way to help Fredy. Several close friends are equally dedicated to helping in any way they can and call Todd regularly, including Lori, who asked to meet with Todd in person today.

"How is it possible that someone like Fredy can't have better options than some Hail Mary asylum application?" Lori says, still pacing the small amount of free space in Todd's office. "I mean, this is exactly the kind of immigrant we should *want* in this country. I just don't understand it."

"Well, the law says—"

"The law is stupid!" Lori interrupts.

Todd laughs, nodding his head in agreement.

"I'm not kidding, and if I have to hear one more of these fools say 'the law is the law' again, so help me," Lori says passionately, lifting and shaking her hands in front of her as if she were strangling an invisible adversary. "Ugh!" she shouts in frustration, thrusting her arms down to her side. "It's all just so infuriating!"

"I know, I know," Todd says. "But the problem is that not enough people in this country have a Fredy in their lives to put a face on these legal debates."

"Tell me about it," Lori says. "Four months ago, *I* was saying 'the law is the law' with the rest of these idiots."

Todd laughs again.

"And if it weren't for all those people like my own sweet, stupid husband who helped vote Donald Trump into office, we probably wouldn't even be in this mess in the first place."

"Well, I'm not one to rush to the aid of President Trump on the immigration debate," Todd says. "But the biggest problem we have in Fredy's case now is because of the laws passed twenty years before he was even elected. It was a Republican-pushed bill, but it wouldn't have passed without the help of more than a hundred Democratic Congressman and Democratic President Clinton, who signed it into law. There's plenty of blame to go around about how we got into this mess, but not enough people in power who care enough to get us out of it. And honestly, I doubt that the vast majority of U.S. citizens have any real idea of what the laws they're defending actually say and do."

"If we could just show them somehow," Lori says. "I mean, now that my husband's seen just how some of these laws actually affect people like Fredy, he's completely changed his view on the whole thing. I've even caught him using terms like *undocumented immigrants* and *noncitizens* all of a sudden." Lori laughs shortly before continuing. "So can't we do something to try to show *everybody* what's happening to some of these good people like Fredy? Like go to the media or something? If they don't know what the laws are doing and who they're hurting, then somebody needs to show them. Why not us?"

Todd sits quietly, considering the option. Certainly he doesn't expect any media coverage of Fredy's story to trigger a change in the law fast enough to actually benefit him before his hearing, if ever. But could it at least change some minds? Maybe it could give the judge just enough pressure to do the right thing if it's a close case. He has already tried everything else he can think of. But he has no idea where to even start, nor does he have the time to make such an effort.

"That might not be a bad idea," Todd says. "But I don't have any media contacts, and I don't think there's much I could do to get things rolling."

"Say no more, Todd, my boy," Lori says, picking up her purse and putting it over her shoulder. "Leave everything to me."

Without saying another, word Lori turns and walks out of Todd's office. Todd smiles as she leaves.

...

DAY 82

Monday, May 21, 2018

It's just past six o'clock in the evening when the ringing of Todd's phone interrupts his dinner with his wife and daughter. The mere presence of a phone at the dinner table is a clear violation of the duly enacted Becker house rules, but it's one broken equally by both Todd and Julie despite their best efforts. Todd takes the phone out of his pocket but doesn't recognize the number of the incoming call. His curiosity prompts him to ask his wife for her blessing in breaking an even more serious Becker house rule by actually taking the call. To his surprise, Julie grants his request without any pushback. He's greeted by the voice of a woman he doesn't recognize.

"Hello, can I speak to attorney Todd Becker, please?" she says.

"This is Todd," he says. "Who's this?"

"My name is Trudy Robinson. I'm a reporter with the *Deseret News* and I'm working on a story about one of your clients, Mr. Fredy Gonzalez. Are you still representing Mr. Gonzalez?"

By this point, Todd has forgotten about Lori's plans to try to somehow get the media involved in Fredy's case, and he seriously doubted that she would be able to get anywhere. Now that she apparently has, Todd is unsure about how to respond, particularly without discussing everything with Fredy first. He replies cautiously.

"Well, I can't really get into specifics about any of my cases because—"

"Oh, yes," Trudy interrupts. "I know, I know, attorney-client privilege and all of that. I mostly wanted to get your comments on the current state of the immigration laws that are impacting people like Fredy. ICE hasn't let me speak directly to Fredy, but I've already talked to his family and some friends about some of the specifics of his life. It just seems so crazy that the government is going so hard after this guy, who, by all accounts, is just an incredible person."

Todd feels reassured in part by the claim that Fredy and his family are apparently already on board with this, but more so by the fact that his contribution would be limited to providing some insights (and animosity) on the law.

"Yeah," Todd says. "I could talk your ear off on everything that's wrong with our immigration laws."

"Well, great," Trudy says. "By all means, talk it right off. I've got one to spare."

"Can you hold for a second?"

"Sure."

Todd brings his cell phone down to his side, muting it against his thigh.

"Is it okay if I take this in the other room, babe?" Todd whispers to his wife, who has stopped eating to listen to Todd's conversation. "I'll try to make it quick."

"Go ahead, Mr. Bigshot Media Man," Julie says with a smile, having heard enough to know what this call is for. "The public awaits."

"Whatever," Todd says, laughing.

He stands up, walks out of the kitchen, and begins talking as soon as he reaches the hallway leading to his bedroom.

"I guess it's just you and me tonight, kid," Julie says, turning to Nora in her highchair. "You up for another girls' night?" she says, reaching over and poking Nora in her belly, triggering a soft giggle.

...

DAY 86

Friday, May 25, 2018

Julie is sitting on her bed smiling, looking at her new smartphone, which is connected to her home's wireless internet. Two significant upgrades in the Becker home. Todd opens the door to their apartment, drops his laptop case next to the couch to his immediate left, and intentionally collapses over the armrest onto the couch.

"Sorry I'm late, babe," he says, his voice muffled by the back of the couch where he is facing as he continues to lie on his stomach. "I'm so ready for the weekend."

"Did you see it?" Julie says excitedly, walking quickly down the hall to the living room. "Did you see it yet?"

Todd can hear Nora start to cry from her bedroom.

"Do you want me to go get her?" he asks, turning over onto his back towards the sound of Julie's voice and Nora's crying.

"She's fine," Julie says, now in Todd's view but still walking towards him. "We can't have her spoiled now. It's about time she grew up a bit and quit all this belly achin' all the time."

"Yeah," Todd says, sitting upright. "Ten months *is* a little old for all this crying, I suppose. Don't you think it's about time she got a job already?"

"Shut up," Julie says, laughing. "Just read this already."

She hands Todd her cell phone open to the *Deseret News* website. He reads the title, *Utah husband, father and volunteer fights deportation from behind bars.*

"You're famous now," Julie says before Todd can read further. "They quoted you and everything."

Todd smiles with a combination of hope and pride.

"Tell me, Mr. Becker," Julie says, deepening her voice with exaggerated pouty lips, as she slowly straddles him on the couch and puts her arms around his neck, tilting her head to the side. "What's a girl gotta do to get an autograph around here?"

"Just an autograph?" Todd says, pulling her in close and attempting to kiss her.

"Not so fast now, Mr. Becker," Julie says, pushing him to the back of the couch by his shoulders. "I'm a married woman, you know."

"Yeah, *I* should know," Todd says. "I'm still paying interest on that wedding band upgrade I got you last year. Now get over here, woman!" he says, pulling her close to him again.

"I'm sorry, Mr. Becker," Julie says, pushing Todd back again and starting to step backwards off of the couch. "But my body is still recovering from the trauma of childbirth. No funny business. Doctor's orders. You understand."

"That was more than ten months ago!" Todd retorts. "You haven't tried to pull that excuse in months!"

"What's that?" she says, now walking towards Nora's room, playfully cupping her right hand around her right ear, pretending to strain to make out his words. "I can't hear you, Mr. Becker. My sweet infant is crying. I must tend to her needs now."

"She's almost a year old," Todd says. "Shouldn't she be moving out by now?!"

"I'm so sorry, Mr. Becker," Julie says, now at the back end of the hall. "But I really must be going now. My parents must be worried sick."

"Curse you, evil temptress!" Todd shouts towards the now empty hallway, to which Julie responds with laughter.

Todd sits for a moment, staring at the entrance to the hallway, pursing his lips and furrowing his eyebrows into a mild grimace, and then smiles. He looks down to the couch cushion to his left where Julie left her phone. He swipes away the blackened screensaver to read the story.

Utah husband, father and volunteer fights deportation from behind bars

By Trudy Robinson

Published: May 25, 2018 2:15 p.m.

SALT LAKE CITY — Long-time Utah resident Wilfredo "Fredy" Gonzalez has been detained in Utah by Immigration and Customs Enforcement (ICE) since March 1. His "crime"? Being brought to the United States illegally by his parents as a young child almost thirty years ago. Fredy's predicament provides a real-life example of a child paying the price for the sins of the parent. But in this case, it is not just the child who is paying the price. Fredy's detention has had a negative ripple effect throughout his community.

Prior to his detention, Fredy provided for his U.S. citizen wife and three children. Despite graduating high school with honors, Fredy's undocumented status prevented him from pursuing his dream of becoming an architect or an engineer. Undeterred, Fredy explored self-employment options, eventually starting his own landscaping business. At the time of his arrest, his business was flourishing, providing full-time employment for as many as ten Utah residents. But now, that business is in danger of closing.

"We can only get along so long without Fredy," said Trevor, a U.S. citizen and an employee of Fredy's since 2014. "He's like the glue that holds this place together."

Fredy's wife, Sarah, has done her best to fill in where she can but has admittedly fallen short. With three young children—the oldest diagnosed with cystic fibrosis and the youngest only fifteen months old—she said it's taken all of her strength just to keep her home in order. For the first time in her life, Sarah has had to apply for government assistance to provide for her family.

"We don't have family nearby, so we've been relying a lot on friends and neighbors, but they can only do so much," Sarah said. "They have their only families to worry about."

Those friends and neighbors have similarly found a void in their lives in Fredy's absence.

"Fredy is the ideal citizen," said one neighbor and close family friend, Lori Reed. "He has given more of his time and energy to this community than almost anybody I've ever met. And this is how we thank him?"

Lori's ten-year-old son, Ethan, has been playing on a soccer team both created and coached by Fredy since last year. According to Lori, Fredy got the idea to start the team after he heard his own son, Oscar, talking enviously with Ethan about the soccer jerseys some of their peers were wearing to school.

"[Fredy] was always out with the boys, teaching them how to play and building on their strengths and helping them over-come their weaknesses," Lori said. "And it was just like a light bulb went off in his head, and he knew he had found a way to help the kids in the neighborhood who wanted to play soccer but couldn't afford to sign up for the expensive leagues in the community."

That "light bulb" led to what would ultimately be a group of 21 children spread throughout Salt Lake and Davis county. Without Fredy, the driving force behind the team, the free community soccer league is on hold indefinitely. "We miss you, Coach!" said Lori's son, Ethan. "We love you!"

With an increased focus of the deportation of "criminal" aliens throughout the United States, it may seem strange that Fredy would be deemed a priority. Although he was initially stopped and investigated for a possible DUI last March, that investigation came up empty and no charges were filed by the police. However, that was enough to catch the attention of ICE. The government went on to argue that Fredy's misdemeanor citation for shoplifting in 1995, which was later dismissed and expunged, was an "aggravated felony," preventing him from being released on bond or applying to cancel his deportation.

"Immigration law is its own twisted world where dismissed cases are treated as convictions, misdemeanors are treated as aggravated felonies, and good members of our society, like Fredy, are treated like hardened criminals," said Fredy's attorney, Todd Becker.

Becker is representing Fredy pro bono but is concerned that the harsh and unforgiving immigration laws of the United States have prevented Fredy from getting legal status despite his strong ties to this country.

The Justice Department declined to comment about Fredy's case because his removal case is still pending, DOJ spokeswoman Barbara J. Clemens said.

Fredy is in the middle of the fight of his life. In many respects, it is a fight *for* his life. His ultimate fate lies in the hands of immigration judge Samuel O. Lanzotti, who will be conducting a final individual hearing in Fredy's case next month.

Todd smiles throughout the entire reading.

This is perfect, he thinks. *Well written, persuasive, and accurate. Perfect. This is exactly the kind of information we need to get out there.*

He's encouraged further to see the story has generated a lot of public interest with already over one hundred comments online. His optimism is quickly replaced with cynicism after he reads the first few pages of comments. In general they seem to be variations of only a few different types of responses. Some, like MackDaddy from Nephi, Utah, made broad statements without addressing the substance of the issues in the story:

MackDaddy - Nephi, UT

May 25, 2018 3:15 p.m.

Somehow the terms "deportation" and "assimilation" have taken on negative meanings. We must correct that or lose our nation to the third world.

10 Likes

"What?" Todd says out loud in confusion. *That has nothing to do with the story, he thinks to himself. Who could be more assimilated than Fredy? Did this guy even read the story?*

As Todd continues, the comments seem to become more passionately uninformed, polarizing, and combative.

Truth_Troller - Orem, UT

May 25, 2018 2:37 p.m.

Wait, what??!!? Illegals get to "FIGHT" their deportations??? No wonder this country is such a mess and drowning in debt. These illegal aliens sneak in here to steal our jobs, steal our identitieis steal our benefits, pay no taxes, and then they get it hang out in jail wtih three meals a day & cable tv to "fight" their deportations on MY tax money!!!!!!! If his attorney doesn't like our immigration laws we should deport him along with the rest of teh criminals. SMH... #notmycountryanymore

21 Likes

Sean M - Park City, UT

May 25, 2018 3:15 p.m.

We all know that if this immigrant's name was Rupert instead of Wilfredo, and he was from England instead of Mexico that he'd be walking the streets and none of you would think twice about it. What would you do if you were in his shoes? Your all bunch of crazy racists up in here.

13 Likes

@Sean M

JonDoe - Junction City, KS

May 25, 2018 3:17 p.m.

You mean, YOU'RE a bunch of racists? As in, "YOU'RE welcome for the lesson in elementary school grammar." MORON!!!

31 Likes

@JonDoe

Sean M - Park City, UT

May 25, 2018 3:21 p.m.

Whatever, you knew what I meant. It'd be nice if people on here would actually respond to people's comments instead of criticizing there grammar.

3 Likes

@Sean M

JonDoe - Junction City, KS

May 25, 2018 3:22 p.m.

You mean, THEIR grammar?... ROFL!!!

43 Likes

The toxicity of the public comment board, which Todd generally avoids, has never felt so personal and cruel. Although Todd did find some measure of amusement at Truth_Troller's call for *his* deportation. But Todd is most discouraged by what proves to be the most well received of all the comments, from a Mr. or Ms. Mind-Blower of Durham, North Carolina.

MindBlower - Durham, NC

May 25, 2018 4:37 p.m.

Ever wonder why the media tries to bury the TRUTH about illegals with fluff pieces like this? If you want to see what we're really fighting against here, take a look at this story: http://www.therealworldnews.org/us/2018/05/19/illegal-immi-grant-who-rapes-and-murders-child-had-been-deported-two-times.html

107 Likes 57 Shares

Todd frowns at the number of likes and shares before even following the hyperlink, which proves to be a far more influential story. After reading the title he has already read enough: *Illegal immigrant who rapes and murders child had been deported two times.*

Of course, Todd thinks to himself. *Perfect timing.*

Fredy's story is now buried under a national story validating the fears and stereotypes of those Todd had hoped to actually influence. Todd realizes there are some minds, on both sides of the debate, that are incapable of change or compromise. But he had hoped that Fredy's story may have at least impacted some. It *is* a great story, he thinks. The most relevant opinions, Todd resolves, are those least likely to be shared online on a comment board. Maybe the judge will read the story. Or maybe the government attorneys. He feels an immediate sense of guilt at the passing thought that maybe, if nothing else, the story will help him build up his business. It's an ongoing inner conflict for Todd, balancing the desire to help other people with the unavoidable need to make money. But how much money does he really need?

Of course, Todd has his own family to worry about, and they have to come first. But he often finds himself feeling inwardly embarrassed by his worries about his comparatively minor financial and family challenges. He often thinks back on the culture shock of returning to the United States after his mission in Argentina. While in some parts of Argentina Todd felt like he was still in the United States, other parts exposed him to a level of poverty he had never imagined. He recalls some areas with "houses" thrown together with the types of wood scraps he might find at the local dump, with open sewage lines dug out of the dirt outside the homes. And this was in one of the more advanced and wealthy countries in South America. The happiness he felt when he returned to his family's home for the first time was tarnished by feelings of discomfort, to the point of sadness, in their "modest" U.S. home five times the size of any he had been inside for two years. He recalls tears building up in his eyes as his bare feet felt the frivolous comfort of *carpet*, while his siblings quickly walked across it without a second thought.

Todd recognizes he is blessed far beyond the vast majority of the world for little reason other than the country and family he was born into. While he doesn't necessarily feel guilt for these luxuries, he also doesn't feel pride for what he's accomplished in a country and a family that paved so much of the way for him. It's allowed him to have the good fortune of being able to both help others *and* his own family at the same time. The decision of Fredy's parents to bring him to the United States as a child afforded Fredy much of that same good fortune. Todd realizes that many immigrants have not made good use of those opportunities to the extent that Fredy has. But, of course, the same is true of many of those born on the "right" side of the line, who similarly did nothing to earn the opportunities that they neither appreciate nor take advantage of.

Not even Todd himself knows for sure whether or not his intentions were entirely pure in helping publicize Fredy's story, and he's all but accepted the fact that it will make no meaningful difference in Fredy's actual case. But his resolve to keep fighting on Fredy's behalf remains unchanged.

CHAPTER 21

DAY 109

Sunday, June 17, 2018

SARAH SLOWLY WALKS OUT OF HER BEDROOM, RUBBING THE SLEEP OUT OF HER EYES AND THEN STRETCHING HER ARMS TOWARDS THE CEILING IN AN EFFORT TO FORCE HER BODY AWAKE. Her hair is messy but still held partially back in the loose bun she didn't bother taking out before going to sleep. She's wearing one of Fredy's old t-shirts, which drapes over her grey sweatpants. She slides slowly across her old hardwood hallway floor in the socks she wore the day before. Fredy always enjoyed teasing her for her habit of sleeping in her socks, but she refused to give in to his peer pressure. She said she always found it comforting somehow. Fredy, in contrast, insisted that his toes demanded to be free.

As Sarah turns from the living room into the kitchen, she's greeted by two mostly eaten bowls of cereal stacked inside of each other on the table, surrounded by pieces of cereal and small puddles of milk, next to a half-empty gallon of lukewarm milk missing a lid. Two spoons are on the floor under the table, surrounded by pieces of cereal that missed both the bowls and the mouths of her children. She finds comfort in this semi-regular morning mess, knowing that it means she now only has to worry about feeding breakfast to one of her three children. She hears Veronica now crying in her crib after having entertained herself to her breaking point of fifteen minutes. As she turns to the sound of her cries, she is visibly surprised when she notices the time for the first time since waking up. It's now 8:35, and church starts at 9:00.

Sarah quickly clears off the kitchen table and puts the milk back into the fridge without bothering to look for the lid. She ignores an incoming call to Fredy's cell phone, which doubles as his business line, and continues cleaning. She knows she's short on time to get herself and three children ready, but for a moment is motivated by the possible luxury of returning to a reasonably clean home. That moment passes quickly, and she walks away from the remaining mess to a door at the far end of the kitchen leading to the basement stairs, where she can hear a television blasting at a volume far louder than the authorized 25.

"Oscar! Katie!" she shouts down the stairs. "Get dressed! We gotta go to church soon!"

She can just barely hear the unintelligible grunts of disappointment from her son over the television.

"Turn off that TV!" she shouts. "Let's go!"

After what seems to be a deliberately delayed moment, she hears the television turn off.

"I don't wanna go to church, Mom," Oscar says after walking from the couch to the bottom of the stairs, where he is now looking up to his mother. "I wanna go play soccer with Ethan. I haven't played in like a hundred days."

"You know we don't play soccer on Sunday, Oscar. I need you to get ready and to help Katie. But first, go and check on Veronica and get her out of her crib, please."

Making sure his opposition doesn't go unnoticed, Oscar dramatically drops his head and shoulders, moans emphatically and slowly walks up the stairs as loudly as possible. Sarah accepts this begrudging compliance as a victory and walks back through the kitchen, out to the living room, and then to the hallway leading to her bedroom. She hears a notification from Fredy's cell phone indicating that the caller left a message. Taking advantage of the few minutes she has saved by sending Oscar to check on Veronica, Sarah picks up her phone to listen to the message.

"*Mr. Gonzalez,*" a woman says. "*This is Barbara King over at the Lush Garden Condominiums.*"

The voice is unfamiliar to Sarah, but she immediately recognizes the name as the president of the homeowners' association of one of Fredy's biggest clients.

"*I'm sorry to call you today, or I should say I'm sorry that I have to call you today,*" she continues with a tone that is equally pretentious and annoyed. "*But I have some serious concerns with the lack of attention and care our community has received from your company this year. We have been loyal customers to you for four years now, and for the most part have been very happy with your work. But it seems to me that our loyalty is not as appreciated as I had previously assumed.*"

Sarah sighs in desperation and brushes the loose strands of hair covering her face behind her ear as the message continues.

"*It has been more than three months since you have even bothered to show your face at our community or even call me. These half-wits you've been sending to cover for you might work for some of your clients, but they are not cutting it for us. I've told a Mr. Trevor Something-or-other, on more than one occasion, to have you contact me about my concerns, but I guess you couldn't be bothered. So let me be very clear, Mr. Gonzalez. If I do not see you personally this next Saturday, I will have no choice but to take our business elsewhere. As much as I'd hate to do that, I'm afraid that's what this has come too. Thank you.*"

Sarah drops the phone onto her bed. She turns quickly to the sound of little feet running down the hall and sees Veronica, naked from the waist down, laughing as she clumsily runs away from her room holding her own diaper.

"Oscar!" Sarah yells. "What are you doing?"

"You told me to check her diaper!" Oscar yells back, walking out of Veronica's room, adjacent to Sarah's. "But then she ran away."

"No, I said to check on *her*," Sarah says in frustration. "Just to entertain her for a couple of minutes, not take off her diaper. I'm happy to hear that your ears still work, just not your ability to follow simple instructions."

Sarah grabs a clean diaper from Veronica's room and chases her down as Veronica continues laughing at what appears to her to be a game. After putting on the diaper, Sarah quickly takes her back to her room and puts on the first dress she sees lying on the floor, without confirming it is clean and suspecting it likely is not.

"All right," Sarah says to Oscar. "Now go and put on your dress shirt, hurry up."

"I told you, I don't wanna go to church," Oscar says defiantly. "I'm gonna go play soccer."

"Oscar," Sarah says with a sigh, attempting to regain her composure. "Even if we didn't have church, I wouldn't want you out there playing today. We've had too many red air days this summer; it's not good for you."

"Who cares? Dad would take us up to Bear Lake on bad air days."

"I told you, Oscar, we're going to church."

"I *hate* church! I don't wanna go, I told you."

"I don't care!" Sarah shouts, giving in to her frustrations. "I didn't ask for your opinion. Just do what I told you."

Oscar grunts in defiance before turning abruptly and stomping down the hallway as loudly as he can walk, pounding a couple of times on the wall with his fist just in case his mother didn't hear him.

Sarah puts Veronica back in her crib to momentarily contain her, which triggers immediate screams. She closes Veronica's door behind her and then walks back into her own room, also closing the door in an attempt to mute the crying as much as possible. She picks up Fredy's phone and quickly scrolls through his work contacts until she comes to Trevor and pushes his name with her finger. After several rings he answers.

"Good morning, Mrs. Gonzalez," Trevor says facetiously, seeming to mimic the tone of an elementary school student greeting his teacher.

"Trevor, what's going on?" Sarah says curtly. "What happened with the Lush Garden job yesterday?"

"Nothing happened. That crazy ol' broad complains just to hear herself talk sometimes. I don't know what her problem is."

"This is serious, Trevor. This is one of Fredy's biggest clients. We can't afford to lose another contract right now; you know that."

"Look, Sarah. I'm telling you, I did the job and I did it right. There's nothin' I did that Fredy woulda done any different if he was there himself. She's just one of these high-maintenance, VIP customers who thinks she's entitled to some kinda special attention. It's like some psychological thing with her or somethin', like she thinks if we don't got the owner of the company out there on every single job, then we must be cuttin' corners or whatever. And I gotta tell ya, I'm sick of being told how to do my job by people who don't know what they're talking about. And with all due respect, Sarah, that includes you."

"You are way outta line, Trevor," Sarah says, raising her voice to the level of her frustration. "This is not the first problem we've had with a client in the past couple of months. And then we missed the quarterly tax deadline, and have to pay those penalties for—"

"Oh, come on now, again with the taxes?" Trevor interrupts in frustration. "That's never been a part of my job, and you know it!"

"Trevor," Sarah says. "I'm just trying to keep this business alive until Fredy gets back, and you—"

"*If* Fredy gets back," Trevor interrupts again.

Sarah grimaces in shock at the comment, initially unsure of how to respond.

"Excuse me?" she says with an annoyed tone after a brief pause.

"Nothin', just forget it. But let's be honest here, Sarah, it's *me* that's kept this business goin', not *you*. I'm the one that's been working extra hours with all this managing and hand-holding. All based on a promise that Fredy will be out soon and do right by me and compensate me for all this extra work I've been doin' alone. But I can't promise I can keep doin' this much longer. Especially when this is the kinda thanks I get."

"What are you saying, Trevor? What? You're gonna quit? We got a lot of other employees who depend on this business too, you know. It's not just you. It's not just us."

Sarah waits for a moment, expecting a response but receiving none.

"Trevor?" she says. "Are you still there?"

"All right, look, I gotta go," Trevor says. "Thanks for the call, Sarah. Tell Fredy I said hi."

"Trevor?" Sarah says to a now empty line. "Trevor?!"

She throws down Fredy's phone in frustration, unsure of what to do or where to begin. Ultimately, she accepts the fact that there's little she can do right now to solve any work issues, and she decides to give Trevor some space before calling him back. After almost four months without Fredy, Sarah knows she is drastically limited in what she can accomplish in any given day. Having concluded that nothing more can be done in this moment to help Fredy's business, she turns her full attention—and frustrations—to getting her kids to church.

She opens her bedroom door to check on the progress of her older two children but finds Oscar in the hallway wearing his soccer jersey, shorts, and cleats, holding a soccer ball.

"Oscar!" Sarah yells with the force of all the rage built up through the morning. "What's wrong with you?! I need your help now with Dad gone, and you're just making things worse! You *promised* him you'd be my big helper until he got home."

Oscar stares in silence at his mother with an expression of increasing rage, which quickly explodes.

"He's *never* coming home!" he says, throwing down his soccer ball before running back towards his room.

Whatever feelings of empathy Sarah would normally feel in this moment are lost under her own still-increasing frustration and anger. Motivated by a combination of these two feelings, she runs after Oscar, forcibly removes his jersey, drags him by the arm down the hall into his room, and awkwardly forces a blue polo shirt onto her still-resisting son. With an unbending determination to get her kids to church on time, she manages to get her other two children and herself dressed and reasonably presentable in less than ten minutes—a new record for the Gonzalez family, but not one likely to be celebrated today.

...

Sarah is sitting at the end of a church pew with her elbow resting on a wooden armrest, fanning herself with the paper program handed to her as she walked into the chapel at her church. This is the second week in a row that the air conditioning has been broken, prompting the "less faithful" to sit out in the cooler lobby of the building. She's holding Veronica with her other arm and ignoring the feeling of a half-chewed, soggy graham cracker falling out of her daughter's mouth and onto her arm. Katie is lying on her stomach on the bench next to Sarah, coloring in an already mostly colored coloring book. Oscar sits on the other side of Katie, folding his arms with a scowl that Sarah has been ignoring since the meeting began about fifteen minutes earlier.

In the aisle to Sarah's immediate left, six young men in shirts and ties walk towards the front of the chapel carrying metal trays full of small, now empty plastic cups. They have just finished passing to the congregation bread and water representing the body and blood of Jesus Christ, referred to as the sacrament in the Church of Jesus Christ of Latter-day Saints. They take turns handing their trays to two older young men at the front left corner of the chapel. They put the trays down on a table in front of them covered by a white cloth, and then drape another white cloth over the trays. After doing so, all the young men return to sit with their families in the congregation, prompting one of three men sitting on the stand at the front of the chapel to walk up to the pulpit.

"I'd like to thank the priesthood youth for the reverent manner in which they administered the sacrament today," he says to the congregation.

Sarah is staring blankly at the back of the head of the person sitting in the pew directly in front of her. She's barely cognizant of what is being said as the man continues speaking.

"Before we hear from our first speaker," he continues, "we'd like to invite all of our primary children up for a special musical number."

Several children, including Katie, stand up and begin walking towards the front of the chapel. Sarah turns instinctively to Oscar.

"All right, that means you too, bud," Sarah says coldly, followed by a head motion instructing him to follow the other children.

"I'm not going," he says defiantly.

Sarah leans in towards her son with a facial expression reminding him that she still hasn't gotten over the morning's frustrations.

"Go, and go *now*," she says quietly but forcefully. "Today is not the day to try my patience, son."

Oscar stares quietly and coldly at his mother for an extended moment with a look of quiet anger before forcing his way past her to the aisle leading up to the front of the chapel. A minute later, all of the children are up in the front of the chapel and a woman directs some of the shorter children to move up to the front. After finding their placement acceptable, she walks over to the microphone.

"Good morning, brothers and sisters," she says to the congregation. "Your children have been working really hard together these past few weeks on this musical number, and we just wanted to wish all of our daddies out there a happy Father's Day."

Sarah's head jerks up abruptly and she sits upright as if about to stand at the mention of Father's Day, which she completely forgot was today. She feels sick as she makes eye contact with her son, whose face seems now more sad than angry. She turns to Katie, who is smiling and talking to the girl next to her, seeming to be completely oblivious. Sarah wishes she could immediately walk up to the front of the chapel to save her son, but the pianist has already started playing.

"*I'm so sorry, Oscar,*" she mouths to her son, slowly shaking her head. "*I'm so, so sorry.*"

After a brief introduction on the piano, all of the children begin to sing, except for Oscar. The first line seems to echo through Sarah's mind and repeat throughout the performance.

> *I'm so glad when daddy comes home,*
> *Glad as I can be;*

Sarah immediately recalls Oscar yelling at her less than thirty minutes ago that his daddy was never coming home, as she now watches him surrounded by children, including Katie, singing about the joy they feel when their dads come home after work every day. The frustration and anger Sarah felt this morning feel so petty and trivial now. Her son was trying to communicate his pain with her, the best way a ten-year-old knows how. But she missed it somehow. What else has she missed?

The children continue singing, with corresponding actions to compliment the lyrics.

> *Clap my hands and shout for joy,*
> *Then climb upon his knee,*
> *Put my arms around his neck,*
> *Hug him tight like this,*
> *Pat his cheeks, then give him what?*
> *A great big kiss.*

The words remind Sarah of Oscar's disappointment during their first visit with Fredy when he couldn't hug him. It's now been almost four months since Oscar has been able to touch his father. It's been just as long since he's had much of a mother, Sarah feels.

As soon as the children finish the song, and before they can begin a second one, Sarah is standing in the aisle, holding Veronica and motioning for Oscar and Katie to come down. Oscar quickly complies, taking Katie by the hand, which prompts the woman leading the music to turn her head in confusion, appearing unsure of how to respond. Sarah waves to her in a motion attempting to tell her to continue without her kids, who are now by her side. Sarah bends down and looks in Oscar's eyes.

"Let's go play soccer," she says.

Oscar smiles.

...

Sarah and Lori are sitting alone at a table under a pavilion at a park with a large grass field and an old wooden boardwalk leading to Bear Lake. It is a two-hour drive from their home, but it had become a favorite for the Gonzalez family on days when they wanted to play outside but the air quality was poor at the lower elevation near their home. It's a small accommodation for Oscar's cystic fibrosis that the family willingly made regularly before Fredy's arrest, but this is the first time they've come here this year.

Katie is helping Veronica slowly walk towards a playground, while Oscar and Ethan are in the middle of the field wearing their matching jerseys and running some of the practice drills Fredy taught them. A cool breeze softens the already moderately warm afternoon.

"I'm a terrible mother," Sarah says, shaking her head in desperation. "I don't even know what I'm doing anymore."

"Oh, stop it," Lori says. "You're a *human being* in a terrible situation. And none of us know what we're doing. We all just fake it the best we can."

"I guess," Sarah says with a tone suggesting she's not convinced. "Thanks again for coming with us. I feel so bad dragging you away from home on Father's Day of all days. Does Greg hate me?"

"Are you kidding me?" Lori says with a face of genuine surprise at the suggestion. "This is exactly the kind of Father's Day he's always asking for. One where he can just be alone and *forget* that he's a father for a few hours."

Sarah laughs.

"I'm sure that's not true," she says.

"Believe me, he's fine," Lori says. "As long as I'm back by six to make his favorite barbecue ribs, he doesn't care about anything else. So please, don't feel bad at all. And Ethan's having a great time."

They turn briefly to their boys, who are still running after a soccer ball in the middle of the field.

"Oscar and I had a pretty good talk on the drive up here," Sarah says. "Well, as good as you can expect from a ten-year-old boy, but I finally got him to open up a bit about some of his feelings and how things are going in his life."

"That's good," Lori says. "What'd he say?"

"Well, I knew he was missing his dad, obviously, and that he was feeling sad and nervous. But he's also been very scared about what's going to happen to himself. He's been afraid that *he* was going to be taken to jail and be deported too."

"You're kidding me! That's terrible. How'd he get that idea in his mind?"

"I guess he's been getting bullied at school from some kids who somehow found out about Fredy. Saying we're gonna build a wall so his dad can never come back or something like that. But someone was even telling Oscar that *he* was going to be deported along with his dad."

"That's awful," Lori says, shaking her head in disbelief. "Did you call the school about that?"

"No," Sarah says. "Like I said, he just barely told me about this today, and school's been out for a couple of weeks now. But apparently elementary school is just as awful as I remember it. It's just crazy to me how cruel some of these kids can be to each other."

"Well, that sounds more like a kid mimicking his parent than anything else," Lori says. "There's no way some nine- or ten-year-old is coming up with something like that on his own."

"Exactly," Sarah says. "So I'm not sure it'd do any good to say anything to the school."

Lori frowns and shakes her head, seeming unsure of what to say. Eventually Sarah ends the silence.

"I'm just really worried about what this all has already done to my kids," Sarah says. "Even if everything goes perfect at Fredy's hearing, I have this fear that the kids, or at least Oscar, won't bounce back from this."

"Oscar's a tough kid," Lori says reassuringly. "I'm sure he'll be back to his old self as soon as Fredy walks back through your front door. It might even make them closer."

"I hope so," Sarah says, looking down. "But—"

She pauses before finishing.

"I—I just," she continues, stumbling through her words as she attempts to control her emotions. "I mean, Fredy is always so sure that everything will work out. He won't even entertain a discussion about what we're going to do if it doesn't. He has this perfect faith that God will save us, and I don't know if it's completely sincere, or if he's just trying to reassure me just like I keep trying to reassure the kids. But I don't know, Lori. I just don't know if I believe it. I don't know."

Lori reaches across the table and takes Sarah's hand but doesn't speak. A moment later Sarah continues.

"I just don't know what I'm supposed to be telling my kids," she says. "It's not like when my parents got divorced when I was a kid. Even when my dad was *physically* in our house, he wasn't really there. He had checked out on us all years ago. If he wasn't yelling at me or my brother or my mom about something, he wasn't talking to us at all. It was almost a relief to have my parents not living in the same house anymore, ya know? And we'd still see him when he cared enough to show up, but we knew what to expect. If we didn't see our dad, it was because *he* made the choice not to see us. Eventually that reversed, and we were the ones who chose not to see him.

"But when I married Fredy, I made sure I was not marrying my dad. I was *not* gonna put my kids through what my brother and I had to go through. Never feeling like we were good enough to be loved by our own dad. And Fredy's *nothing* like that. He's got his flaws for sure, but no one can say he doesn't love his kids, or that he wouldn't do anything for them to give them the best life possible. And they know that; they all know that. I could always at least dull the pain of my childhood by just convincing myself that I didn't care since my dad didn't care. And that was still hard. *So* hard. It took me years to get over that, and to feel like I had any real worth, ya know?"

Lori nods her head.

"I'd always tell Fredy that it would've almost been easier for me if my dad had just died," Sarah says.

"What do you mean?" Lori asks with tone of genuine interest.

"That way I could've just mourned for the loss of my dad without knowing he's still out there and *choosing* to not be in my life," Sarah says.

She smiles sadly, now looking past Lori.

"I used to sit in front of my bathroom mirror," Sarah continues, still not returning eye contact with Lori. "I would pretend I was speaking at my dad's funeral or talking to a close friend about my dad's death or something like that. Talking about what an amazing father he was, and how much he loved me, and how much I missed him. I'd picture myself placing flowers in front of his tombstone. And I'd just cry, devastated that my daddy had died at such a young age. And those feelings were so real to me in those moments, like he had actually really died, and like I actually cared. But that was so much better than the reality that he *chose* to leave me."

Sarah looks back at Lori, who raises her eyebrows softly in a silent gesture of empathy. She's surprised when Sarah suddenly laughs.

"Fredy would always joke with me that he'd never leave me even if he wanted to because he's afraid of what I'd do to him," she says with a smile. "Because he knows I'd rather have my kids have a dead dad than a deadbeat dad."

Lori smiles.

"Well, that's one thing you'll never have to worry about with Fredy," she says. "He'll always be there for all of you, no matter what happens. Forever. You know that."

"Yeah," Sarah says, looking down somberly. "I know."

CHAPTER 22

DAY 111

Tuesday, June 19, 2018

TODD AND EMMA WALK INTO THE FAST FOOD RESTAURANT WHERE
THEY HAVE THEIR WEEKLY "FREDY MEETINGS," AS THEY'VE STARTED
CALLING THEM. It's a tradition that continues even now that Todd
has his own office space and no longer needs to rely on the free Wi-
Fi. After seeing a longer-than-usual line to order, they decide to sit
down in their usual booth and start their meeting until after the lunch
rush. The last semester of Emma's second year of law school ended
a couple of weeks ago, allowing her to dedicate a significant amount
of time to Fredy's case. Through her research, she has collected hundreds of pages of evidence of the dangerous country conditions in
Mexico, all of which she has highlighted and emailed Todd for them
to review together.

"So I think the best place to start would be with evidence from
our own government," Emma says after directing Todd to the first
page of the most recent U.S. Department of State Human Rights
Report for Mexico. "Obviously there are problems with gangs and
cartels in Mexico, but this report says the most significant human
rights issues in Mexico just last year 'included *involvement by police, military, and other state officials*, sometimes *in coordination with
criminal organizations*, in unlawful killings, disappearances, and even

torture.' It also says 'there were credible reports of police involvement in kidnappings for ransom,' and that they often did so '*with impunity.*'

"The next document is also from the U.S. Department of State, but this one is the most recent travel warning for Mexico. This one, I think, is very helpful to show how bad things are specifically in the Mexican state of Guerrero, where Fredy's from. It has the whole state ranked as a Level 4 Do Not Travel area, which appears to be the highest possible level. It goes as far as saying that all U.S. government employees are *prohibited* from even entering the state. Can you believe that?"

"Yeah, it really is a mess down there," Todd says. "Guerrero is actually the Spanish word for *warrior*, which seems fitting."

"I didn't know that," Emma says. "There's some criminal organization down there I read about called the Guerreros Unidos. So I'm guessing that would mean the *united* warriors, right?"

"*Muy bien, Emma!*" Todd says, with exaggerated enthusiasm. "*Estoy super impresionado con tu español.*"

"All right, you lost me after *muy bien,*" Emma says, laughing.

"Sorry," Todd says with a smile. "Go ahead."

"So, yeah," she continues. "I was actually reading something about the Guerreros Unidos. I guess just a few years ago, some local police detained over forty student protesters for some reason and then just handed them over to the local Guerreros Unidos, who killed them. I don't know much more about it, but can you believe that? What's wrong with that place?"

"Wow, that's awful," Todd says, shaking his head.

"That's why I wanted to focus as much as I could at first on reports directly from our own government describing Mexico," Emma says. "So it can't be so easily dismissed as an exaggeration or something. Plus, I figured a U.S. government attorney can't argue that Fredy will be fine in Mexico if the U.S. government reports clearly contradict that."

"You would think so," Todd says. "But I wouldn't be surprised if they did anyway. Have you heard of MS-13?"

"Yes, I have," Emma says, still seeming excited every time she has an answer to one of Todd's questions. "I read a lot about them in my research, actually. They're a gang that started in California but spread all over Central America after a lot of the gang members were deported, right?"

"Yes," Todd says. "They're pretty much running large portions of Central America now, and the U.S. Human Rights Reports acknowledge that. That's a main reason I've seen that so many families are fleeing their countries to the United States in hopes of protection from groups like that. They're constantly threatening to kill—and *do,* in fact, kill—people who can't pay their extortions, boys who refuse to join them, and girls who refuse to be their property."

"Yeah," Emma says softly. "It's so sad."

"I know," Todd says. "It's terrible. But the point I was getting at is that even though our own government acknowledges these facts, it still argues that it doesn't matter in most asylum cases. It's very ironic to me, because the way our president and attorney general talk about the dangers MS-13 poses *the United States,* you'd think we're on the verge of the apocalypse or something. But they have no problem sending women and children back to countries where MS-13 is a significantly greater problem. I don't mean to minimize the things they've done here in the U.S., but there's not a Central American country in the world that wouldn't swap their MS-13 problem for ours in a second."

"But I still don't see how these undisputed facts and country reports could be irrelevant to Fredy's case," Emma says. "Especially after his sister was murdered there."

"It's because of how our asylum laws are written, and then how they've been interpreted," Todd says. "It's not enough to prove that Fredy would be threatened, or persecuted, or tortured, or even killed. There are so many other requirements. Even if we fail to meet just one of the requirements, that's all it takes for the judge to deny the whole case."

"Right," Emma says, looking down at her computer screen at her notes. "We have to also show that the reason for the persecution would be because of Fredy's race, religion, nationality, political opinion, or membership in a particular social group. Which I was gonna ask you about. Which one are we arguing applies in Fredy's case?"

"It seems that the only one that would work for Fredy would be a *particular social group*," Todd says. "But before we can even get to that argument, there are some issues that may prevent the judge from even considering asylum."

"Like what?" Emma asks.

"Like a conviction for an aggravated felony, which Judge Lanzotti still thinks includes Fredy's twenty-year-old shoplifting offense, even after I reduced it to a class B misdemeanor. You can't get asylum if you have an aggravated felony conviction."

"Oh, that reminds me," Emma says with excitement. "I heard about some new Supreme Court case about aggravated felonies, something about it being unconstitutional. I haven't had a chance to read it yet, but I made a note about it."

"Was it *Sessions v. Dimaya*?" Todd asks.

"Yeah, that sounds right," Emma says. "Do you think that will help Fredy?"

"Unfortunately not," Todd says. "You probably remember from your research that there are dozens of different types of aggravated felonies, some very serious crimes, some minor ones like Fredy's. But in the *Dimaya* case, the Supreme Court was just reviewing a portion of a statute defining a *crime of violence*, which is obviously not the type of crime Fredy was convicted of. But then again, nothing is ever as obvious as you'd think when Congress redefines commonly understood terms, which we've already seen plenty of in Fredy's case. Congress did the same thing with the simple term of *crime of violence*, defining it so broadly that it didn't require the crime actually involve any *violence*. The problem was Congress defined it so vaguely that the courts struggled and disagreed for years on what did and didn't meet that *re*-definition. So the Supreme Court held that it was unconstitutionally vague, and therefore no longer legally enforceable."

"If only the Supreme Court would find that the laws that apply to Fredy's case were unconstitutionally stupid," Emma says, appearing to be only half joking. "So can Fredy even apply for asylum then?"

"Well, I'm still going to submit some written arguments on the aggravated felony issue to try to convince the judge to change his mind," Todd says. "I have to file that tomorrow with all of the evidence we got. But even if we won that argument, we still have the problem of the one-year filing deadline."

"Yeah, I was gonna ask you about that one too," Emma says. "How could Fredy have been expected to file an asylum application one year after coming here when he was a kid? That's ridiculous."

"I know," Todd says. "There's an exception for the filing deadline for *unaccompanied* minors, but Fredy came with his parents. So once again he's potentially being punished for the action—or inaction—of his parents. But even if we could excuse his failure to apply as a kid, he's forty-one years old now. I'm still going to at least try to argue for an exception based on changed country conditions or other extraordinary circumstances, but that will be an uphill battle too."

"Let me make sure I'm understanding this," Emma says. "You could, in theory, convince a judge that you meet every single requirement for asylum, but then still have it denied if you file it even one day after the deadline? And then the judge will send you back to a country where he himself believes you'll be killed?"

"Unless you meet one of the limited exceptions, then yes, that's true," Todd says.

"So that's it then, right?" Emma says, in desperation. "It's over."

"No," Todd says. "If we lose those arguments, then we can still argue for a variation of asylum called withholding of removal."

"What's the difference?" Emma asks.

"It has a lot of the same basic requirements," Todd says. "We still have to show the harm Fredy would face would be because of a protected ground."

"So the 'particular social group' you said, right?" Emma asks. "What does that even mean? Like a member of a club or something?"

"No," Todd says. "It's actually one of the most complicated areas of asylum law. I'm still trying to wrap my brain around it myself. Apparently, it has to be some well-defined, recognizable group of people who share some common characteristic that they can't or shouldn't have to change."

"I can't even think of what that would mean," Emma says.

"I know, it's super complicated," Todd says. "But then you've got all these thousands of unrepresented people seeking asylum at the border who are supposed to be able to recognize their membership in one of these groups, and all the while, lawyers and judges and the government can't agree on what that even means."

Emma sits quietly, unable to think of even a single particular social group based on Todd's description, much less one that would apply to Fredy.

"But there have been at least a couple of times where everyone has been on the same page on what could qualify as a particular social group," Todd continues. "The most recent one I can think of was in certain cases of extreme domestic violence. The Department of Homeland Security agreed with the argument that one particular social group could be defined as 'married women in Guatemala who are unable to leave their relationship,' and the Board of Immigration Appeals accepted that agreement."

"Okay, wait," Emma interrupts, still confused. "Walk me through that group again."

"No problem, it's a mouthful," Todd says. "So there are certain women in Guatemala, and other countries too, who are married in relationships they can't get out of without risking their lives. They make up a well-defined *group* of sorts, with the immutable characteristics of being women and being in a relationship they can't leave. That's something they can't change about themselves. They're recognized by their community as members of this group and are considered property of their spouses. Even the police treat any complaints of horrific domestic violence as 'family matters' that they won't get involved with. So it meets the general requirements of a particular social group, which is presumably why even the Department of Homeland Security accepted it as such."

"That's awesome that everyone could agree that our asylum laws can at least protect those poor women," Emma says with a sweet smile, forgetting for a moment her growing skepticism towards Fredy's case.

"You're not gonna like the next chapter in this story though," Todd says.

"Oh no," Emma says, her smile collapsing. "What?"

"This comes from another troubling part of our immigration laws," Todd says. "Our politically-appointed attorneys general can refer *any* specific immigration case to themselves and then impose a binding decision on the whole country with their own personal interpretation of our immigration laws. They can change the law overnight, or at least the interpretation of the law. I think it was just last week that Sessions did that on an asylum case, where he reversed the domestic violence protections that everyone had agreed on."

"Are you serious?" Emma says. "That's awful. So what's going to happen to all of those women now?"

"They'll probably be deported right back into those situations they were fleeing from," Todd says. "But the reason I wanted to bring up this decision from Sessions is because I think it just made Fredy's very difficult case even more so. Even though that case was based on domestic violence, Sessions went out of his way to simply state in his decision that most asylum cases involving *gang violence* should also be denied."

"So was all my research for nothing then?" Emma asks in frustration.

"No," Todd says. "I don't think so. Even Sessions said that there would still be some *exceptional circumstances* where people could still get asylum based on feared persecution from gangs or other criminal organizations."

"What kind of exceptional circumstances?" Emma asks.

"I don't know yet," Todd admits. "That's what I've been trying to figure out. I'd like to think that the murder of Fredy's sister would be exceptional circumstances, but I can't get any specifics from anyone. Sarah got me a copy of a vague death certificate confirming it was a homicide, but nothing more. Fredy's dad died before it even happened, his mom died last year, and the family has lost all contact with his sister's husband, so that's all we've got. Sarah doesn't even know the specifics after all these years, and just keeps telling me that Fredy 'doesn't talk about that.' I've tried talking to Fredy a couple of times about it, but he shuts me down pretty quick."

"So how are we supposed to show that Fredy's case is any different than any other person who may be deported?" Emma asks. "Obviously these immigration judges aren't going to grant asylum to every Mexican who applies. They deny most of them as it is."

"I don't know," Todd says with a frown that he quickly buries under a forced smile in an effort to restore Emma's hope. "But seriously, all this evidence of the country conditions you got me will help a lot. It will paint a very helpful picture of what is waiting for Fredy in Mexico. Sarah and Lori have also brought me a ton of other evidence to prove the very strong ties he has to the United States, and how he would stand out so much in Guerrero."

"But we'd have to show he's a member of some particular social group, right?" Emma asks. "What would his particular social group be? And what extraordinary circumstances can we show without knowing the circumstances?"

Todd sits pensively for an extended moment.

"I don't know," he says.

He looks over his shoulder and confirms that the lunch rush has ended.

"Do you wanna get something to eat now?" he asks.

"I'm not hungry," Emma say.

"Me neither," Todd says.

CHAPTER 23

DAY 119

Wednesday, June 27, 2018

TODD IS WALKING THROUGH THE LOBBY TOWARDS THE EXIT OF THE BUILDING SHARED BY THE IMMIGRATION COURT AND ICE AND ITS ATTORNEYS. He's just finished what has become for him a relatively straightforward master calendar hearing for the filing of another application for relief from removal. Unlike Fredy, this particular client actually *was* charged, and ultimately convicted, of a DUI this year, in addition to a recent class B misdemeanor retail theft. But also unlike Fredy, under the law this client was eligible to be released on a bond and to apply for cancellation of removal, which application Todd just filed. Because of the ongoing backlog in immigration court, this new client's final merits hearing was just scheduled for October 7, 2019, almost a year and a half from now. Todd has learned that several other immigration courts throughout the country are taking significantly longer than that, despite Attorney General Jeff Sessions' recent imposition of case quotas on immigration judges.

Having finished all the work he planned to do for other clients today, Todd's thoughts naturally turn to Fredy, whose hearing is scheduled for tomorrow afternoon. Todd immediately feels the familiar burden of the pressure from all of the people depending on him to save Fredy. He wonders if he's really done all that he can at this point. Last week, he filed all of the evidence he and Emma had gathered together, plus a legal brief he'd prepared outlining most of the legal issues. But without the knowledge of the details of Fredy's sister's death, he's been unable to identify Fredy's particular social group or the extraordinary circumstances that would justify approval of his case. He wonders again if Fredy would have been better off finding someone else to take his case.

As Todd exits the building into the hot summer air, his attention turns abruptly to the sound of a small group of protestors on the sidewalk running between the street and the large black metal security gates of the immigration court. Rather than turning left towards his parked car, he turns right and slowly walks in the direction of the small group to get a closer look. He stops as soon as he's close enough to read some of their signs. The informal feel of the group and the absence of the typical unified chants lead Todd to assume this is more of an impromptu gathering than an organized political protest. Just a small group of regular people unhappy with what's happening and wanting to at least do something to feel heard.

Some signs and sporadic individual chants are pleading for the government to keep families together, while others are calling for the complete abolishment of ICE. But one sign in particular stands out to Todd: "We Care And We're Everywhere!" It feels to Todd almost as if it were a message prepared specifically for him, as he has found himself wondering more and more just how much anyone actually cares about what some U.S. immigration laws are doing to people. While recognizing that this small group will make no meaningful impact on the ICE officers or immigration judges inside the building, they've made an immediate impact on him. He feels a renewed sense of hope and validation that what he's doing matters.

Todd smiles and waves to the group before turning around to walk towards his parked car. He stops abruptly at the sound of a familiar voice coming from the crowd.

"Hey, Todd! Is that you?"

Todd turns around and begins to walk towards a woman waving at him. He shades his eyes and squints as he continues walking. He is surprised to finally recognize the woman.

Todd laughs. "Lori?" he says as he continues walking towards her. "What are you doing here? Did you set all of this up?"

"Yeah," she says with a smile, putting down her sign for the moment. "Maybe a last-ditch effort, I guess, with Fredy's hearing tomorrow, but I couldn't just keep sitting around doing nothing. I figured with all the national outrage about the families being separated at the border that I could take advantage of that before everyone goes back to not caring."

After Attorney General Sessions announced his zero-tolerance policy two months ago, thousands of people detained while attempting to cross the southern border have been held for prosecution prior to any immigration action or enforcement. Even first-time offenders who could be charged with nothing more than a misdemeanor offense were detained. This was an abrupt change from the policies of prior administrations of selectively prosecuting and not detaining people charged with non-violent misdemeanor offenses. More significantly, this change did not make exceptions for those people who entered the United States with their children.

Within a short time of this new policy, well over a thousand children were separated from their parents. Widespread public outrage followed as images and audio of children crying for their parents were distributed through all forms of the media. Reports followed of lost children and parents deported prior to family re-unification. It was no surprise to Todd that there were still plenty of people dismissing the crisis as a media exaggeration, or nothing that prior administrations did not also do on some level. But he has been pleasantly surprised to see how many people were not persuaded by these arguments and justifications.

Sessions himself invoked the Bible to support his actions, calling upon the words of the Apostle Paul and his "clear and wise command in Romans 13, to obey the laws of the government because God has ordained the government for his purposes." Some critics argued the scripture was taken out of context. Others noted that the same scripture was cited in the past by loyalists to the crown who opposed the American Revolution, and subsequently by Southerners defending slavery. What's more, many churches and religious leaders, including Pope Francis, rejected this scriptural justification and strongly criticized the family separations. Todd was particularly encouraged last week when his own church issued a public statement reiterating its belief "that immigration reform should strengthen families and keep them together" and strongly condemning the "aggressive and insensitive treatment of these families" at the border. He went out of his way to bring up the statement during conversations with other members of his faith, and posted about it heavily on his social media accounts.

For his part, President Trump argued that his hands were tied by laws he attributed to the Democratic Party, and he urged them to change them so the families would not be separated. *There's nothing I can do,* he argued. However, Trump ultimately gave in to the mounting political pressure and signed an order last week preventing the separation of *future* families detained at the border. But as of today, thousands of children remain separated from their parents, and Todd has his doubts about whether Trump's proposed alternative of prolonged family detention would be practical or legal. Nationwide protests continue, including this relatively small one outside of the immigration court in West Valley City, Utah.

While the large-scale family separation at the border sparking this nationwide outrage is relatively new, families like Fredy's have been separated for decades now, through detention and deportation. Todd can't help but wonder how sustainable the current movement will be when (or if) families detained at the border are no longer separated. Will thousands and thousands more families continue to be *permanently* separated through the immigration courts without any meaningful opposition? Pushing aside his justifiable skepticism for the future, Todd returns his focus to the optimism of the present. Right now, in this moment, people are coming together to show that they care, and that they're everywhere, even in a small town in one of the most conservative states in the nation.

"This is so awesome, Lori," Todd says after she finishes describing her online efforts to gather this group of mostly strangers. "And who's this little revolutionist you brought with you?" Todd asks, pointing to the young boy standing behind her.

Lori turns and puts her arm around her son, bringing him forward next to her.

"This is my son, Ethan," she says. "My husband has the day off but he said he had some errands or something, so I brought my little partner in crime with me."

"Well, it's nice to meet you," Todd says, looking down at Ethan and extending his hand, which Ethan accepts and shakes lightly with a nervous smile. "Do you guys have an extra sign?" Todd asks, turning back to Lori.

"You can have mine," Lori says with a smile.

Todd reaches for Lori's sign but is startled by a sudden outburst from another member of the protest.

"Quit your job, Nazi!" yells a man holding a sign saying "CRUSH ICE," as an ICE officer leaves the building towards the parking lot. "How'd you like us to cage *your* kids, you animal?!"

A few others in the crowd begin booing and heckling the lone officer as he continues walking.

"Should I be worried about them sicking the police dogs on us?" Todd asks, turning back to Lori with a half-smile. "Because this is my only good suit."

"Maybe," Lori says, laughing. "We have a few *enthusiastic* supporters of the cause here. But what do they say—beggars can't be choosers, right? I'm not one to discriminate."

Todd smiles and then turns his attention to the ICE officer, who's now almost out of his view. What do these people think would actually change if that ICE officer *did* quit his job? Todd wonders. He thinks of the reports he's seen announcing nationwide "Abolish ICE" protests planned for this Saturday. Congress can't even agree to pass the relatively uncontroversial DREAM Act. What makes anyone think they'd ever agree to completely dismantle an entire immigration enforcement agency? But what if they did? That wouldn't do anything to change the substance of the law. Congress would just create a new agency, perhaps with a friendlier-sounding acronym like ICE-*CREAM*, which agency would carry on the legacy of *the wrath of Ira.*

Todd certainly believes ICE is far from a perfect organization and in need of reform, but the root of the problem goes so much deeper. After two and a half years of working full-time in immigration law, Todd feels like he can barely understand it himself. How, then, can he expect a nation of generally well-intentioned people on both sides of this complicated issue to understand the problem, much less settle on a viable solution?

...

Fredy walks past a guard through a door that quickly closes behind him into the room reserved for personal video visits. He hasn't been here since Sarah's visit to the jail more than three and half months ago, after which they decided to opt for the more convenient at-home video visits or phone calls. His visits with Todd have always been in a much more personal setting, where they can actually see each other on just the other side of a glass window. As Fredy appears to speculate on who could be visiting him, his expression of puzzlement is quickly replaced with one of happy surprise after looking closely at the image on the small television screen in front of him.

"Greg?" Fredy says with a tone matching his expression of

surprise after picking up the phone. "Is that you?"

"Yeah, it's me, Fredy," Greg says. "How are you doing?"

Greg immediately regrets the question in light of the circumstances, but Fredy responds casually.

"A little better now," he says. "It's good to see you. You look good on television."

"You too," Greg says, laughing shortly.

Neither of the men seem to know what to say next. For the past several weeks, during the sporadic, passing quiet moments between his busy work and family schedule, Greg's thoughts have consistently drifted to Fredy. Despite initially making light of his wife's offer for them to sponsor him, Greg was discouraged to later learn that wouldn't be possible. His discouragement only increased as more and more time passed with Fredy in jail for reasons he still can't fully understand. He knows Fredy is a good and honorable man, and he doesn't doubt he made sincere efforts to make things right with the law as an adult. He has also met with Todd and is confident in his ongoing efforts to do the same. So why is Fredy still in jail? There must be more to Fredy's story, Greg continuously finds himself thinking. Motivated by a desire to comfort both a friend and his own conscious, Greg has wanted to visit Fredy for weeks. Although he remains convinced that the law will sort things out in an ultimately fair way, he can't help but think that today, the day before Fredy's final hearing, may be his last chance to visit him.

"So I've been wanting to come down here for a while," Greg says in an effort to break the uncomfortable silence. "I even stopped by the jail a few weeks ago when I had to come up to Logan for work, but they got so many government hoops you gotta jump through for these jail visits. I had to fill out some online application and wait for it to be approved, and—"

"Don't worry about it," Fredy interrupts. "How are Lori and Ethan doing?"

"Great," Greg says enthusiastically, happy to have the

conversation directed to a less awkward topic. "Ethan just finished school for the year, so he's excited about summer. Lori's supposed to be planning some family trip for next month, but she hasn't filled me in on the details yet."

"You're just along for the ride, I take it," Fredy says with a smile. "That sounds familiar."

"Exactly," Greg says, laughing. "I just go where she tells me when she tells me and smile when she says there's some camera pointed at us. Rockin' the boat usually just gets me kicked out of the boat, so like you said, I just go along for the ride."

Fredy laughs. "That's great," he says. "I'm sure you'll all have a great time."

"Yeah," Greg says, smiling sadly as his thoughts return to Fredy's uncertain future. He looks downward, then back at Fredy, then down again, as if searching for the right thing to say next. He finds nothing, and his discomfort increases with each passing second of silence. Perhaps sensing as much, Fredy continues.

"So, have you seen much of Sarah and the kids?" he asks.

"Yeah," Greg says, looking back at Fredy. "Well, not as much as Lori, obviously, but I still probably see them once or twice a week when I'm not on the road for work."

"How do they seem to be doing?" Fredy asks. "We talk pretty much every day, but it's hard to get a good read on everyone without being there in person. Sarah was really worried about Oscar for a while, but lately I feel like she's holding stuff back from me since there's not much I can do to help right now. Do they seem to be all right?"

"Oh, yeah," Greg says reassuringly. "They're doing fine. I mean, obviously they want you home as soon as possible, and it's been tough, but they're doing okay from what I can tell. Nothing that you need to be worried about. Plus, you'll be getting out of here soon anyway, with your hearing tomorrow. It seems like you've got a good, honest lawyer, so pretty soon everything will be back to normal."

"Yeah, I've been praying every day for things work out, and I feel peaceful about it all," Fredy says.

"Oh, me too, me too," Greg says.

"You?" Fredy says, in disbelief. "Praying?"

"Well, you know what I mean," Greg says. "Just thinking good thoughts or sending positive vibes or whatever. But I feel the same, um, same *peace* about it all."

"Thanks," Fredy says.

A brief pause follows, which Greg abruptly ends after settling on an opening question intended to steer the conversation to answers to some of his many questions.

"So, how's jail?" he says awkwardly.

"It's awesome," Fredy says sarcastically with a laugh.

Greg laughs nervously. "Sorry," he says. "Obviously it's not *good*. But, I mean, is anyone giving you any problems or anything?"

"No," Fredy says. "No real problems like that. Nothing like you see in some of the movies, but it's hard being away from my family for so long."

"How are your roommates or whatever?" Greg asks. "Or do you have roommates? I don't really know how it works, I guess."

"Yeah," Fredy says. "I had my first cellmate for a few weeks. But since then, they've been moving everyone out pretty quick and transferring them to Nevada or Colorado. I'm usually not with the same person for more than a few days or so, so it's hard to really get to know anyone. Most of the time it's just me and one other person since we only got two beds to a cell, but sometimes we get too full, so we have someone sleeping on the floor for a night or two."

"What are they like?" Greg asks, feeling encouraged by Fredy's willingness to answer his questions. "I keep thinking how they must have you locked up with a bunch of serious criminals."

"They're all different," Fredy says. "Some were picked up by ICE after getting convicted for DUIs or assault. Some came here after long prison sentences for much worse stuff like you might expect.

But there's been plenty of people with clean records too who were just in the wrong place at the wrong time. I met one guy who had no criminal history at all, who got arrested at an immigration interview he went to after his U.S. citizen wife filed a petition for him."

"Wait, what?" Greg says in disbelief. "So he was actually trying to *fix* his status and they arrested him? Why?"

"I don't know all the details," Fredy says. "He wasn't here with me long, but he told me he missed some hearing when he was a kid back in the 90s and so he got ordered deported. His mom was supposed to go to court with him, but I guess it didn't matter that it was her fault. So he had that old deportation order on his record and immigration scheduled an interview for him as a trap or something so they could just arrest him and deport him."

"So he's been deported already?" Greg asks. "Even though he has a U.S. citizen wife?"

"Yeah, and some kids too," Fredy says, shaking his head. "And since he had that old deportation order, he didn't even get to see a judge. They deported him within just a couple of days."

Greg sits pensively in silence before responding.

"I guess this just isn't how I thought the system worked," he finally says. "And not the types of people I assumed would be impacted. I mean, I've known you a long time, Fredy, and you've heard all my political rants on immigration and stuff like that. All my *solutions* for what to do with all those *illegals* and *aliens*, but I never had you in my mind, Fredy. I didn't know—I never would've thought in a million years that—"

"I know, I know," Fredy interrupts. "Don't worry about it. I always knew your intent."

"What do you mean my intent?" Greg asks, thinking to himself that Fredy surely must *not* have known his intent if he feels as if that somehow softened his past arguments.

"It's not that hard to get what someone means if you actually listen to them and try to understand them," Fredy says. "That's more important, I think, than the words they use to say it. I always knew what you were trying to say, even though I probably would've said it different and didn't always agree with your solutions. I get it. People want to feel safe and want to live in a country with law and order and want to know who's in their country. They want to make sure there are enough good-paying jobs, and that everyone is paying taxes and all of that. I've never had a problem with those arguments. That's not what feels dehumanizing to me."

"Then what is it?" Greg asks, genuinely interested in Fredy's response.

"I guess it's just this feeling I get that I'm not even an individual person to some people," Fredy says. "I don't necessarily care about being called an *alien* or an *illegal* or whatever. What's always bothered me is this false idea that we're all the same. That we all look, act, and think exactly the same. So it doesn't matter what I do or say or think as an individual anymore, because I'm not really an individual at all. I'm just a part of the problem, like some kind of virus or something, instead of a person. I mean, how I got to this country is such a small part of who I am. Most people didn't even know that about me, and a lot of the time I almost forget about it—at least until I got here. But when it comes to politics and the law, it's like it's the *only* thing that matters about me anymore, and the only thing people have to know about me to sum me up as a person."

Greg looks down below the screen in front of him and frowns. While Fredy may not include Greg among those dismissing the individuality of millions of people, Greg feels that's where he belongs. Or at least where he *belonged*. He's not as quick as Fredy to forgive his prior generalizations as well-intentioned. He's grateful for this new perspective Fredy is giving him, but at the same time almost resents him somehow for leaving him no clear idea of the right thing to do. This pushes his thoughts back to those Greg views as the original culprits, Fredy's parents.

"I hope this isn't too personal of a question," Greg says sheepishly, "but do you know why your parents didn't just do things the right way before coming? I mean, I'm sure it would've taken a little longer and cost more money, but you wouldn't be in this mess now, at least."

Fredy pauses for a moment, leaving Greg concerned that he may have taken his desire for answers too far. He feels a sense of relief when Fredy answers the question without any indication of offense.

"I asked my parents about that a few times before they died," he says. "Especially once it really started to affect my life when I was trying to get better jobs or apply to college. They'd always just say they couldn't come legally. I could never really get much more out of them than that, and it seemed to me that's all they knew, that we couldn't come here legally for some reason."

Greg feels unconvinced, suspicious even. Encouraged by Fredy's apparent willingness to share these personal details of his past, Greg continues his soft interrogation.

"So did they actually look into it then?" he asks. "Or it was just too hard to do it all legally?"

"I don't know exactly," Fredy admits. "But I think they looked into it. I've talked to my lawyer a lot about this kinda stuff. To figure out what we all could've done different, and what we can do now to fix it. He said that everyone thinks it's just a matter of filling out some paperwork and waiting your turn, but I guess it's not that simple."

"So what are you supposed to do then?" Greg asks.

"I mean, I'm not an expert on any of this," Fredy says. "But Todd said there's not just some single line that everybody waits in. There are multiple lines, and some move faster than others, but you have to qualify in the first place to get in one of those lines. Todd mostly does work for people who qualify based on family visas, but my family didn't have any U.S. citizen family members, so they couldn't get in any of those lines. But there are also different types of work visas you can get, but you need a sponsor for those too, I guess, and you need to show you have some special skill for some job that nobody here will take. Something like that. Todd says that most of his clients who are here illegally never qualified to immigrate legally, so it sounds like my parents were right, that they just *couldn't* come here legally in the first place."

Greg pauses for a moment, unsure of whether he should press the issue further but ultimately giving in to his curiosity.

"So why'd they come then?" Greg asks. "I mean, I don't want to come off like I'm attacking your parents or anything, but do you know why they decided to take that risk?"

"For us," Fredy says, followed by a brief pause. "They did it for me and my sister. My parents couldn't get much education growing up. They could barely even read. Same as their parents, and their grandparents, and who knows how far back it goes. They both had to start working when they were just kids still, which supposedly is illegal, but it still happened all the time in Mexico back then. I'm pretty sure it still happens today. So my parents always had to work, but never got any kind of education that could ever get them any decent work.

"I remember we were all living with my grandparents, one of my aunts, and her three kids. There were ten of us altogether, in a two-bedroom house without running water. We'd have to actually go to a well to get water to drink and clean with, and we shared a latrine with our neighbors. I don't remember thinking anything about it at the time; it just seemed normal to me. But then my mom got hurt on the job and they fired her. Up until that point we'd been able to stay in school, but once my mom lost her job, we knew pretty quick we weren't going to be able to make it in Mexico unless Veronica and I quit school and started working. My parents refused to let us do that. They wanted to break the Gonzalez family cycle I guess, so that we could have a better future than they did, and so that our kids would have it even better."

Greg finds himself reflecting upon his own childhood, moments when he felt growing up that he didn't have as much as some of the other kids at his school. Even with much more than the basic necessities of life in the wealthiest country in the world, Greg resented his parents at times for not always providing him the newest and trendiest clothes, toys, and *things* in his youth. Although he long ago recognized his childhood feelings of entitlement as petty, they feel more so now, after hearing Fredy's watered-down version of what Greg has no doubt remains commonplace for children throughout the world.

"And there was really no other way for your parents to just apply for a visa?" Greg asks in a final attempt to elicit the type of answer he both wanted and expected.

"I guess not," Fredy says. "We didn't exactly look like the type of people that would do this country any good."

Fredy's response triggers even more uncomfortable self-reflection for Greg. He knows he would have never supported allowing immigrants he perceived would be nothing more than an immediate drain on resources and government assistance. But as a father, he also knows he would've done the same thing Fredy's dad did were their roles reversed.

"But," Fredy says emphatically, "my dad provided for us here. He worked almost every day, it seemed like, and rarely got all the overtime pay he earned. But it was enough for us. We weren't rich by any means, but we always had enough without any help from the government or from anyone else. Which just makes me feel like a failure now."

"Why?" Greg says in genuine surprise.

As far as Greg can tell, Fredy is a success story. Far from a millionaire, but from where Fredy started, Greg struggles to see how he could view himself as a failure.

"After all my dad did for me," Fredy explains, "all the opportunities he gave me that he never had, I haven't been able to do the same for my own family."

"What are you talking about?" Greg asks, feeling almost offended somehow by the suggestion. "You've done so much for your family."

Fredy shakes his head. "Not enough though," he says. "All it took was a few months of me in here, and my family had to turn to government aid and help from our church to get by. My dad never had to do that, and never would've either. It almost makes it feel like it was all for nothing."

"Well, that's not your fault," Greg says emphatically. "If you were still at home right now, I'm sure that wouldn't have happened. And once you're back, everything will just go back to normal."

"But it *is* my fault," Fred insists. "Half of my problems now are because *I* made the decision more than twenty years ago to steal something. I don't know if Lori or Sarah told you, but I got cited for shoplifting when I was eighteen, which is why I haven't been able to get a bond. That was *my* decision, and as much as I've tried to minimize it now, there was no excuse for that. And now my family's paying the price for it."

Greg is surprised. Only partially by Fredy's admission of a crime, but more by the impact it has had so many years later. Greg thinks back on his own youthful indiscretions. *What if my family were impacted like this because of all the dumb stuff I did as a kid?* Greg wonders. But why should all of that matter now? Obviously that says nothing about who Fredy is today. Greg now feels he has a better grasp of the facts, which has strengthened his confidence that everything will get straightened out tomorrow. He has now passed the point of reconciling his former political opinions with the reality before him, and he feels a greater sense of clarity.

"All right, this is all just stupid," he says, shaking his head. "None of this is important. What matters is who you are *today*, and all the good you've done in this country. It's not as quick and easy of a fix as I assumed, but Sarah and Lori and Todd have been working like dogs on this for months now, and they've presented as compelling of a case as I think you could ever see. Lori even got the media involved in this. They got all kinds of evidence of all the good you've done for your family and everyone around you. And tomorrow, the judge is going to have to look you in the eye, face to face, after seeing all of that, and he'll make the right decision—the *only* decision that makes any sense."

Fredy smiles. "Thanks, Greg," he says. "To tell you the truth, I've been feeling some doubts today. I'm really glad you came."

"Of course, buddy," Greg says. "We're all here for you. I'm not sure I'll be able to be there tomorrow though, with work and everything, but—"

"Don't worry about it," Fredy interrupts. "Sarah will be there with the kids, so I'll be fine. I'll see you again soon."

"Barbecue this weekend?" Greg asks as he stands up from his seat, getting ready to end the call.

"You got it," Fredy says with a smile. "I'll have Sarah make her *in*famous potato salad."

CHAPTER 24

DAY 120

Thursday, June 28, 2018

FREDY IS SITTING AT THE DESK RESERVED FOR ALIENS IN FRONT OF AN EMPTY JUDGE BENCH. ICE Officer McAllister is the only other person in the courtroom. Fredy looks up at the circular wall clock. It's now 7:46 am. He looks behind him to the empty gallery and frowns. They said they would be here fifteen minutes early. They're late. He's reminded of his first hearing, when the gallery was filled with thirty-two other aliens but he felt equally alone, without an attorney or any supporting family or friends.

"They'll be here," he says quietly to himself before turning back to the front of the room.

Officer McAllister has already uncuffed Fredy's right hand, leaving the other cuffed to the chain around his waist. He uses his free hand to support his head as he leans forward on the desk, but then he turns back abruptly at the sound of people walking into the courtroom. He sees Todd carrying three very large files, and a woman he doesn't recognize, but no one else.

"Hey, Fredy," Todd says. "Sorry I'm a little later than I said I would be."

"I didn't notice," Fredy lies with a smile.

"This is my wife, Julie," Todd says, looking back to Julie.

"Oh, it's so nice to meet you," Fredy says, standing.

"So you're that handsome fellow my husband has been running around with behind my back late at night for the past few months," she says with a lighthearted grin.

"I guess so," Fredy says, playing along. "Don't tell my wife though; she'll be here soon. Did you see her out there? She said she'd try to bring the kids this time."

"No, I didn't see her," Todd says, looking back towards the open door to the courtroom. "But I'm sure she's on her way. Sometimes it can take a while to get through security."

Todd directs his wife to take a seat in the empty front row of the gallery and opens the wooden gate to go sit next to Fredy. They spend the next few minutes talking about what to expect at this last hearing until they hear the government attorney walk in. Jonathan Richter has been assigned to the case, triggering unpleasant flashbacks to Fredy's first hearing without an attorney. But now he has Todd. *Todd will know what to say and what to do*, Fredy reassures himself. While Todd and the government attorney discuss the intended format of the hearing, Fredy checks the time again. It's now 8:01 am. He looks to the gallery behind him and exchanges a short smile with Julie as the judge walks into the courtroom. Although there is no clerk in the courtroom to instruct everyone to rise upon his entry, both attorneys do so intuitively, prompting Fredy to do the same. Julie stays seated with a defiant smile, in her small personal protest against the judge who has been responsible for many of her husband's multi-weekly rantings and ravings.

"Good morning," the judge says. "It looks like you didn't get the memo. We've moved these proceedings to Courtroom 3 so we can have enough room for everyone. I'll meet you over there," the judge says before walking out the back door without saying more.

"Are there any other hearings today?" Todd asks Mr. Richter.

"I didn't think so," Mr. Richter says. "At least not with Lanzotti this morning."

Officer McAllister walks over to Fredy to escort him over to Courtroom 3, and the others follow closely behind. Fredy can hear the increasing sound of quiet conversations as they walk towards an open doorway. Upon entering, a large crowd of people instinctively rise to their feet at the sight of Fredy, causing a wave of emotion to completely engulf and overpower him. His eyes scan the crowd until finding his wife, who is holding Veronica. Oscar and Katie stand on the bench to get a better view of Daddy, whom they start calling for until Sarah instructs them to be quiet. Beyond his wife and kids, he sees Lori and Greg with their son, Ethan, followed by several other kids from his soccer team and their parents. He sees Emma, who came with Todd on one of his visits to the jail. He sees dear friends from church—from the missionaries who baptized him, to his current and former bishops and their wives, to Brother Moore from the jail church services. He sees his brother- and sister-in-law from California with their son. He sees several of his former co-workers. Fredy smiles and begins to softly weep as Officer McAllister escorts him past his dearest friends and family, just out of his reach.

"Thank you," he says somberly to the crowd. "Thank you."

He takes a seat at the desk reserved for aliens, and Todd sits down next to him, smiling as he puts his hand gently on Fredy's shoulder.

"You did this, didn't you?" Fredy asks Todd.

"You did it, Fredy," Todd says. "You impacted all of these lives, leaving them with no option but to do whatever it took to be here for you now."

"You may be seated," the judge says to the crowd, as if they had stood on his account.

The crowd sits down as the judge removes the large rubber bands from the three overflowing files now dedicated to Fredy's case. After organizing his desk, he starts the recording of the proceedings and begins his standard introduction. He then acknowledges the numerous filings Todd has made since the last hearing, including evidence and written arguments.

"Any objection that these documents be added to the record of proceedings?" the judge asks Mr. Richter after briefly describing the filings.

"Just a few, Your Honor," Mr. Richter says.

Todd looks over abruptly at Mr. Richter with a look of disdain and confusion. *What objection could he possibly have?* he wonders. By this point, Todd has practically memorized the Immigration Court Practice Manual. His filing is timely, paginated, has the required certificates of services, proposed orders, and so on.

"Mr. Gonzalez is only eligible for withholding of removal or protection under the Convention Against Torture," Mr. Richter continues. "He must show that it is sufficiently likely that he would be persecuted on a protected ground, or tortured—"

"I'm quite familiar with the requirements, Mr. Richter," the judge interrupts. "Where are you going with this?"

"Well, Judge," Mr. Richter says, "the respondent has submitted over two hundred pages of documents that are completely irrelevant to the relief he actually qualifies for. This is not an application for cancellation of removal or for lawful permanent residency. I understand he's still arguing he doesn't have an aggravated felony, and that he's eligible for asylum, but this evidence is irrelevant for asylum too. He's submitted over twenty years' worth of taxes, birth certificates for his U.S. citizen wife and kids, evidence of volunteer work, and a bunch of certificates and an honors diploma. And then he has over fifty character statements from friends, family, neighbors, church members, and co-workers. None of this is relevant to whether Mr. Gonzalez would be harmed in Mexico."

The judge frowns then turns to Todd.

"Do you have a response, Mr. Becker?" the judge asks.

"I certainly do, Your Honor," Todd says. "Mr. Gonzalez faces a greater risk than most native Mexicans precisely because of his extraordinarily strong ties to the United States, which this evidence supports. We have also submitted another two hundred pages' worth of country reports and travel warnings supporting our position that individuals like Mr. Gonzalez are more likely to be targeted because of their strong ties to the United States."

"That may be, Judge," Mr. Richter says interrupting. "But come one, let's be serious here. *Fifty* character statements? Volunteer work? That is not needed to show he has been in the United States for many years."

"Mr. Richter," the judge interrupts. "Your objection is overruled. I'm finding that all of the evidence is relevant to Mr. Gonzalez's applications for relief, particularly on any potential discretionary issues."

"Well, Judge," Mr. Richter continues, "the government would concede the issue of discretion if that makes a difference. This evidence is clearly designed to persuade this Court to feel sorry for Mr. Gonzalez just because—"

"Mr. Richter," the judge interrupts sternly, "I've heard enough. Your objection is overruled. If it makes you uncomfortable to have an extraordinarily clear picture of the kind of person your clients are attempting to remove from the United States, that is a personal problem that does not concern this Court. Furthermore, your suggestion that I am incapable of faithfully applying the law in this case because of the apparent good character of the respondent is troubling to this Court. I might advise you to exercise a little more restraint. Anything else, Mr. Richter?"

The judge's rebuke leaves Mr. Richter unable to immediately respond, an uncommon scene after more than ten years working as an attorney for the Department of Homeland Security. Todd doesn't even attempt to conceal his smile as a giddy spectator of the nerdiest brawl he's ever has the pleasure of witnessing.

"No, Judge," Mr. Richter ultimately says in an uncharacteristically timid tone. "Nothing else at this time."

"Mr. Becker," the judge says, turning back to Todd. "You have, in fact, submitted a substantial amount of evidence. I have reviewed it all carefully, in addition to your written arguments which I very much appreciate. Do you have anything else that you would like to submit before I issue my decision today?"

"Could I have one moment with my client, you honor?" Todd asks.

"Certainly," the judge says, turning to his computer equipment to stop the audio recording. "We're off the record."

Todd turns to Fredy and puts his arm around the back of his chair.

"All right, Fredy," Todd says quietly. "We have a ton of evidence already on the record. We can easily show that Guerrero is incredibly dangerous, and that you don't have the resources to be able to live anywhere else. We have your sister's death certificate, but it's very vague. We don't have anything giving the details about what actually happened. I tried as much as possible to not have to require you to testify about all that, and you still don't *have to*, but I really think that's our best chance of you being able to win this case."

"Even with all that evidence?" Fredy asks, looking back at the judge's desk. "He has three huge files of evidence. Is that really not enough?"

"I don't think so, Fredy," Todd says. "That evidence is not enough to show that you *specifically* would be at a heightened risk in Mexico. Your sister gives the judge a real-life example of exactly what you fear in Mexico."

Fredy sits in silence for a moment. He hasn't even told his wife the details about what happened to Veronica. He turns to the gallery full of family and friends. The reservations he had about testifying just a moment ago are instantly buried under feelings of confidence and strength from the love and support behind each of those faces. Motivated in varying degrees by a combination of these emotions, Fredy takes a bold and defiant stand.

"I guess I'll see what I can do," he says.

Todd notifies the judge that they are ready to go back on the record and that Fredy will be testifying. The judge instructs Fredy to take a seat at the witness stand next to an empty desk at the front of the courtroom typically reserved for the Spanish interpreter. Before sitting, the judge instructs him to raise his right hand to take an oath to testify truthfully. With the judge's permission, Todd begins with a number of preliminary questions about Fredy's entry to the United States, his school and work history, and his family and community ties. Fredy testifies that he didn't know about the requirement to file an asylum application within one year of his return to the United States, and he explains that he didn't contact an attorney because of his prior bad experiences with attorneys or notaries. Having thus set the stage, Todd asks Fredy to specifically describe his relationship with his older sister, Veronica. Fredy pauses for a moment and sighs heavily before responding.

"Veronica was my best friend," Fredy says. "She was my only sibling. We were already really close when we first came to the United States, but once we got here, we were all that we had. Nobody else knew what we were going through. It was an adjustment for our parents too, but we were living in a mostly Hispanic neighborhood, and my dad had a job in construction where pretty much everyone spoke Spanish. For my parents, it was almost like we were still in Mexico except that all of a sudden we had enough money to eat three meals a day and an apartment with running water. But for Veronica and me it was different. Very different."

"How was it different?" Todd asks.

"We were living in two different worlds," Fredy says. "During the day we were in a school where pretty much every face was white except ours, and we couldn't understand anything anyone was saying. I mean, we knew enough to know that the other kids were making fun of us, but it took months before we could understand enough to know exactly what they were saying about us. So we kept working harder and harder to not talk funny, but our parents kept trying to make us speak Spanish and hold on to our Mexican heritage at home. It was kinda like we were outcasts everywhere we went, even at home. I don't think I could've made it through those years without Veronica. She was always there, defending me against the kids at school and our family at home."

"Did you stay close after high school?" Todd asks.

"Oh yeah," Fredy says, nodding his head emphatically. "By that point, we were bonded for life."

"Can you tell us why she went back to Mexico?" Todd asks.

Fredy pauses before responding and looks down towards the floor. "She had to," he says.

"Why?" Todd asks.

"She married to this guy, Steve, who's a U.S. citizen," Fredy says. "He was a great guy. I really wish we hadn't lost contact. But they'd been married for a while, and they just kept putting off getting her papers fixed."

"Why did they put it off?" Todd asks.

"Because her attorney said that she had to go back to Mexico to finish the process, and that she had to get some forgiveness or something," Fredy says.

"A waiver?" Todd asks.

"Yeah, that's right, a waiver," Fredy says. "I guess she only needed the waiver if she *left* the U.S., but they told her she had to leave the U.S. to finish her process. I don't know exactly, it all never really made any sense to me. I think that's why she just kept putting it off, because she was scared to go back to Mexico and there was no guarantee that she'd be able to return or how long it would take. And then my wife and I hired someone here who said we could apply without leaving the U.S., so she wanted to wait to see how that turned out for us. But the person we hired was wrong, I guess, and my application was denied. After that, my sister's husband convinced her to leave, but he had to stay here to keep working. She went to her first interview at the U.S. embassy in Mexico, and then they said she had to make a second appointment to file her waiver application. So she did that, and then she was just waiting and waiting for a decision. She had already been waiting in Mexico for about four months when it happened."

"When what happened?" Todd asks.

Fredy sits silently, as if debating whether or not to continue. Todd, not daring to press him further just yet, patiently waits for a response. Even the judge is uncharacteristically patient, allowing almost a full minute of silence to pass without intervening. Finally, Fredy speaks.

"It was on March 1, 2013," Fredy says. "Veronica called me, but I was working so I couldn't take her call. She left a message, but I guess I forgot about it. I finished work late, so I just went straight to bed when I got home. It wasn't until the next morning that I remembered she had called me. So I just called her back instead of checking my voicemail, but it went straight to her voicemail. I left a message telling her I was just calling her back and to call me later that night if she wanted to talk. Then I decided to listen to her voicemail."

"What did it say?" Todd asks.

Fredy sits in silence, looking down now.

"I know this is hard, Fredy," Todd says. "Take all the time you need."

Fredy continues to sit in silence for a moment before responding.

"She was crying," Fredy says, his voice lowered as he is now softly crying himself.

"Why was she crying?" Todd asks.

Fredy wipes the tears from his face and takes in a deep breath before continuing.

"She said that some people had taken her, that they knew she had family in the U.S. who must have a lot of money. She said they were going to kill her if her family didn't send them money immediately. She was begging me to call her back."

"Did she say anything else?"

"Yes, but I didn't listen to it all that first time," Fredy says. "I disconnected from my voicemail and I called her again and again. I left messages saying I would help, that I would do whatever they wanted. Anything."

"Did she call you back?"

"No," Fredy says. "I never heard from her again."

"Why didn't you hear from her again?"

Fredy sits silently without responding.

"Fredy?" Todd says, as if to remind him of the question still unanswered.

"Because they killed her," Fredy says numbly, still looking downward. "I was too late. I couldn't save her. It was *my* fault. I should've answered my phone. I could've saved her, but I didn't. I know that she would've answered any time I ever called, no matter what she was doing. But I was *too busy* to be bothered while my sister was being murdered. While they were—"

Fredy pauses, tightly clenching his lips together as if some natural defense reflex is preventing him from continuing. He forces open his mouth, releasing a heavy sigh, and continues. "While they were hurting her," he says.

"I'm sorry, Fredy," Todd says. "I have to ask. How do you know they *hurt* her?"

"Because of the autopsy."

"What did the autopsy show?"

Fredy slowly lifts his head, making eye contact with Todd for the first time during the past several questions.

"Do I have to answer that?" Fredy asks timidly.

"No, Fredy," Todd says mercifully. "Not if you don't want to. Would you like to stop?"

Fredy considers the question at length. He turns to the faces filling the gallery behind his attorney. His thoughts turn immediately to his wife and children. He's sickened at the thought of potentially losing them because it was "too hard" for him to continue. But more than that, he feels strengthened by their love and support and the silent prayers he knows they must be offering on his behalf.

"Can someone please bring my kids out of the room?" Fredy asks, turning to the judge. "They don't need to hear any more of this."

The judge sits back and raises his eyebrows, apparently surprised by the request, but he agrees and calls for a short recess. Lori is standing and reaching for the hands of the children to walk them out to the lobby before Sarah even has time to think to ask. She closes the door behind her and the judge restarts the proceedings.

"Whenever you're ready, Fredy," Todd says.

Fredy pauses and takes a deep breath before responding.

"They raped her," Fredy finally says through gentle sobs, turning back to Todd. "All of them did. Again, and again, and again. And they didn't just rape her; they tortured her. They beat up and cut up her body. They used her to send a message to everyone else."

Fredy covers his face with his hands and drops his head down. Other than his now poorly restrained weeping, the courtroom is completely silent. Todd, processing the new information, stares blankly at Fredy, unsure of how to respond. It all feels so inhumane to him. He should be comforting Fredy right now. Instead, he is forcing him to publicly relive the most traumatic experiences of his life in some backwards effort to help himself now. But the law is the law, and the law has no emotion, so Todd knows he must continue and reluctantly does so.

"I am very sorry to continue to push you on this, Fredy," Todd says. "Obviously this is a very difficult thing to discuss. But what do you mean that they were trying to *send a message*? What message?"

"*Paguen la renta*," Fredy says.

Todd is surprised by the use of Spanish and its meaning at this point, but Fredy continues.

"The police found her head in a bag lying in the street with a note saying *paguen la renta*."

Todd pulls his head back abruptly in shock at Fredy's description, as if the harrowing image created in Todd's mind carried some physical force. Shaking off this initial impact, Todd's focus shifts back to Fredy's statement about the note left behind. "What does that mean?" he asks, wanting to make sure the Spanish is translated for the benefit of Judge Lanzotti.

"'Pay the rent,'" Fredy says, still sobbing. "The police couldn't find her actual body for a week. That's when they did the autopsy."

The pain accompanying Fredy's words is palpable to everyone in the room. Fredy turns to his wife, whose hand is still cupped over her mouth with tears freely falling down her face, having heard for the first time the details Fredy has kept to himself for so many years. He then turns back to Todd.

"No further questions," Todd says.

"Mr. Gonzalez," the judge says. "Would you like to take a break before I ask the government if they have any questions?"

"No, sir," Fredy says, taking in a deep breath, sitting upright, and straightening back his shoulders. "Let's just do it now."

"Mr. Richter," the judge says. "Any questions?"

"Just a few, Your Honor," Mr. Richter says. "Mr. Gonzalez, you said that the police discovered the body after your sister's death. Did they do an investigation?"

"They said they were going to, but we never heard anything more from them," Fredy says.

"Who ordered the autopsy?"

"I dunno," Fredy says coldly, avoiding eye contact with Mr. Richter and consciously providing as little information as possible in response to each of his questions.

"Do you think it was the police?"

"Maybe."

"Did you or anyone in your family make a request by phone or other means that an autopsy be done?"

"No."

"Then it's safe to assume that the police took that initiative, isn't it?"

"Yeah, I guess."

"And were *you* ever threatened or physically harmed while you were in Mexico?"

"No, but I was only there for about four months."

"No further questions."

"Any questions on redirect, Mr. Becker?" the judge asks, turning back to Todd.

"Just a couple, Your Honor," Todd says. "Fredy, other than possibly ordering an autopsy and filling out a report, are you aware of *anything* else that the police did in your sister's case?"

"Nothing," Fredy says. "Like I said, I was down in Mexico for four months, following up with the police and trying to help my mother. They just kept blowing us off, telling us to follow up in a few weeks, and then a few weeks more. They finally asked us to stop bugging them about it, and said they'd done all they could do and that we should just move on already."

"Okay, just one more question," Todd says. "How do you know they conducted an actual autopsy rather than just a visual examination of your sister?"

Fredy is somewhat surprised by the question, having never given the point much thought.

"I guess I don't," he says. "They never actually used that word themselves, and they told us their conclusions the same day that they found her body. So maybe they just did some visual examination of her and were able to tell what had happened to her. I really don't know. I just know that the whole supposed investigation seemed to come to a stop pretty quick."

"Thank you, Fredy," Todd says, almost apologetically. "That's all."

With the judge's permission, Fredy stands up and walks back to his seat next to Todd, forcing a slight smile as he makes eye contact with his wife. As Fredy sits down, he feels a strange sense of empowerment. He has completely exposed himself before everyone he cares about, and before a man who holds in his hands the fate of him and his family—and he survived. Regardless of the outcome, Fredy feels a comforting sense of assurance that he has given all that he has to give. Judge Lanzotti asks Todd if he would like to make any closing arguments, which he enthusiastically states that he would, but first he asks the judge, as requested by Fredy, if he could invite his children to return to the courtroom. The judge agrees and sends his clerk to find them in the lobby, where they are restlessly waiting with Lori. After they have taken their seats on the bench next to their mother, the judge invites Todd to make his closing arguments.

"Your Honor," Todd says. "Fredy is as American as any person born in this country. It was not his choice to come here, but it was his choice to embrace this country in every aspect of his life. He speaks better English than Spanish. He has a U.S. citizen wife and three beautiful U.S. citizen children. They are faithful members of an American-born religion. He is living the American dream. He has his own American business; he has paid all of his American taxes; and he is employing other American citizens even as he is supporting his own American family. The government is not trying to send him back to his country. The United States of America is *his* country. Mexico will be as foreign to him as it would be to you or me. Quite frankly, I find it incomprehensible that our government is spending thousands of dollars to deport someone who has done nothing but help this country."

With Todd's last statement, he can almost feel Mr. Richter's urge to object, which urge he ultimately ignores. Todd continues.

"The evidence before this Court paints a pretty clear picture about what Fredy can expect to find if he is deported to Mexico," Todd says. "He will be a completely obvious outsider in any community he goes to. He will be easily identified as one deported from the United States, and as such, a highly likely target for money, or 'rent.'

In fact—"

Todd stops abruptly as he remembers a part of Emma's summary of the country conditions at their last "Fredy meeting." He quickly opens Fredy's large file to the tab saving the place of the most recent Human Rights Report for Mexico, skimming through the portions Emma highlighted until he finds the portion he was looking for.

"I think it is highly relevant, Your Honor," Todd continues, "that our own Department of State has recognized that in Mexico just last year there were, quote, 'credible reports of *police* involvement in *kidnappings for ransom*,' end quote. It also states that the police acted, quote, '*in coordination with criminal organizations*, in *unlawful killings, disappearances*, and *torture*,' end quote. These country reports support the conclusion that the police's failure to actually investigate Veronica's kidnapping for ransom, torture, and unlawful killing may well have been because of their own involvement in the crime."

Emma sits up abruptly, seeming to glow with pride from Todd's inclusion of her contributions to Fredy's case.

"This Court doesn't have to look any further than Fredy's own family to know what is waiting for him," Todd continues as the missing pieces of Fredy's case seem to come together in his mind right when he needs them most. "Like his sister, Fredy is a member of a particular social group I would define as '*Mexicans whose nuclear family members are all U.S. citizens*.' They shared these common, immutable characteristics, which were easily recognizable in the community that recognized them as outsiders and perhaps even believed them to be U.S. citizens themselves, having lived virtually their entire lives in this country. *This* is why his sister was killed. The horrific abuse and murder of Fredy's sister, his dearest and closest friend, goes far beyond what is required to show persecution or even torture under the law. And this was followed by the complete lack of any meaningful investigation into a crime that would without question be a highly publicized national story if it had happened on *our* side of the line, to one of *our* people. But Veronica and Fredy are *our* people. The product of *our* schools, *our* churches, *our* communities, all of which benefited from *their* membership.

"Your Honor, I am not simply asking you to do the noble or compassionate or right thing for an at-risk immigrant seeking refuge within the borders of this great nation. I am asking you to do the selfish thing. We need and want people like Fredy in this country. It's not in our interest to give them away. We want to keep him for ourselves. And lucky for us, the evidence in this case would fully justify such a selfish decision under the immigration laws of this country. Thank you."

Todd feels an almost immediate release of the heavy emotional load he has been carrying ever since agreeing to take Fredy's case. He has given everything he feels he could have possibly given, and is almost surprised by how well it all seemed to come together in the end. He feels as if the hopes and prayers of the gallery full of people behind him has carried him further than he could have ever gone on his own. There is now nothing more he can do.

"Thank you, Mr. Becker," the judge says. "Mr. Richter, anything from the government?"

"Your Honor," Mr. Richter begins. "It's the Department's position that the asylum application is untimely, and that his theft conviction bars him from asylum, despite how old it is and the subsequent reduction. But even if he were not disqualified from asylum, he has not met his heavy burden of proof."

As Todd expected, Mr. Richter's arguments highlight the fact that even if Fredy meets some or most of the requirements for relief, unless he meets them all, the judge will have to order him removed from the United States.

"The respondent himself has never been the victim of any kind of persecution," Mr. Richter continues. "Even after at least four months in the same area of Guerrero where his sister was murdered—not so much as a threat. But even if he were to have issues in Guerrero in the future, he would not be *required* to live in that area.

Having some distant family members there may make that initially an *easier* option, but I don't think he's shown that it would be the *only* option. But even if that were the only option, the respondent's fears of persecution would not be based on any legitimate protected ground. It seems clear to me that the reason the respondent's sister was targeted was not to punish her for having U.S. citizen family or ties, but to get money. The message they sent with her death was not towards a particular social group, but rather to anyone debating whether or not to pay their extortion demands. Tragic as that may be, it's not enough to meet the respondent's burden.

"But even if this were a valid particular social group, and even if that were the reason his sister was targeted, and even if the same exact thing were to happen to the respondent, that would still not be enough. He has not shown that the persecution he fears would be at the hands of a government actor, or someone the government is unable or unwilling to stop. The Mexican government may be inefficient, and even corrupt in some cases, but even in the case of the respondent's sister, they attempted to investigate the incident and ordered an autopsy, or at least did some kind of examination. Now, maybe they didn't do as thorough of a job as they should have, but Mr. Becker's unsupported speculations that the police may have been involved somehow are completely inappropriate. The same country reports submitted by the respondent show that the Mexican government is making efforts to address their problems, and making progress in some areas.

"For these reasons, Your Honor, whatever unfortunate dangers may await the respondent in Mexico, our immigration laws do not provide him *any* option to stay here. And on that point the government rests."

CHAPTER 25

DAY 120

(continued)
Thursday, June 28, 2018

JUDGE LANZOTTI SITS IN SILENCE WITH A PENSIVE LOOK ON HIS FACE, SEEMING TO CAREFULLY TAKE IN ALL OF THE EVIDENCE, TESTIMONY, AND ARGUMENTS MADE FOR AND AGAINST FREDY. Todd studies his face and expressions in an unsuccessful search for any indication of what he may decide.

"This is a very difficult case for me," the judge finally says. "I would like to thank both parties for their excellent advocacy. As an initial matter, Mr. Gonzalez, I am finding that you testified credibly regarding your fears of returning to Mexico. In other words, I believe you. Your testimony was internally consistent and sufficiently corroborated by the evidence in the record. I am finding further that you testified credibly that you were unaware of the one-year filing deadline for asylum, that you were unaware asylum was even an option for you, and that you filed as soon as you knew that it was. But this does not, in the court's view, meet the requirement of changed circumstances that materially affect your eligibility for asylum. You certainly had a viable claim to pursue upon your return to the United States. However, you did not file your application until several years after your return. Unfortunately, the law does not permit me to consider your asylum application under these circumstances, no matter how viable your asylum claim may be. But even putting aside the one-year filing deadline, the record still suggests that your prior shoplifting offense is an aggravated felony, which would also disqualify you from asylum.

"But your prior conviction is certainly not a particularly serious crime, and so you remain eligible for either withholding of removal or relief under the Convention Against Torture. To that end, Mr. Gonzalez, I believe you have, in fact, established that there is a very real possibility that you will be harmed or even killed were you to return to your home in Mexico. *Home* may not be the best word, given the limited time you actually lived there. However—"

Todd feels as if his heart has stopped and dropped into his stomach at the sound of Judge Lanzotti's ominous *however*.

No, no, no, no, he mutters under his breath.

"However," the judge continues, "I am unable to find that this reasonable fear of persecution would be based on a protected ground, such as your race, religion, political opinion, or membership in a particular social group. I am sorry to say you have presented today what is an all-too-common case of a long-time resident of the United States returning to a dangerous country where you will likely be targeted by criminals as a source of potential wealth. The country conditions and the experiences of your own family confirm that this is a very real risk, perhaps even more likely than not. But persecution or even torture and death for the purpose of getting money is insufficient for withholding of removal. I'm afraid I must agree with the government that this would be the reason for any difficulties you may face, rather than your membership in a particular social group.

"Of course, for protection under the Convention Against Torture you need not show that the reason for your feared torture would be based on any protected group. Showing you would be *tortured*, even if the reason were just for money, would be enough to meet that requirement. However, you had to show that public officials in

Mexico would be the ones committing the torture, or that they would turn a blind eye to the same. You testified and submitted evidence of a number of problems with the police in Mexico with corruption and, in some cases, complicity with criminal organizations. However, the evidence is insufficient to establish that it would be more likely than not, *in your specific case*, that the authorities would torture you or turn a blind eye to any person or persons who may attempt to do so. And I would note that the country reports do indeed also indicate that the Mexican government is making some efforts to combat corruption and to enforce the law. Certainly they have a long way to go, and your return to Mexico will not be without great risk. But I simply cannot find that you have met your heavy burden of proof under the very high standards established by our nation's immigration laws."

A brief pause in the judge's oral decision, which has been amplified by the microphone on his desk, allows the sound of soft sobbing from the gallery to echo through the courtroom.

"I am very sorry, sir," the judge continues. "As an immigration judge, it is not my place to create or critique the law. I must apply it as written, even when I may be compelled to do otherwise. By all accounts, you appear to be an upstanding human being who has been an asset to your community. I would not hesitate to find that you warrant favorable discretion, if this case came down to an issue of discretion. But I am afraid that the law dictates that I must deny your applications."

Fredy turns back to Sarah, who is tightly holding their children, who he can hear asking Mommy what's happening and why she's crying. *Is this really happening?* Fredy wonders. *Is it really all over?* After nearly thirty years of building a family and a life and a future, somehow everything is taken away from him forever in an instant. Deep in the corner of his mind, buried under all of his faith and hope, there has always been a knowledge that this day might eventually come. Even before his arrest. But it was never a knowledge he was able or willing to confront seriously enough to even begin to answer all the *what ifs*. Now that's the only thing he can think of. His family is all that matters to him. It's all that has ever mattered to him, but he sees no possible way he could ever be any kind of meaningful husband or father to them now. His heart aches for them more than anything, leaving no room for even a passing thought or concern about the uncertainties of his own future in his foreign native country.

Todd has already explained to Fredy that because of his supposed false claim to U.S. citizenship to his first employer, he will never be able to legally immigrate to the United States. His strong family and community ties, his good character and community service, and the far-reaching void he will leave behind are completely irrelevant under the law.

"Does either party wish to reserve appeal?" the judge asks, wrapping up the proceedings with the final formalities.

"The government will waive appeal, Judge," Mr. Richter says.

Fredy's prior insistence that everything would somehow work out has made it difficult for Todd to have a detailed discussion about what he wanted to do if the judge denied his case. Todd doesn't have an answer, and wonders if Fredy doesn't either.

"Your Honor," he says, "May I have a moment to talk to my client before deciding?"

"Certainly, Mr. Becker," the judge says. "Will fifteen minutes be sufficient?"

"Yes, thank you," Todd says.

After pausing the audio recording of the hearing, the judge stands, stops his clerk from attempting to have everyone rise, and informs the parties that he'll be back in chambers for the next fifteen minutes. Mr. Richter stands up after the judge leaves, closes his file, and excuses himself to the restroom.

"I am so sorry, Fredy," Todd says.

"You have no reason to be sorry, Todd. I know you did your best. I don't think anyone could've done any better. Not even Mr. Shane

Radley. So I guess this is goodbye then."

Fredy's response startles Todd.

"No," Todd says, "not necessarily. We can appeal the judge's decision to the Board of Immigration Appeals and try to convince them to let you stay here."

Fredy looks down, snickers softly under his breath, and shakes his head with a sad smile. He turns back to the gallery of family and friends and then back to Todd.

"Maybe I should've been a little more specific with all of my praying," Fredy says.

Todd's confused expression prompts Fredy to elaborate.

"I've been praying every day and every night that God would have mercy on my family and help them get through this trial," he says. "I guess I always assumed it was understood that that was supposed to mean keeping me here with my wife and kids."

Fredy turns back briefly to the gallery and then back to Todd.

"But maybe God is answering my prayers through all of them instead of through me," he says. "Not exactly what I was hoping for, but I'm grateful that my family will have so much support when I'm gone."

"Wait, Fredy," Todd says anxiously. "This doesn't have to be over yet. Even if we lose your appeal with the Board of Immigration Appeals, I've already started looking into getting admitted to practice before the Tenth Circuit Court of Appeals, and even the U.S. Supreme Court. There's always a chance that we could still—"

"Just stop, Todd," Fredy says calmly. "We all know where this ends. Whether it's today, or next year, or five years from now, I am going to stay in jail until the government takes me to Mexico. I can't keep pretending there is any other possibility for me than that. I can't keep my family sitting around with false hopes while I sit in jail doing nothing. I can't keep asking you to do all this work for me for free, and I can't ask my family and friends to pull together all their resources to pay you what you deserve when that money would be so much better spent helping my wife and kids move forward without me."

"Come on, Fredy," Todd says. "I want to do this. I wouldn't offer to if I didn't."

"I know, Todd. And that means a lot. You've been a great friend to me during the worst part of my life. I will never forget that, and I will thank God every day for meeting you. But I can't and I won't ask any more from you. You have your own family to worry about. And there's nothing I can do for my family from behind bars. We've all given all we had to give, but that wasn't enough. So I don't want to appeal, Todd. I feel very sure about that now."

"Fredy, do you know what this means? You can *never* come back. It doesn't matter if your U.S. citizen wife and all of your U.S. citizen kids, and a dozen U.S. businesses petition for you all together. There's no fine you can pay, no waiver you can file. Nothing. This is permanent, Fredy."

"I understand that—well, I guess I don't really *understand* that; I don't think I'll ever understand that. But I know that's the reality. Dragging this out longer won't change that reality. It's an ugly reality, but it's one that me and my family have to start facing now."

Todd sits silently, searching in vain for a viable argument against the reality Fredy has seemed to accept.

"Okay, Fredy," he finally says. "Do you have any other questions for me before the judge comes back?"

"Can my family bring a suitcase or anything for me with some of my stuff?"

"Yeah," Todd says. "They can schedule an appointment with ICE to drop off a suitcase up to fifty pounds."

Fredy sits quietly thinking without responding. After three decades' worth of life, love, and memories, what would he put in that single suitcase of up to fifty pounds? They may as well have limited it to five pounds.

"Only fifty pounds?" Fredy says. "Even with all of Sarah's running, she'd be more than fifty pounds. So much for that plan." He forces a smile. Todd is unable to do the same. "Will you please tell my wife that I did all that I could, that there was nothing more that could be done?"

"Of course, Fredy," Todd says, his voice cracking through his tight throat. "Anything else?"

"No. I just wish I could hold them one last time before I leave. I haven't touched them for months."

"Hey, Fredy," ICE Officer McAllister says, interrupting. "Come here."

Neither Fredy nor Todd responds for a moment, until Todd ultimately asks what the problem is, only to have the same order repeated. Fredy stands up and slowly walks over to the officer.

"I'm sorry, man," Officer McAllister whispers to Fredy, looking over his shoulder. "This isn't what I signed up for. I'm—I'm just sorry, man. Look, I can give you two minutes, but don't you *ever* tell anybody I did this, got it? I could get fired for this, you understand?"

Fredy nods his head without saying anything, tears beginning to pour down his face as Officer McAllister uncuffs his hand and pulls open the wooden gate, on the other side of which Fredy's wife and kids are now standing and waiting for him, having been motioned over by the officer. Fredy and Sarah fall to their knees as the small family holds and hugs each other in a tight huddle. For the next two minutes they do not move, and say nothing more than various forms of "I love you" between sporadic bursts of a strange combination of sobbing and laughter. Their shared devastation is softened for a moment in some small degree by the immense joy they feel the second they touch each other for the first time in months.

Grateful for Officer McAllister's gesture, and not wanting to push his luck, Fredy asks his children to go sit back down with Lori after telling them one last time that he loves them forever. He asks Sarah to stay for one moment longer, after getting a nod of approval from Office McAllister. They stand and he pulls his wife close to him.

"Sarah, I love you so much," Fredy whispers in her ear, his face pressed tightly against hers.

"I love you too," Sarah says.

"And I'll love you forever," Fredy continues. "But listen to me. I *died* today. Do you understand me?"

"What are you talking about, Fredy?" Sarah says, pulling back abruptly with a face of anguish.

"You can*not* bring our babies to Mexico," Fredy says quietly but forcefully. "Not even to visit, even if we could afford it. It's not safe for them. It's not safe for you. There's no way for me to come back. There's no way for me to provide for you. There's no way for me to be your husband and their father in this life anymore. I don't want our kids growing up like you did, with a dad who wouldn't or couldn't be there for them, whatever the reason may be. When the time is right, tell our babies that their daddy died, but that he is always watching over them, and that he loves them forever."

"I'm not going to do that," Sarah says. "I would never do that. You're their father. You're my husband. That doesn't make any sense at all!"

"It makes more sense than all of this," Fredy says. "I need you to move on, baby. I can't and I won't expect you to live alone for the rest of your life. Just remember, we got sealed to each other. So you can find some other guy for the rest of your life, but you're mine for eternity. Don't forget that. You're mine for eternity, and I'm yours. Man cannot break what God has sealed."

"Don't do this to us, Fredy," Sarah says desperately, shaking her head in despair. "Don't you quit on us. We can't survive without you. How can you abandon us like this now?!"

Her words cut deeply through the numbness that seemed to consume Fredy's soul immediately after the judge's decision. He feels a pain unlike any he has ever known, and one he could not even begin to describe. A pain that steadily increases with the agonizing thought that those he loves most must be feeling this same exact pain in this same exact moment, and there is nothing he can do to stop it. Like rays of light forcefully piercing through rapidly fading clouds, reality is mercilessly breaking through Fredy's defensive barriers of denial and naiveté. He grimaces tightly, looks down at the floor and begins sobbing heavily.

He doesn't need to say a word for Sarah to know exactly what he's thinking and feeling. She knows that she isn't any more broken or devastated by the judge's decision than he is, but her reluctance to accept the practical finality of it all has triggered feelings of anger and resentment at Fredy for seeming to just give up. She knows that her words have extinguished the one lingering piece of hope that Fredy had, that his family will somehow be fine without him. Without that hope, even if a false one, he has nothing. Seeing that this emotional load is about to break him, perhaps beyond repair, Sarah forces aside her own feelings in a final act of love and support for her husband and best friend.

"I'm sorry, Fredy," Sarah says instinctively, pulling him close to her and squeezing as tightly as she can, her face pressed forcefully against his. "I'm sorry. Don't worry about us, lovey."

Sarah pulls back and looks behind her at the gallery of people behind her, prompting Fredy to do the same.

"Look at all of these people the kids and I have to help us," she says, forcing a strong face. "We're going to be all right, Fredy, I promise. We'll be fine."

This is the first time Sarah has lied to her husband. By this point she knows from months of personal experience that no number of friends or family, and no amount government resources, will ever begin to fill the hole Fredy will leave behind. But she also knows that the hope or faith that he could be so easily replaced will at least fill a small portion of the hole in Fredy's own heart as he embraces a new life alone in a country far more foreign than native.

"But I need you to promise me that you will take care of yourself and be safe too," she says, looking back at Fredy. "At least promise me that."

"I promise," he says.

Without speaking, Fredy and Sarah stare into each other's eyes, reflecting on the lives they built together and the incomprehensible misfortune that brought them to this point. There's not much more that can be said, they seem to decide.

"I love you," Fredy says.

"I love you more," Sarah says.

Fredy returns to his seat next to Todd. A couple of minutes later, Mr. Richter returns to the courtroom just as Judge Lanzotti is doing the same. Todd solemnly tells the judge that Fredy has decided not to appeal his decision. The judge sits silently with a sad countenance for a moment, as if he was secretly hoping a higher court would tell him he was somehow wrong. He wishes the best for Fredy and his family, signs his final order, and hands two copies to his clerk to provide to Mr. Richter and Todd.

"These proceedings are closed," the judge says.

CHAPTER 26

DAY 123

Sunday, July 1, 2018

"Are we going to your family's house for dinner tonight?" Todd asks his wife, initiating the traditional conversation out of habit.

"We don't have to tonight," Julie says.

It's been a difficult few days for Todd, who has struggled to motivate himself to continue with his work, but he's still surprised by Julie's response. Not surprised that she would spare him from a family dinner if he genuinely didn't want to go, but surprised that she knows him well enough to know he's still struggling despite his best efforts to hide his sadness. Todd pauses briefly, debating whether or not to accept his wife's offer for a night off.

"But we always do on Sunday," he says.

"Who cares?" Julie says. "John Jacob Jingleheimer Schmidt will be there, and you know how Nora feels about him."

"She'll survive," Todd says with a timid smile. "Let's get ready."

Todd is quiet when they arrive, avoiding any comment that could possibly lead to any kind of political discussion. But even his silence proves insufficient to prevent the inevitable, as the conversation, quite unnaturally, turns to immigration. Julie's mother, Rose, makes a simple and innocent observation that her next door neighbor, "Bless her heart, she just cannot seem to stay on top of her own gardening now that she no longer has a gardening service." Just a little harmless gossip and a passive-aggressive jab referencing the dandelions peppering her neighbor's front yard, causing Rose to cringe every time she walks past her house.

"Small price to pay, Ma, to finally get these illegals outta here," Jesse says with a smile as he glances over at Todd. "We have to do our own gardening and roll our own burritos, but we'll survive."

Todd sighs heavily and looks up as if ready to engage. Julie puts her hand on his thigh and squeezes in her unspoken way of asking him to *please just ignore them and eat your peas.* Todd looks back down at his plate and takes another bite of mashed potatoes. He's never liked peas.

"Do you got somethin' to say, Todd?" asks Jesse, having noticed he's struck a nerve. "Certainly you have an opinion on the subject, Counselor."

Todd doesn't respond or even make eye contact as he takes another bite of mashed potatoes.

"Oh, Jesse, just leave him alone," Rose says. "You know he doesn't like to talk about these things."

"Well, maybe it's about time he did, Ma," Jesse says. "I mean, if he's gonna provide for *my* sister with untaxed wetback money, then I think he should have to explain himself."

This prompts a course of laughter from all the male J's.

"Oh, you all stop that now," Rose says, gently slapping Jesse on his shoulder. "I'm sure *some* of those people are very honest and good people. It's just too bad they decided not to do things the right way when they came here."

"What did *you* do, Rose," Todd says, turning to his mother-in-law, "to *earn* the right to live in this country?"

"Excuse me?" she says, clearly taken aback.

"Todd, please don't," says Julie quietly, starting to stand up. "Let's just go home."

"No, no, I can't do this anymore," says Todd emphatically to

Julie before turning back to his in-laws. "I am sick to *death* of this. If you all are going to have such strong opinions on the subject, I think you need to at first have a minimum level of knowledge."

"Well, forgive me, Todd," Rose says defensively, "if it *offends* you that there is a right way and a wrong way to do things, and that there are consequences for doing things the wrong way."

"What is the *right* way?" asks Todd. "Can any of you please explain that to me?"

"It's not that complicated, Todd," says Jesse loudly, emboldened by Todd finally taking his bait. "You wait your turn like everybody else, at the *end* of the line. No cuts, no buts, no coconuts. Easy peasy."

"That's my point," says Todd. "You have no idea what you're talking about. You're all so ignorant it's painful. I have a client who has lived in this country for almost *thirty* years, has a U.S. citizen wife and kids, and now he has to leave forever. There is no line! He's gone *forever*, shipped off to a country that's as foreign to him as it is to me, or even you. How would you like that?"

"Well, he obviously shoulda done things right in the first place," says John, coming to Jesse's aid. "It's too bad he screwed over his whole family with his bad choices, but his wife shoulda thought about that before she shacked up with some illegal."

"His *parents* brought him here!" Todd yells. "He speaks better English than all of you do! Which I realize isn't saying much, but he didn't do anything the *wrong* way! Unless by wrong way you mean he should've told his parents when he was twelve years old that he was going to stay in Mexico alone so he could do things *the right way*. But there never was any right way for him or his family. That's the point. There was no *line* they ever qualified to get into, so they couldn't have come here legally in the first place. It was between starving in Mexico or crossing some imaginary line without asking first, so they did the exact same thing that you would've done."

"Well maybe that's so; you should know better than we do, Todd," says Julie's father, Randy. "But we can't just open our borders to every person in the world that wants to come here. Some people are just not going to be able to come here, and I think that's a good thing. We only have so many jobs and resources in this country, so we gotta take care of the people we got here first."

"That's fine, but do you really think our immigration laws are taking care of the people here?" asks Todd. "That's the biggest lie of all. A lot of these laws are hurting our country, not helping it. My client *was* taking care of a lot of people here. He was providing for his wife and three kids. He was a volunteer soccer coach. He owned his own business. He was paying his taxes. But our government, in its infinite wisdom, just spent thousands of our tax dollars to hold him in jail for four months in *civil* immigration proceedings. That's four months longer than he ever served for any actual *criminal* offense. Our government is now paying for food stamps and Medicaid for his family and will probably continue to do so for years. Meanwhile, they'll be doing so without the income taxes of my client or his ten former employees, who are still looking for new jobs. But this guy was more than just an economic plus to our community. He was a good neighbor, a good friend, and a good person. Everyone who ever knew him is the better for it—*including me!*"

"Well, so big deal," Jesse says. "Maybe you found the *one* illegal who doesn't quite fit the mold. We're in a war here; there are bound to be some civilian casualties. That's called collateral damage. It's the price of war."

"This is not just one person!" Todd says. "We're doing the exact same thing a thousand times over every day. But that's what you idiots all want, isn't it?! So congratulations, Rosie!" Todd says, turning back to his mother-in-law. "*The wrath of Ira* wins again! Chalk up another victory for the '*real*' Americans. All it cost us was just a little piece of our souls."

"Whoa, dude," Jesse says, laughing heartily now. "You have finally lost your mind completely, Todd."

"Well, I'm in good company for that then, aren't I?" Todd says.

"So how about we all just shut up until we have the slightest idea of what we're talking about."

Todd abruptly pushes back his chair, stands, and walks out of the kitchen. The rest of the family sits silently for a moment. They hear an echo through the house of the opening and slamming of the front door.

"Well, it looks like somebody's lady's days came a little early this month," Jesse says.

"Shut up, Jesse!" Julie says as she quickly stands up, taking the cloth napkin from her lap and dropping it on her plate before running after her husband.

"Julie, wait!" her mother says, starting to stand.

"Just let her go, mom," Jesse says, gently grabbing her arm and pulling her back down to her chair.

Todd is sitting just outside the front door on the steps leading up to the porch. He's leaning forward on his knees, staring blankly into the night. Julie sits down next to him and gently touches his arm, which seems to trigger his emotional collapse. His head drops to his arms, which are folded across his knees, and he begins sobbing heavily. In five years of marriage, she's never seen him cry more than a few times. She enjoys bringing up periodically the fact that he didn't cry when they got married or even when their daughter was born, yet she will occasionally find him misty-eyed during emotional moments of children's movies starring animated animals. But never anything like this. Tears begin to well up in her own eyes as she leans over onto her husband and puts her arm around him, squeezing him close to her. They sit without speaking for several minutes.

Todd sits up, wipes both hands down his face, turns to his wife, and forces a smile before looking back down.

"I'm sorry," he says, sighing heavily. "I don't know what's wrong with me. Should I go apologize to everyone?"

"Absolutely not," she says, sitting up abruptly. "My brothers are idiots. That was *long* overdue. If anything, I should apologize for always holding you back."

"What about your mom?" Todd says.

"Eh," Julie says, shrugging her shoulders. "She'll be fine. She could use a healthy dose of reality every once in a while."

"Thanks," Todd says, half-laughing. "It wouldn't have been a very sincere apology. This is all just too much for me sometimes. I love my job; there's no better feeling in the world than when I can really help some family. But it feels so pointless sometimes."

"Todd, you did a great job in Fredy's case," Julie says. "The law was just against him. But don't forget that you have helped *a lot* of people. Remember that guy from Guatemala? The one who ICE had taken and already had his plane ticket out of here when his wife came to your office? You helped him reopen his immigration case and get him residency. His wife still stops by every once in a while with those tamale things. I can't remember what she calls them. Or what about that lady you helped get asylum after she had been raped and tortured by the police in that horrible place in the Middle East? You even got the rest of her family over here. And dozens of others, I'm sure."

"Yeah, I know," Todd says. "But it doesn't make Fredy's loss any easier. It was all just so senseless. I think that even your brothers would've said we should let Fredy stay here, if they actually knew him. Anybody would've made an exception for Fredy. But Fredy's not the exception; that's the problem. I've met a hundred Fredys, and I've only been doing this for a couple of years so far. But nobody knows this—or cares to know this. Everyone in this country just has their immovable opinions on the issue, whether they know what they're talking about or not, and nothing ever changes. You've got the one side saying everyone who disagrees with them are ignorant racists and Nazis, and the other responding that they're all anti-American, bleeding-heart hippies. So they feel they don't even need to acknowledge the opposing views because of this generalized idea they have of who they're opposed to. And it feels like there's nothing I can do to change that. I'm probably as big a part of the problem as anyone, just dismissing your brothers as uninformed racists as quickly as they dismiss me."

"Well, in your defense, my brothers *are* uninformed racists," Julie says.

"Yeah, I know," Todd says with a short laugh, shaking his head and looking down. "But plenty of people agree with their points who aren't. And everyone that's supposedly on 'my side' of the debate just calls them *all* racist instead of acknowledging their points and trying to compromise. That's never going to change anyone's mind.

"Jesse summed the problem up perfectly when he acted like Fredy is the *one* illegal immigrant who doesn't fit the stereotypical mold. The other side would say that Fredy is the stereotypical illegal immigrant who actually gets deported, and the hardened criminals are the very rare exceptions. Both sides painting with these broad brushes, dismissing anything or anyone that doesn't fit into *their* world view. Because it's easier to just assume that the *truth* just happens to align with whatever version of reality we happen to be more comfortable with. Heaven forbid anybody ever have to consider changing their mind about anything or compromising.

"Did I tell you my old friend Simon from high school called me up the other day?" Todd asks, to which Julie shakes her head. "Yeah, so we were talking for a while about the good ol' days and all that, when somehow he started talking about some Mormon guy who he's working with down in Tucson now. And so I'm just listening, and he goes off on the guy for a while, and then he starts talking about how they're all the same, just socially awkward, racist homophobes or whatever. I can't remember everything he was saying. But he knows that I'm a member. So finally, after a while I say, kinda joking and keeping it light, that, 'Ya know, Simon, *I'm* one of these guys you're talking about, in case you forgot.' And he just laughs and says, 'Yeah, but you're not a *real* Mormon.' And that caught me by surprise, so I ask him why, and he says because I'm not *weird*."

"He must not know you that well after all," Julie says with a smile, trying to lighten the mood.

"I know, right?" Todd says, smiling back briefly before continuing. "But I guess I'm not the right kind of *weird* or something, the kind of weird that Simon, for whatever reason, has decided is a necessary characteristic of all *real* Mormons. So since I don't fit that mold, he's found a way to hold on to his stereotype about Mormons by making me a *fake* one. And I'm not a *real* immigration attorney because I don't think we should have completely open borders, and I'm okay with some people actually getting deported after a fair hearing under reasonable laws. So I guess I don't even know what I am. I'm a fake Mormon and a fake immigration attorney representing a bunch of fake immigrants. This world is so full of grey, but everybody refuses to leave their preferred black or white. It's all so stupid, and real people are getting hurt every day because of it."

"But not everyone's like that," Julie says. "That's just the loudest people on both sides."

"I know, that's what I keep telling myself too," Todd says. "But what are all the quiet people *doing*? Is there some action they're taking to make up for their silence? Or do they think it's enough to just quietly disagree?"

Julie sits quietly, seeming to ponder the question without yet finding a convincing response.

"We all keep looking for someone to blame," Todd says. "ICE— let's just abolish ICE and then it will all go away. Or let's impeach Trump. Or let's blame Obama for not doing anything significant when he had the chance. Congress is always an easy target too. The media. God. But the reality is it's *our* fault. All of ours. We don't care enough about the people our laws are hurting to actually demand that the laws be changed. Or maybe we just don't take the time to even understand what the laws say before picking a side. Most of the country doesn't even vote unless there's a presidential election, and even then, just over half of us do. We have these passing moments where we can actually gain a consensus, like when they started separating families at the border. We had strong majorities demanding immediate action. Republicans, Democrats, Independents, apathetics, everybody. And Trump kept saying *my hands are tied, my hands are tied, I can't do anything*. But we refused to accept that and he caved. He did exactly what he said he couldn't do because we demanded it. At least partially. That's what's so infuriating. We don't have to allow this to keep happening, but we do it anyway. And as soon as we inevitably ease up the political pressure I'm sure we'll start to just see more of the same—maybe worse."

"I think it comes down to priorities in the end," Julie says. "It just feels like life is so busy sometimes that we don't have time for anything extra that doesn't directly impact us or our families. It doesn't help that these laws are all so complicated. I just pretend to understand half the things you tell me about. Do you really think that the average person could understand all of these immigration laws and issues? Even if they took the time to study up on it I don't think they'd really get it. I doubt half the politicians who even passed these laws actually understood them."

Todd releases a heavy sigh and leans forward, resting his head on his hands. The couple sits in silence looking forward, accepting for the moment that there is no immediate solution. Julie leans again on Todd's shoulder. The comfort this provides him reminds him of how Fredy will find no such comfort when he steps off of a plane in whatever random Mexican city he's dumped into next week with a couple dozen other aliens. Todd feels conflicting feelings of guilt and gratitude as his thoughts turn to his own small family. He will hold his wife a little closer tonight. He will hug his daughter a little longer. He knows he did everything that he could for Fredy and his family but that it wasn't enough. He reluctantly accepts the fact that he can't change the world overnight, if at all. He's just one person in what feels like a losing battle that will likely never end. But he also knows there's still much more he can still do for his own family, and the families behind the faces of his fifty-plus open cases, faces that slowly begin to consume his thoughts. He mourns for the heartache he cannot remove from an imperfect world, while finding some measure of peace in knowing there is still much good he *can* do.

After an extended moment of quiet reflection, Todd breaks the silence. "Did I seriously just yell, '*The wrath of Ira wins again*' at my mother-in-law?" he asks, turning to his wife.

Julie smiles and nods. "That was my favorite part," she says before resting her head back on Todd's shoulder.

TO THE READER

I AM SINCERELY GRATEFUL TO ANYONE AND EVERYONE WHO HAS TAK-EN THE TIME OUT OF THEIR BUSY LIVES TO READ THIS NOVEL. While I have always loved writing (and arguing), which is part of the reason I decided to become a lawyer, I never aspired to be a novelist. But after several years of confronting head on the many absurdities of U.S. immigration law, I have convinced myself that we as a nation would stand up and demand change if we all knew exactly what our laws say and do every day. I can't help but believe that a majority of us would agree that "the right way" is often times *wrong*, and the mere fact that a law exists does not mean it should not change. This novel is just one of many efforts I have made and will continue to make on behalf of my immigrant brothers and sisters in order to inform the public to the best of my ability.

While Fredy's story is not based on any specific client of mine, every law and policy that impacted him and his family in this novel is a real law or a real policy that impacts real people everyday. This novel provides the reader with just a small taste of what I have re-grettably witnessed on more occasions than I care to recall. But there has been nothing sweeter than the feeling I have had when I've been able to help a client and his or her family make it safely through this daunting process. I hope that you will join me and others in learning more, and then turning your informed opinions into action until we see real change in the law through reasonable compromises from both sides. I will continue to provide suggestions on what you may be able to do to help as an individual on the advocacy page of my law firm's website: **www.AndersonAndBenson.com/Advocacy/**

You can also keep up to date on developments in imm gration law by following me here:
www.facebook.com/UtahImmigrationAttorney/

Finally, you can reach out to me directly here:
Skyler@AndersonAndBenson.com

—Skyler Anderson

Made in the USA
Lexington, KY
22 June 2019